A
REBEL
WITHOUT
A ROGUE

BLISS BENNET

Copyright © 2015 by Jackie C. Horne

Cover design by Historical Editorial
Cover photograph copyright © 2015 by Jessica Boyatt
Cover image of Scottish Steel and Silver Scroll Pistol, by Christie & Murdoch, Doune, courtesy of Lyon & Turnbull Auctioneers
Fleuron from Vectorian Free Vector Pack: http://www.vectorian.net

This is a work of fiction. Names, characters, places, and incidents are the product of the author's imagination or are used fictitiously. Any resemblance to actual events, locales, or persons, living or dead, is purely coincidental.

ISBN: 978-0-9961937-1-9
Paperback Edition

For permission requests, please contact the author: blissbennet@gmail.com.

To Keith, who has always supported my dreams

ACKNOWLEDGMENTS

It's been a long and detour-filled journey, this road to romance publication, and there are many people to thank for helping me navigate it.

The many, many inspiring teachers who have influenced me over my long educational career: Augusta Thomas, Anne Maerklein, and Kathleen Ryan; Sandra Coyle and Jennifer Bagley; Cathryn Mercier and Susan Bloom; John Plotz, Sue Lanser, Beverly Lyon Clark, and Susan Staves. Special thanks to Laura Baker for helping me brainstorm about Kit's and Fianna's characters, and the major turning points in their story.

Romance writing friends and colleagues, in particular my fellow NECRWA chapter mates and the members of the Beau Monde (especially my Beau Monde mentor, Kate Pearce). Thanks for sharing your knowledge and expertise about this crazy business of romance with an eager newbie.

Readers and critique partners who have known when to offer praise, when to raise eyebrows in confusion, and when to give me a swift kick in the pants: Dan Feinberg, Fran Fowlkes, Jane Lesley, Audra North, Trey Peck, Sabine Priestley, and Myretta Robens. Special thanks to Cecilia Grant for taking a look at the opening chapters of this story and giving me invaluable feedback on how to improve them.

My publishing support group, including: My editor, Meredith Efken of Fiction Fix-It Shop, who protects me from committing the sins of painfully contrived plotting and overly purple prosing. And my copyeditor, Carolyn Ingermanson, who graciously but meticulously points out all my typos and corrects my wanton misuse of the hyphen. And the designer of my web site, Denise Biondo of Biondo Studio; thanks for taking my sketchy vision and turning it into gorgeous reality. And Jenny Q of Historical Editorial, for creating such a wonderfully evocative cover. You all are the best!

The many, many readers who have commented on, and/or disagreed with, the blog posts my alter ego, Jackie Horne, has written at _Romance Novels for Feminists_. I love the way you challenge my ideas, and push me to think harder about the hows and whys of feminist romance.

My toddler dinner neighbors. Have we really been getting together every week since the last century? Thanks, Jessica, Trey, Anita, Norbert, Anne Marie, and Roger for not just listening to all my talk about romance, self-publishing, and sex, but actually being curious enough to ask questions about it. And special thanks to Jessica for the lovely author and cover photos.

Dan Brenner, who has helped me through many dark days, and always encourages me to see the light.

Mr. Bennet (my own, not Elizabeth's), who is so supportive of all my goals, and who laughs out loud whenever he reads Jennifer Crusie's _Bet Me_. And my own young Miss Bennet, even though she'd far prefer to read fantasy than icky romance. I love you both so much.

And last, but certainly not least, my readers and reviewers. Thank you for taking a chance on a new author. There are so many romances being written and published today; it is an honor to know that you've chosen to spend your time with mine.

CHAPTER ONE

London, February 1822

Fianna Cameron—at least that was what she called herself today—slipped a hand inside her cloak pocket and curled her fingers tight around the butt of her father's pistol. Her long, hurried strides had sent it bouncing hard against her thigh, but even that pain wasn't enough to reassure that her the weapon hadn't disappeared, that she hadn't only imagined hiding it there before she'd finally tracked her prey to his lair. Still, she couldn't shake the fear that when the time came for her to act, she would find herself confronting the man empty-handed, shaking in impotent fury as Major Christopher Pennington offered her a condescending smile and walked on, just as he had so many times in her dreams.

The memory of Grandfather McCracken's soft, broken voice reading the Bible verse that had first inspired her—*For he is the minister of God, a revenger to execute wrath upon him who doeth evil*—brought her back to her sense of purpose. She could not fail, *would* not fail, not now, not when she'd given nearly everything for this chance to bring her father's killer to justice and redeem the honor of his name. And to prove herself, bastard though she might be, worthy of her rightful place in the McCracken family.

The only family she had left—

Eyes darting between strangers and shop windows, carriages and carts, she searched the unfamiliar street for her destination. She'd feared being followed and had altered her path to throw any pursuer off her trail. But the evasion must have pulled her off course as well. She'd come too far, missing Pennington's reputed favorite haunt.

Retracing her steps, she discovered the Crown and Anchor Tavern lay not on the Strand itself, but behind that bustling street's houses and shops. Stepping into the long, narrow passageway between two shopfronts, she forced herself to slow to a pace painfully at odds with the rapid beating of her heart.

The sight of the Crown and Anchor's spacious stone-paved foyer brought her up short. In Dublin, no place this grand would ever be termed a mere tavern. Ornate columns, a sweeping staircase with iron rails and what looked to be handrails of some dark, expensive wood—why, it seemed as elegantly appointed as the Lord Lieutenant's mansion. And so many people! How would she ever find her quarry amidst such a throng?

A man in dark livery broke through her dismay. "May I direct you to the Philharmonic Society concert, ma'am? Or Mr. Burdett's meeting to discuss the wisdom of abstaining from intoxicating spirits? Both may be found on the floor above."

Not just a tavern, then, this Crown and Anchor, but a public meeting hall of no small repute. What a lackwit, to call attention to herself by staring at its grandeur like the greenest bumpkin. Lucky, she'd be, not to be judged an impostor and thrown out on her ear.

Run! her body urged. *Hide!*

Instead, forcing her hand from the comfort of the pistol, she pushed back the hood that hid her face.

The porter took a step back, his eyes widening. How predictable, the catch of breath, the poleaxed, besotted expression. She'd long ago stopped wondering why God had gifted her with a face that no man could seem to pass without falling guilty to the rudeness of staring. Lucky for her, men only seemed to care about the deceptively lovely husk of her face, never giving a single thought to what ugliness might lie beneath.

Lowering her voice to a murmur, she forced the porter to step closer. "It is so crowded here." She widened her eyes. "My footman seems to have gone astray."

"Might I send a man in search of him for you, ma'am?" he asked, a blush spreading over already ruddy cheeks.

"My uncle," she said, taking care to add a shy, embarrassed frown. "The footman was to take me to my uncle, Major Pennington. Would you know where I might find him, sir?"

The man took another step closer, as if drawn to her by an invisible wire. "Major Pennington? Ah, let me see. There is to be a meeting of military gentlemen in the Small Dining Room this evening, but I believe they are men of the navy. I do know of a *Mr.* Pennington, though, a Mr. Kit Pennington. Brother to Lord Saybrook, he is. Might he be the gentleman you seek?"

"Ah yes, *Mr.* Pennington. I nearly forgot, he sold out some years past. My mother always called him the Major, you see."

"Of course, ma'am. I believe he is up in the news room, reading the papers. I'll send someone to fetch him immediately." Reluctance and relief warred over his face as he turned toward the stair.

"Oh, please don't," she cried, placing a palm on the man's arm. No need to give the Major any warning.

She felt the porter start, watched him stare at the hand from which she'd deliberately removed a glove. "It was meant to be a surprise, you see, for his birthday," she added. "I'm sure I can find my way to this news room, if you give me the direction."

"But women don't typically frequent the news room,

ma'am, and—"

Lifting her chin, she turned the full force of her green eyes upon the hapless servant. "You wouldn't spoil my uncle's surprise, would you?" she pleaded, adding the softest exhale of a sigh to draw his attention to her wide, full lips.

The quiver of his arm under her fingers told her all she needed to know.

Her mouth grew dry as they ascended the prodigious stone staircase and made their way across the second-floor lobby, passing a large assembly room. The strains of a tuning violin, its strings wound tight as her nerves, assaulted her ears. "Haydn's Requiem," the placard outside the room read. How fitting, that the Philharmonic Society should be playing a mass for the dead.

His death, not mine, she offered in silent prayer, even as a shiver slid down her frame.

"The news room, ma'am," the porter said, stopping beside one of the many doors lining the passageway and reaching toward its handle.

She raised a silencing finger to her lips before he could step inside.

"A surprise, do you not recall?" she whispered. He mimicked her action with his own finger, pleased to be privy to the secrets of such a creature as she. At her nod, he reached for the door and opened it just a crack. Then, with a flustered bow, he retreated down the passageway.

She stood for a moment, then another, until she was certain he had gone. Then, with a quick inrush of breath, she drew her father's pistol from her pocket. Her fingers shook as she cocked it, then hid it between the folds of her skirt. Pulling the concealing hood of her cloak back over her head, she forced her icy hand to push the door wide.

The floor's thick carpets and the door's well-oiled hinges allowed her to slip in unremarked. In her eagerness to finish the business, she'd stupidly assumed he'd be alone in the room. But she'd been mistaken; several groups of gentlemen were scattered about the large room. Damn, how her wits had gone astray since she'd arrived in London.

It would have been far wiser to leave before she attracted notice. But somehow, she could not pull her eyes away. Which of the room's occupants was the man responsible for her father's death? One of the knot of men debating earnestly around a table? The single man in a rumpled suit by the window, scribbling notes with a stubby pencil? Surely not one of the pair of gentlemen barely old enough to sprout whiskers, frantically pulling books off the shelves, nor their companion, dazed, even cup-shot, in a chair beside them.

She frowned. None had the stiff, upright bearing of the British military man, as had the soldiers she'd seen in Dublin and Belfast. Were they more relaxed, these English fighters, when in the safety of their own country?

"Mr. Pennington?" she asked, taking a few steps into the room. Her eyes cut between the lone man by the window and the group on the left. "Is Mr. Pennington present?"

She could barely hear her own words over the pounding of blood in her ears. But her voice must have been louder than it seemed, for each man raised his eyes. Most seemed shocked to see an unescorted woman in their midst, although several looked as if they wished they could answer in the affirmative.

But none did.

Had the porter been mistaken, then? Her eyes narrowed, her teeth biting down hard against her lower lip.

Before she could draw blood, a supercilious English drawl caught her ear.

"Kit, how amusing. For once, a lady appears to want you, not me."

The voice had come not from the group on her left, but from the one on the right, the one now slightly behind her. She froze, waiting for the response.

"Pennington, pay attention. There's a *lady*, here, in this very room, asking for you," a second voice added. One voice to her left; the other to her right.

"A lady? Looking for *me*?" A third speaker. She heard one of the three take a step in her direction.

She cursed her shaking hand, clutching the butt of the pistol, her feet frozen to the floor. What, could she be losing her will now? Simply because this last act of retribution, unlike the others, demanded that she not simply humiliate or shame, but threaten real violence?

No. She steeled herself to charm Pennington into leaving the room. Once they were alone, she could beguile, or, if necessary, threaten, until the cursed man signed the recantation that would restore her father's honor.

Taking a deep breath, she turned to face him. The hand holding the hidden pistol gripped tight, angling the weapon away from her body. Upward, to ward off any potential threat.

But her finger, slippery with sweat, slid against the trigger—

The unexpected force of the shot sent her reeling back toward the door.

Time hung suspended as, through the dissipating smoke, she struggled to make out her target.

Golden curls. Blue eyes, wide with shock. Blood, drip, drip, dripping from an arm to the carpet below.

A face even younger than her own.

A Mháthair Dé!

Mother of God. Not only had she fired too soon.

She'd fired upon the wrong man.

CHAPTER TWO

"Shot by a spurned lover? When would I have had the time to find such a creature, never mind spurn her? For pity's sake, Benedict, I've only been in London a fortnight."

Christian Pennington's boots beat a sharp tattoo of disgust against the Grosvenor Square pavement. Being shot by a woman he'd never met, for God knows what reason, had been bad enough. Being confined to his bed for the better part of a week to ensure the bullethole she'd left in his arm did not fester had been worse. But hearing from his brother Benedict that he'd been cast into the fiery furnace of the *ton*'s lust for gossip, and for something not even remotely close to the truth—Lord forgive him for wanting to do something far more violent than wail, weep, or gnash his teeth.

"I've only been back in England for a week," Benedict answered, "but I haven't been able to take a step outside my door without someone making snide inquiries about the state of my youngest brother's health."

Kit scowled. He couldn't even put the whole humiliating incident decently behind him, not now that this ridiculous rumor that he'd been shot by a former mistress had begun to race through ballroom and breakfast parlor alike. And just when he most needed his reputation to be spotless! If he wanted to clear his name, he had to make that pistol-wielding woman admit he'd done nothing to her to warrant such violence. It ought to have been as simple as visiting her in prison and extracting a confession.

Only somehow, in the melee after she'd pulled the trigger, the maddening witch had disappeared without a trace.

Kit wished he could howl out his frustration to the stars.

But even this late in the evening, Mayfair thronged with denizens of the *ton*. Lord knew he had no desire to provide additional grist for its rumor mill. And poor Benedict was only the messenger, after all, not the source of the tale. Judging from the expression on his face, his brother was as embarrassed to relate the tittle-tattle as Kit was to hear it. Still, if the rumor had reached the ears of the reclusive Benedict, there was little chance it had escaped the attention of their far more sociable eldest brother, the current Lord Saybrook. A realization certainly worth the choicest oath in Kit's vast and varied repertoire.

"Glad you've still enough life in you left to curse," Benedict said. "Rumor had you bleeding out your last on the Crown and Anchor's best carpet."

"I'm not quite ready to go the way of all flesh, I as-sure you," Kit replied, shooting a quick glance at his austere brother. Had Benedict just tried to make him laugh? As a child, Ben had been the least playful of the Pennington siblings, but Kit knew little of this brother as an adult. They'd been sent to different schools, and had grown even further apart when Benedict traveled to the Continent to study painting.

No matter. Benedict was a Pennington, and for a Pennington, loyalty to family always came first.

"If only I knew what she looked like! But with that hood pulled down over her face, all I caught was the merest glint of her eyes," Kit said as he followed his brother across a quiet street. "I pray that your friend Ingestrie will be able to help."

Kit hefted the weight of the firearm he'd placed in his greatcoat pocket, the very weapon the woman had dropped in her haste to flee. Not the tiny muff pistol one would expect a woman to carry, but a flintlock, similar in size to the cavalry pistol their uncle Christopher had used during his years fighting against the Irish and the French. It had no prancing lion stamped on its lock, as had their uncle's, nor was it marked with any other stamp that might indicate its place of manufacture. But the light engraving tracing down the pistol's butt—*Tá na téada curtha go húr agus cloisfear í*—might prove an even better clue.

"Ingestrie's no friend, merely an acquaintance," Benedict said. "Stupid as a stick, and a whiner, too. Not likely he picked up enough Gaelic to be able to translate for you, even after spending two years in Ireland."

"Pity Uncle Christopher's hatred of the Irish meant we never had an Irish maid or footman. A servant might not be able to read, but might recognize the sounds of the words."

"The same might be said of Uncle Christopher. And he spent far more time in Ireland than Ingestrie ever did. I still think you should ask him first."

Kit shook his head. "Have you forgotten how angry he gets if anyone even mentions Ireland, Ben? And his antipathy for that country has only grown more extreme since you've been away. Every physician he's consulted has warned him against raising his temper, and if I ask him, he's sure to blaze on for hours about the barbarity of the Irish race. Which you'd know, if you'd do your familial duty and pay him a visit."

Benedict grimaced. "Sure you just don't want to tell him you allowed a woman to get the better of you?"

Kit just grunted as his brother came to a stop in front of a small townhouse on Seymour Street.

Ingestrie's rooms. Would he find an answer here?

The snap of the flint against the frizzen. The sudden spurt of fire. The smoke, acrid and bitter. . .

Kit looked down as he felt his brother's hand cover his own, stilling its restless movement over his wounded arm. When had his hand strayed from his pocket?

"Don't want the bandage pulling loose," Benedict said, a glint of sympathy lightening the severity of his countenance.

A raucous shout split the night, followed by a burst of male laughter. Light streamed from an upper floor; loud voices drifted down from open windows. Damnation! Was Ingestrie entertaining?

Benedict's head cocked toward the windows above. "Shall we come back another time?"

In reply, Kit raised the knocker on the townhouse door.

Voices blared and liquor flowed as Kit followed Benedict through the crush of warm bodies in Ingestrie's rooms. How charming they were, *ton* gentlemen at play. Kit choked back his disgust as a clearly inebriated young fop tripped on the carpet, tipping half his glass down another's back. The smell of fresh whitewash, mixed with the stench of spilled wine, made Kit's head pound. How long would it take Benedict to run Ingestrie to ground?

"Yes, Saybrook's brother, the youngest one. Studying to be a parson—ha!"

Kit stopped in his tracks. Damnation! What was the latest round of rumormongering saying of him? He edged closer to a crowd of young bucks laughing in the corner.

"I'd just stepped out of the hall to fetch refreshments for Lady Butterbank—you all know how that woman loves to eat!—when suddenly, I heard the report of a pistol. A pistol, right in the middle of the Philharmonic concert. Why, I nearly spilled Lady B's ratafia all over my waistcoat!"

Kit snorted at the appreciative gasps of alarm. He wasn't certain, but the storyteller's voice sounded as if it might belong to Lord Dulcie, one of the *ton*'s prime gossips. Kit craned his neck, struggling to catch sight of the speaker.

"There I stood, all agog, wondering if Napoleon himself had risen from the grave to lead one last attempt to invade England, when a hooded figure of the feminine persuasion rushed right by me and flew down the staircase."

"A woman?" one wide-eyed listener asked. "What of the shooter?"

The speaker chuckled. "One and the same, my dear, one and the same! And imagine—I almost called out to ask if she required assistance! Why, I, too, might have fallen victim to her bloody reign of terror."

"What, was she your lover, too, Dulcie, as well as young Pennington's?"

The crowd around the viscount shouted with laughter.

"Have you a taste for violent females, my lord?" Kit called, raising his voice so that it might be heard above the din.

The crowd parted to reveal Lord Dulcie, dressed with a flair in marked contrast to the dishabille of the men around him. At the sight of Kit, a sly smile curved up the corners of his mouth.

"Why, young Pennington, as I live and breathe! I would have sworn that lightskirt of yours had sent you to count the worms."

"My brother is not quite ready to stick his spoon in the wall, Dulcie, I assure you," Benedict replied, his voice cold and tight.

The viscount's eyes narrowed. "All too ready, though, to stick his knife somewhere equally unsuitable, Pennington. And he almost a clergyman! For shame, sir, for shame." Dulcie shook his head at Kit with mournful mockery.

"That woman was not my lover," Kit bit out, taking a step in the viscount's direction. Wounded arm or no, he'd not let any man insult him, especially a dandy such as Dulcie.

"Not your lover? Why else would she have shot you? Come now, you'll not convince me the wench simply took exception to a poorly delivered sermon."

A restraining hand descended on his shoulder as Dulcie's audience roared again with laughter. Kit turned to see Benedict give him a warning shake of his head.

"Allow me to deal with my Lord Dulcie," Benedict said in a low voice. "Ingestrie just made his way into the next room."

Kit glared at Dulcie, then turned back to his brother. The scowl slashing across Benedict's face suggested that something more than an insult to Kit lay between him and the foppish viscount. Something quite memorable, if the animosity between them still flamed after all the years Ben had been out of the country.

He'd almost forgotten how good it could be to have a brother at his back. Since their father's death, the new Lord Saybrook had certainly not been in any shape to offer support, drowning his grief in wenching and wine. But Benedict's austere expression promised that retribution would be swift.

With a nod, Kit left Dulcie to his brother's wrath.

The door Benedict had pointed to led not to another parlor, but to a bedchamber, although the number of rowdy gentlemen it contained suggested anything but peaceful slumber. A young man held court here, the stiffness of his starched collar at odds with the lazy slump of his body against the mantel. Smiling, he waved one arm, mock conducting the chorus surrounding him as it swayed and chanted:

And where are your maidenheads,
You maidens frisk and gay,
We left them at the alehouse,
We drank them clean away—

Charles Chetwynd-Talbot, Viscount Ingestrie, Kit

presumed. Eldest son of Earl Talbot, the recently re-called Lord Lieutenant of Ireland.

As the chorus came to a rousing, if somewhat slurred, conclusion, his host caught sight of Kit. "And who might you be, sir?" he asked, his words deliberate and slow.

Kit bowed. "Christian Pennington, my lord. You are acquainted with my brother Benedict, I believe?"

"Ah, the youngest Pennington! Another man who has won out against sore affliction," Ingestrie cried, raising his glass in tribute. "I survived the depredations of barbaric Ireland, and Pennington here endured the attack of a vindictive female. But where is your brandy, man? Someone bring this fellow a glass!"

Kit refused several overflowing tumblers thrust in his direction. "Ingestrie. Might I have a word in private?"

"Oh, oh, don't let him foist his baggage off on you, Charlie!" a portly man called from the corner. "Last thing you need, a woman with a pistol!"

"Ingestrie'd never be so daft!" another voice shouted. "'Sides, haven't you seen the prime 'un he brung back from his travels?"

"I'd take a clean Englishwoman over an Irish whore any day, even one with her own fire-arm."

"Ah, is yours so lacking, Pierson, you need a woman to bring her own?"

Suggestive sniggers followed as Kit towed the half-inebriated Ingestrie out into the passageway.

Best to be as quick and direct as possible, especially if Benedict was right about the sluggishness of Ingestrie's wits. "I find myself in need of a man with a reading knowledge of Gaelic, sir. As you've just re-turned from Ireland, my brother thought you might be able to help."

Ingestrie gave an ungentlemanly snort. "I can't even understand it when they *speak* the blasted words, Pen-nington. Never thought it worth the trouble to learn to *read* it. Besides, in Ireland, anyone who's anyone speaks

English."

Kit crossed his arms, struggling to contain his disappointment. Would he have to ask Uncle Christopher after all?

Obviously impatient at having been pulled away from his guests, Ingestrie's eyes wandered back toward the bedchamber. With a sudden start, he pulled himself away from the wall against which he had slumped, knocking Kit's injured arm as he pushed past. Kit struggled to hold back a curse.

"Fianna!" Ingestrie slurred, tottering down the passageway.

Had he been thoroughly dismissed? But then Ingestrie flapped his hand in Kit's direction and pointed down the hall. "Fianna might be able to help."

Kit followed Ingestrie's gaze to see a woman—the only woman in the room—calling to someone over her shoulder. Her dark hair, unbound, spilled in thick, flowing waves down to her slender waist.

An unexpected chill traced down his spine. A woman, in the midst of this rabble?

"Brought her back with me from that godforsaken land across the sea," Ingestrie proclaimed with drunken pride as he grasped the woman by the waist and turned her to face Kit. "Fianna, my very own wild Irish girl."

Green eyes, green as a summer lake in shade, met his.

Did the English hang attempted murderers as quickly as they executed rebels?

Fianna's heartbeat pounded in her ears as Ingestrie pulled her to his side. How had the man she's shot found her? Had she been so mad with fear that she'd not sensed she'd been followed as she fled?

Her mind detached itself somehow from her body, floating above, observing rather than participating in this fearful, deadly farce.

She waited for the ringing denunciation, the outraged calls for the constable or the watch. But the man across from her remained blessedly silent. Did he truly not recognize her? Or did he only wait for a private moment to take her into custody?

He hardly looked much older than Ingestrie, this man she'd shot, just shucking off boyhood, coming into the first bloom of his manly strength. It irritated her, the way his tousled blond curls, ripe for a woman's hands, fell over his high forehead, though she kept her face impassive. His square chin and thin lips suggested a determination far more stern than Ingestrie's ever would be, though she saw something sweet, untouched, lurking in the depths of his blue eyes. Easily hurt, this one would be, and not just by the pain of a bullet.

Might she turn such innocence to her advantage? A sentimental tale of woe to explain her mistake? With the addition of batting eyelashes, and a gentle clasp on the arm, might she even keep herself out of gaol?

"Anna," Ingestrie said, his hand sneaking down from her waist to curve around the jut of her hip. "My friend Kit Pennington here needs a bit of the Irish translated. Told him you were just the chit for the job."

She'd shot a Pennington, then, at least. Just not the right one.

Might he be a relation, though, of the man she sought? She'd paid little attention to the family lineage in *Debrett's Peerage*, casting aside Ingestrie's copy of the book when it gave no hint of Major Pennington's current abode. Might this young man be the Major's son? Or perhaps his nephew?

Her mind raced, working to spin this disaster into opportunity.

"Anna?" Ingestrie prompted, pulling her from her own thoughts. "Will you help?"

"Of course." She turned her head away so that his slobbering kiss, half thanks, half heavy-handed claim, landed on her cheek rather than her lips.

Ingestrie gave her hip a squeeze before releasing her, reminding her just whose bed she was expected to warm after this evening's guests returned to their own. With a quick nod, she grabbed a decanter from the table and filled his empty glass just before another of his boisterous friends pulled him back into his bedchamber. If her luck held, he'd be in no shape to partake of her charms after they all finally departed.

If her luck held, she'd not be forced to leave herself.

Drawing in a deep breath, she tucked her hand beneath this Mr. Pennington's arm. The arm she *hadn't* shot.

When she needed to guile a man, she'd sometimes force herself to press her breast against the side of his arm, as if charmingly unaware of the distance between his body and hers. Yet tonight she refrained, worried that the pounding of her blood would give away her fear. Instead, she blinked her eyelashes and gazed up at him with her most artless expression.

"Tell me, sir, how may I be of help?"

So many fops and fribbles degenerated into a foolish stupor when she turned her face to them, their eyes widening as if they wished to swallow her whole. But this man's gaze only narrowed.

"Do you have a surname, ma'am?"

If he only knew how many! And some of them even legally her own.

"Why yes, of course, sir. Cameron, it is."

"Well, then, Miss Cameron. May we not remove from the din of Lord Ingestrie's guests, so I might ask you about this?"

Her father's pistol lay in the man's gloved hand.

Kit's injury must have addled his brain as well as dam-
aged his arm. For a moment, he'd taken the woman
standing before him to be a spirit or a wraith; surely,
such strange, eldritch beauty could belong to no mere
creature of bone and flesh. With skin as pale as moonlight, wide green eyes hiding behind a spill of sable hair,
a veritable *leannán sídhe* she seemed, a fairy so ethereal-
ly lovely that a mere mortal would overcome any obsta-
cle to win the chance to touch his lips to hers, lips as
ripe with promise as a lush summer plum. He'd always
scorned them, the foolish men in the tales Uncle
Christopher had brought back from Ireland, sacrificing
everything in their all-consuming passion for a mere
fairy girl. A *leannán sídhe* might gift the man of her
choice with artistic inspiration, but she'd demand his
life force in recompense. What rational man would give
up his very life for a mere woman, fairy or no, he'd
challenge his uncle, his words redolent with adolescent
disbelief.

One glance at this haunting creature and suddenly
Kit knew how utterly foolish his doubts had been.

But then Ingestrie had groped her, and slabbered
over her, and the illusion had fallen away. She was only
human after all. Less than human, if one took the
church's strictures against whoredom as guide, a low
wretch who'd forfeited the character of woman. He'd
preached against such creatures once, with a discomfiting sense of his own hypocrisy, in the days before he'd
become disillusioned with his divinity training.

He'd come here tonight for information, not to judge
anyone's morals. But the memory of his father's death
from the pox—a disease he'd picked up from his own
kept woman—still sent a shiver of disgust tracing across
his frame.

She must have felt it, for her hand dropped from his
arm. Was that hurt that flared in those wide green eyes?

If it was, blinking lashes and a teasing smile soon hid it from view.

Surely the feelings of a courtesan need be no concern of his. "The landing outside, perhaps, Miss Cameron?"

She nodded, then took the stairs to the floor above, away from the male shouts and laughter. The light from a gas lamp on the street set a halo around her hair, but kept her face in shadow.

"What is it you wish from me, Mr. Pennington?" she asked, her low voice nearly as enticing as her face. "I've no knowledge of firearms."

"Viscount Ingestrie suggested you might be able to aid me with a translation."

Her lips curved in an insolent arch. "Oh, are the lines your Latin tutor set beyond your ken, young sir?"

"I'm hardly of an age to need a tutor, ma'am." The petulance of his tone, though, would scarcely persuade her of the fact. Forcing himself to speak more evenly, he added, "What I require is someone who can read Irish."

"Read Gaelic?" She laughed, her arms crossing tight over her chest. "When the schools insist we learn only English?"

"But surely, outside of school—"

"In Ireland, sir, English is the language of power. Gaelic's only spoken by the poor. And what cause have they to learn to read or to write it?"

Kit frowned. He'd hardly expected to find a political radical in the midst of a viscount's revels. "Why, then, would someone go to the trouble to engrave Gaelic words on a flintlock?"

She took the pistol he held out to her, squinting at the letters in the dim light. After staring at it for several minutes, turning it to and fro in her small but strong hands, she shook her head, looking up with strangely blank eyes. "I'm sorry, sir. I wish I could help."

She held the pistol out to him, but just as he reached for it, she tucked it back against her chest. He jerked his hand away before it accidentally brushed against the small but lush curves of her breasts.

His eyes narrowed. Had she intended to discompose him? Or was it only his own lust, reasserting itself after lying so conveniently dormant these past months, that urged his body forward?

He took a step back, once again placing a decent distance between them.

"Why would an English gentleman take any interest in Gaelic words, sir?" she asked, gazing not at him but at the weapon in her hands.

"Not the words, but the man to whom they might lead. I'm searching for the owner of the pistol, and the engraving's my only clue."

"You seek to return the firearm to its rightful owner?"

"No, I intend to send the woman who borrowed it to gaol."

She frowned. "To gaol? Merely for borrowing a pistol?"

"No, for firing it in my direction."

She laughed, then flung the gun out, pointing it at his chest. "A mere woman had the gall to attack a strapping lordling such as yourself?" Her lips turned up in the merest wisp of a smile as her thumbs raised the flint to full cock.

A strange mix of shame, fear, and desire clenched Kit's gut. "My Lord Ingestrie may take pleasure from such games of violence with his paramour, but I have little liking for insult guised as flirtation." He stepped forward, capturing the hands clutching the weapon between his. "Only a fool points a pistol in a man's direction, even an unloaded one."

"Unless that fool wishes to do him harm," she answered.

Her breath, redolent of wine and spice, warmed the air between them. But even through his gloves, the cold of her hands bit into his palms.

"Tell me, what harm did you do her, to drive the

foolish wench to fire upon you?" she asked.

"Rumor has it that she's my discarded mistress," Kit said as he drew the pistol from her grasp. Frowning, he strode to the window. "But I swear I never laid eyes on her before that night. Not that anyone will believe it, not after Lord Dulcie and his fellow gossips finish spreading their tales."

"And why should such rumors upset you? Do not men of fashion take pride in the irrational lengths to which they can drive their discarded lovers?"

"Men like Ingestrie, perhaps," Kit accorded, glancing back at her over his shoulder. "But some gentlemen place a higher value on their honor. I assure you, I have no wish for such a reputation. Particularly not now." Not unless he was prepared to allow his political aspirations to die stillborn.

"How remarkable. An Englishman who'd rather not be known for his amorous exploits." Silk skirts swished across the landing, and an icy palm lit upon his back. "Perhaps, if you left this pistol with me, I might make some inquiries on your behalf?"

Kit shrugged off Miss Cameron's hand, then turned to face her. "No. This pistol's the only lead I have."

Her face remained impassive, but something in her eyes, glinting in the gaslight from the window, made him feel as if he had done her an injury by refusing.

"But if you've paper and ink, I could copy the words," he said, the words a reluctant concession.

"Indeed. And if I were to discover their meaning? Might I demand something in recompense?"

"You wish to be paid for such service?" Why should he be surprised by such a demand? Was not financial recompense the reason women such as she engaged in harlotry?

"Not coin," she said, reaching out to trace the engraving on the pistol with one delicate finger. His eyes followed as it whorled and stroked over the sinuous curves of the Gaelic letters. The small hairs on the back of his neck began to rise.

He jerked his eyes up to her face. "What else do I have to offer?"

"Your aid in my own search," she said, her hand dropping from the pistol. "I've not come to London simply for my own pleasure, sir. I'm looking for an Englishman, one who served in the British army in Ireland. It's vital that I find him, and as quickly as possible."

"Do you not know his direction?"

"No. Only his name. And that he once served in a regiment stationed in my homeland."

"Have you checked *Boyle's Court Guide*? And *Debrett's*?"

"Of course. What, do you take me for a simpleton?"

Kit grimaced at the sharpness of her words. "And who is this man to you? Has he done you harm?"

Her eyes glittered, though with anger or with tears, he could not decide. "Will it satisfy your curiosity if I say that my family will not be complete until I find him?" she whispered.

Damnation! Had some dishonorable English soldier trysted with an Irish wench and abandoned her with child? An illegitimate child, now woman-grown and standing before him? If so, he understood her reluctance to openly admit the truth of such parentage. But he would not cast aspersions. He'd never agreed with the church's insistence on blaming the child for the sins of its parents, one of the many reasons he'd grown disenchanted with the profession his father had insisted he pursue.

Had she agreed to become Ingestrie's mistress solely so she might travel to England and search for this man? And if Kit helped her find him, would she leave Ingestrie far behind? Even if he no longer wished to pursue a life as a clergyman, he'd far rather a woman follow a godly path than one of debauchery and sin.

Besides, if she were able to help Kit in return, he'd

not have to trouble Uncle Christopher, risk endangering the man's already precarious health.

He stared down at her a moment, allowing his instincts to weigh the benefits against the dangers. Then, removing his glove, he held out his hand, as if she were a fellow with whom he was conducting a financial transaction rather than the mistress of another man.

"A fair trade. Your help, in exchange for mine."

She hesitated for a moment, then, unsmiling, placed her much smaller hand in his.

A brief snap of electric fire shocked through his fingers. But instead of pulling away, he grasped her hand more firmly.

Only a superstitious man would take such a commonplace occurrence as an omen, a warning to a mere mortal presumptuous enough to strike a bargain with a *leannán sídhe*.

CHAPTER THREE

"Why are you in London in the midst of term, Christian? Is this how you repay the kindness of the dons, by slacking off your duties?"

Kit looked away as his uncle struggled to shift his unresponsive legs higher up in the bed. Though some might think him callous, Kit knew better than to offer help to a man as proud, or as sharp-tongued, as Colonel Christopher Pennington. Especially as this seemed to be one of his uncle's poor days, when the pain of his lingering war injuries forced him to remain in bed instead of sitting up in a chair. As Kit had learned all too well during his visits over the past nine years, any offer of help would only result in his being filleted on the edge of his uncle's ire, dressed down as harshly as a private who'd had the unmitigated gall to question the orders of his commanding officer. Not at all the right way to soothe a tetchy man.

Nor would telling him about being shot help, either. No, Kit would be keeping that little incident to himself, especially his suspicion that his attacker had ties to Ireland. Penningtons did not speak of Ireland, not in front of Uncle Christopher.

The table beside his uncle's bed held only maps and books, with none of the usual powders, pills, or other medicines common to the sickroom. Not even Great-Aunt Allyne, who'd been kind enough to offer the wounded soldier a place in her own home after his brother, Lord Saybrook, had died, was allowed to physic Uncle Christopher, not even with a tot of brandy or rum. She wasn't *his* wife, nor even his aunt, after all, only the aunt of his brother's long-dead wife.

Kit pretended not to notice the sweat breaking out on the Colonel's brow as he used his strongly muscled arms to lever himself into a comfortable position. If the man felt any pain, he refused to show it.

Uncle Christopher cocked an eyebrow as he settled himself against the pillows. "Well, sir? Explain yourself."

"It was kind of the dons to extend my fellowship for another year, was it not?" Kit began.

"They didn't do it out of love for you, my boy, and don't you forget it. 'Twas on your father's account, and in the hopes of continued Saybrook patronage. Felt such a generous benefactor deserved a full year of mourning from his sons, they did. Pious bastards."

Kit smiled. Uncle Christopher had never had much use for the more sedentary professions. "No matter on whose account the offer was made, I was only too glad to delay my ordination another year. In fact," he continued, rising from his chair and grasping his hands behind his back, "the extra time helped me realize that I don't wish to be ordained at all."

A fierce scowl slashed across the Colonel's freshly-shaved face. "Just because your father's dead, Christian, do not think you'll persuade Saybrook to purchase you a set of colours."

Kit's shoulders tightened. If only it were as simple as an army commission.

"No, sir. I've quite reconciled myself to not following the drum. But you know I've never been entirely happy at the idea of becoming a churchman."

"Yes, but no Pennington worthy of the name just sits about on his arse, sucking the estate dry. I could write to Talbot, now that he's back from that godforsaken

Ireland, see if I could secure you a diplomatic post—"

"Thank you, but no." His secrets wouldn't last very long if Uncle Christopher began exchanging gossip with Lord Talbot, Viscount Ingestrie's father. "I've something else in mind."

"Pray don't tell me you've decided to set up as an artist like Benedict. Why, you'll have your father rolling in his grave."

"No, the work I plan to pursue would have been far more acceptable to him, I believe, even if it's not what he would have chosen for me." He paused, his hands grasping the back of his chair. He'd forgotten how much he valued his uncle's good opinion. "I don't know if you're aware, sir, but Mr. Norton, the man Father chose to represent our district in the House of Commons, has begun to throw his lot in with the Tories."

"Ah, something that truly would have your father rolling in his grave. I imagine Theo has rebuked him for his disloyalty?"

"My eldest brother is an indifferent politician, sir." And far too taken up with drowning his sorrows to pay much attention to politicking, it seemed; he'd not deigned to answer any of the many letters Kit had sent calling his attention to Norton's perfidy. But Kit valued family loyalty too much to tell tales on his eldest brother.

"But if you help me persuade him, surely Theo will see that Norton must be replaced," Kit said, stepping closer to the bed. "We need someone we can rely on, someone who will be loyal to the Whigs, and to Pennington interests. Someone who will carry on my father's legacy, support the principles he held dear."

The Colonel raised an eyebrow. "Someone such as yourself, Kit?"

Kit refused to turn away from the gimlet stare that had set many a younger officer a-quaking. "Yes," he said in as firm and assured a voice as he could muster. No need for his uncle to know it was guilt, as well as principle, that had set him upon this course.

The Colonel did not burst out laughing, for which Kit was deeply grateful. Shifting higher in the bed, he eyed his nephew from crown to boot, as if inspecting one of his troops on parade. Shaking his head as if not entirely satisfied with what his scrutiny revealed, he crossed his arms over his broad chest.

"So you want to be a politician, do you? But that's your brother's concern, now, his and all the men who own land. What reason have you to become entangled in such matters?"

"Not everyone has a nobleman, or even a gentry landowner, to look to his concerns, Uncle." Fianna Cameron certainly hadn't, not if she'd had to come all the way to England herself to find the father who'd abandoned her.

But the plight of an Irishwoman would hardly move Christopher Pennington. Kit aimed his argument in a more likely direction. "What of the people living in the towns? The ones working in the factories that keep springing up like weeds across England? Who will represent their concerns?"

Uncle Christopher frowned. "A candidate for reform? Truly, Christian?"

"Yes, sir."

"Do you not realize the dangers of such a position? Few radicals find themselves welcome in the homes of the aristocracy."

"Should I care more for the opinion of the gossips and idlers of the *ton* than I do about my duty as a Christian? I may not wish to take on the collar, sir, but I still remember my Bible. 'Do justice and righteousness, and deliver the one who has been robbed from the power of his oppressor,' God tells us. What more just and righteous cause than working to aid the disenfranchised?"

Uncle Christopher shifted his gaze away from Kit's face, struggling to contain what looked suspiciously like a chuckle. Damnation! Had he bungled it, crowing in priggish self-righteousness like a cock at the dawn?

But when he spoke, Uncle Christopher's words held no note of derision. "I could almost imagine my brother still alive, you sound so much like him. Why didn't you tell him of your political ambitions?"

Kit shrugged. "He was so ill those last years, and so set on my joining the clergy. With Theo showing such a marked lack of interest in running the estate, and Benedict outright refusing to return to university, I didn't want to add to his share of disappointments."

A rare smile flitted across the Colonel's face. "Do you know, Kit, your father hoped to name you after me? But your dashed mother insisted on christening each of her sons with a suitably sacred epithet. A compromise, Christian was, but a well-chosen one, I see. You've a soft heart, sir, underneath that argumentative front."

"I must have a soft heart, to put up with all your bluff and bluster these many years," Kit ventured, taking advantage of this rare softening in his uncle's mood. He returned to the chair by the Colonel's bed. "But now you'll return the favor by putting them to good use on my behalf. If you back my plans, Theo won't just grudgingly accept them, he'll actively support them."

His uncle grimaced. "Well, the new Lord Saybrook isn't much for visiting, I've discovered. But if his uncle sends him a summons, I suppose he'll deign to call."

"I should hope so." Kit struggled to keep the frustration out of his voice. "He's been dodging me for the past fortnight, but surely he won't show such disrespect to the senior member of the family."

"Damned well better not," his uncle growled, pushing himself back up in the bed. "Unworthy of a Pennington, such behavior."

Kit reached out and grasped the man's hand, eager to direct the conversation away from his brother's faults. "You won't regret it, sir. I will make the Pennington name proud."

"Enough, sir, enough," the Colonel said, pulling his

hand free of Kit's. "You can return the favor by keeping your ears open around your political friends. I've heard rumors of Irish radicals infiltrating London, looking for some way to destabilize our government. If you hear tell of any such men, you come to me. Why they do not ban the vermin from entering our country I will never understand."

"Of course, sir," Kit answered. He'd not encourage his uncle's virulent prejudices by asking any questions about such a purported Irish plot. All just a figment of his uncle's overly vivid imagination, no doubt, a way to stoke the fire of his biases against the Irish.

The Colonel reached for a small bell resting on the table beside him. "Now that I've granted you your blasted boon, let me ring for refreshments. And while we wait, you can show due admiration for my latest acquisition."

His uncle's eyes lit at the sight of the small box in the hands of his valet. Another Waterloo relic, no doubt. Though Uncle Christopher's wounds had prevented him from taking part, the final defeat of Napoleon held an indefinable fascination for him, and he had taken to collecting tokens from that memorable battlefield. Each rested in its own special case, as precious as a lady's jewels.

Uncomfortably morbid, touching the detritus of such a battle. Yet the old man took such obvious pleasure from his bullets and badges, and from showing them off. Kit suppressed his distaste as his uncle handed him the latest treasure, wondering instead how he might use it to turn the conversation to his other task: the search for Fianna Cameron's father.

"Do you have any idea to whom it belonged, Uncle?" Kit asked after offering the requisite praise of the lion head boss that had once decorated the helmet of a French lancer. "Could you find out, if he were still alive?"

"I wouldn't have the least idea how to go about

tracking down a Frenchie, even if I had the inclination," the Colonel said, turning the lion over and over in his palms. "But if this had belonged to an English officer, I'd certainly try to find him and return it, to him or to a member of his family."

Ah, just the entry Kit needed. "How would you go about such a search, sir?"

"If I knew the fellow's name and regiment, I'd start with the *Army List*, of course." His uncle laid a hand on a book sitting on the table beside him. "See if he's still in service or no."

Kit eyed the slim volume under his uncle's palm. "Yes, then you'd find out where the regiment was stationed, and you could contact him there. But what if he'd left?"

"Been pensioned off, you mean? Well, that'd be a bit more difficult. I'd start by writing to the regiment's commanding officer, see if he knew where the fellow'd taken himself off to. If he didn't, I'd ask 'em to check the regiment's muster roll; sometimes they write down where you signed on, and I could track him down that way. Couldn't go myself, of course, but I could send a hale nephew to nose around on my behalf," he said with a grin.

Kit smiled in return. "And if that didn't work?"

"Why, then it'd be off to the War Office for you, my boy. Up to their ears in records books there. Bound to be something that'd tell you a fellow's whereabouts amongst all that paper."

With a sudden frown, the Colonel leaned forward and placed a hand on top of Kit's. "But your interest seems more than idle, Christian. Why are *you* in search of some military man?"

The cold metal of his uncle's signet ring against his hand brought back a sudden memory, the grating disappointment of the day he'd finally come of age, when he realized that his father, so ill, had forgotten the tradition of gifting each Saybrook son with a signet of his own.

Though he'd said nothing at the time, Uncle Christopher must have guessed his feelings; only a week later Kit had found a box by his breakfast plate, one containing a ring that matched his uncle's, the initials they shared entwined in elegant monogram on its lapis lazuli bezel. How proud he'd felt, finally slipping that sign of his manhood, his connection to the house of Saybrook, to his family, over his bare finger.

He could hardly imagine not having such a family to rely upon. But Fianna Cameron surely could.

"Such a quick mind you have, Uncle," he said, pulling his hand from his uncle's tight grip. "The search, though, is not on my own behalf, but on behalf of an acquaintance. And that acquaintance has not given me leave to share the details."

"Sounds a havey-cavey affair. Not involved in anything untoward, are you, sir?" he asked, folding his arms across his chest.

"Of course not, Uncle. But might I borrow your *Army List*, to share with the young la— with my friend? I promise to return it forthwith."

Uncle Christopher laughed. "A lucky young la—, to have your aid in her quest. A comely wench, is she?"

Kit hesitated, at first from surprise, then from reluctance. Embarrassing, just how much Miss Cameron's person had affected him.

The Colonel nodded. "Yes, I see. Very comely. Well, no keeping her all to yourself, young man. Bring her round, so I can see if she's deserving of a Pennington." He sighed, rubbing a hand against his immobile thigh. "Would do me a world of good to see a handsome countenance around these dull rooms every now and then. Lord knows your great-aunt Allyne is bracket-faced enough to turn the milk sour."

Kit forced a laugh, though he felt more like grimacing. How quickly his uncle's sigh would turn to outrage if he had any idea from whence the lovely lady in question hailed.

No need to feel disloyal, was there, just for keeping a few secrets from his uncle?

CHAPTER FOUR

"Blister it, but my head aches. Anna, have you seen my other boot?"

Across the room from Fianna, a bleary-eyed Charles, Lord Ingestrie, sat on the side of the rumpled bed, his as-yet-untied neckcloth hanging limply over his shirt. Late nights of cards, wagers, and, most of all, raising celebratory glasses with every son, brother, or distant cousin of the lords of the land did not have the poor boy looking his best.

Not that Fianna would ever say a word against such behavior. Didn't his all-hours carousing give him little time for anything to do with the bedchamber besides dressing for his next bacchanal? Grateful, she should be, that she'd not had to lie with him since their arrival on his beloved English soil. Ridiculous to keen like a *bean sí* over the death of her own innocence as she'd done this morning when she'd awoken alone. He'd not stolen her virtue from her, after all; she'd offered it of her own free will, desperate to take advantage of this rare chance to afford passage to England.

England, where her father's final betrayer awaited the justice it was her duty to deal.

No, she'd made this bed, and now she'd lie in it, no matter how distasteful she found the task. And surely it was far better to sleep on a mattress beside a fool than amongst criminals in the filth of a gaol cell, accused of attempted murder? Her hands clutched at the frame of the door by which she stood, pushing away the memory of young Pennington catching her eyes across Ingestrie's crowded room the night before. Indulging in guilt and fear over shooting the wrong man would only churn her insides raw.

"Could Davenport have chucked the damned boot out the window?" Ingestrie pushed himself up off the bed, rocking on his feet as if they were still aboard the ship that had taken them across the Irish Sea. "Or used it to sip his champagne? Anna. . ."

The way he whined, one might be forgiven for thinking Ingestrie two instead of twenty. For all that Christopher Pennington had looked so young, his manner and speech indicated a man far more mature than the one beside her.

Fianna shook off the thought and trudged away from the door to engage in the search. Poking a foot under a fallen coverlet revealed two mismatched shoes, but no boot.

She didn't like playing mother or maidservant to the ridiculous boy any more than she liked playing his lover. Yet it would not do to alienate him, not yet. Not until she'd mastered her own fear, and secured the full cooperation of young Pennington to help her track down her true target. Most likely a relative, given their connection to the house of Saybrook. An uncle, perhaps?

Getting down on her knees, she groped under the bed, pulling out a wine bottle, the half-burnt end of a cheroot, and, at last, the wayward boot. Repressing a sigh, she tossed the errant footwear in Ingestrie's direction.

"Ah, you're a bonny lass, my girl," he said, sitting on the floor to pull it on. "If the pater weren't so eager I dance attendance on him this morning, I'd take you for a drive in the curricle, demmed if I wouldn't. Make all the other fellows' jaws drop, spying me with such a prime article."

She hid her grimace as she hauled him to his feet, then brushed the dust from the back of his coat. "Do up your neckcloth for you, shall I?"

"No time. Do it in the hack." He drew a quick comb through his hair, then tossed it back on the dresser. "Good Lord, why don't you put on one of the gowns I bought for you instead of that drab thing? I've wagered Kirkland and Cabot a hundred guineas each I've the most delicious piece in all London, but they'll have to see a bit more of your charms before they concede."

He gave her breast a quick, careless squeeze before turning and leaving the room.

Fianna stared in the mirror long after the slam of the door faded, willing her insides to still. She'd chosen to take on the role of courtesan; she'd no right, then, to take umbrage at being treated like one. Besides, a true McCracken would never allow such an insignificant snip of a man to wound her feelings. Grandfather, Aunt Mary, the uncles and cousins and wives—all the Mc-Crackens kept their emotions decently in check. A girl who let her passions flow without restraint would never deserve a place amongst them.

So. It was nothing.

He was nothing.

The clock on the mantel struck the hour. Turning away from the mirror, she pulled on a hat with a heavy, concealing veil. She missed the reassuring weight of her father's pistol against her thigh. But no matter. The razor she'd stolen away from Ingestrie's valet would have to suffice.

All she need do was dupe young Pennington into revealing the whereabouts of his relation, without giving herself away in the process.

He stood by the door of the coffeehouse, the man she'd mistakenly shot a mere seven days earlier.

He looked even younger in the daytime than he had during the night. Younger than her own thirty years, certainly; a year or two older than Ingestrie's twenty, perhaps. What a tiny cherub of a babe he must have been, with those celestial blue eyes and those fat, golden ringlets that wouldn't stay brushed back over his forehead. Even now, young girls just awakening to the wonders of the other sex likely made calf eyes at him in droves. Fine to dream about stolen kisses with a fellow whose sweet face promised no real threat to that virtue you were just beginning to understand the necessity of guarding.

Even though he stood with a certain stiffness, his expression stern and unsmiling, still, something about him urged one to give him one's trust, to hand it over as one might the only cup in one's tea service with the tiny nick in its rim, certain that he'd take care to not make it worse, nor have the bad manners to comment on its defects.

What would it be like, to share one's burdens with such a man?

She shook her head, flinging away such a ridiculous yearning. She was no young moonling, eager to spill her secrets to the first handsome face that passed. Leave the romantic reveries to the innocent young misses of the English *ton* for whom he was destined. The terrors of the night, with their fiery visions of vengeance, must be enough to sustain her.

What an irony it would be, though, if angelic Kit Pennington should end up being her guide to the very devil.

She crossed the room, all too aware of the blatant speculation in the eyes of the men she passed. Each assuming her presence in the all-male domain of the coffeehouse indicated her lack of respectability. Each wishing that he might be the one to reap the benefits of that lack. Lord, that one by the window—if she sent a smile in his direction, promised to spend a night in his bed, why, the stupid fellow would likely declare himself her slave.

She enslaved him, that leannán sídhe! Aunt McCracken's bitter voice rang in Fianna's head. *My brother never would have done it, not any of it, but for your mother, that Irish witch,* she'd hissed as she and Fianna had watched the cart carrying her mother, grandfather, and young uncle Sean crest the hill and pass out of sight. *Far better rid of her, you are, Maria, rid of all of them. No McCracken girl will ever tempt a man to his downfall, we'll make certain of that. . .*

How utterly wrong her aunt's prophecy had turned out to be.

Fianna straightened her shoulders, shaking off a fleeting pang of remorse. She had another man to tempt today.

When she reached Kit Pennington's side, she lowered into her most graceful curtsy. "Mr. Pennington. I'm sorry to have asked you to come so far out of your way."

"Miss Cameron." Doffing his hat, he gave her a short bow, as if she were any other gentlewoman of his acquaintance. "It was no trouble, I assure you."

She caught back the deep breath her body wanted her to take, cursing the part of her that obviously still feared him, feared he'd recognize her and call for the watch before she had a chance to finish what she'd come to England to do. No, even in the brighter light of day, he did not see her for what she truly was. And she'd be damned if she allowed her body to give him any reason to doubt her.

He remained unsmiling, but no expression of contempt marred his countenance. "Shall we find seating? I've some information I hope will be of benefit to you." He crooked an elbow in her direction.

Reaching out a tentative hand, she rested her fingertips on the wool of his greatcoat, careful to keep her gaze directed demurely at the floor. Because it was part of her masquerade, of course, not because she was afraid.

Or because his eyes were the least bit compelling.

He led her to a table and settled her in a wooden chair. "Coffee?"

"Chocolate, if you please."

He signaled to the server, then shrugged out of his greatcoat, reaching into a deep pocket before setting it on the chair beside him. He slid a small volume across the table, indicating with a nod that she was to open it.

She removed her gloves, then trailed her fingers over the golden lions embossed on the red leather cover before turning to the first page. *A List of all the Officers of the Army and Marines on Full and Half-Pay.*

Could it truly be so easy, the Major's location written down in a book for anyone to see?

"You did say the man you sought was an officer, did you not?" he asked, reaching out in his eagerness to ruffle through the pages. "Do you know his regiment?"

She shook her head. "Only that it was stationed in Ireland during the 1790s. I do know he was a major, though."

He pulled his chair around the table, setting it right beside hers. Her breath caught in her throat. At the thought of how close she was to her father's killer, of course.

"That should be enough," he said. "See, here, right at the front, all officers, from general to major. Not alphabetically, but by date of commission. Of course," he acknowledged with a self-deprecating smile, "it might be easiest just to check the index. You do know his name, do you not?"

His sleeve brushed against her arm as he thumbed to the end of the book. No odor of smoke or stale, unwashed bedsheets hung about him, as it always did about Ingestrie. Kit Pennington's scent soothed, like freshly washed linens hanging to dry in the sun, or perhaps the rich, fertile earth after a summer rain. Warm, friendly even.

With a jerk of her head, Fianna focused her attention back on the book. "Pembroke," she said, remembering the small, wheeled table from which Grandfather Mc-Cracken took his meals when he was too ill to come to table. In an index, surely Pembroke would not be too far away from Pennington.

"But I needn't take up your time now," she added, placing a quelling hand over his. It would do her little good to raise his suspicions now, when she was so close.

Today luck appeared to be on her side. She waved a hand toward the entrance of the coffeehouse. "If the arrival of that large group of gentlemen is any indication, the antiquarian meeting about which I was told is soon to begin."

"Antiquarian meeting?" he asked. He looked not at the door, though, but down at their hands. When had his fingers curved around hers?

"Yes," she said, startled by the low pitch of her own voice. With a shake of her head, she slid her hand from beneath the warmth of his. "As difficult as it may be to believe, some Anglo-Irish Protestant antiquarians have become quite interested in the past of the country they oppress. We might even find a scholar who knows enough Gaelic to tell you what your mysterious words mean."

No, not Kit Pennington's words, but *Father's*. Not long after Aunt Mary had taken her away from her mother and brought her to Belfast, during that short time she'd lived in the McCracken home before they'd sent her away to school, she'd found it, her dead father's pistol, buried in the attic of Grandfather McCracken's house. Deep in a box, it had been, hidden beneath the neatly folded letters Aunt Mary had exchanged with her brother the year he'd been held in Kilmainham Gaol, accused of fomenting rebellion. She'd taken care to conceal the letters, and the firearm, from prying eyes after she'd stolen them away to her own room. Not out of fear of being connected to the disgraced rebel to whom they had belonged, but from a fierce, angry desire to keep the only mementos of her father she possessed solely to herself.

She'd never dared ask anyone what the words he'd had engraved upon the pistol meant.

Kit Pennington rose, holding out his arm once again to her. How could anyone smile with such ease, as if he were certain nothing in the world would do him harm? No, he had no idea that the pistol belonged to her.

Together, they made their way across the room to where the party of gentlemen had begun to confer over a pile of books and manuscripts.

With a bow and a genial smile, Pennington introduced himself. "Pardon my interruption, good sirs, but I was given to understand the most knowledgeable antiquarians in all the city met here. Might we have a word?"

For all his youth, he had the easy assurance of the aristocrat born and bred. How simple he made it seem, evoking both deference and curiosity from the group of scholarly men with his confident bearing and friendly mien. If she'd been by herself, she'd never have been able to set them at their ease so quickly, nor to gain their respect or trust.

"You've an intelligent informant, then, sir, at least if your interests lie in the history of the land to our west," one of their number replied, removing his glasses and bowing in return. "Artemus Callendar at your service. Have you an inquiry you wish us to undertake? An old manuscript you wish to have copied?"

"A task far less daunting, I promise. Just a line or two of translation, if any amongst you can read Gaelic."

"What, that jargon still spoken by the unlettered vulgar?" muttered a man from across the table, casting a scornful glance in her direction.

Although Pennington's countenance remained cordial, the muscles beneath her hand tensed. Had he taken umbrage on her behalf? Fianna gave his arm a light squeeze, warning against alienating their best chance of finding the answers they sought.

Mr. Callendar frowned at the sharp-tongued man, then smiled in apology. "I'm sorry, sir, but Gaelic is a difficult language to master. We tend to rely upon native scholars and scribes when a bit of treasure still locked up in the Irish language needs unraveling. But few such men choose to leave their homeland, alas."

"What of that political fellow, the one from Cork, come to raise funds for the destitute?" another member of the group asked.

"Ah yes," the rude gentleman acknowledged. "That sly gent, who made the utterly ridiculous claim that the barbaric Gaels valued learning as much as they did military skill."

"Yes, that's the one," Callendar said, with a slap of his hand on the table. "And he said he'd come again today, did he not? Now, what was his name?"

A chorus of "O'Hanlon?" "No, O'Hanley?" "You're wrong, I'm certain it was O'Hara!" flew about the room, the antiquarians squabbling over the name like fowl over freshly strewn feed. Kit Pennington cut his eyes to hers, quirking a sardonic eyebrow.

How long had it been since she'd felt such an urge to smile at a man in shared amusement?

A heavy tread behind her checked the unwise impulse before it had a chance to take root. "O'Hamill, sirs. The name for which you seek is O'Hamill."

Fianna stilled, all her senses snapping to painful attention. A common enough name in Ireland, O'Hamill. But a man from Cork, in the south of Ireland, would never set the syllables dancing with a musicality found only in the north. Why would he lie?

She turned, half a beat after all the others, to find her

gaze caught by a pair of eyes as green as her own.

Kit had been born with the gift of intuition, at least when it came to sensing the emotions of others. A quick glance at a person's face, or the way they held their body, and the edge of irritation, or disappointment, or fear that lay beneath the polite exterior seemed as clear to him as if they'd spoken their true feelings out loud. How often he'd winced as others foundered, misreading others' feelings, until he'd realized that most people could not see beyond social façades as he could.

But his usual skill had failed him when he'd met Fianna Cameron. Even given her impassive, cold demeanor and the stillness in which she held her petite frame, it had taken him aback, his inability to read beyond her glittering surface.

How odd, then, to sense her sudden disquiet now, even as she stood behind him, out of his line of sight. He could feel it quivering in the air, like the trembling tension of a rabbit immobilized by the sight of a predator yet unable to still the wild beatings of its heart. What had shaken her so?

Her countenance, when he turned to face her, proved just as unrevealing now as it had been two nights earlier. But when he followed the direction of her gaze, he found a possible answer.

One of the two men making their way across the coffeehouse was as familiar to him as were his own brothers. More so, perhaps, given how little time he'd spent with either Benedict or Theo of late. But surely his friend Sam Wooler wouldn't make any woman uneasy. Kindly and even tempered despite his radical politics, Sam rarely allowed strong emotion to overset him.

It must be the man beside Sam, then, a man Kit did

not recognize. Did Miss Cameron know the burly, stern-faced fellow? Impossible to tell, for by the time the two men reached them, she had turned her eyes modestly to the floor.

"Kit!" Sam grasped his hand with eager welcome. "Why did you not send me word you were up and about again?"

"Because attempting to amicably settle your argument with Abbie was what led to the trouble in the first place," Kit said, quirking up one corner of his mouth. "I'd no wish to listen to the two of you continue to squabble over my sickbed."

The night he'd been attacked, he'd been searching the news room at the Crown and Anchor for a copy of the second volume of *The Rights of Man*, in an attempt to settle a ridiculous quarrel between Sam and their friend George Abbington-Pitts over the precise wording of one of Mr. Paine's pithier pronouncements. Witnessing a fellow being shot would have sent such petty quibbles straight out of the heads of most men, but once Sam and Abbie sniffed out a bone of contention, neither was likely to let it drop.

"Ah, you already know our friend Mr. Wooler, do you, sir?" Callendar exclaimed. "But not Mr. O'Hamill, I'll warrant. How fortuitous!"

Callendar nodded to the Irishman, then gestured him toward their group. "Mr. Pennington, may I introduce Mr. O'Hamill? Pennington here is in search of a Gaelic scribe."

"Is he, now? And cannot the lovely *cailín* do the honors?" the stranger asked, nodding toward Miss Cameron, who stood a bit apart from their group. "I'd wager my last groat that she's the blood of the Irish flowing through her veins."

All the antiquarians had responded to Fianna Cameron's disquieting beauty in one way or another—darting glances, shuffling papers, a quick hand smoothing over an unruly head of hair. And even Sam, usually indifferent to the attractions of the fairer sex, kept turning his head in her direction before jerking it back to the conversation of the men.

But none had the effrontery to stare at her the way this O'Hamill did.

Oddly, though, nothing of lust, nor even of admiration, warmed his eyes. His workingman's clothes, his grim, creased face, both said here was a man inured not just to want, but to the deadening certainty of want ever unsatisfied. But still he stared at her, his eyes narrowed, considering. What could he mean by it?

With a frown, Kit made the introductions. Neither Miss Cameron nor Mr. O'Hamill gave any indication that they knew one another, but tension still charged the air. Kit made sure to keep himself between the burly man and the far smaller woman. To reassure her? Or to warn O'Hamill off? He wasn't quite certain.

"I've no knowledge of the Gaelic, alas," Miss Cameron said, eyes downcast. "Mr. Pennington had hoped these kind gentlemen might be able to aid him."

"But your antiquarians, even the Anglo-Irish ones, rarely have much facility with the language, do they?" the man answered, his smile edged more with contempt than collegiality.

"But they've been kind enough to recommend your skills," Kit replied before any of the antiquarians could take offense. "Might you be able to oblige?" Kit gestured to a table apart from the others.

"Your servant, sir." Turning to Callendar, O'Hamill added, "Please, do not hold off on your meeting for my sake. I'll join you presently."

"Mr. Pennington, do not hesitate to call on us if you find you need the advice of an educated man," Callendar called before turning back to his group. Miss Cameron's mouth tightened, but O'Hamill's steps did not even pause. Had the Irishman become so used to such casual slights as to render them insignificant?

Kit reached to pull out a chair for Miss Cameron, but

O'Hamill was quicker. Kit's jaw clenched at the sight of the Irishman's hands as they remained on the back of her chair, even after she'd taken her seat. It would hardly be gentlemanlike to point out the impropriety of how close they were to her person. Especially if Miss Cameron did not object. Kit scraped his own chair across the floor and sat down opposite her.

Sam hovered beside the table. "Is this a private matter, Kit? Uncle's asked me to write an article for the paper about Mr. O'Hamill's efforts on behalf of Ireland's poor, but I've no need to intrude upon your concerns."

"Please, Sam, sit down. You may be of as much help as either Miss Cameron or Mr. O'Hamill, as you were actually there when the shooting took place."

"Shooting?" O'Hamill's work-roughened hands flattened on the table. "You begin to interest me, sir. Come, tell me all about it."

Between them, Kit and Sam related the events that had occurred at the Crown and Anchor a week earlier. O'Hamill listened intently, his occasional interruptions to clarify a point or to draw out a pertinent detail demonstrating a quick, analytical turn of mind. Miss Cameron remained silent.

"And the inscription on the pistol is the only clue you have? Might I see it?" O'Hamill asked when Kit reached the end of the embarrassing tale.

"You will understand my reluctance to tote the firearm about London, I'm certain." Kit grimaced as he pushed a paper across the table. "But I've written down the words from the engraving. I believe they're Gaelic, but whether Scots or Irish, I've no idea."

O'Hamill glanced down at the paper, then frowned. "Irish Gaelic, it is, not Scots—see, no grave accents, only acutes. *Agus* means 'and,' and this, here, the *Tá* and *curtha* together make 'has been.' Something about strings, here, and hearing—a reference to a harp, perhaps?"

"A harp?" Kit's forehead creased.

"The harp is the most common emblem of Ireland," O'Hamill replied, placing the paper back on the table. "Does not your king himself include the harp on his coat of arms, as reminder of England's union with our fair nation?"

"Domination of our land, more like," Miss Cameron said in a flat, expressionless voice.

"So one might say, if he'd little care for keeping his neck out of a noose," O'Hamill replied with an affable nod.

He hadn't thought Fianna Cameron's face could grow any less revealing, but O'Hamill's words seemed to shear away every shred of expression from her eyes. Was the man threatening her in some way?

"The harp's also a symbol used by radical groups in Ireland," Sam added, rubbing the back of his neck. "Although I can't see you being the target of a politically motivated shooting, Kit. Even though your brother's a viscount, your views hardly qualify you as an enemy of radical causes. Not since Peterloo, at least."

"Were you in attendance at that horrific event, Mr. Pennington?" O'Hamill's eyes lit with interest. "How difficult to believe the accounts of the English soldiers' brutality toward the innocent populace who had gathered to hear Mr. Hunt speak on behalf of universal suffrage."

Miss Cameron's lips parted, as if to scoff at the Irishman's assertion. But Sam, who loved to tell the tale, spoke first. "We both were there, although not together. At least, not until Kit saved my friend and me from being skewered by a slightly overzealous member of the yeoman militia."

"And Abbie's been scolding me ever since for pushing him out of the way. How dare I muddy his clothing!" Kit said, hoping to turn the conversation. He hated it when Sam told the story, making it sound as if Kit had been some kind of damned hero that day. Would Sam be as eager to claim friendship with an aristocrat if he'd come across Kit even a few moments earlier, moments when Kit had stood, frozen in disbelief, as that maddened militia began to attack the crowd? As he'd watched a soldier slash at an old man, another cut down a woman with a babe in arms, without making a single move to intervene? Only when a sword had come swinging in his direction had Kit jerked free of the shock and begun to push other unarmed members of the crowd away from the attacking soldiers.

"The harp is also a symbol of Irish culture," Miss Cameron said with a quick glance in his direction. Had she picked up on his discomfort, as he had begun to recognize hers? The thought brought a smile to his lips.

"You think the pistol's owner may be a musician?" he asked.

She nodded. "Is there a section of London where the Irish generally reside? Perhaps you might extend your inquiry to that neighborhood's taverns."

Sam leaned forward. "St. Giles, mostly, and Seven Dials. But you'd best take a pistol with you if you venture into the rookeries, Kit."

Kit turned back to the Irishman. "Do the words truly suggest a musician? What is the exact translation, O'Hamill?"

The Irishman tapped a finger against the paper, glancing not toward Kit but toward Sam before he spoke. "Wouldn't want to say for certain, sir, least not before confirming my reading. Could ask a friend or two, ones who have a bit more knowledge of the Gaelic than I, if you'd like, and let you know what I find."

"Of course. Here is my direction, if you discover anything of interest." Kit took out a pencil and scribbled a few lines below the Gaelic, then slid the sheet back across the table. "I'd be most grateful for any help."

"No trouble, no trouble at all, sir." O'Hamill nodded in Sam's direction. "Mr. Wooler, shall we join the antiquarians, as we had originally planned?"

"I'll be with you in a moment, O'Hamill," Sam said. "Just need a word with Pennington first."

Taking up his hat, O'Hamill gave a short bow. "Your servant, sir. Ma'am."

Kit watched the sturdily built man thread his way across the crowded room, glad to see the back of him despite his offer of aid. Even after O'Hamill took a seat amongst the antiquarians, though, Fianna Cameron's posture remained rigid. Had O'Hamill not been the only cause?

With an abruptness that took him by surprise, she pushed back her chair. "I, too, must bid you good day, sirs. I'm afraid another engagement awaits."

Kit rose, oddly reluctant to let her go. "Please, allow me to see you to it."

He held out his arm, but she only shook her head. "Do not concern yourself, sir. Arrangements have already been made for my safe return. Mr. Wooler, a pleasure."

If Miss Cameron were a lady, he'd have insisted she not leave unaccompanied. But would a courtesan resent the courtesies a gentlewoman would demand as her due? Unsure, Kit returned his hand to his side.

She smiled and curtsied, then walked in the direction opposite to the one taken by O'Hamill. Her reticule, heavy with the weight of the book he'd lent her, swung below her hip.

"Pennington?" Sam asked, his voice low and tight. "Kit, are you involved with that woman?"

Kit gave a start. How long had he stood there, staring at another man's lightskirt?

"Involved?"

"Yes, involved."

"Sam. Please. She's Ingestrie's mistress, not mine. Even if he didn't accompany her here, he knows she offered to help me." Praise heaven Sam had far less skill reading others' emotions than he. "Do you know some ill of her?"

"No. In fact, I'd believe I'd never met her before in my life, except for this feeling, right here"—Sam's palm rose to tap against his chest—"that I have. And not under pleasant circumstances, either."

Kit forced a grin. "Come, Sam, aren't you the one always mocking Abbie for his irrational superstitions? How he'd laugh to hear you, you and your mysterious 'feeling'!"

"It's not the same, Kit, not at all. If only I could put my finger on where I'd seen her before!" Sam shook his head in frustration. "But she's a danger, I'm sure of it."

"A danger? That little slip of a chit?"

"Another slip of a chit aimed a pistol at you only a week ago, Kit! And if she'd had better aim, you'd not be here to argue the point."

"Granted. But would you have me place every woman in London under suspicion?"

"Perhaps, at least until you've run your attacker to ground." At Kit's grunt, Sam took a step closer. "Look, Kit, you need to take better care of yourself. We've few enough men amongst the gentry willing to take up the cause of parliamentary reform as it is. Don't risk decreasing that number out of some childish belief in your own invulnerability."

Sam laid what was surely meant to be a comforting hand on Kit's shoulder, but the gesture simply increased Kit's frustration. Shrugging out from under Sam's fingers, Kit took a step closer to the door through which Fianna Cameron had left. His untoward response to Ingestrie's mistress was anything but childish.

"At least have a care of that Cameron woman," Sam said, worry making his voice uncharacteristically gruff. "Meeting with a fellow's mistress behind his back isn't the wisest thing you've ever done, Kit, even if she's not a threat herself."

"No, it's not, is it?" Kit murmured. Especially for a man attempting to clear his name of another scandal.

Why, then, did the very air of danger that hovered

around Fianna Cameron entice him so?

CHAPTER FIVE

"More tea, miss?"

Fianna sighed as the sole serving girl in the nearly empty pastry shop interrupted her yet again. The fashionable hour for indulging in bonbons and ices had yet to arrive, it would seem, and the girl had little to occupy her time besides offering to refill her cup every five minutes.

Fianna shook her head and turned back to the window. Foolish of her not to put as much distance as possible between herself and the men in the coffeehouse across the street. She'd almost choked on her heart when Pennington's friend strode toward her, recognizing him from the night of the shooting. And his Irish companion, with his sharp green eyes and his too-familiar surname—her own family name, at least for the first six years of her life, before she'd been taken away from her mother—had made all her self-protective instincts prick.

Mr. Wooler, just like Kit Pennington before him, might have failed to recognize her. But that Irishman had far too much of the look of the O'Hamills for her comfort. What if he knew her, or the family from which she had come? What if he suspected her? Revealed her original identity to Kit Pennington? She must find out who he was, no matter the danger.

The imaginary appointment she'd invented gave her

all the excuse she needed to leave alone, freeing her to lie in wait for the Irishman. Whether she'd confront him or simply follow him remained to be seen.

But O'Hamill had tarried at the coffeehouse far longer than she'd expected, so long that she hadn't been able to resist glancing through Kit Pennington's *Army List* while she waited. Well, she'd been fittingly rewarded for indulging that bit of impatience, now, hadn't she? For while the book's index listed *Pennington, Lowther, Pennington, Thomas,* and *Pennington, William,* of *Pennington, Christopher* it made no mention. Nor did the name appear on the book's list of army majors, amongst the officers of the Royal Regiment of Artillery in Ireland, or on the list of officers on the Irish half-pay. She'd even begun to search the lists of more senior officers, in case the man's scurrilous actions in Ireland had earned him a promotion or two. But for all this book had to report of him, Major Christopher Pennington might never have existed.

"Miss? A cup fer yer man?"

Fianna's eyes jerked away from the window. "My man? What man?"

The apron-clad girl shrugged a shoulder toward the door. Twisting in her seat, Fianna caught sight of a stocky, stern-faced male, his hand raised in greeting.

O'Hamill.

Her instincts had not played her false, then. There *was* some connection between this man and the family of her birth. She gripped the edge of the table, her knuckles growing white.

"Ah, I'm that sorry, *cailín*, for making you wait," he said as he reached her table, his tone suggesting they were the oldest of friends. "But prying coins from the hands of an Englishman's worse than prising a stick from a starving dog. Begging your pardon, ma'am."

The smile he tossed at the serving girl did not come close to reaching his eyes. But she hardly seemed to notice. "Tea, sir?" she asked.

He nodded. As the girl scurried away, he pulled out a chair and sat down across from Fianna, as comfortable as if she'd invited him into her own house.

Her eyes narrowed. "Mr. O'Hamill. Why did you follow me?"

"Do you call a quick glance out the window, noting the path taken by a pretty wench, 'following'?"

"Yes, I do." Lowering her voice to barely above a whisper, she hissed, "I want nothing to do with you, sir. Nothing. And if you think to importune me, you'll find yourself regretting it."

The stocky man clasped his hands on the table, then leaned toward her, his countenance grim. "It appears that someone else has already done the importuning, *cailín*. If yon Pennington's ruined you, I'll make sure he'll regret it, to the very end of his days."

She nursed her anger, willing it to drown the uneasiness his words inspired. Worry not on her own behalf—she'd been taking care of herself for far too long to allow a simple threat to give her pause—but on behalf of the far-too-innocent Kit Pennington. And what if he was in danger—what was it to her? She'd be a right fool to give in to such ridiculous sentiment now.

"I believe you've misunderstood our relationship, sir," she said, smoothing all expression from her face. "Mr. Pennington is simply an acquaintance to whom I offered my aid." No need to inform him of her less-than-respectable relationship with another young member of the English *ton*. Especially if O'Hamill turned out to be kin. Irishmen did not look kindly on their womenfolk taking up with the English.

"Pleased I am to hear it," he said, sitting back in his chair. "I'd not be shocked to find you despairing of your treatment at his or any other Englishman's hands, what with the way the brutes ravish our women with as little concern as they despoil our land."

"I am no Mary Le More, sir," she replied, her hands clenching tight under the table. How she scorned the heroine of that popular ballad, driven mad after her rebel menfolk were killed and herself debauched by marauding English soldiers. As if crying and raving were all a woman could do in the face of such bitter injustice.

No, she'd done far more than weep and wail in her campaign against those who'd betrayed her father. She'd not been Ingestrie's victim, nor any other man's, but their hunter, ensnaring each in order to achieve a larger, more worthy goal. And she'd be damned if she shied away from using Kit Pennington, or even this grim-faced Mr. O'Hamill, if the using would help gain justice for her father and his family. She wasn't the daughter of Aidan McCracken for nothing.

"From Cork, are you, sir?" Fianna asked as she leaned forward across the table. "Englishmen may have little ear for the speech of our countrymen, but I assure you, I can tell the difference between a man born and bred in the south and one who hails from Antrim or Down. What cause have you to lie, sir?"

A grim smile played about O'Hamill's lips. "A smart one, aren't you? But not as smart as you think. A truly intelligent wench would be far less worried about from whence I hail, and far more about the fire with which she plays. *Tá na téada curtha go húr agus cloisfear í*, indeed!"

Fianna's lips thinned. "Then you do know what the words on the pistol mean. Why did you not say so?"

"Because young Mr. Wooler, involved as he is in radical politics, would have recognized them immediately. And I believe, Miss *Cameron*," he said, his tone giving a derisive edge to her name, "you would not have liked that at all. No, you would not have liked that one little bit."

She pulled up the memory of the words he had offered—*a harp, strings, hearing*—allowing them to tease at something long forgotten, tucked away far in the back of her brain. Her father's voice, deep, impassioned, proclaiming not just a slogan, but a creed. . .

"*Equality—It is newly strung and shall be heard*," she whispered, her eyes widening in both awe and dismay. The sheer audacity of Aidan McCracken, to translate the seditious motto of the United Irishmen into Gaelic and inscribe it on his pistol for all to see. Flaunting it right under the noses of the English oppressors, mocking them not only for their arrogance toward the people they looked down upon as so very inferior to themselves, but also for their ignorance of that people's language and culture. She'd never been prouder of her daring father.

And she'd never been more frightened of another man than she was of the one sitting across from her. O'Hamill knew. Somehow, he knew she was the one who had taken that pistol and aimed it at Kit Pennington, the son and brother of English lords. She could see the knowledge of it in the loose, confident way he held himself in that chair, in the shrewd, cunning glint in those dark green eyes. And he meant to use that knowledge to his own advantage. Despite whatever kinship lay between them.

He took up her cup and downed a large gulp before dropping it back in its saucer with a loud clink. "Bah. It's gone cold. Why doesn't the wench bring any fresh?"

Fianna pushed back her chair, groping in her reticule for coin to throw on the table. She had to leave. Now.

But he followed her out the door and over the rough cobbles of the street. Could she lose him in the alleys behind the tea shop?

"I'm to have no thanks for my friendly warning, then, *cailín*?" he called. "To be sure and I thought you had the look of an O'Hamill, but no child of our Mairead's would have shamed her family with such a show of ingratitude."

Fianna stilled in her tracks. "Mairead? Mairead O'Hamill?"

"Heard of the O'Hamill, have you?" he said, taunting

her by focusing on the least important of the two names. "Descendants of Binneach, son of Eoghan, son of Niall of the Nine Hostages, founder of the Uí Néill dynasty? Poets and wise men, advisers to the mightiest of the land, they were, before the English sullied Éire-ann shores."

He paused, as if waiting for her to speak. Did he expect her to claim a place in such an exalted lineage? She would not give him the satisfaction.

Booted footsteps rang against the cobbles, bringing him one step closer, then another. "A *McCracken* might have forgotten such a proud heritage," he whispered over her shoulder. "But a daughter of Mairead's? You'll never convince me of it."

Fianna allowed the shudder to finish its course through her body before carefully turning to face the man who should have been a stranger, but was not.

"Oh, and haven't you just the way of her?" he asked, the ghost of a smile whispering across his lips. "That nose up in the air, those green eyes flashing, cutting a man down to size quicker than a sword. A brave *fear*, Aidan McCracken, to take up with a *sidh* such as our Mairead."

A chill shivered down Fianna's spine. "Who are you?" she whispered, needing him to say the words out loud.

He took a step closer, lowering his voice as he pulled the cap from his head. "Sure and you're not knowing your own uncle Sean, Máire O'Hamill?"

Fianna jerked back. This dark, hard man, her mother's young brother? The same eager boy who'd followed Aidan McCracken about with the devotion of an apostle? Not a distant connection, but the closest of kin?

She shook her head. "But they left—*you* left. You all fled, before the soldiers could come and take you away. Aunt McCracken, she told me she gave you the money to go to America, so they wouldn't capture you and hang you, as they did my father."

He nodded. "'Tis true, my father and my sister sailed for America. But not I. I'll not be abandoning the cause of Éirinn so quick as all that."

The Sean O'Hamill she remembered had been a boy, only a handful of years older than herself, far too young to take part in any of the fighting the rebels had planned. But he'd hung on Aidan McCracken's every word, whispering under his breath the pledge taken by the United Irishmen, determined someday to play a role in bringing liberty and equality to their people.

Her mother, Mairead, would sit and watch, pride warring with worry, as her young lover set her even younger brother aflame with visions of Irish freedom.

Her mother—

Fianna's breath caught in her throat. "Is she here with you? Mairead?" she whispered.

He considered her for a long moment before answering. "She is not. Did I not say she'd gone to America?"

"Where?"

"I know not."

Fianna pressed a fist against her chest. How quickly thoughts of vengeance had been forgotten, overshadowed by the yearning for a mother's arms.

But Mairead O'Hamill did not deserve the name of mother. No, not after abandoning her to the McCrackens, their beloved Aidan's only child, in exchange for mere coin. Not after purchasing her own freedom at the expense of her daughter's. Not after leaving Máire behind.

No, Mairead's daughter was a McCracken now, not an O'Hamill. She'd prove it, or perish in the attempt.

But might even an O'Hamill still be devoted to the memory of a hero such as Aidan McCracken?

She stepped closer to Sean, laying a hand on the man's rough sleeve. "Help me find someone, *Seanuncail*?"

He laughed at that, the joke of the old nickname, as

if a boy only four years her senior could be counted among the doddering old men typically granted the respectful title of "grand-uncle." Rougher and lower than she remembered, that laugh, yet in it she finally recognized her childhood playmate, a boy who'd always had time for an illegitimate niece shunned by neighbor and parish alike.

"Come to London chasing after a long-lost love, have you, then?" he asked.

Her hand tightened on his arm. "A lover? Say instead a killer."

"Aidan McCracken's killer? Ah, so that's why you're hanging after young Pennington. Not being much of a help to you, is he, though, I'd wager. And what's a wee slip of a *cailín* such as yourself going to do to the likes of the Major, even if the boy were to lead you to him? Bat your eyes at him until he cries sorry?"

Fianna's hand jerked away, her stomach seething at the derision in his voice. But instead of backing down, she took a step closer, hands clenching tight by her sides.

"Mayhap, *Seanuncail*, you've not heard what's become of the other men who betrayed my father? How Samuel Russell lost all his money at cards, trying to win enough to please a ladylove? Or how Alan Simms's wife won't let him near his children after catching him with another woman, his trousers down about his ankles? Or of that gaoler at Kilmainham, how his own brother beat him within an inch of his life, all over a mere *sidh*? Curious, how each lost what he most desired, far beyond the means of its recall. And all taken away by a wee slip of a *cailín*. Or so I have heard."

The lines around Sean O'Hamill's eyes deepened, almost as if they were tempting him to smile. But his lips held fast in a grim line. "Sure, are you, that Old Scratch's not already called the devil home to hell?"

"Certain," she lied with practiced ease. Surely the Lord would never be so cruel as to steal Major Pennington away before she had had her chance at him.

Sean stared at her then, his eyes as deep and green as her own mother's. Could he see it, the hope that burned in hers? The only thing that kept her moving, day through deadened day? The hope that by bringing the men who had harmed her father to justice, and by forcing Pennington to recant his vicious lies, she'd still her grandfather's pain, and finally prove herself worthy of the McCracken family? A real family to love, one that would love her back?

"They do say no one rejoices more in revenge than a woman, don't they, now?" Sean said at last. "But the Major's no player in the current game, even if he is still alive. Why should one bother with the likes of him?"

She swallowed, hard. She should have expected it, yet another rejection from her Irish family. Well, no matter. She'd done all the rest by herself, and she'd not shy away from doing this one last thing alone, either.

With a nod, she turned away and began to trudge down the street.

But before she had taken three steps, a weighty hand on her shoulder drew her back.

"For Mairead's sake, though, and for Aidan's, I might be persuaded to spend a few hours looking for yon Major," Sean said. "That whoreson refused my sister even the small comfort of cutting a lock of hair from the head of her own true love before hanging him dead, didn't he, now? And turned him into a figure of contempt, rather than the martyr he was, all with a few lies whispered in the right ears. What idiots, to believe a man such as Aidan McCracken would ever betray his men."

A grim smile slashed across his face. "Perhaps such a fiend deserves the fate a mere *cailín* has in store."

The bond of common purpose tightened around her then, almost as strong as the ties of kinship she had felt for Sean in their youth.

"And Ireland will soon have need of a daughter who

teaches her enemies the price of betraying her," Sean continued. "One who can do more than just breed, nurture, and give over her men to the republican cause. One ready and willing to exact vengeance upon its worst enemies. Might you be such a daughter, Máire O'Hamill?"

For the first time in a long time, Fianna felt the hint of a smile tugging at her lips. Sean had not come to England simply to raise money for the poor, then, had he? A wily man, this newly rediscovered uncle of hers. Was he bent on political reform? Or did he think to organize another armed revolt?

No matter. He'd not turn her from her own purpose. At least not yet.

"Perhaps I might put my hand to your cause," she said, her tone a tempting drawl.

A dark, satisfied spark brightened his green eyes. He gestured back toward the tea shop. "Then come, and I'll tell you why I'm here."

But Fianna remained where she was. "I'll be more than ready to help you, Sean. But only after you've first helped me."

She reached out a gloved hand and squeezed his arm in a viselike grip. "I need to deliver God's justice to a killer, *Seanuncail*. Find Christopher Pennington for me. If not for my sake, then for my father's. So he may rest in the peace he deserves, with the glory of a hero, not the shame of a turncoat."

Sean looked down at her hand for a long moment, then back up to her face. Slowly, the hand of his other arm reached out to cover her own, clenching until she thought her fingers must surely break under the pressure. But the nod of acquiescence he gave left no room for any feeling but elation.

Christopher Pennington would not remain hidden much longer. Not with both Fianna and her uncle now on the hunt.

CHAPTER SIX

Kit should have been home, preparing for his meeting with Theo and Uncle Christopher. But instead, he found himself again at the door of number 12 Seymour Street, eager to find out if Fianna Cameron had found a clue in the *Army List* he'd lent her. He had the excuse of returning for the book, of course, but perhaps he should have send a note inquiring whether his visit would be welcome. If Ingestrie hadn't left yet for his daily rounds of the clubs, would he think Kit had designs on his mistress? It wouldn't do to get the fellow's back up, or he might find himself in the midst of a ridiculous duel. Perhaps he should send round a boy with a note?

But as Kit searched for a likely messenger, Ingestrie himself stepped onto the pavement. His face the picture of petulant ire, he waved toward two men who followed, urging them not to dawdle. Hauling heavy, hastily packed trunks on their shoulders, the men pushed past Kit to drop their burdens with grunts of relief into a waiting dray, then turned back, presumably for another load.

"Hold there, driver! I've need of your services," Ingestrie shouted as the cabbie Kit had hired began to pull away. Catching sight of Kit, the viscount gave a puzzled frown, as if he couldn't quite recall who this other gentleman was, though he knew that he ought. "Done with that cab, are you, sir?"

Kit nodded. "Setting off on another voyage already, Ingestrie? Benedict told me you'd just arrived in London." Would Miss Cameron be accompanying the young lordling on what looked to be a journey of no short duration?

"Benedict?" Ingestrie's eyes clouded, then widened. "Ah yes, Pennington's brother, ain't it? Good chap, Pennington. Give any brother of Pennington's a drink, I would, 'cept it's all packed up in the cart there."

"Removing entirely, are you? Surprised to hear it."

"Yes, so was I when the pater called me up on the carpet," Ingestrie said. "No need to rusticate, not over a mere wench. But would he listen? Never saw a man take anyone into such dislike, and for no cause whatsoever! Not as if I'd bring her to Almack's, or Gunter's, or any place a respectable girl's likely to frequent."

"That's the last of 'em, yer lordship, 'cept for the ones belonging to the lady," one of the carters interrupted as he sidled past them to add another box to the pile.

Ingestrie gave an impatient yank to one of the many capes of his greatcoat, pulling it free from where it had caught under his collar. "Be sure you return for the others, man, after you've delivered these. And don't allow her to abscond with them; they've all got to go back to the blasted dressmaker."

"Miss Cameron does not accompany you, then?" Kit asked, working to mask his surprise.

"Haven't I just been saying the pater's taken against her? And how he got wind she'd accompanied me here, I'll never know. Traveled steerage on the way over, far away from his sharp eyes, didn't she? But somehow fathers always know, damn their eyes."

Ingestrie threw a coin in the direction of one of the carters, then bounded up the steps of the waiting carriage. "I envy you, Pennington, having only an elder brother to answer to. Especially one who enjoys his pleasures as much as does yours. No need to worry about the antecedents of one's lady friends, not with a fellow like Saybrook as the head of one's family."

Kit scowled, but the obtuse fellow paid no heed. Hanging from the open window of the hack, he called, "Wish me luck in finding a girl as lovely as Fianna back in Staffordshire. I dare say she'll have an easier time finding a new companion than I, more's the pity. Do you think Saybrook might take an interest? Oh, no need to scowl so, just because you've not the blunt to keep her."

Kit banged a fist against the carriage door, sending the startled lordling flying back into the squabs. "Drive on, growler!"

"Impudent dandiprat," he muttered as he made his way up the stairs to Ingestrie's former lodgings. Miss Cameron was no kin to the viscount, but he'd left her behind with as little compunction as if she'd been a soiled napkin, or a wine bottle emptied to the dregs. No matter her own failings, Fianna Cameron was well rid of such a blackguard.

The carters hadn't closed the door behind them; it swung open at his touch. Miss Cameron sat perched on top of a trunk in the otherwise empty room, her thin brows arching over a small volume she held open in her ungloved hands. No sign of tears, or even of anger, marred her pale skin; from the sight of her, one would never have thought she'd just been abandoned by a feckless lover. Indeed, dust motes stirred in the shaft of late morning sun surrounding her, almost as if they danced at her fey command.

Some strange part of Kit wanted to dance, too, almost as if knowing she was no longer tied to Ingestrie had freed something wild inside him, something he'd not even known he'd been keeping under tight rein.

Mere lust, most likely.

He welcomed the feeling, even while recognizing the need to restrain it. No one in the family had ever spoken of it, but they all eventually realized that the late Lord Saybrook had suffered from a venereal disease. And ever since Kit had realized the true cause of his father's decline into death, he'd found himself indifferent to, put off, even, by the fairer sex. That said indifference was proving to be of limited, not protracted, duration reassured him no end. Yet Ingestrie, damn the insolent pup, was certainly correct that he was in no position to take on a high-flyer. More importantly, he'd promised himself never to allow his baser urges to put him at risk of becoming diseased, as his father had been.

Even in the face of temptation as alluring as Fianna Cameron.

His footsteps echoed against the newly uncarpeted floor as he made his way into the empty room. At the sound, she looked up, her wide green eyes drawing him toward her.

"Mr. Pennington. How kind of you to call." She closed her book and set it on the trunk beside her. Not the *Army List* he'd lent her, but some other, weightier tome.

Kit cleared his throat. "Miss Cameron. I came to inquire about your search. But I fear you have more important matters occupying your time."

"Indeed, sir, you find me woefully unprepared for entertaining." Her gaze swept over the empty room as if she could not quite believe how quickly it had been denuded of its furnishings. But her voice betrayed no unease. "If you've no objection to using a box for a chair, you are more than welcome to keep me company whilst I await the carter's return."

Instead of sitting on the box, which rested against the far wall, Kit took up a stance beside the trunk on which she perched. The sunlight lit the back of her head, where her dark, thick hair was dressed in a decorous knot. Tiny wisps along her hairline had pulled free, though, drawing his eyes to her nape. If he blew a puff of air across it, would she react to the glissading curls?

Shaking his head free of the whimsical urge, he tucked his hands behind his back. "Did the *Army List* prove of help, ma'am?"

"I'm afraid not, Mr. Pennington. Although it included several men of the same surname, none of them were
the man for whom I search." She sighed, drawing the
cloth of her dress tight across her small breasts. "If only
you had served in the military, you might advise me on
how to go on."

Kit forced his eyes back to her face. "I may not have
served myself, ma'am, but I do have friends amongst
those who have. Horse Guards should be your next
stop, I believe. The records of every man who has served
his country are stored there, in the War Office."

"The War Office? But will they allow a woman, particularly an Irishwoman, access to such records?"

Kit frowned. As the son of a nobleman, he took it for
granted that any government official would be more
than happy to help him with any inquiry he might pose.
But of course, the same would not be true for a woman
such as Fianna Cameron. "Perhaps not. But if I inquired
on your behalf, I could send you word of my
discoveries. If you'll give me your future direction," he
ended awkwardly.

"Ah, there's the rub, sir. I've little idea where I might
find myself tomorrow, and none at all where I'll be at
some unspecified date thereafter." Remarkably even, her
voice. And her face, unsmiling but unruffled. As if being
abandoned by a callow protector were as expected as
the daily rising of the sun.

Perhaps for someone like her, it was.

Still, a despicable excuse for a gentleman, Ingestrie.
"Did the viscount not provide adequate funds to see you
home?" he asked, his hand reaching for his pocket. Did
he have any banknotes with him?

Her ungloved hand reached out to stop his, then
jerked away as another electric spark shot between
them. She tucked her hand back in her lap. "More than
enough for the mail to Holyhead, and the steam packet
back to Ireland. Apparently 'the pater' wants this wild

Irish girl as far away from his errant heir as possible."

His eyes narrowed. "You're not going, though, are you?"

"I am not going. Not until I've completed the task I came here for. I've not sacrificed so much only to be put aside now."

Had it been a sacrifice, suffering the attentions of a puppy such as Ingestrie? Her beauty struck him as without age, yet nothing about her suggested the first blush of youth. Nor that she'd suffer the foolishness of a child such as Ingestrie with any degree of pleasure.

"Will you search out another protector, then?" he asked. Why? What she did with herself was certainly no concern of his.

"That would be the wisest choice for the likes of me, would it not?" Her eyebrows arched, challenging him to deny it.

"What if I were to offer you another choice?" he heard himself say.

"Another choice?" The brittleness of her laugh scraped against his ear. "What, do you offer yourself up for the role? I'll confess, I'd not thought you the type. You seem remarkably unmoved by my womanly assets."

"You mistake me, ma'am," he bit out, clenching his hands behind his back. "The choice I offer does not involve trafficking in those, as you so charmingly describe them, womanly assets. In fact, it would require you to keep them under proper restraint. But it would offer you a safe place to live, and honest work. If, that is, your only goal in coming to England is to find the man who will complete your family. But perhaps I mistake the matter. Even after you've finished your search, do you intend to continue on as you've begun? Taking up with someone a bit more experienced than young Ingestrie next time, perhaps?"

Miss Cameron's lips thinned. Ah, at last, a crack in her icy calm. A minuscule one, but a crack nonetheless. Even that regal raise of the chin, meant to convey how wide of the mark his ill-bred barbs had flown, could not mask the intensity of her words when she finally deigned to speak.

"My only goal, sir, is to repair my broken family."

"Then allow me to conduct you to a place from which you may do so free from the importuning of persons who do such little credit to the title of Englishman as does my Lord Ingestrie."

With a sweep of his hand, he invited her to take the first step through the open door.

Only after she'd accepted, crossing to the landing with a mien as lofty as any queen's, did he think to question the wisdom of becoming even more entangled in the affairs of Fianna Cameron.

As the carriage wheels bumped over cobbled pavement, Fianna cursed herself for a thrice-bedamned fool.

Hadn't she used her head-turning looks to bend a man to her will dozens, nay, hundreds of times, during her quest for retribution? Of late, she'd relied on their power so often she hardly had to think, deploying a gaze here, a touch there as instinctually as a general deployed his troops on the battlefield. Distasteful, indeed, even loathsome at times, to do it, but such qualms had never kept her from her purpose before.

Why, then, had she scrupled to turn the force of that beauty on the man who sat across from her in the hack?

She'd certainly beguiled far uglier men. That fat old turnkey from Kilmainham Gaol, for one, the one who'd taken Father's money but then not given him the food or books he'd promised in return. And those three other rebels imprisoned alongside her father, who'd all pledged to stand with him in protest against English oppression, but then, as the weeks dragged on into months, begged their relatives to petition for their individual releases. She'd been all of four when that had happened, but she'd waited until time, and her looks, had ripened, then flirted and flaunted until she had each ancient apostate panting for a mere glance from her. How satisfying, to betray each in her turn, just as they'd betrayed her father, and then to write to Grandfather McCracken, sending word of the punishment God had seen fit to visit upon each sinner.

Only by using the one execrable endowment with which the Lord had seen fit to gift her had she been able to bring such treacherous men to justice, to prove herself worthy of the McCracken name.

Why, then, did she not have young Mr. Pennington begging even now to make her his mistress? To carry her back to his own rooms, where she might find some further clue as to the whereabouts of his uncle, instead of off to God only knew where? Or if she couldn't bring herself to use him, why did she not tell him to instruct the hack to take her to St. Giles, where Sean O'Hamill had taken lodgings?

Fianna stared from under lowered lashes at the man on the seat opposite, willing his eyes to hers. But unlike every other male she'd deliberately enticed, Kit Pennington did not stare back. Instead, his gaze stayed fixed on the book she'd been reading back in Seymour Street, flipping through its pages with eager interest.

How was she to beguile a man who regarded her with such indifference? Nay, who barely regarded her at all?

She rustled her skirts, even gave a little cough. But still his eyes did not wander.

Might this one need to be approached through his mind, rather than his body?

She cleared her throat. "He's an intemperate liar, that Sir Richard. Not that an Englishman such as yourself would see it."

That had him raising his eyes. "Is he, now? Why

then did you purchase his"—he paused, his finger tracing the title embossed on the book's spine—"*Memoirs of the Different Rebellions in Ireland*?"

"Because I wanted to see what falsehoods the English public is being fed about my country, my people." Because she'd hoped to find mention of her father, more fool she. But none of the Northern rebels warranted mention by name, at least not in the mind of a conservative such as Sir Richard Musgrave.

"And what lies did you discover?"

"That the Irish Rebellion of 1798 was just a Catholic conspiracy against the Protestants, not a quest for political rights and freedom from oppression. And that all Catholics and Protestants were mortal enemies, rather than partners in calling for an end to religious discrimination and a greater franchise for the people."

"But Musgrave writes with such authority. And here, he vows he makes the truth his 'polar star.'"

Could the man truly be so naïve? Or was that a hint of irony edging his words?

"And look, here, he writes that the officers of the military, as well as the civil magistrates, confirm the accuracy of his account." He held out the book for her inspection.

Yes, that merest wisp of a smile surely hinted at a far keener intelligence than one so easily taken in by the blatantly biased arguments of a Sir Richard Musgrave. How novel, to be invited to engage in a war of wits with a man, rather than serve as the object of his lusts. Fianna quelled the unfamiliar urge to offer her own hint of a smile in return as she took the volume from his hands.

"Ah, the officers of the *English* military. But I see little mention of him speaking to any Irishmen to discover their motivations."

"And you have? But no, how could you? You couldn't have been more than a babe when these events took place."

"A bit older than that, sir. And even the youngest

child can listen to the stories her elders tell, can she not? Stories they'd never share with a man such as Sir Richard, one who deems them savages, barbarians, and fanatics."

"And what do you deem them?"

Words her McCracken relatives had used when speaking of her father swirled in her brain. *Courageous. Idealistic. Impetuous. Rash.* She finally settled on the one nothing she could do would ever change.

"Dead."

The bitterness of that one word would have pushed another man away. But she had gauged him well, this Kit Pennington. Though he sat abruptly back against the squabs, his back taut, she had seen the sudden pity flaring in his eyes.

Sit beside him. Place your hand on his arm. Whisper in his ear.

But somehow her body would not obey.

Why? Why should she be plagued by such reluctance now, when her final quarry was almost within reach?

"Where are you taking me?" No sweet whisper that, but a rasp as harsh as a file against steel.

"To the Guardian Society." He crossed his arms and gazed out the window. "A benevolent institution for the reform and rehabilitation of penitent prostitutes. My aunt is one of its patrons."

Her fisted hands pressed hard against her stomach, as if she'd received an actual blow. Mother of God, he thought her a prostitute. Of course he did. He only knew Fianna Cameron, the mask of the practiced courtesan she'd worn to lure Ingestrie, to persuade him to pay for her passage to England. Be glad that he'd never see past it, never catch sight of Máire O'Hamill, or Maria McCracken, the child and woman buried far beneath.

Ignore that weak, gut-sick feeling. Think instead about this philanthropic aunt, the one simple enough to take pity on the fallen women of the world. A lady of such sensibility would surely be less of a threat, and far easier to fool, than the man opposite. Perhaps she might even prove to be the wife of Major Pennington.

Yes, far better to keep this one at bay, and use her wits on another.

It must have been the devil in her, then, that pushed the goading words from her mouth. "You think me capable of reform, do you, Mr. Pennington?"

"All God's creatures are capable of reform, ma'am."

"Capable, of course. But desirous of?"

Good, that made his eyes widen. But after considering a moment, he shook his head. "A lady who has traded her person only to help her family is no hardened whore."

"And who's to say I've not traded my person to others? Why, for all you know, I might have sold my body up and down the coast of Ireland long before I ever took up with young Ingestrie."

He shook his head. "You've not the look of a practiced jade."

"Are you so familiar with the look of a jade, sir? No wonder you think yourself unsuited to the clerical life. But then, what Englishman truly is?" Ah, that should set his hackles a-rising.

But instead, he reached out his hands, taking one of hers in his gentle grasp. "You've been deeply hurt by an Englishman, haven't you, Miss Cameron?"

She found herself frozen in his gaze, unable even to blink. So long, it had been, so long since anyone had spoken to her thus, not with disgust or desire, but with simple kindness. Touched her intent on offering sympathy, rather than satisfying lust.

Back in Ingestrie's rooms, she'd accused this Kit Pennington of indifference. But *his* indifference wasn't the trouble, was it? The real trouble was her own unexpected, unwelcome awareness of him, of the compassion written as clearly on his face as the crimes of a wanted man screamed from a broadsheet.

How she longed for it, that fellow feeling, that sharing of a burden with another.

But how quickly such compassion would be jerked away, once he discovered her true reason for pursuing him.

With a sudden rush of breath, she pulled her hand free, staring down, away, anywhere but into the charity of his eyes.

"A miracle, it would be, to find any Irishwoman who'd not been harmed by the English in some way or another, Mr. Pennington," she said, her voice flattened of all emotion.

The carriage bucked to a halt before he could answer.

"And this must be the Guardian Society of which you spoke. Will I be able to keep my own clothing, do you think, or must I garb myself in sackcloth and ashes, like a true penitent of old?"

He reached out for the door's handle, but she was there before him, nearly tumbling down the metal steps in her eagerness to escape the close confines of the carriage. Yes, the sooner she could find Mr. Pennington's aunt and play upon her sympathies, the sooner she could leave this dangerous man far behind.

CHAPTER SEVEN

"Pacing back and forth like a caged beast won't bring your brother here any sooner, Christian. Nor does it demonstrate the patience required of a successful politician. Sit down, if you please, before you wear a hole in your aunt's carpet."

The sharpness of his uncle's tone stilled Kit in his tracks. Aunt Allyne hadn't mentioned that her boarder was having a difficult day. But the strange restlessness that had driven Kit the past week, ever since he had left Ingestrie's mistress in the hands of the Guardian Society, would not be confined to a chair, even to soothe a fractious invalid. Instead, he perched against the sill of the bedroom window, crossing his arms over his chest to keep his hands from tapping out a rhythm as irritating to his uncle as the pound of boots across the floor.

The sooner Theo agreed to support his political aspirations, the sooner Kit could travel back to Lincolnshire and begin the work of canvassing for support. Lincolnshire would be a welcome distance from London and from the all-too-alluring Fianna Cameron. More than once this week he'd found his steps taking him in the unlikely direction of the Guardian Society, even though his inquiries at the War Office had yet to be answered. The lust inspired by that sharp, icy beauty— against that he could stand firm. Why, then, should a mere hint of sadness, one that had fluttered across her face when he'd asked about the pains of her own past, prove so much harder to resist?

Kit pushed aside the curtain yet again to look for a sign of his brother. But the street below remained cursedly empty.

"You're certain it was the fourth and not the fifth?" he asked.

The Colonel shook a piece of foolscap in Kit's direction. "The fourth of March, clear as day. But look yourself if you think me so feeble as to misread your brother's own hand."

"No, no, of course I believe you. And being in good time was never one of Theo's virtues. But I did think he'd show more respect to you than to forget the appointment completely."

"Not everyone regards their elders with as much consideration as you do, Christian. Witness Ingestrie, Earl Talbot's heir, kicking over the traces in Ireland when the poor man had all he could do to keep the peace in that godforsaken land. At least he's back now in a civilized country, where a man can exert due control over his wayward sons."

Kit rose, striding back toward his uncle's bedside. Had the earl's talk extended to his wayward son's mistress?

"Did the earl pay you a visit, sir? Tell me, what news had he of the unrest in Ireland?"

"Now, no more of that political talk, boys, not when Mr. Acheson has come for a match with the Colonel," Aunt Allyne said, bustling into the room with a chessboard in hand.

Kit bowed to his uncle's physician, a man whom his uncle would only allow in his rooms on the pretext of a game of chess. If Aunt Allyne had thought it necessary to summon Acheson, his uncle must be feeling far worse than Kit had realized.

"My apologies, Uncle, for taking up your morning on

this sleeveless errand. Shall I send a note to Saybrook and arrange another time for us to meet?"

Uncle Christopher gave a short nod, his lips pursed tight. Against pain? Kit cursed himself for an unobservant fool as he followed his aunt from the room.

"Why did you not inform me, ma'am, that my uncle felt poorly?" Kit asked as they reached the bottom of the narrow staircase. "I could easily have postponed our meeting until another day."

"Oh yes, feeling poorly, to be sure, Christian," Great-Aunt Allyne answered, her brow furrowed. "What a sad excuse for a nurse you must think me, not to realize the pain the boy must be suffering. But he never spoke a word of it, truly, not to me, at least, and not to Peg, either, for all the silly creature must have seen the blood on the bedsheets when she changed them this morning. And to think I would have missed it, too, if I had not taken a moment from my packing to make sure that wasteful girl did not use too much lye in the washing."

Blood. From bedsores? Or something worse?

Damn his uncle for valuing his privacy over his health. But haranguing poor Aunt Allyne would do little to persuade the Colonel to be more forthcoming.

Before the diminutive woman could set off on another self-deprecating lament, Kit placed an arm around her and gave a reassuring squeeze. "Do not trouble yourself, Aunt. Acheson's sure to have him on the mend before you even leave for Lincolnshire."

"But there is so much to do before I may even step foot in the post-chaise!" Aunt Allyne gave a deep sigh. "Saybrook depends upon me not just to bring your sister from Lincolnshire to London, but to oversee the hiring of more staff for the London house, and to ensure it is in a fit state for entertaining. And how can I depend on Peg to properly convey Mr. Acheson's instructions after this morning's debacle with the sheets? Oh dear, how long does it take to play a round of chess?"

Theo must be in a truly bad way, to fob off his own

duties onto another family member like this. Especially one as aged and anxiety-prone as Great-Aunt Allyne.

Kit caught his aunt's heavily veined hands in his, stilling their anxious fluttering. "You need not take everything upon yourself, ma'am. Go, meet with the housekeeper, and tend to your charities. I'll speak with Acheson and leave you a note detailing his instructions, one you can share with the nurse."

"Oh, Christian! Are you certain? What a dear boy you are! But pray, do not let your uncle hear the word 'nurse' pass your lips. He'll put a bullet in anyone so presumptuous as to play that role toward him, he assures me."

Kit smiled to cover his worry as he helped his aunt into her cloak and set her and her footman on their way to Pennington House. After a quick glance up the staircase, he made his way into the small drawing room that fronted the house, searching for a newspaper or book with which to pass the time until he could speak with the physician out of his uncle's hearing. But all he could find were improving volumes aimed at the education of young ladies. Intended for his unruly sister? Or perhaps for the downtrodden women he'd seen at the Guardian Society? He smiled in truth at the haughty disdain with which Fianna Cameron would likely greet the improving words of a Dr. Fordyce or a Hannah More.

The thud of the door knocker jerked him free of the enticing but unwelcome image. Had Theo come after all?

Unwilling to wait for the hapless Peg to pull herself away from the laundry, Kit strode into the front hall, repressing the urge to ring a peal over his dilatory brother.

But when he pulled open the door, it was not Theo who stood on the step, hat in apologetic hand.

It was Fianna Cameron.

Fianna willed herself to stillness, though her every nerve thrummed at the sight of the man who stood before her, blocking her entry to the small, neat house she'd walked several weary hours to reach. No one would mistake Kit Pennington for a footman, even if he'd been dressed for the part. Not with that assured air, those clear blue eyes staring down at her without the least hint of deference or shame. After she'd banished him from her mind during those dark, solitary nights in the Guardian Society dormitory, how dare he suddenly appear where he was least wanted? Damn her body for urging her to throw herself against his comforting bulk. And damn it a second time for pressing her to flee like a coward in the face of such unwonted longing.

Before raising the knocker, she'd donned her own deferential mask, readying herself to play the role of remorseful fallen woman, overcome with gratitude at the kindness of charitable Mrs. Allyne. That mask had won her the regard of Kit's pious aunt, not to mention an invitation of employment in her home, and after only two encounters at the Guardian Society. If Mrs. Allyne had been the one to answer the summons of the plain iron ring of a door knocker, Fianna would have known precisely how to act.

But deference would hardly fool a man to whom she'd shown far more cunning disguises. Especially a man to whom she found herself so inexplicably, dangerously drawn. She had to gain the upper hand here, and quickly, before he recognized the power he might wield over her.

Lowering her eyes, then, in a semblance of sensual appreciation, she drew her gaze slowly down Kit Pennington's person, then back up again, pausing on the places most likely to raise a flush in the inexperienced.

"Never say you are the invalid whom Mrs. Allyne wishes me to nurse?" she asked, pitching her voice sultry and low. "Have you done yourself an injury since we last met, Christopher Pennington?"

"My name isn't Christo—" he began, then stopped, frowning.

"Oh, do you insist that everyone call you Kit? Afraid of not measuring up to the lofty example of your patron saint, are you? Or were you named in honor of a relative, perhaps, one whom you've taken into dislike?"

While her insolent gaze had left him unruffled, this verbal barb had his eyes widening. He grabbed her wrist and pulled her down the front steps, the door banging closed behind them.

The valise she held in her other hand struck painfully against her side. She stifled a cry and tried to pull free, but his grasp bound her tight. Struggling not to trip on the uneven cobblestones, she swore under her breath as he pulled her into the alley that ran beside the house.

"You met my aunt at the Guardian Society?" he asked.

"She is one of its patronesses, is she not?" She rubbed a hand over the wrist he had so rudely clasped, but he paid no heed to her silent rebuke.

"And she took pity on you, such a lovely creature fallen so low?"

She raised her chin. "A kindly woman, your aunt, ready to offer what aid she can to all God's creatures. "

"*All* God's creatures? Then why are you the only one here? Or am I to expect the rest of the Society's inmates to arrive on the doorstep within the hour?"

"Only if you have a position to offer them, Mr. Pennington. But given your vaunted self-control, we know that to be unlikely, do we not?"

A muscle along his smooth jaw clenched. "A position? Caring for the aforementioned invalid?"

She nodded. "When Mrs. Allyne heard how I had

nursed my own dear aunt during her last days, she said it was as if heaven itself had answered her prayers."

Caring for an invalid had certainly not been the answer to any prayer of Fianna's. After discovering fairly early during their first encounter at the Guardian Society that Kit Pennington's aunt was not married to the man she sought, was in fact only related to the Pennington family through marriage, she hadn't petitioned the heavens, but cursed them. Said curses grew more wicked when her cautious attempts to draw information from Mrs. Allyne only gained her the elderly woman's tedious laments over the overwhelming tasks with which she was burdened.

But by the time the aunt returned a few days later, Fianna had rethought her strategy. All it had taken was a woeful sigh or two, a fond if not entirely truthful remembrance of a dearly departed aunt of her own, and a specious thanks to the Lord above for granting her the patience and skill to nurse poor Aunt into the kingdom of heaven. Too-trusting Mrs. Allyne had all but persuaded herself that offering Fianna the position of caring for her petulant relative was her own idea, rather than that of the penitent to whom she'd proposed it.

Such a move would allow Fianna to meet with Sean again, or at least send him word. Even if she'd wished to tell him of her new residence, the Guardian Society's matrons did not allow inmates to correspond with anyone outside its walls.

And if she were truly lucky, she might even uncover a clue to Major Pennington's whereabouts in the home of this distant relative.

But not if Kit Pennington never allowed her inside.

"So, sir, if we are quite finished, may I enter the house and discover from Mrs. Allyne something of my duties? I understand the sick boy is prone to fits of peevishness when vexed. Another brother of yours, perhaps?"

"The boy?"

"Yes, the boy who is to be my charge whilst your aunt makes a short journey on another relative's behalf."

"The boy. . ." Kit Pennington stared for a long moment back in the direction of the house, then gave a short, sharp shake of his head. His mouth firmed with resolve as his eyes returned to hers. "Unfortunately, Miss Cameron, the boy would be more than peevish if you were to enter his room."

Fianna's eyes narrowed. "Teaching them anti-popery in the nursery now, are you? Or does the young master fear that he'd be sullied beyond recall if he were touched by a lowly Irisher?"

"No, Miss Cameron. But my aunt seems to have forgotten that the boy's nursemaid, the one who died from the same fever from which he is struggling to recover, was Irish. And as much as he'd like to deny it, he loved her, and mourns her deeply. You'll forgive me for believing your presence, no matter your intentions, likely to do more harm than good."

Fianna knew the signs of a lying man, and Kit Pennington showed them all. What cause had he to keep her from the position Mrs. Allyne had offered? Her nationality couldn't be the reason, not if his family had employed an Irishwoman before.

Her eyes narrowed. All fine and well for an aunt to give charity to the downtrodden, it would seem, but to invite a fallen woman into the bosom of her home—no, no man as family proud as was Kit Pennington would allow a female of his family to risk her reputation so.

Frowning, she crossed her arms. "And so once again I find myself without shelter or protection?"

"I would be happy to accompany you back to the Guardian Society, and explain why you are still in need of its services."

"No!"

Kit Pennington was not the only one surprised by the vehemence of her refusal. How unwise, to show this man that the constant reminders from the asylum's inmates and staff that she was no better than a dirty Irish whore had any power to hurt her. Fianna wished for a mental knife, one sharp enough to cut out that last bit of softness within her, the one that still sought consolation against the quotidian cruelties that continued to shape her life.

Turning away from the expression of pity suffusing his face, she schooled her voice to impassive coldness. "You did not inform me that the Guardian Society would be no better than a prison, sir. How did you imagine I would find the man for whom I seek when I am not even allowed to leave its premises?"

He took a step back, clasping his arms behind his back. "I told you I would see to it, Fianna."

"Since I've not seen hide nor hair of you since you left me there, *Kit*, you'll forgive me for presuming that you have not, in fact, seen to it."

Lord, had he actually blushed at that reminder of the rudeness he'd shown in using her given name? If playing on his carnal instincts seemed doomed to failure, perhaps invoking his chivalrous ones would meet with greater success.

"Am I wrong, sir?"

"No, but—"

"And there is no employment for me in Mrs. Allyne's home?"

"I am afraid not."

"Then I beg you excuse me," she said, raising the small valise at her feet and dropping him a polite curtsy. "I must resume my search. If I have to find another protector in order to do so, well. . ."

She shrugged, then turned her back and stepped toward the entrance to the alley. As if she'd ever consent to such a degradation again! The mere thought of placing her body in the hands of another fumbling nobleman sent the bile rising in her throat.

But she had to make the threat convincing. One step,

then another—

"Miss Cameron, wait!" She tried not to shudder in relief as a restraining hand grasped her elbow. "You know no one in London—how will you find a suitable. . ."

Fianna donned her most brittle smile before facing him again. "The word is 'protector,' Mr. Pennington. 'Protector.' A man must have coined the term, do you not agree? Alas, the irony of the appellation tends to escape those who employ it. As for suitability, well, nice manners and expeditious dispatch in the bedroom would both be more than welcome. But little beyond the pecuniary is truly required."

His brow furrowed again. Curse her hand for that momentary twitch, as if it would reach out to smooth the lines away. Time to twist the knife deeper, not pull it free.

"Are you acquainted with a Mr. Davenport, sir? Or Lord Kirkland? Both of the gentlemen expressed some interest in my future plans, despite purporting to be friends of Lord Ingestrie's."

"No." The hand on her elbow tightened. "No protector. I'll provide for you."

"You'll provide for me?" He would do her such a kindness? Treat her as a friend?

No, of course not. He thought to take Ingestrie's place, to make her his own lightskirt. To think she'd been so naïve as to think chivalry would ever win out over lust.

She shook her head, fighting against the rush of disappointment tightening her chest. "But what of your reputation, sir? How will you prevent rumors of a new mistress from spreading?"

His posture stiffened. "You misunderstand me, ma'am. You will be my guest, not my mistress."

Why such a rejection should bite even more sharply, Fianna could not begin to fathom. Dropping the valise at her feet, she stepped closer until she sensed his body's warmth inches from her own.

"You think to reside in the same house, yet not long to take me to your bed? What, are you alone among men impervious to lust?"

The color in his face heightened, but he kept his hands still at his sides. "All men are subject to lust. But not all allow it to rule them."

"And you, of course, are one of the latter?"

"I am a gentleman, Miss Cameron."

She moved even closer, so close that the buttons of his coat pressed against her breasts. "But am I a lady?"

Reaching up to grasp the back of his neck, she pulled his mouth to hers.

And fell, not into the shallow puddle of an inexperienced fumbler, but a swirling maelstrom of passion.

CHAPTER EIGHT

Since leaving Fianna Cameron at the Guardian Society nearly a week earlier, Kit had prided himself on the strength of his self-control. Not once had he allowed his waking mind to dwell on the enticing possibility of her mouth upon his, no matter how often his nighttime dreams drifted in that direction. Yet as her cool, full lips pillowed against his own, he realized it might have been better if he had given due consideration to the possibility of being kissed by a woman as bewitching as a *leannán sídhe*. Then, he might have been able to stop himself from responding with a groan as those cool lips warmed, then opened beneath his, allowing the tiniest of teeth to nip against his soft flesh. Might have been able to keep his arms impassive by his sides rather than reaching around and pulling her small, yielding body tight against his own. Might have been able to prevent his all-too-unruly cock from rising to painfully uncomfortable attention, greedily pressing itself against the softness of her belly.

Might not have forgotten the suspicion that had flashed through his brain when she'd called him—

"Christopher." Her whispering lips traced a path up his jaw to the lobe of his far-too-sensitive ear.

Yes, there, she'd said it again, just as she had on the front steps—not *his* given name, but his uncle's. His uncle, who'd been a major when he'd served with distinction in Ireland during the Rebellion of 1798. A conflict about which he would never speak. A conflict in which this woman had shown inordinate, angry interest.

Could the man whom she sought be his uncle?

He pulled away from her, searching for the truth in her face.

Fey green eyes, sharp as the needles on a pine, stared up at him, enticing him to set aside all suspicion, to tumble back into their drugging depths.

His uncle had been right to warn against the terrible power of the *leannán sídhe*. For even now, with doubt teasing at the corners of his brain, every fiber in his body urged him to crush her back within his arms and never let go, to bind this fairy mistress so that she might never offer the balm of her cool lips to another.

If it had only been a matter of himself, he might even have done it.

But if she meant to ruin the good name of his uncle —

Should he summon the watch? He had no real evidence that she wished to harm Uncle Christopher, only the surety of his intuition. Many a London constable would be all too happy to throw a lowly Irishwoman into gaol on little else than the word of a viscount's son. But Kit's sense of justice would not allow it.

No, first, he needed to find out more. Not only *if* his uncle was truly the man for whom she sought, but *why* she was in search of him. Her words had led him to assume she sought her natural father who'd abandoned her, an assumption she hadn't denied. But what if she had a more malevolent reason for her pursuit?

Bloody, bloody hell. What if she'd been the one who'd shot him at the Crown and Anchor? Not intending to harm him at all, but mistaking him for his uncle?

"Mr. Pennington. Kit." He felt her shrug beneath his hands. "You're hurting me."

He looked down, confused. When had his fingers

curled so cruelly about her arms?

He released her, but then caught her back again, his arms pulling her tight to his chest. One palm cradled her head close against his shoulder, keeping her from watching his face as a tangle of suspicions whirled through his brain.

To ferret out the secrets of such a guarded woman, he'd have to keep her close to hand. Not as close as his uncle's bedchamber, of course. But perhaps as close as his own? That's what she'd assumed when he'd told her he'd provide for her, that he meant for her to be his mistress, wasn't it?

The thought of having her beneath him sent a shiver, part fear, part desire, racing down his spine. But it would be sheer madness to actually take up with a woman he suspected might be intent on harm. If he extended the offer to be her new protector, but did not immediately partake of her charms, how long would he be able to keep her from suspecting his true motives?

And if word got out that he'd invited a woman to take up residence, rumors about him would once again run rife through the *ton*. He could just hear Dulcie and his cronies now, trading tales about the youngest Pennington's new paramour. Or perhaps they'd even say he'd made up with the one who had shot him. . .

Would such rumors damage his political aspirations beyond repair? Not if he could keep her presence a secret from the gossips. And from Uncle Christopher. And Theo.

But even if word did spread, Kit would sacrifice more than a seat in Parliament to ensure his uncle's safety. Nothing was more important than family. Nothing.

He clenched his hands against Fianna's back, steeling himself for the task ahead, then stepped away from the enticing creature in his arms.

"It seems I'm not as much of a gentleman as I might wish, at least where you are concerned, my dear," he murmured, looking down as if abashed. His body might be only too happy to cooperate in such a deception, but it would all be for naught if his expression gave his doubts away. He reached out and took her hands in his. "Will you let me take care of you, Fianna?"

He waited, his body tensed.

Until at last her fingers gave a wordless squeeze of consent.

Kit Pennington was not living in his family's London home; the knocker had not been on the door at Saybrook House when she'd gone there in search of Major Pennington the day she'd arrived in London. No, Kit's lodgings lay only a few streets away from Ingestrie's. Yet they might have been a world apart, so different did they seem. And not only because Kit's lay in Mayfair, and Ingestrie's in less fashionable Marylebone. In fact, the furnished rooms the viscount hired had a decided air of style about them, with their rich red walls and gilt-embellished picture frames, a style the forgiving shadows of lamp and candlelight only enhanced. But in the bright glare of day, the cracking paint and worn upholstery, the stains from spilled wine and burns from countless careless cigars, were harder to hide. Ingestrie's penchant for leaving his soiled clothing and other belongings scattered about only added to the dilapidated air. Fianna had been glad to wander London's streets each day in search of Major Christopher Pennington, if only to escape the dispiriting pall that fell on her whenever she found herself alone in those rooms.

But as soon as she stepped inside Kit's chambers, an unfamiliar serenity settled about her. The woodwork in the two main rooms, painted in a dark green that might have been oppressive, instead warmed. During the day, the room would likely be awash in sunlight, given its tall windows topped only by the smallest of swags. Green-and-white striped upholstery, and a lighter green stripe on the papered walls, contributed to the open, airy feel. Though she stumbled over a footstool—covered with fabric of the same color and pattern as the carpet below it, masking it from her eyes—the room still made her feel as if she were walking amidst a stand of springtime trees, drinking in the promise of new life, new growth.

How ironic, that he would bring a harbinger of death to such a vitally alive retreat.

"My brother's doing, not mine."

She frowned at Kit as he walked into the room and set her valise on the edge of the carpet.

"Benedict, not Theo," he answered, gesturing to the room around them. "My middle brother, the artist of the family. Though of late he's been pouring his energies into portraits, he's not above raising a brush to a wall if the color of a room's not to his liking."

"You share chambers with him?" she asked, careful to keep her distance. How foolish she'd been, throwing herself at Kit that way, with no clear aim in mind. And to allow it to go on so! With the exception of Ingestrie, her rule had been to allow the men she cozened only a taste of her favors, enough to entice but not satisfy, so that they would grant her whatever she wished in the vain hope of winning more. That it had been Kit, not she, who had been the one to break their embrace had disconcerted her more than she cared to admit.

Only the memory of Grandfather McCracken, his bent finger tracing over and over the letters that inscribed his lost son's name in the family Bible, could persuade her to accompany the far-too-self-possessed Kit Pennington to his rooms.

"No, these are Benedict's rooms, not mine. He urged me to exchange with him after the shooting, so that my attacker would not be able to find me so easily."

Her back stiffened. But when her eyes darted to his,

nothing in his face suggested any hidden meaning lay behind his declaration. No, he still did not suspect her.

He moved toward a window, pulling the curtain shut against the darkening evening. "And when he discovered the light for painting was even better in the attics at Pennington House than it is here, he vowed he'd never return. You've no cause to worry; he'll not bother us."

It was not Benedict Pennington who caused her hand to stroke over and over her sleeve, chasing wrinkles that even she could not see. Why had all the boldness with which she'd kissed Kit earlier suddenly abandoned her? Fianna removed her gloves and set them on a side table.

"Are you the youngest Pennington, then?" she asked, perching on the edge of a sofa. She'd not be the one this time to make the first move.

But he remained standing, his hands clasped behind his back. "No. In addition to my two brothers, I have a younger sister, Sibilla. Aunt Allyne will soon be traveling into Lincolnshire to bring her up to town."

"For her debut? Your mother is unable to oversee it?"

"We lost our mother some years past."

"And your father, too, as your brother now holds the title?"

He gave a short, sharp nod.

She tamped down the unwelcome stab of sympathy. "You rely on Mrs. Allyne, then, for counsel and support? Have you no other elder relations upon whom you may call?" *An uncle, perhaps?*

"Oh, the stray distant cousin or two," he replied, turning back to her with a shrug. Sitting down in the chair opposite, he leaned forward, elbows perched on his knees. "What of yourself? Is your father still living?"

A vision of a much younger Sean, holding her small body high above the crowds so she might bear witness, shot through her mind. Her own father, leader of the Antrim rebels, standing tall and calm by the gallows. Nodding to Major Pennington, who had overseen his imprisonment and trial. Ascending the scaffold, attempting to address the people who had gathered not just for the spectacle, but in tribute to his leadership, his courage, his friendship. Smiling as the rope was put around his neck.

And behind him on the Market Hall spikes, the heads of four other rebels, sightless eyes staring out over the crowds, flies lazily buzzing about the festering flesh. . .

Máire—*no, Fianna, your name is Fianna*—jerked to her feet. May the cat eat her, and the devil eat the cat, if she were fool enough to share such a memory with the likes of Kit Pennington.

Ever the gentleman, Kit stood as well. But something stronger than mere civility had him taking a step toward her. "Is there something wrong, Fianna?"

"I find I am rather tired this evening," she said, folding her hands tight below her breasts.

"Then perhaps we should retire early. May I show you where you'll sleep?"

Somehow she nodded, even as her mouth grew dry. Would he remain with her the entire night? Or take himself off to other pursuits, as Ingestrie often had after taking his pleasure of her?

Taking up her valise, Kit guided her down the passageway. Opening a door at its end, he gestured her inside a simply furnished room. As she stepped inside, her eyes went straight to the plain white dimity curtains hanging from the half-tester bed. A bed only large enough for one.

"If you find yourself in need of anything during the night, my room is just across the hall," Kit said. With a stiff bow, he retreated into the passageway, closing the door gently behind him.

CHAPTER NINE

"My sincerest apologies, sir. I can find no record of a Major John Pembroke in any of this year's muster rolls." Ensign Farmer bobbed his head with red-faced deference not in Kit's direction, but in Fianna's. "Have you asked the Clerk for Widow's Pensions? Or examined the *Army List*?"

Pressing folded hands into the small of his back, Kit suppressed a grimace. The ensign was the fourth clerk at the War Office to whom they'd been shunted off, all in search of a man whose existence might, if his suspicions were true, be only a figment of Fianna Cameron's cunning imagination.

Given said suspicions, he should be pleased, not chagrined, at the continued inability of the War Office's clerks to uncover any sign of the man whom the Irishwoman continued to imply was her natural father. Yet some soft part of him clearly wished the assumptions he'd initially made about her search to be true, wished her a righteous innocent rather than the creature of guile he feared she must be.

It hadn't been his aristocratic connections that had persuaded anyone at the War Office to aid them in their search, as he'd assumed, but rather the power of Fianna Cameron's strangely compelling countenance. At the sight of disappointment on her narrow, fey face, each War Office clerk had moved a little closer, as if he would gladly offer himself as sacrifice if he could but lift the burden of dashed hopes from her dainty, fragile shoulders. That tiny moue turning down the corners of her mouth even affected Kit, though he'd watched her don it, then remove it now several times in a row.

And yes, there went Ensign Farmer, right on cue, leaning over the wooden counter like a fish ensnared on a line. Kit held his own body still, refusing to give in to the same compulsion. Damn them both for fools.

"Please don't apologize, Ensign. Of course a man as busy as yourself hasn't the time to examine *all* the lists." Miss Cameron laid a gloved hand atop Farmer's ink-stained fingers. Would the familiar squeeze she gave them leave the boy as addlepated as the last clerk she'd enthralled?

"If I might just look at the older records myself? I've come so far, you see, and my poor mother is so very distraught. . ."

Ensign Farmer bit his lip. "I truly wish I could help, ma'am. But I'm not allowed to bring members of the public behind the counter."

Fianna's lowered lashes, so dark against her pale cheeks, hardly fluttered; her quiet sigh raised her small but enticing bosom only the slightest bit. But her subtle machinations proved quite enough to entice the hapless ensign.

"I suppose—I might bring the ledgers here? If you wouldn't mind standing while you examine them?" he asked, as if she, not he, had the right to grant such an indulgence.

"What a wonderful idea, sir. How clever of you to think of it!"

The clerk slowly backed away from the counter, unable to tear his eyes away from the demure look of adoration with which Fianna gifted him. Only after his backside caught the edge of a desk and sent a pile of papers flying did he turn to search for the ledgers in question.

Kit could not stop himself from smiling a little at the poor man's discomposure. When he turned to Fianna to share the joke, though, all he saw was a frown. Why would a woman so skilled in manipulation not show some triumph, not even the least bit of pleasure, at her success?

"Here are the ones from the 1790s, ma'am, one for each regiment," Ensign Farmer said as he returned with an armful of dusty books. "Are you certain you don't know his regiment?"

"Unfortunately I do not," Fianna said as she examined the words scrawled on each cover. "Only that it was stationed in Ireland in 1798."

Ensign Farmer frowned. "In Ireland? Oh, I do wish you'd said so earlier. Ireland's an entirely different matter, indeed."

"Different in what regard, sir?" Kit asked.

"Why, before the Act of Union in 1800, troops stationed in Ireland were paid for not by the English Parliament, but by the Irish one."

"And the significance of the distinction?" Kit asked.

"I'm afraid, sir, those muster rolls are not kept here, at the War Office, but at Dublin Castle."

Fianna's face fell. "Do you mean I've come all this way, only to discover the information I need is right there, in my own country?"

"Oh, I hope not, ma'am! Surely the records must have been transferred here after the Union. Perhaps Ensign Timms will know where they've been stored." Farmer gazed toward the back of the office, where another man sat scribbling.

Kit snatched up a piece of foolscap and scribbled down his direction. "Perhaps you might send a note, informing us if you come across them, Ensign?" Tossing the pencil on the counter, he took Fianna's elbow. He'd not spend another hour kicking his heels in this drafty, dusty place, watching yet another young clerk succumb to Fianna's far-too-compelling charms.

The sound of the ensign's sighs dogged them until Kit yanked the door closed behind him. How long would they have to prolong this wild goose chase before he could catch her in a falsehood? And how many more smitten clerks would she leave in her wake?

As they left Horse Guards and made their way toward St. James' Park, Miss Cameron pulled her hand free of his arm, presumably to retie her bonnet ribbons. But she did not retake it as she fell back into step beside him. "If the War Office is to be of no aid, perhaps the regimental agents should be my next line of inquiry. Do you know if there is a place where such men typically congregate?"

Her tone held none of the honey she'd poured out so freely to the clerks at the War Office. Why was her tone far more brusque, her words more direct, when she spoke to him, a man whom she'd agreed to bed? Did she guess he was growing suspicious? Or did she simply believe him already so in her thrall that no further effort on her part was required?

"I've not the least idea," Kit bit out, taking her hand and placing it back upon his arm. Ah yes, petulance was always so very charming.

They walked in silence for some minutes, Kit taking care to keep his gaze straight on the pavement before him. Even if he turned his head, the deep poke of her bonnet would likely hide most of her face. But he'd rather not give her any more hints of just how easily she might beguile him.

They'd come to a stop at Charing Cross, waiting for the crush of traffic to lessen. After a few minutes, he spied an opening and stepped forward. But she pulled heavily against his grip, her slight weight still enough to jerk him back from the road.

"Fianna?"

She made no answer, just stared at a raucous circle of red-coated soldiers blocking the walk before them. One of the men laughed as he held a bag over his head, just out of reach of two small, grimy, barefoot creatures clambering before him. As one of the urchins jumped and swore, the soldier tossed the sack to one of his fellows, over the child's head.

With the boy's attention on his prize, he must not have seen the boot the first soldier intruded into his path. The redcoat holding the bag laughed even louder than the first as the boy tripped and fell heavily to the pavement. His smaller companion raced to his side, throwing a protective arm about him.

But the first boy would have none of it. Popping up quick as a jack-in-the-box despite the trail of blood flowing from the scrape on his forehead, he raced to confront his new tormenter. "*A thabhairt ar ais, car ar oineach!*" he cried, his skinny arms flailing to little avail.

Fianna jerked at the words, her hands fisting in her skirts. What, did she mean to launch herself into the midst of a street brawl? Kit reached out an arm and pulled her behind him.

At her cry of protest, he stepped forward himself, jerking the contested bundle from the second soldier's grasp. He'd not stand by idle and watch children be tormented. Especially not by a soldier. Uncle Christopher had drilled it into him that it was a soldier's duty to protect, not to harm, the innocent, something he'd taken for granted until Peterloo.

The soldier whirled, his grin changing to a snarl as he realized the sack had been taken not by a fellow redcoat, but by a stranger. Kit dropped it and held out a placating hand, offering peace but ready to curl fingers into a fist if the man proved belligerent.

Before the soldier could utter a protest, though, Fianna Cameron had slid between them. She raised her hand and whipped a biting slap across the man's beefy cheek.

"How dare you bedevil a poor child so!"

The soldier raised a slow hand to his face. Dazzled by the pain of her blow? Or by the beauty of the woman before him? The tussle had knocked the bonnet down her back, revealing her dark curling hair, cheeks ablaze with ire, eyes wide with scorn.

Kit's gut tightened. He had thought this woman cold, without passion?

The soldier who had tripped the boy—an officer, much to Kit's disgust—stepped to their side of the circle and laid a quelling hand on his subordinate's shoulder. "My apologies, ma'am. We'd no wish for our little joke to upset a lady's sensibilities."

The lieutenant's self-assured smile faded as Fianna turned her disdain on him. "And what of the child's sensibilities?"

"Sensibilities? A lowly sweep? Surely, ma'am, you jest."

"Besides, he's an Irisher," offered the soldier she'd slapped. "Everyone knows they don't feel as deep as we do."

"Do they, now?" she muttered, pushing her way between the two men to crouch beside the unkempt children.

The boys' eyes darted between her and the soldiers, each narrow chest heaving from their exertions. Defiance and fear warred over their sharp features. Would he have to protect her not only from a troop of soldiers, but from these feral children, too?

Fianna, though, seemed undaunted by the boys' sullen glares. Holding a handkerchief in one outstretched hand to the injured one, she tossed her head in the direction of the soldiers. "*Car ar oineach*, indeed."

Startlingly white teeth flashed in the midst of that grimy face before a small hand reached up to cover it. But the hand could not hide the laughter that sparked in the boy's eyes.

"*Shit on honor*," she translated, before reaching out to dab at the blood on the boy's brow. "As everyone knows His Majesty's soldiers are all too wont to do. Every Irisher, that is."

"See here, now, ma'am," the officer began, belliger-
ence edging his voice. "There's no call to besmirch—"

"No call for arguing with a lady, Lieutenant," Kit
said, using his body to block the man from stepping any
closer. "Or harassing hardworking children. You'd do
better to gather your men and return to your duties."

The man glared, but took a step back, clearly reading
the implicit threat in Kit's crossed arms and narrowed
eyes. "Your servant, sir," he offered, with the briefest of
bows.

Kit kept his eyes on him as he gathered his fellows
and hustled them back in the direction of Horse Guards.
Only after the entire troop had turned the corner did he
pick up the sack he'd dropped by the side of the street.

"Me soot," the boy clutching Fianna Cameron's
white handkerchief against his begrimed forehead cried.
He abandoned the scrap of linen to grab the heavy bag
from Kit. "Master 'ud whip me sore if I'd lost it."

"Does he beat you, your English employer?" Miss
Cameron asked, taking a step closer to the child. She
looked ready to rebuke said employer with as much
vehemence as she'd used to slap the soldier.

"Oh, not regular-like, miss, not like some," the other
boy answered with a shake of his head. The soot that
flew from his hair had Kit forcing back a sneeze. "But
there'd be no coins for our supper without the soot to
sell. Put it in the ground, farmers do, Lord knows why.
Not me place to ask, not if I gets me dinner at the end of
the day."

"Best run along, then, and see your precious cargo
safely where it belongs," Kit said, laying a gloved hand
on the boy's lean back.

The child gave a quick nod. Hefting the sack over his
bony shoulder, he took the hand of his smaller companion and scampered off in the direction opposite that
taken by the soldiers.

"The boy may have forgotten his manners, but I
certainly haven't," Fianna's low voice whispered in his

ear. "Thank you, Mr. Pennington, for intervening on that child's behalf. It is more than many a gentleman would have done, especially when the child in question is Irish."

Kit bent down to retrieve the handkerchief the boy had dropped, returning it to her with a cautious smile. "I have no jewels to offer you, Miss Cameron, but a new handkerchief is well within my means. I fear the soot on this one will be impossible to remove."

"Perhaps. But it will serve me well as a talisman. A reminder of the casual, workaday cruelty of His Majesty's army. Especially toward those of us from Ireland." She folded the linen carefully before placing it inside her reticule, closing it with a quick snap.

Kit doubted Fianna Cameron had need of any such reminder. Animosity as biting as hers surely stemmed from some act far more brutal than the unthinking teasing of a pair of poor sweeps. What had English soldiers done to her people, her family?

To her?

And had his uncle been the soldier responsible?

Kit shook his head, banishing the traitorous thought. No Pennington would ever harm an innocent, especially a Pennington as honorable as his uncle Christopher. If his uncle was the major for whom she searched, she must simply have the wrong man.

He swore under his breath as Fianna once again began walking away without taking his arm. He couldn't afford to leave her alone, not for a minute, not until he'd had the chance to take steps to ensure his uncle's safety.

Kit rushed across the street to catch up to her, thanking the heavens he'd been wise enough to write to both Theo and Benedict this morning. Surely one of his brothers would have enough family feeling to answer his summons without demanding all the whys and wherefores beforehand. Whys and wherefores he was strangely reluctant to share before he understood just what game the woman beside him played.

So far, he'd been able to stand his ground against the strangely enticing aura she seemed able to summon at will. But the crusading, vulnerable Fianna she'd just revealed—that Fianna had the potential to make him forget himself entirely.

Yes, having a brother beside him would help him remember what he owed himself and his family. Especially his uncle, who had sacrificed so much for them all.

He quickened his pace, forcing his eyes not to stray to hers. It simply didn't matter what sacrifices Fianna might have been driven to make, or why. Not if those sacrifices brought danger to one of his own.

CHAPTER TEN

Fianna's ungloved finger traced down the column of army agent names listed in the *Post-Office Annual Directory for 1821*. Such agents served as go-betweens for gentlemen who wished to purchase cavalry or infantry commissions and those who wished to sell out. If Major Pennington had left the army, he might have sold his commission through such an agent, and said agent might have a record of his current direction.

Not as many men as she had expected currently served as army agents in the city and its environs. If she knew London as well as Belfast or Dublin, reorganizing the names and addresses by neighborhood would be the simplest of tasks. But many of the addresses here included only a street name; to track down many of the men listed, she'd need a map of England's capital. An irksome task, without doubt.

She'd throw herself with diligence into one far more tedious, though, if such work would keep Kit Pennington from asking her any more intrusive questions. He'd nearly driven her mad yesterday with his far-from-subtle attempts to pry into her concerns as they'd made their way to and from the War Office, then again this morning as they'd broken their fast. Pretending not to hear, or turning the conversation in another direction, did not stop his inquiries; neither, surprisingly, did any of the subtle sensual lures she attempted to cast his way.

He was not indifferent to them, no; his eyes would follow the line of her finger as it carelessly grazed the line of her neck or the top edge of her gown until he realized what he was doing and jerked them away. But he had kept his hands entirely to himself. Not just in public, either, but in private, too.

It was not like her to be so impatient. Far stronger men than Kit Pennington had eventually spilled their secrets in the face of her enticements, had they not? This strange, discomfiting restlessness she felt in his presence must stem from being so close to her final quarry without being able to bring him to heel.

Her restlessness certainly wasn't from his decision to sleep in his own bedchamber, rather than hers. Two nights ago, when her plea of tiredness had forced him to play the gentleman, she could understand. But last night, when he left her standing by her door to continue down the passageway to his own without even demanding a touch—what could he mean by it? Her thumb riffled down the side of the directory's stacked pages, but the book held no answers.

"You don't truly think to inquire of each and every agent listed in that blasted thing, do you, Fianna? There must be more than a hundred."

Hands clasped tightly behind his back, Kit Pennington paced with barely restrained energy through the patches of sunlight and shadow dappling the sitting room floor. Was he even aware how he'd slipped into informality today, calling her by what he thought was her Christian name? And how she, too, had begun calling him by his, as if they were the lovers in fact that her presence in his rooms suggested?

If only he would treat her with the careless regard a man typically showed his mistress. Visiting with her for an hour or two of love play before deserting her for other concerns would have given her time enough to search for Major Pennington without his interference. But Kit had remained inconveniently close since bringing her to his rooms, so close that she'd had to wait until he was fast asleep last night before slipping out and summoning a street boy to deliver the note she'd penned to Sean, telling him of her new location.

How much longer would she have to pursue this task before tedium drove him from her side?

"Not quite that many," she said in a provokingly even tone. "And once I've finished copying down each and every name and address, I'll need you to help me sort them by the part of London in which they are situated. For instance, I've no idea where one would find Hatton Garden, do you?"

"And here I thought all we'd need do was have a little chat with a fellow or two at the War Office. Who knew there were more than"—he reached over her shoulder to poke an accusatory finger at the numbered list she had begun compiling—"fifty men who earn their daily bread bartering commissions for His Majesty's regiments?"

Fianna stilled, far too aware of the chest only a whisper away from her back. "Have a care. If you upset the inkstand, I'll have to send you off to find another *Directory*."

With a grimace, Kit moved away to resume his pacing. But before long he'd returned to peer once again over her shoulder. Fianna bit back the urge to shove him bodily away.

"Why, they're not all London addresses," he exclaimed. "Look, Armit & Borough does its business in Dublin. And so does Cane & Son. And Corry & Bristow. No street addresses, though. Do you have any family in Dublin who might search them out on your behalf? Your mother, perhaps?"

Her hand wobbled, allowing a blot of ink to mar the *T* in *Bormor, Thomas, 25 Spring-garden*. Such obvious, clumsy questions would hardly trick a child into revealing its secrets. Still, one had to admire his persistence.

Laying her quill down beside the directory, she

rubbed an ink-spotted finger against the blotter. "You are welcome to take up the search again yourself, Kit, while I finish here. I assure you, I've no need of a watchdog to keep me company, especially one as restless as you."

But Kit only shook his head. "No good rushing around like a chicken with its head cut off. Plan before acting, my father always counseled, though at times I think he despaired of both Sibilla and me, headstrong, tearaway madcaps that we both are. Why, one time, she and I—"

A sharp rap from the entryway, followed by a key turning in the lock, brought him up short.

"Ah. That must be Benedict."

Quickly, she gathered up the directory and her writing tools, careful to keep the ink from dripping from the quill. "If you keep him from the bedchambers, he should have no idea I'm here."

"Why should you hide?" He spoke in his normal tone, not in the whisper she'd employed.

Fianna brushed a hand down her dress in exasperation. "I'm no longer wearing the clothing from the Guardian Society, Kit. This isn't as fine as the gowns Ingestrie gave me, but your brother would hardly mistake it for the dress of a servant. He might even recognize me from Ingestrie's party."

A slow smile began to creep over Kit's face. "Have a care for my reputation, do you, Fianna?"

Her lips tightened. "It would be unwise to assume I have a care for anyone's reputation but my own, Mr. Pennington. Now, if you'll excuse me—"

He laid a hand on her sleeve, pulling her to a halt. "Don't concern yourself, Fee. Benedict won't tattle, on me or on you. He's family. Besides, I invited him here specifically to meet you."

As she opened her mouth to raise an objection, he pulled the quill from her hand, then tapped its tip against her lips. He grinned at her widening eyes, tossing the feather back on the table before striding out to greet their visitor.

As the sound of his friendly tenor mixing with the far deeper voice of his brother drifted down from the passageway, Fianna gave herself a brisk shake. Just because he was the only man for as long as she could remember who treated her with such playfulness was no reason to allow her mask to slip. No man would ever want her, not if he truly knew her. The heartless actions she'd taken to avenge her father might earn her a place in the McCracken family, but they'd hardly endear her to a man as untouched by tragedy as was Kit Pennington.

A loud series of thumps and grunts, a muffled curse, and Kit's warm laugh preceded the two men into the sitting room. A liveried footman hefting a weighty trunk atop his shoulder followed.

"Put the crate by the bookcase," Kit's brother directed the servant, "then you may return to Pennington House."

"Very good, sir."

Taller and darker than his brother, Benedict Pennington was all sharp planes and angles. His downturned mouth and creased brow suggested a temper far less open than Kit's, a sullenness that fairly shouted, "Keep your distance." But something else lurked behind his narrowed eyes, something she recognized from seeing it in her own face when she stood in front of a mirror and stripped away her social mask. Something young and yearning. Something unwilling to give up all hope.

He scowled, yanking his eyes away from her unflinching gaze. Yes, very unwise, not to keep such weakness carefully hidden. Especially from someone who might turn it against you.

"Benedict, may I introduce you to Miss Cameron? Fianna, my brother Benedict."

Fianna gave the requisite curtsy, but the brother

showed no similar courtesy. Shrouding himself once again in arrogance, he crossed his arms and examined her from toe to crown, as if she were something he could purchase rather than a fellow human being. But she'd suffered far more dehumanizing scrutiny in the past. She gazed back, unflinching.

"Damnation, Kit, you weren't lying. If he weren't such an imbecile, one could almost be grateful to Ingestrie for bringing her over. Now, where did I leave that sketchbook?"

"Sketchbook?" Fianna looked at Kit as his brother rummaged noisily inside a cupboard.

Kit grimaced. "I had to offer him something in exchange for pulling him away from his precious studio, the selfish beast. Aunt Allyne needs my help finalizing her plans for her journey, and as I'm assuming she'd not take kindly to seeing you, I thought it best to leave my brother here while I'm gone."

He didn't wish her to be alone. Out of politeness? Or suspicion?

"I've no need of a nursemaid, Kit."

"Truth be told, it's Benedict who's in need of one. Or perhaps a muse? He's had terrible trouble with his art since he's come back to England, haven't you, Ben?"

A dark head emerged from the cupboard. "Can't paint anything worth a damn. Bloody damp climate."

"Bloody damn temper," Kit whispered with a conspiratorial wink. "See if you can't soothe the brute while I'm gone, will you? He won't interfere with your list making as long as you don't move about too much while you do it."

Taking up hat and gloves, Kit called to his brother, "I don't know if I'll be back by dinner. Make sure you feed her if I'm delayed."

Benedict grunted, then emerged once again from the cupboard, a sketchbook clutched in his hand. "Now where are those blasted charcoals?"

Only the click of the front door answered. Kit had

left her alone with his brother.

Might this Pennington male be more susceptible to her charms?

Fianna glanced out of the corner of her eye at the mantel clock, then gave a discreet kick at the charcoal-smudged papers littering the floor. Four hours. Kit had left her with this grunting, foul-mouthed scribbler of a brother for four interminable hours. During which time Benedict Pennington had not had the courtesy to respond with more than a "yes," "no," or noncommittal "mhhmmm" to the politely worded questions about his life and family she lofted in his direction. But his single-minded focus on his art seemed to do him little good; each time he roughed out a sketch, he would stop and examine it, then shake his head and tear it from the pad, crushing it into a ball before tossing it on the carpet. His curses grew ever more repellent as the day's light waned.

And she'd thought an artistic Pennington would be easier to charm than a morally conscious one. But no. Even when she'd given over friendliness for enticement, had begun stroking the tip of the quill against her lips, then along her collarbone, willing him to imagine his own fingers in its place, he'd simply barked at her to hold still and allow him to capture the pose on paper. Oh, he admired her, yes, but just as he would an aesthetically appealing field of flowers or artfully arranged bowl of fruit. Not as a woman whose physical secrets he'd do anything, say anything, to plumb.

She should have found such indifference infuriating. But all she could summon now was a feeble frustration, underscored by—could it be relief?

"You must excuse me, Mr. Pennington," she said,

rising as the clock struck the hour. "I'm afraid I must take a turn around the room, else I'll fall to nodding in my chair."

He grunted—in assent or dismay?—but made no further comment as she paced before the hearth. After she added coal to the fire, her eye caught on the trunk Pennington's footman had left by the empty bookcase. Personal items of Kit's, perhaps? Lifting her skirts to avoid brushing against the charcoal from the discarded sketches, she crossed the room and lifted the trunk's lid.

No letters or personal papers on top, at least as far as she could see. She glanced over at Kit's brother as she lifted a pile of dusty pamphlets from the box and set it on the shelf, but he offered no objection, too involved in his sketching to pay her any heed. Stifling a sneeze, she pulled out another stack, then another.

The trunk seemed to contain little of a family nature, only newspapers and pamphlets and books. Political works, they looked to be, and more than a few of a decidedly radical nature. Surprising, to find such in the possession of an aristocrat's son. Might one be the news sheet for which Kit's friend Mr. Wooler wrote?

What did English radicals have to say about the way their government oppressed the peoples across the Irish Sea? She scoffed at an account of George IV's recent visit to Ireland, and His Majesty's reported pleasure at the so-called loyalty and attachment manifested by all classes of his Irish subjects. Setting the paper aside, she hoped Benedict Pennington had not heard the derisive snort she'd not quite been able to contain.

Only after she'd nearly emptied the entire trunk did she come across anything the least bit useful. A stack of letters, bound together with rough twine that had caught on a piece of wood splintering from the chest's side. Her breath caught as she read from whom they were sent: *Maj. Christopher Pennington.* The ones on the top of the stack had been sent from Dublin, she saw as she flipped through the bound stack, the lower ones from various locations on the Peninsula. Her father's executioner had continued to serve, then, after his regiment had left Ireland. And been promoted, as well— the last letter had been addressed not by a major, but by a colonel. Of course. The English army rewarded its butchers well, did it not?

What were they doing in Kit's possession? More importantly, would any give a hint as to the Major's current location?

But it wouldn't do to be caught showing an interest in personal communications from a man of whom she was supposed to know nothing.

Happily, Kit's brother's attention still remained on his sketches. Her hands tingled as she slipped the letters into the pocket hidden in her skirts. Time enough to plumb their secrets later, in the privacy of her own bedchamber.

If Kit continued to grant her that privacy.

"Bah, the light's going," Benedict Pennington grumbled, kicking at the balls of paper scattered about his chair. "And not one halfway decent sketch to show for an entire afternoon's work, devil take it. You've been far more productive, unpacking that. Now I can use it for my own books and prints."

"Do these belong to your brother, then?" Fianna asked, waving a hand toward the shelf behind her.

"Our late father. Liked to keep abreast of all the political rumors bruited about town, no matter how ridiculous."

Might Kit's brother be more inclined to talk now that the sun had gone down? Fianna donned her most ingratiating expression as she helped him pull a portfolio of prints down from the shelf. "What a kind brother you are, to bring them here for Kit. You must be a very close family."

"Nothing kind about it," he replied, stooping to collect the discarded sketches. "Just wanted the clutter out of my studio."

"Ah yes, your brother did mention something about superior light in Pennington House's attics."

"Yes, I'd finally got them all cleared out, and was just setting up my easel when Aunt Allyne demanded I hide this lot away up there." Benedict kicked at the mostly empty trunk. "Been sweeping through Pennington House like a whirlwind, she has, trying to rid it of anything she deems the least bit objectionable before she allows our sister to take one step inside. Just imagine the gossip if she allowed Sibilla within a mile of a radical newspaper!"

"Why bring them here, then? Why not simply toss them on the dustheap?"

Benedict grimaced. "Should have. But if Kit found out, I'd never have heard the end of it."

"Does your brother take an interest in politics?"

"Kit? Politics?" Benedict laughed. "My brother is far too quick-tempered to meet with success in that field, I assure you. Sibilla's the only Pennington who shared our father's interest in politicking. More's the pity, as she's a girl. Still complains that it was Kit, not her, who had the luck to be in Manchester during the massacre. As if anything about that infamous day could be considered the least bit fortuitous."

"Your brother was at Peterloo?" Mr. Wooler had commented upon that strange detail, too. Whatever had Kit been doing at such a place?

It had been hard not to take grim satisfaction in the news from England during the summer of 1819, hearing that British soldiers had turned their weapons for once not upon her countrymen, but upon their own. That a peaceful gathering to hear radical orator Henry Hunt urge parliamentary reform had turned into a bloodbath had not surprised her in the least. But that the English newspapers had decried it, printing not only damning accounts, but engravings of unarmed women and children being cut down by English soldiers, had shocked her to her very marrow. What had Kit been doing there?

"Ironic, isn't it?" Benedict said. "Growing up, all my brother ever wanted was to go for a soldier. And there he was, defending innocent Englishmen from the very men whom he'd always idolized."

"Kit wished for a military career?"

Benedict nodded. "Army mad, for the longest time. Sucked up all that patriotic drivel about defeating Napoleon's tyranny and bringing justice to the world as if it were mother's milk. But Father refused to purchase his colours. Packed him off to university instead, to study for the ministry. Kit, dutiful child that he is, did not fight his fate. Takes loyalty to his family quite to heart, does my younger brother."

Her lips thinned at his derisive tone. "Unlike yourself?"

"I find that, as a virtue, loyalty is often overrated."

"And justice as well?"

"A lofty ideal, to be sure. But as with loyalty, more often boasted of than actually practiced. Particularly among the members of the upper ten thousand."

"And yet these two ideals form the very heart of your brother's character."

Benedict Pennington's jaw set. "Recognized that already, have you, Miss Cameron? You, though, seem a bit more difficult to read. I wonder—to whom do you owe your loyalty?"

Ah, the man's sharp tongue could lash out at someone besides himself, could it? But such attacks were easy enough to parry. "A courtesan's loyalty is always to her current protector, is it not?" she replied, careful to keep her face turned downward in a pretense of brushing dust from her skirts.

A long beat of silence followed, which he broke only after she had raised her eyes to his. "And Kit's first loyalty will always be to his family."

Not to you, his crossed arms and stiff posture implied, without any need to speak the words aloud. For all Benedict Pennington scoffed at familial fidelity, he seemed remarkably protective of his young brother. And not only because the two shared a surname.

How might her life have been different, if she'd been worthy of such family loyalty? If her mother had refused to give her up to Aunt Mary, refused to leave her behind? If Grandfather McCracken had allowed her to stay with them in Belfast, rather than sending her away to school, and then out to work as a governess? Might they have grown to care for her, despite her faults, rather than seen her simply a burden that duty required them to bear?

She gave a light laugh, then bent to smooth out the crumpled sketches he had collected from the floor. "La, sir, you begin to frighten me. What, will your brother throw me over because I failed to adequately inspire your artistry?"

"No, that fault lies entirely with myself, I'm afraid." He moved to collect the rejected efforts, but she pulled them closer, grateful for the distraction they provided.

"Not all your efforts are failures, sir. At least not the ones where you sketched from memory rather than from life. Look, this one of Kit, and this one, of the fashionable, animated fellow—someone from Ingestrie's party, is it? Lord Dulcie? Why, he fairly leaps off the page."

With a grunt, Benedict Pennington swept the sketches back into an untidy pile, then stuffed them into a portfolio. "You flatter me, ma'am. The only place these will be leaping is straight into the dustbin. Now, the hour grows late, with no sign of my brother's return. Shall I send a boy to the chophouse around the corner to procure our dinner? Or shall we brave the streets ourselves?"

She answered by taking up her redingote from its peg in the entryway.

Who was the bigger fool, she wondered as they made their way down the stairs. A man such as Kit Pennington, who believed in justice, and loyalty to family, with such youthful naïveté? Or a woman such as herself, chasing after justice in the hopes of catching hold of a family loyalty always just out of reach?

Kit blew on his gloved hands, though it did little to warm them against the damp March chill. His afternoon had been spent better than his morning, dodging the raindrops as he arranged for extra footmen to be installed in Aunt Allyne's house. Now, he could only watch and wait. Would Fianna take the bait he'd laid, and prove his suspicions warranted?

He'd been skulking about for the better part of an hour now outside his own rooms, trying to appear as inconspicuous as possible as he waited for her and his brother to return from wherever they'd gone to procure dinner. He hadn't been quite ready to share his misgivings about her with Benedict, not without any actual evidence of wrongdoing on her part. But Ben had answered his summons, and not demanded any explanations in return. A sign of fraternal loyalty? Or had the offer of a beautiful woman ready to serve as model been explanation enough for his forbearance?

His breath huffed out, sending a cloud of amused steam into the icy night air.

A low, sardonic laugh drew him back into a shadowy doorway. Yes, there, just turning down from Oxford Street, the dark figure of his brother, beside him the far smaller one of Fianna Cameron. Was it his fancy, or simply the fog swirling about their feet, that made it look as if she drifted above rather than walked on the cobbled pavement?

Benedict turned the key in the front door lock, then ushered her inside. Kit paced, beating his numb hands against his chest, resisting the urge to race up the stairs and hurry his brother along. This time, praise heaven, he had far less time to wait; within a few minutes, Benedict returned to the street, his quick steps taking him toward Grosvenor Square.

A light flared in the window above, then moved deeper into the rooms. A part of him stubbornly believed that she'd remain inside, prove his suspicions unfounded. But when the light above snuffed out, and a tiny caped figure tripped down the front steps to the pavement, he pushed that obviously false wish aside.

She did not seem to have the *Army List* in hand, though, nor the note he'd left with it, the note with instructions that it be returned to Christopher Pennington at 7 Curzon Street. A location far from Aunt Allyne's actual Bloomsbury townhouse. Perhaps she'd simply memorized the address?

Her small size and dark clothing allowed her to blend with ease into the evening shadows. It took all his attention to keep her in sight without alerting her to his presence, so much so that he paid little heed to the streets they walked. Yes, she headed in the direction he'd anticipated, skirting the edge of Mayfair, making her way on to Bloomsbury.

To his surprise, though, she passed right by the turn that would take her to Curzon Street. Nor did she loop back after a few streets, realizing she'd missed her direction. No, she trod straight through Bloomsbury, then on into the City. Where could she be headed?

His boots, not intended for such lengthy walks, had long set to blistering his heels when she finally drew up outside a nondescript building in Bishopsgate and slipped inside.

He cursed when he caught sight of the coffeehouse's sign swinging lazily in the wind. What the hell was she doing at the Patriot, a known haunt of radicals and reformers?

If she'd come here to meet with someone, he'd best not scare the person off by trailing her too closely. He waited in a doorway across the street, his foot tapping out the minutes. When he could restrain his patience no longer, he followed.

Something about the low-ceilinged house struck him as familiar, though to his straining eyes it looked no different from a dozen other such establishments he'd been to during his years at Oxford. After his experiences at Peterloo, he'd searched out the hauns of others who found the government's actions there, and the coercive bills it passed to restrict public protests, intolerable. Peering through the clouds of smoke, he scanned the room.

A few tables of idealistic gentlemen sat by the door. Some surely fired by the passion of youth to protest injustice, others drawn less by political reasons and more by the thrill of attending a potentially seditious meeting. A larger number of tables were occupied by older, hardened workingmen, men who'd be intent not on abstract justice, but on more specific political reform. Universal suffrage, most likely.

And there, sitting in the shadows at a table far from the fire, the slight figure of Fianna Cameron, the sole woman in the room.

She still wore her cloak, and had her back to the door. But there was no mistaking the proud, straight set of that spine, the stillness with which she contained her wary energy.

No one sat across from her.

He edged away from the door in case the person whom she planned to meet had yet to arrive.

But before he could take up a strategic position at the bar, a large hand clapped him on the shoulder. "Pennington! Never thought to see a nob like yourself gracing our fair tavern."

The room's noise would have swallowed up many another man's words. But not those of George Abbington-Pitts. A thin man, but Abbie had a voice that could rival that of the brashest costermonger hawking his wares in the streets. Hadn't Kit and Sam Wooler been taunting him about that very thing as they'd left the political meeting for the Crown and Anchor's news room the night Kit had been shot?

How far had Abbie's cry carried? Kit darted a wary glance toward the depths of the room.

Glittering green eyes stared back at him, unblinking.

"Another time, Abbie," Kit said, his chest tightening as he shrugged off his friend's hand. "I've an important appointment to keep."

Abbie was clearly half cup-shot now, as he'd been that night at the Crown and Anchor. Still, the intoxicated were often strangely canny. Might Abbie, unlike Sam, recognize Fianna as the woman who'd shot Kit?

Why should the thought give him such a hollow feeling?

He pushed through the crowd toward Fianna's table.

He'd expected her to show guilt, or at least a hint of dismay, at the sight of him. But instead, she wore that impassive, imperious expression, the one that suggested he was merely another foot soldier summoned to hear her queenly command.

His eyes narrowed.

"You read my note," she said with a quick nod. "But why did you not stay out of sight as I requested?"

Kit frowned. She'd left him a note? What in hell was she about?

"No lady should sit in a London coffeehouse unaccompanied," he replied, deploying politeness to cover his confusion. "In fact, we should leave. Immediately."

She pulled back from the hand he offered. "Ah, but we've already established my lack of ladylike credentials, have we not? Why should I let such a paltry concern stand in the way of finding the man for whom I seek? Did I not write that my informant specifically instructed me to come alone? And now you burst in, instead of keeping hidden as I had instructed."

Informant? She'd come here seeking information—

but about whom? Her mysterious father? Or Major Christopher Pennington?

Her eyes swept the room, then narrowed as they returned to him. "You've frightened him off, no doubt."

Kit held out his hand again. "Oh, no doubt at all. So you should have no objection to leaving."

Her lips pursed. A small dart of satisfaction arrowed through him. Not used to someone who sparred against her scorn rather than apologized, was she?

Before she could rise, though, Abbie pushed aside Kit's arm and slid onto the bench opposite her. "No wonder you had not the time of day for me, Kit, what with this prime article awaiting you. Please, sweetling, tell me you've a sister just as pretty as yourself waiting around the corner."

Devil take it! Kit grabbed at his friend's cuffs, jerking his hands away before he could capture Fianna's. Leave it to Abbie, as arrogant as any aristocrat despite his father's background in trade, to try to ingratiate himself with a woman even in the midst of a public coffeehouse.

Abbie, like Sam, showed no sign of recognizing her. Could his suspicions be wrong?

"If she'd a sister, she'd not want anything to do with you, you half-sprung lout. Take yourself off, that's a good fellow."

"Now is that any way to treat a man whose life you've saved?" Abbie slung a careless arm about Kit's shoulders, pulling him down to the bench. "At least do me the honor of granting me an introduction before banishing me from your lady's presence."

Fianna stared with brazen directness straight at Abbie. "Saved your life? You must tell me all about it, sir."

Even the self-assured Abbie seemed momentarily bewitched by those compelling green eyes, for he paused instead of jumping immediately into his tale.

Before he could begin, Sam Wooler rushed over to their table, waving a newspaper dangerously close to the sputtering candle. "I've already told the story to Miss

Cameron, Abbie. Besides, we've far more important things to discuss before tonight's meeting starts. Miss Cameron," he added, his acknowledgment of her far more short and clipped than Kit would have expected.

The usually friendly Sam folded his arms and frowned at Fianna, then at Kit. Kit glared right back at him. He wasn't a child in need of Sam's protection, or his disapproval.

He stood, nudging Sam out of the way so he could again extend his hand. "Miss Cameron, I believe we must—"

"Sam, how many times must I tell you how rag-mannered it is to barge in on another's conversation?" Abbie interrupted, pulling Kit back down beside him. He batted down the news sheet blocking his view of Fianna, then set his chin atop his steepled hands with an exaggerated sigh of longing.

"Won't you introduce me to your friend, Mr. Pennington?" Fianna's expression remained serene, although amusement, and perhaps a hint of scorn, tinged her voice. Did she find Abbie's immediate infatuation worthy of contempt? Or was it only his own vile temper that wished it so?

"What a lovely voice you have, Miss Cameron," Abbie said after Kit had made the introduction. "Nothing charms like the lilt of an Irishwoman's voice, does it, now?"

"Yes, Ireland," Sam repeated. "I don't believe the Union of Non-Represented People of the United Kingdom of Great Britain and Ireland allows women to join, Kit. Perhaps Miss Cameron should leave before the meeting begins?"

Fianna's green eyes narrowed. "Should only men be encouraged to throw off the fetters by which they have so long been bound? Is it not time for the clouds of error and prejudice to disperse for all parts of the Creation, female as well as male?"

The silence that followed her impassioned pronouncement was broken by a slow, steady clap.

"It is time, is it not, *cailín*, for the great nation of Ireland to set the example to her neighbors?"

Kit jerked in his seat, fists clenching. The expression on the face of the man who approached signaled approval, not derision, but Kit's eyes still narrowed when he realized who had spoken.

Sam jumped up from his seat and held out a hand in welcome. "Welcome, sir, welcome. Kit, Miss Cameron, surely you remember our speaker for this evening. Abbie, may I introduce Mr. Sean O'Hamill?"

CHAPTER ELEVEN

"And this is the wretched state of the Irish population, and the manifold grievances under which they suffer. Absentee landlords; a ruinous collapse in grain prices; tithes levied only upon those who till the land, not the cattlemen and sheep masters who might better afford them; the most crippling of taxes falling upon those least able to pay them. And so I ask you tonight, good gentlemen, to offer what you are able in aid of my long-harassed and afflicted people. Support our efforts to gain equal rights for *all* Irishmen!"

Applause rang out from all corners of the room as Sean O'Hamill made his bows. But Fianna kept her hands clenched in her lap. How young they all seemed, these men, many just boys, really, thronging in the tight confines of the coffeehouse, their dreams fired by the idealism of the yet untried. Did they truly think their paltry donations would do anything to help a land that had suffered the tyranny of English rule for centuries?

And what of Sean? The boy she remembered from her childhood had always grown red with frustration whenever he'd tried to persuade others to join the cause, the very fervency of his beliefs overwhelming his ability to speak. How had he learned to address an audience like this, with conviction stirring enough to lead strangers not only to praise his words, but to open their purses?

The boy she'd known then would have done anything for his family, even a bastard niece. But would the man?

From across the room, Sean caught her eye, then moved on to stare fixedly at Kit. The smile he wore to greet others faded, giving her a glimpse of the far more bitter man secreted behind the genial front. Had he discovered information about Major Pennington's whereabouts in the week since they'd first met? Or had Sean summoned her here for some other purpose of his own?

By her side Kit stared just as intently at Sean as her uncle glared at him. Before his speech, Sean had followed her lead when Mr. Wooler introduced him, pretending he and Fianna had no prior acquaintance besides their meeting of the week before. But if he continued to glower at Kit with such obvious dislike, he'd be bound to raise suspicion. As if Kit weren't already likely to find her actions tonight suspect. How many more tales could she spin before she trapped herself in the tangle of her own falsehoods?

"A powerful speaker, is he not, Miss Cameron?" Kit whispered. "He's taken the entire crowd here well in hand."

"Powerful indeed. But the Patriot is known as a gathering place for London's radicals and reformers," she answered, gesturing to the men crowding around her uncle. "I doubt few others in England would be as receptive."

"Or less willing to consider what he *hasn't* said, as well as what he has," Kit replied, rising as Sean made his way through the crowd to their table. She frowned at his cryptic words.

Sean greeted them affably. "Thank you again, gentlemen, for attending my talk this evening. And for bringing such a flower of Irish womanhood to listen, too." He nodded in her direction as he took the seat offered him by Mr. Wooler. "Mother Erin and her real-life daughters ever inspire us to sacrifice in the cause of our aggrieved nation."

As he sat back beside her, Kit's arm pressed casually but firmly against her shoulders. Damn these forward Englishmen! Even if he meant it as a sign of protection, not possession, Sean would likely read it as the latter. Kit was not the only man whose suspicions would be raised this night.

Leaning forward out of Kit's embrace, she set her hands on the table. "Are Irishwomen to play no role in the struggle for freedom, then, besides that of muse?"

"Oh, surely not, Miss Cameron," Mr. Abbington-Pitts exclaimed. "Governing is the work of men, not of ladies."

"Women do seem somewhat unfit for the action and decision required of such work, do they not?" Mr. Wooler said with an apologetic nod in her direction.

Yes, no matter how taken with her beauty, any man could regain a modicum of control by asserting his superiority over her sex. One reference to the purported inferiorities of women, and all the males in the room, even one as seemingly shy of females as poor Mr. Wooler, could rest safe in the knowledge of their God-given masculine advantages over the likes of her.

Of course, such mistaken assumptions were precisely what had allowed her to triumph over so many of the foolish men who had betrayed her father. Somehow, though, in the presence of those who claimed to support the rights of all mankind, she could not forbear from protest.

"What of the women revolutionaries in France?"

"Indeed." Kit's sleeve brushed against hers as he placed his folded hands on the table, sending a rill of awareness up her arm. "From what I understand, many Frenchwomen participated in the calls for freedom, and even in the workings of government that followed the downfall of the monarchy."

"Only acting under the influence of their menfolk,

surely," Wooler said.

"Or led astray by their willful natures. Quite unsexed by designing men." Abbington-Pitts nodded in agreement.

"Hardly women at all," Wooler added.

Did Kit find such women's actions admirable? Or did he share the disparaging opinion of his friends?

Her eyes narrowed. Not that Kit's opinion mattered to her in the least.

"They do say that all a woman can give to her country is her sons, and her tears." Sean nodded at the two men, then turned sharply back to Fianna. "But perhaps you see yourself playing another role, *cailín?*"

Did Sean hope to draw her into his intrigues? To urge her to leave off her own quest to take up his? Raising funds to assist widows and fatherless children was the least of his reasons for coming to London, of that she was certain.

Might she find the acceptance she sought, the family she longed for, with Sean? The possibility tempted her. But how long could she keep Sean from the knowledge of her illicit arrangement with Ingestrie, and her new one with Kit? Few Irishmen looked with anything but contempt upon a kinswoman who had been taken without leave by an Englishman; she could only imagine the curses likely to rain down on the head of one who had entered into such agreements of her own free will. No, far better to keep to her own chosen path. The Mc-Crackens need never know the lengths to which she'd gone to secure retribution against her father's betrayers.

Fianna's lips narrowed. "Whatever role my God and my family deem me worthy of, that I will take."

"And for now, your family requires you remain in London?" Sean asked, echoing her slight emphasis on the repeated word. At her nod of assent, he added, "Then I have not a doubt that whatever you seek will surely be discovered within its bounds."

Did a message lie beneath the simple platitude? Was

the Major somewhere in London? She grasped her own wrists, feeling her pulse quicken beneath her palms.

"But family ties lead us in many directions, I find, do you not?" Sean added, leaning forward in his chair. "When you have completed one task, may not another one take its place?"

Beside her, Kit stiffened at the clear invitation in Sean's voice.

Mr. Abbington-Pitts slapped Kit on the back with an uneasy laugh. "Better watch yourself, Pennington, old boy, or O'Hamill here will have spirited poor Miss Cameron away to help with his campaigning before you can blink an eye. Lord knows I'm far more likely to turn out my pockets if a pretty woman does the asking, no matter what the cause."

Abbington-Pitts gestured to the man standing behind Sean, whose upturned cap held a small collection of banknotes and coins.

"My uncle will be sorry he missed you, sir," Sam Wooler said, rising to add his own contribution. "I'm certain if you cared to write down your speech, he'd be most interested in printing it in his paper."

Sean glanced down at the news sheet resting under Kit's free hand. "Ah, the radical press. How lucky you are here in England. In Ireland, we rarely have a chance to read dissenting views, as your government pays the publishers to print only its version of events."

"And you're certain there is no truth at all to such accounts?" Kit asked, leaning forward and setting his palms on the arms of his chair. "I am, myself, much disturbed by their reports of violence in your country. And not all of it perpetrated by English troops."

"'Whoever shall smite thee on thy right cheek, turn to him the other also'? A worthy sentiment, sir, but not one likely to lead to political change." Sean smiled dismissively, then turned toward Mr. Wooler. "Will you join your friends in supporting—"

"And will thievery and murder bring about change,

Mr. O'Hamill, when turning the other cheek will not?"

The room fell silent.

Her uncle rose and faced Kit. "Do you accuse me of a crime, sir?"

Kit rose, too, leaning on fisted hands set on the scarred wood of the table. "No, sir, I do not. But I do wish to know whether this money you collect tonight will pass into the hands of those in need, or instead to those who see violence as the means to freeing themselves from oppression. If the latter, I'm afraid I will not be able to contribute."

Fianna stared at the stern set of Kit's jaw, willing the fluttering in her belly to still. Could this forceful man be the same one she'd regarded as a mere stripling only a few days earlier?

Sean sneered. "Ah, one of those who believe only the deserving poor merit help, are you? Only those who snivel, and grovel, and accept that it's God's will that they be forever ground beneath the heels of their 'betters'—these are the only ones who merit our aid?"

Kit raised his voice, just loud enough to be heard over the renewed murmuring of the crowd. "You misunderstand me, sir. I have no argument with those who openly resist such false, pernicious doctrines. Only with those who believe using force is the best means of so doing. I've heard reports that some Irish insurgents, under the guise of collecting for the destitute, use those funds to purchase firearms. I've heard they conduct raids and thefts to secure additional weapons. I've heard they've beaten and mutilated those who protested such infringements of their property and persons, or who reported such attacks to the constabulary. And yes, I've heard they've even committed murder, when such raids go awry. According to reports in the *Dublin Evening Post*, the county coroner conducted twenty-five inquests for murder in Limerick alone these past six months, the majority reputedly perpetrated by insurgents. Do you wish to claim that all these accounts are false?"

Several hands besides Mr. Wooler's pulled back from the collecting hat, waiting for an answer.

Fianna bit down, hard, on her lip. To contain the torrent of denial his words provoked? Or the shocking smile that rose in admiration of the skill, and passion, with which he had uttered them?

The taste of blood on her tongue jerked her free from the tumult of her emotions, sharpened her focus once again on the murmurs of the men circling their table. Sean was not the only accomplished speaker in the coffeehouse tonight. Which man would the crowd follow?

Sean's hands fisted, then slowly unfurled. "You would be right to call me a liar if I made any such claim, sir. Men who have watched their children wither and die from want, watched their daughters and wives insulted and abused by English 'gentlemen'"—Sean's eyes shot in her direction before returning to Kit's—"such men sometimes find themselves overtaken by uncontrollable anger. Yet should the innocent many be made to suffer for the sins of the few?"

"Not if you assure us that these funds you collect will be used to support the innocent, not those who raid gentlemen's homes in search of cash and arms."

"You would accept the assurance of a man such as myself?" Sean scoffed, his smile tight with scorn. "An Irisher, with no claim to the lofty title of gentleman?"

Fianna held her breath. How cunning of Sean, not only to recognize the innate sense of justice that lay at the heart of Kit Pennington, but to manipulate it to his own advantage. For somehow she knew, even before he spoke the words, what Kit's answer would be.

"I accept the word of any man, no matter his rank or station. That is, until he gives me cause to doubt it."

The two men stared at each other across the table, the tension between them as palpable as if each strained at opposite ends of a rope.

After nearly a minute's silence, Sean reached out and

took the collection cap from Mr. Wooler. The coins within it jingled as he thrust it toward Kit.

"For the women and children. I give you my word."

Kit reached into his waistcoat pocket and withdrew a sovereign, then placed it with deliberate care into the hat. "For the women and children. And for any who work through peaceful means to secure the rights of all."

Kit stepped away from the table and held his arm out to Fianna. "The hour grows late, Miss Cameron. Shall I summon a cab, and see you back to your lodgings?"

Even now Kit thought to protect her honor, pretending that she had rooms of her own. Would Sean be taken in?

She nodded her assent, then watched as he made his way to the coffeehouse door, his friend Abbie dogging his steps.

"Not willing to wait for my help, *cailín*? I might have saved you from such a fate, trading yourself to your enemy's kin." Sean spoke from behind her, his body turned so as to give the impression he was engrossed by the conversation of the men beside him. "But at least you'll gain something from the devil's bargain, which is more than most *bean na hÉireann* who've had the misfortune to be defiled by an Englishman can claim."

His breath whispered against her neck, raising a horripilation of anger and shame.

"But when your task is done, Máire O'Hamill, you come to me. Young Pennington'll not bother you again, not after these hands have taken recompense for what he's stolen."

Her cloak fell over her shoulders then, held in place for a moment by the heavy weight of her uncle's palms.

She held her shudder in check until they lifted, and Kit was once again by her side. "Bid you good evening, sir," he said to Sean, holding out his arm to her.

Sean bowed and stepped aside.

"*Go mbuailimid le chéile arís*, Miss Cameron," he

murmured as she brushed by him.
Until we meet again.

CHAPTER TWELVE

"See you at Milne's dinner party, Kit? Or do your *affairs* keep you otherwise occupied?"

Abbie's playfully lecherous leer was surely meant to amuse, or even to welcome, a gesture from one fellow man of the world to another newly joining the mistress-keeping club. Yet as Kit watched Fianna disappear behind the door of Benedict's lodging house, he felt none of the anticipation of a man about to join a paramour for a night's pleasure, warmed by the certainty that his lust would soon be satiated. Oh, anticipation, yes, and lust, damn him for a fool, most certainly. But suspicion and self-righteousness, and, if he were being truly honest with himself, the unfamiliar burn of barely suppressed jealousy, promised the next few hours would end with little satisfaction for either party.

"I thank you for the ride, Abbie. And Fianna is *not* my mistress," he heard himself blurt, the feebleness of his response almost as galling as the smile crinkling about Abbie's eyes. With an inarticulate snarl, he slammed the door of the carriage shut in his friend's face.

"Drive on," he called to Abbie's coachman, slapping his hand against the side of the carriage. Even the noise of the horses' hooves against the cobbles could not quite drown out Abbie's shouts of laughter.

Taking the stairs two at a time, he followed Fianna

into their lodgings.

She had not even stopped to light a candle, relying on the thin light of a streetlamp to guide her down the passageway. Did she think to bolt herself inside her bedchamber without even speaking to him? He'd kept his silence in the carriage, not wishing to question her in front of Abbie. But no such scruples restrained him now.

Catching up to her in three long strides, he stilled her hand before it could reach the door's latch.

"Miss Cameron. A word, if you please."

With his free arm, he gestured back toward the drawing room, then turned back down the passageway, silently willing her to follow.

He pulled off his gloves and lit a single candle, then stalked about the room, peering into its shadowy corners. "You left a note for me, you say? I wonder where it could be?"

"Did you not take it with you?" she asked, settling into the armchair, as self-possessed as a queen upon her throne.

"I never read it in the first place." The flame sputtered as he set the candlestick on a table by her side.

She did not flinch at his accusation, merely turned her impassive face towards his. "You had me followed, then."

"No. I followed you myself."

"How tiresome for you." Her laughter bit far deeper than Abbie's, though it tinkled as light as a glass bell. "Or perhaps you enjoyed it, skulking about the shadows like a thief in the night. Not an activity in which many preachers engage, I'll warrant."

"I'm not a preacher, nor do I plan to become one. As you are well aware."

"A preacher, a parliamentarian; little difference between the two," she said with a careless toss of her head. "Both need to avoid offending their patrons. Best not to give alms to the indigent, then, or at least to the undeserving indigent, as Irishwomen such as myself all too often tend to be." She smiled, as if impervious to the insult in her own words. No, as if such a belief reflected poorly upon him and his people, rather than on her own.

He shook his head. Such taunts were meant to distract him. But he'd not be drawn away from his own purpose.

"Whom did you expect to meet at the Patriot? I thought you had no connections in London."

"No protectors, nor friends. But one may always make new connections."

Kit folded his arms across his chest. "Or revive old ones?"

"Mr. Wooler, do you mean?" she asked, her eyes opening wide in mock innocence. "A pleasure to see him again, to be sure. But he was not the connection to whom I referred. Perhaps if you read my letter?" She handed him a sheet of foolscap, pulling her hand away before his fingers could touch hers.

He brought it close to the single candle, reading through it before tossing it back upon the table. Setting the candle on the table beside her, he folded his arms across his chest.

"You would risk your own safety, walking alone about the streets of London at night, just on the chance of hearing word of the man for whom you seek? Why did you not wait until I returned?"

How could she look down her nose at him when he stood so far above her? "You think I need you to keep me safe, Kit Pennington? When I've been protecting myself from the likes of you and every other man for nearly twenty years?"

"Every other man?" A hollow, empty feeling clutched at his chest, but he willed himself to ignore it. "Do you count Sean O'Hamill amongst that number?"

"Mr. O'Hamill? But I'd never met the man before last week."

No, no one seeing the two of them together tonight, or the week before, would have suspected they were anything but strangers. They'd exchanged no whispered words, no half-hidden gestures; not even a hint of recognition had crossed either of their faces. Yet Kit knew as surely as he knew his own name that the two had some prior relationship. It wasn't injustice in the abstract that kindled anger in O'Hamill's eyes as he'd spoken of the insults Irishwomen suffered at the hands of the English. No, such ire could only have been sparked by some deeper, more personal injury. Every instinct told him it was fueled not by the presence of just any female compatriot, but by the proximity of one Irishwoman in particular.

By one bewitching Fianna Cameron.

"Never met him before in your life, you say?"

"Never." Her arm waved away the thought. "I'd not soon forget such a fine speaker as Mr. O'Hamill. Especially after such a passionate defense of Irish womanhood. Would you?"

Kit jerked away from the hearth. He'd never met a person who could lie so easily while staring him right in the eye.

Hands clenched, he strode across the room until he stood directly in front of her chair. Setting a hand on each carved arm, he leaned down, his face within inches of hers.

"You speak a fine game, Fianna. And so does he, your Mr. O'Hamill, protesting the ill-usage of his countrywomen by the likes of me and mine. But what honorable man allows a female relation—his cousin, perhaps, or mayhap even his sister?—to be bedded outside of marriage?"

He'd expected a slap, or at the very least a cry of protest, after the gross insult of this shot in the dark. But Fianna did not even flinch. Her green gaze remained steady, her voice maddeningly silent.

She had never looked so magnificent.

His hands clenched the upholstered arms of the chair, nearly shaking it in his desire to ellicit a response. "Or perhaps Mr. O'Hamill is an even closer relation. Is he your lover, Fianna? Your husband?"

A hint of a smile tipped up one corner of her mouth. Her eyes alight with something far more dangerous than amusement, she reached out a hand and slid it with sinuous intent down the silk of his waistcoat.

"Jealous, are you, Kit?" she whispered, her voice triumphant with discovery of his weakness. "But truly, there's no need. Just let me. . ."

A hand snaked behind his neck, guiding his head down to hers. But before she could lay lips against his, he pushed away, jerking himself upright.

"No. That is not what I want."

"Not what you want?" He shook his head, but still she rose, following him, laying a caressing hand on his arm. "Is it not what every man, the high and the low, the moral and the profane, desires? A woman's lips, teasing against his? A woman's body, compliant and willing?"

"A compliance bought and paid for? I thank you, but such an offer holds little appeal."

"Why, then, did you bring me here? And why do you tremble beneath my touch?"

"Because I imagine your lips tendered in affection, not in trade," he cried, jerking his arm free of her hand. "Your body a gift, not payment for my money, or my secrets, or my willingness to believe your lies."

Fianna stepped back, a sneer marring the perfect symmetry of her face. "Affection? You think me stupid enough to offer my person for free, and do it with affection, no less? When I have nothing else with which to bargain?"

Nothing else with which to bargain? Did she value her intelligence so little? Her strong will? Her dedication, even to whatever misguided cause in which O'Hamill had entangled her?

Perhaps her family never thought to praise such qualities. Never seen beyond the stunning beauty of her face. Never allowed her to imagine what a relationship between a man and a woman not based on barter or trade might be like. . .

This time, he was the one to move closer. "Has no man ever kissed you with affection, Fianna?"

"As if affection would make the experience dissimilar," she scoffed.

But still he heard it, the minute tremor in her words, the slightest catch of breath in her throat.

And, for the first time, her eyes shied away from his.

Two quick steps took him to her. Cupping her head between broad palms, he lifted her green gaze back where it belonged. Staring, haughty and intent, directly at him.

"Just let me," he whispered, then lowered his lips to hers.

Fianna had kept her body as quiet as possible as she parried Kit's words, her poise a shield lest he strike inside her guard. But all the while she'd felt her pulse beating in strange, unfamiliar parts of her body—the base of her throat, the crooks of her elbows, the very tips of her fingers and toes. When he took her face in his hands, that pounding narrowed, converged, as if her heart had decided to emigrate from her breast to her lips. In some foolish, misguided notion, she closed her eyes, as if by blinding herself to the sight of his face lowering to hers, she might keep him from seeing how his touch made her very blood rise.

And still it was a shock when the edges of his mouth pressed against hers, soft and strong and so very, very warm. He didn't thrust his way inside, rushing to find his own pleasure or to impose his will on her; instead, he took his time, bussing his way along the curve of her lower lip, tracing the arches of her upper, using the tip of his tongue like a brush, painting pleasure with tiny, delicate strokes.

And suddenly, it was not his tongue that was limning the seam of their lips, inching inside a mouth. It was hers. Not in sly enticement, as it had with every other man she'd kissed, but in shy, tentative exploration. An exploration he welcomed, moaning deep in his throat, his thumbs sweeping encouragement over the curves of her cheeks.

Fianna pulled away to catch her breath, her lips swollen, ripe. Merciful heaven, kissing Kit Pennington was like biting into the warmth of the first slice of soda bread, fresh from her mother's oven; no, like catching the last drip of clover honey falling from the spoon. A feast of which she would never have her fill.

And then it was Kit who was doing the kissing, tipping her head with gentle hands to angle his lips over hers. The unfamiliar sweetness of his mouth birthed something fragile, almost like pain, deep inside her. At school, she'd never been one to find the gold ring or the coin in the loaf of All Hallows' Eve's *bairin breac*. No, her piece had always held the stick, foretelling a year full of disputes, or worse, the rag, for poverty and bad luck. She'd never deserved any better, had she, a rebel's bastard, abandoned by her mother's family, ignored by her father's.

Who did Kit imagine her, then, that he should treat her with such attention, such care? Make her feel as if bands of gold circled every finger, as if caskets and chests overflowing with gold lay at her very feet?

And who was she, this wanton, needy, vulnerable creature, breathless and trembling with desire?

She stilled, her chest tightening. Damn him. Damn Kit Pennington for making her weak, for making her *want*.

Kit moved his lips away from hers, tracing more tender kisses up and down the line of her jaw. No. No more tenderness. Not from him. And by God, not from her.

With a gasp, Fianna pulled free of his grasp, then reached around his neck and yanked his lips back to hers. With a violent thrust of her tongue, she delved deep, hard into his mouth. She'd not cede control to anyone, especially not a mere stripling such as he.

No, he'd have no gentleness from her. Rough thrusts of her tongue, sharp nips of her teeth, a yank on his hair, that's all Fianna Cameron had to give.

Her roughness, though, seemed to excite him as much as his tenderness had inflamed her. His hands clenched and unclenched against her shoulders, her upper arms; when she jerked down his neckcloth, then circled his Adam's apple with a lascivious lick, his entire body shuddered. Yes, that was more like.

Lowering to her knees, Fianna grabbed his hands and pulled. He followed her down without resistance. But even kneeling on the floor, his larger frame still dwarfed hers. With a groan of frustration, she gave him a sharp push, putting him on his back, putting him in his place.

He made no protest, just lay silent, unmoving, his eyes glinting in the scant moonlight shafting in from the window. Calling her. Daring her.

No. She would not succumb to any foolish urge to rest her head against his broad chest, to burrow her body into his side and nestle within falsely protective arms. Instead, she pressed her palms flat to the floor, one beside each of his ears, looming above him, making it clear who was in charge. Then, with painstaking deliberation, she bent her elbows, lowering her face inch by tormenting inch, commanding his gaze, daring him to look away.

Her hair had come undone, and swung past her arms, cocooning them within a silent, silken cave. She whispered breath over his cheekbone, his chin, the side of his jaw rough with stubble, enticing wordless promises that skimmed, but never quite touched, his heated skin. No, he'd not gain the upper hand over her.

His gulping pants hot in her ear, she pulled away to see the effect of her taunting. Wide, glazed, his eyes burned against the flush staining his high cheekbones; his hands lay empty, clutching, palms up on the floor, knowing to touch would be to burn. Yes, good. Now he was the weak one, the one brought low by his own desire. Not her.

Why, then, could she not calm the pounding of her all-too-susceptible heart? Nor stop herself from bending lower, to touch her lips to his one last time?

"Heaven help me, but I want you," Kit whispered before their mouths could meet. "But will the gifts you offer be worth the cost, my *leannán sídhe*?"

Fianna jerked away, pushing up from the floor, turning her back against the sting of his words. He thought her a *leannán sídhe*? A fae intent on stealing his life force for her own?

Like mother, like daughter, Aunt McCracken's whisper mocked.

Damn her hands for trembling. She schooled her voice to an evenness she was far from feeling. "What know you of the fairy folk, Christopher Pennington?"

She flinched as a finger traced the curve of her cheek, caught a loose curl behind her ear. "I know far more than you could ever imagine, Fianna Cameron," Kit whispered over her shoulder. "If Cameron, or even Fianna, is really your name."

Instead of taking her in his arms again, as a traitorous part of her prayed he would, he turned away, then rose and crossed the room. But instead of leaving altogether, he paused at the door, staring down at its knob. After long, silent moments, he spoke.

"I've heard that the fairy folk need a man's true name in order to work their spells on him," he said, his expression hidden in shadow. "You should know, then, that mine is not Christopher. It's Christian. Christian Pennington."

Fianna's breath caught in her throat. How was she to take it, this simple sharing of a given name? As a warning? Or as a sign of misguided trust?

The door snicked shut behind him, leaving her questions unanswered.

CHAPTER THIRTEEN

Kit tossed and turned in his bed for hours, dreams of Fianna's lush, demanding mouth broken by visions of his uncle splayed out in his bed, in a chair, on the floor, blood oozing from a blackened hole in his chest. How could he be so drawn to a woman he was almost certain intended his uncle harm? And what in the hell had compelled him to tell her his real name?

Kicking free from the twisted bed linens, he sat up and hung his head in his hands. Wounded pride, perhaps, had compelled him, piqued that she could kiss him so simply to serve her own purposes. Or because he'd wanted her to know him, to see *him*, Christian Harlow Pennington, when she pressed her lips to his. Not just some nameless, faceless cog in the wheels of her own machinations.

Damn him for a bloody fool.

The first rays of morning light glazed his window as Kit washed his face and pulled on clean clothing. Uncle Christopher had arranged another meeting between himself and Theo, for ten o'clock this morning. But Kit hardly felt in the mood to discuss his political ambitions with his eldest brother. No, he had questions for his uncle, questions the Colonel might prefer Theo not hear. Such as why an Irishwoman might be in search of a certain English army major. And what cause said major might have given her to want to do him harm.

There was another task Kit had to attend to first, though, before bearding his uncle in his rooms. Checking to make sure Fianna still slept, he moved into the drawing room and pulled the family copy of *Debrett's*, which his father had placed in Kit's care, down from a high shelf. Opening to the section on viscounts, he flipped until he reached the *P*s. With a lead pencil, he added a line to the Pennington entry. Frowning, he set the book on the dining table, where Fianna would be certain to see it. Pray God this trap, unlike the one she'd avoided yesterday, would snare its intended prey.

The mantel clock chimed eight as Kit made his way into his uncle's rooms. Christopher Pennington sat not in bed, but in a chair by the window, pillows and blankets cushioning his legs. One of the invalid's better days, then. Kit's chest tightened at the task ahead of him. Could he truly be so disloyal as to question the honor of a member of his own family?

But the memory of Fianna's face when he'd called her a *leannán sídhe* urged him forward. For the slow smile of triumph he'd expected when he'd uttered the words had been nowhere in evidence, only the blank, frozen stare of one caught out in a secret shame. How could he reconcile such unanticipated vulnerability with the heartlessness of a scheming assassin, one who would murder a man without cause?

"You're in good time, Christian," his uncle said, looking up from the silver medal he held in his hand. Another Waterloo souvenir, no doubt.

"Yes, sir. I have a few things I wish to discuss with you before Theo arrives," Kit said. His usual smile was proving difficult to summon. He hated confrontations, particularly ones with members of his family.

"I'm afraid that Theodosius will not be joining us today, Christian," his uncle answered, his voice holding no hint of welcome. "For I have something I need to discuss with *you*, before you ask your brother to endorse your political ambitions. Come here, sir, where I can see you."

Christopher Pennington straightened his shoulders, then gave Kit a long, cold stare. "Would you believe it possible, Christian, for a man to be shot by a mysterious assailant and not inform his family of the fact?"

Damnation! He'd not expected the gossip to reach as far as his reclusive uncle.

"I informed Benedict, sir," Kit said, meeting his uncle's steely glare. If there was one thing his uncle could not abide, it was a man who would not stand his ground.

"You informed Benedict, you say?" The *tap, tap, tap* of the medal in his uncle's hand, rapping against the table, echoed in Kit's head. "You must forgive me. I was not aware that Benedict had become head of this family."

Kit's chin jerked. "Forgive me, sir, but you are no more the head of the family than is Benedict."

"Oh, Saybrook knows of this little escapade, does he? He is the one who decided to keep me in the dark?"

Kit could not allow such ire to be directed at an innocent. "No, sir. That decision was mine. Mine alone."

The color in his uncle's cheeks rose, then just as suddenly fell, making him look far older than his years. He slumped down in his chair, his eyes shifting away from Kit to gaze, unseeing, out the window.

"So this is what you think of me, is it, Christian? A feeble, sapless old man, unable to withstand even the hearing of bad tidings? Certainly not able to offer help in bearing injury, or to prevent future harms." The man's white head nodded. "Of course. What more could one expect of a man who cannot even move his own legs?"

"Uncle, no." Kit knelt in front of the Colonel's chair, taking the man's hands in his own. The thinness of the skin, the boniness of the fingers beneath his own, shocked him. He gentled his grip.

"Even when Father was alive, you know I held you in the highest esteem," he said, his eyes fixed on his uncle. "And now that he's gone, there is no one in this family I respect more. I only kept the incident from you because your physician told us that undue excitement might do further injury to your health."

"But being quizzed by my friend Earl Talbot about the gory details of my nephew's attack, an attack about which I knew nothing, why, that was sure to keep me in the finest of fettle."

Kit released his uncle's hands and sat back on his heels. The man might be frail of body, but his spirit would not be kept down. "I apologize, sir. I had no idea gossip would spread so quickly."

"Yes, well, you can thank Talbot's son for that. What better could you expect, though, from a boy as crack-brained as to bring an Irish wench back to England to whore for him? Talbot had not the least idea what Ingestrie had done."

"What do you know of Miss Cameron?" Kit asked, jerking to his feet.

"*Miss* Cameron, is it? Since when do you give such courtesies to other men's doxies, Christian Pennington?"

Kit ignored the rebuke. "How could you know Ingestrie had taken up with an Irishwoman?"

"How could I not? The stripling boasted of his 'wild Irish girl' to all the young bucks, including several of the officers formerly under my command. Benedict and Theo may not think it worth their time to visit the senior male of the family, but men of the army do not forget what is due to their superiors."

"And you spread their gossip to Ingestrie's father?

Why?" Kit asked, his voice thickening.

"Why? Because no man minds his son setting up a clean English girl as mistress, or even a Frenchwoman, now that the war's over. But an Irisher? Truly, Kit, how could you think I'd not?"

Kit paced in front of the window. "Ingestrie threw her over, you know. Tossed her barely enough coin for passage back to Ireland, then abandoned her to make her own way home."

"Good riddance to bad rubbish, I say. If they had more than a spoonful of brains between 'em, Parliament'd send the Irish back to their own cursed shores, each and every one."

"Well, there's one who's not returned to her own country," Kit heard himself say before the rational part of his brain could think better of the words.

"What, has the whore wormed her way into the arms of another unsuspecting young cub already?" The Colonel's eyes narrowed. "Into yours?"

Kit crossed his arms over his chest. "Why do you take against her, Uncle? Is it simply your general antipathy for the Irish? Or has she done you some particular harm?"

"Is shooting my nephew, my own flesh and blood, not reason enough?"

Kit stared at his uncle, his stomach sinking to hear the suspicions he'd not allowed himself to acknowledge voiced by another. "You think Ingestrie's mistress and the woman who fired upon me may be one and the same?"

Uncle Christopher frowned. "I don't know, not for certain. But given what I've heard, it's certainly possible, don't you agree? Is she the comely wench of whom you spoke, the one in search of an army officer?"

Kit nodded.

"And the pistol with which you were shot—are the rumors that it is in your possession true?"

Kit just strode to the door, calling for a servant to

bring his greatcoat. He reached into its pocket and retrieved the firearm, then placed it on the table in front of his uncle.

Uncle Christopher took it up, his bony fingers tracing over the long steel barrel. "Christie & Murdoch, if I'm not mistaken. Elegant, they were, those Doune pistols. Favorites with the officers of the Highland regiments."

Leaning over the table, Kit asked, "Highland? Its owner was a Scot, then, not an Irishman?"

"A Scot by birth, but an Irishman by choice," his uncle murmured, his finger tracing over the inscription.

"You know this pistol? And its owner?"

"Aye, Christian, I do." The Colonel's eyes lowered before Kit could make out what hid in their depths. "Or at least I did."

"Who, Uncle?"

The Colonel raised his eyes to Kit's. "Aidan Mc-Cracken. The leader of the Antrim rebels during the rebellion in '98. Mad, he was, and wild, that Scot, believing he and his fellows could bring about in Ireland what the colonists had done in America. As if the ignorant and bigoted Irish would ever join with any men not loyal to the Pope."

"But it was a woman who shot me, not a man," Kit said.

"McCracken lost his life in the conflict. But firearms live on, long after their rabid owners have been put down."

Kit's mind raced. "The woman who shot me—she's a relation of this McCracken's, you believe?"

"There were rumors that the fool had lain with the daughter of an Irish crofter, and had gotten a child off her."

Fianna Cameron, the bastard child of a dead rebel and an impoverished Irish girl? Kit's hands clenched. In anger or in sympathy? He hardly knew.

"And this relation of McCracken's—she meant to

shoot you, then, not me? But why would she wish you harm?"

His uncle tapped a finger against the pistol's inscription. *Tá na téada curtha go húr agus cloisfear í.* "Mc-Cracken thought himself so clever, to have translated their motto into Gaelic. But I soon learned its meaning."

"Their motto? What motto?"

The Colonel pointed to a letter on the table beside his bed. Kit retrieved it, then handed it to his uncle and sat down in the chair beside him.

He thought his uncle would open the letter, but instead he tapped his forefinger against the paper's seal, imprinted in a round of green wax. Kit bent down to examine it more closely. The seal consisted of an oval surrounding an elaborate harp, with two banners, one inscribed "IT IS NEW STRUNG AND SHALL BE HEARD," the other "EQUALITY."

Kit looked up at his uncle. "There's a harp on the Irish flag, isn't there? But I don't recall it bearing such a motto."

"It doesn't. These words have nothing to do with any valid government, Kit." His uncle's voice hardened. "They're the rallying cry of the group McCracken and his cronies founded. The United Irishmen. Those bloody treasonous rebels."

Kit's finger traced the edges of the wax seal. "But what has any of this to do with Fianna Cameron?" he asked, his voice remarkably even given the growing dread roiling his gut.

Uncle Christopher pulled the letter from Kit's hand. "There are rumors of a movement to resurrect the group. And a plan to take their fight beyond Ireland's shores. Here, to English ground."

Kit shook his head. Another of his uncle's unsubstantiated fears? Or was there something real behind this latest claim?

His doubt must have shown on his face, for his uncle grabbed his arm and drew Kit close. The man's eyes bored into his. "Talbot told me, Kit. Earl Talbot, the former Lord Lieutenant of Ireland. He fears there's a plot to assassinate someone, someone high up in the government. And he wants your help to stop it."

"My help?" Kit jerked back in his chair.

"Yes, your help. I told him of your political leanings, and assured him you'd be willing to use your contacts among the radicals to help sniff out the plotters."

Kit's eyes narrowed. "You wish me to betray my friends and allies?"

"No, of course not! No Pennington would ally himself with those who would use violence to bring about political ends. But surely not all the men of your wider acquaintance have such qualms. Or the women." His uncle leaned forward in his chair, bringing his face closer to Kit's. "Take that treacherous wench who shot you. If she's still in London, and she's the child of Aidan McCracken, you can be certain she's at the heart of it. Follow her, find out with whom she associates, and I'll pass on the information to Talbot."

"I don't wish to be impertinent, Colonel," Kit said, his boot tapping against the floor. "But if Fianna Cameron is a political assassin, why would she wish to kill you?"

Uncle Christopher looked down at his hands for a long moment, then raised his eyes to Kit's. "Because she thinks to take the right of the state, and of God, into her own weak hands, before going on to more important prey."

At Kit's puzzled frown, his uncle leaned forward, his fist pounding against the table. "Vengeance, Kit! Vengeance. Because it was I who oversaw the hanging of that damned traitor she likely called father."

CHAPTER FOURTEEN

"Can't go out a-charing for one morning, but what hussies must be a-comin' and 'ticing away me own poor boy to the pub!"

"Hussies? Who you be calling a hussy?"

Fianna awoke with a jerk, her breath catching in her throat. Angry voices—where? Her eyes darted about the room.

"You know right well what I mean, Sukey Timms. Turn me own family against me, will you? Get along with you, afore I tear yer precious hair out."

"You gonna take that, Sukey? Pitch into 'er now!"

Outside. The voices came from outside, from the alley below. No one was accusing her. Fianna rubbed a hand against her throat, urging the race of her pulse to slacken.

Even now the women's quarrel must be ending; she heard no more screeching, or even the sounds of a scuffle, but only the slap of shoes against the cobbles. She reached out to pull up the sheets that she'd kicked off the bed. No need to borrow trouble from a crowd of charwomen, not when she had a quarrel of her own with which to deal.

Fianna dressed quickly, girding herself to face an opponent far less craven than Sukey Timms.

But when she emerged from her own room, she found the sun-filled apartment empty.

"Kit?" she called, stepping into the drawing room. The only answer was a note resting on the mantel. *F— I've an errand to run. Back by midday. —CP*, he'd written, in a bold, slashing hand.

She ran her thumb over the edge of the foolscap, fretting again over the question that had kept her awake until she'd finally fallen into a troubled sleep near dawn. Why had she responded so strongly, so unthinkingly, to Kit Pennington's kiss?

Some foolish part of her longed to believe that no man could kiss a woman with such passion if he cared nothing for her. But all her prior experiences with the other sex suggested that neither moral nor rational faculties held much sway when base lust controlled the reins. No, a man could all too easily woo with hot kisses in the evening and betray with cool detachment in the morn.

And if she remained until this evening, he'd surely expect her to lie with him. A dangerous prospect, given how something weak and craven inside her yearned for the sweetness of his touch, even now, knowing how likely it was he suspected her. No, far better to take the letters and disappear into the teeming London streets, leaving Kit Pennington and his innocent, boyish charms far behind.

She was moving down the passageway, considering what she would take with her, when she realized the one error in her plan. Kit Pennington still had her father's pistol. She couldn't leave without the flintlock, the only memento of Aidan McCracken besides his letters she'd ever had.

Tossing Kit's note aside, she hurried toward his bed-chamber.

He'd not brought many of his personal effects here from Pennington House, it seemed, just a few changes of clothing, a razor and a comb, a brush and some blacking for his boots. His pockets contained no notes, no papers, only a few loose coins and one round bone button, blue thread hanging from its holes. A small cake of hard soap lay in a saucer by the ewer, the cloth beside it damp and redolent of not only the wintergreen of the lather, but the scent of Kit himself. Spicy, pungent even, yet suffused with something that urged her to bring it close to her face and breath deep. Frowning, she set the temptation quickly aside.

She expected a man who valued loyalty to family so highly to keep *some* memento of his relatives about. But no letters, no keepsakes, no cameo portraits cluttered the night table or the small desk by the window. Certainly no books borrowed from a relative named Christopher, with the lender's name and direction conveniently penned on the flyleaf.

And no flintlock pistol.

No excuse, then, to linger by the bed, wondering if its tangle of sheets meant that his sleep had been as troubled as hers. She closed the door behind her with a sharp click.

Perhaps in the drawing room? But the only things in the desk seemed to belong to Kit's brother: a few invitation cards addressed to *The Honourable Benedict Pennington*, bills for paints and canvas, charcoal sketches of unclothed women and unfamiliar countryside scenes. Tamping down her frustration, she placed each back precisely where she'd found it.

Where else, where else? Her eyes scanned the room. Might it be tucked away behind some books? Kneeling by the shelf, Fianna tipped out volume after volume, fingers reaching into dusty, empty crevices before setting each back in disappointment.

As she levered herself up with a hand placed on the table beside her, her fingers grazed a spine of brown kid. The words *Debrett's Peerage,* embossed in gold leaf, sent her pulse racing. How like the arrogant English, to proclaim in print the noble lineages of their ruling families. Charlie Ingestrie had certainly cherished his copy, but it hadn't revealed anything about the whereabouts of Major Christopher Pennington when Fianna had consulted it.

This looked to be a newer edition, though. And might not a copy owned by a Pennington be annotated with more detailed information on the family, as Ingestrie's had about the Talbots?

Kneeling back on the carpet, she thumbed open the book's leaves, turning past the engravings of the coats of arms, past the dukes and marquesses and the endless lists of earls, to the small section of viscounts. And there, on page 279:

ARTHUR PENNINGTON, VISCOUNT **SAYBROOK**, and Baron Pennington, of Much-Easton, and a Baronet; Lord Lieutenant of Lincolnshire: *born* 3 March 1756, succeeded his father Arthur, late viscount, 10 March 1801; *m.*, 22 Oct. 1791, Mary, da. and co-heir of the late Sir James Hammond, of Sleebeck Hall, co. Pembroke, esq., and has issue,— 1. THEODOSIUS, *b.* 16 Sept. 1792; —2. Benedict, *b.* 14 March 1795; —3. Christian, 3 May 1797; —4. Sibilla, 15 Feb. 1802.

Someone had inked in "*d.* 14 May 1821" in the margin by the viscount's title, bringing the listing up to date. Less than a year it had been, then, since Kit had lost his father. Some soft part of her hoped the man's death had been peaceful. Watching a parent die in violence and shame certainly had little to recommend it.

Fianna's finger brushed gently over Kit's name and the date of his birth. Not even twenty-five, he was, with two elder brothers both younger than her own thirty years. She sat back on her heels, shaking her head. As if the difference in their ages were all that kept them apart.

Fianna pulled her eyes away from the viscount's sons, finger skimming to the bottom of the page in search of her real quarry.

And there, at the very end of the entry, the list of the

previous viscount's issue:

2. CHRISTOPHER, colonel in the army, *b*. 28 Feb. 1759.

This book, like Charlie Ingestrie's before it, named no estate, no property where the Major—no, *Colonel* now—might be found.

But it did not matter. For there, penciled into the margin, the letters and numbers blurring before her eyes:

d. 25 Sept. 1818.

A parade of damning memories marched through Kit's mind as he strode from Bloomsbury back to Mayfair, taunting him for doubting his uncle. Fianna's insolence to the soldiers outside the War Office. Her railings against the Englishman who'd written such a partisan account of the Irish Rebellion. Her fiery tirade against English oppression, so intemperate that even the Irishman O'Hamill had warned her against her outspokenness. Confirmation, each one, of the likelihood of the Colonel's suspicions.

In the face of such evidence, what else could he do but assent to his uncle's plan? Trick Fianna, use her as she'd been using him, to lead him on to bigger game.

But what if his uncle were wrong? Or only partly right? What if Fianna were the illegitimate daughter of the rebel his uncle had been charged with executing, but had nothing to do with the plot Talbot had discovered? What if her only goal was personal, not general, justice?

Kit yanked off his gloves, slapping them with frustration against his thigh. To think he should be pleased by the thought of a woman intent *only* on killing his uncle. His grim laugh echoed up the stairwell as he ascended the steps to his lodgings.

He paused outside the closed door, his palm pressed against its frame. By which did he wish to be greeted—an empty room? Or a raven-haired woman whose eyes always hid the truth?

Shaking off his reluctance, Kit pushed open the door and strode down the passageway, marshaling his arguments for the confrontation that was sure to follow. But the sight of stately Fianna Cameron sprawled in an untidy heap on the drawing room carpet, the volume of *Debrett's* he'd falsely amended held slack in her hands, stifled the words in his throat.

When he'd taken up his pencil to falsely record his uncle's death, he'd imagined a Fianna happy to read it, relieved to have the burden of taking Christopher Pennington's life lifted from her shoulders. But no smile, no tears of joy animated the white face of the real Fianna; she stared at the bookshelf beside her, her eyes vacant, unblinking. Even the sharp snick of the door closing behind him did not jar her from her eerie trance. Blank, numb, she sat, as if she'd discovered a member of her own family had died, rather than one of his.

He'd prepared himself to face the familiar Fianna, the cold, enticing *leannán sídhe* bent on his uncle's destruction. Not this wounded, broken creature, slumped on the floor like a rag doll left behind by a careless child.

Surely his uncle had been mistaken. For how could a woman intent on political assassination look so entirely undone by the news of a personal opponent's death? Colonel Christopher Pennington, not some high-ranking government official, must have been her only target.

Even so, he should be angry, incensed at this woman who had done nothing but lie to him. But all he felt was a strange, keen tugging, deep within his chest.

He knelt beside her and lifted the book from her

unresisting hands.

"He was the last one, your uncle," she whispered, so softly he could barely make out the words. "The final one to pay for betraying my father. I left all the others alive, forced them to live with their shame, as I've had to live with mine. For his executioner, though, death alone would serve. But I left it too long—"

A sob broke through her words, stifled by the hands that caught her bowing head.

"Fianna," he asked, his head tipping down to hers, "your father. He was Aidan McCracken?"

A cry—part disbelief, part pain?—tore free from Fianna's throat. Then, her head began to shake from side to side, her unbound hair whipping against his hand. "And I thought you so easy to deceive, so entirely devoid of guile. But you knew all along, didn't you, Kit Pennington? That I was the one who aimed that pistol at you, the one who put a bullet in you. You, an entirely innocent man."

Kit shook his own head. She'd not think him so innocent if she discovered his own deceptions.

"And even after making such a horrible, unforgivable mistake, I still lied to you, still used you." Her voice rasped with self-loathing. "And for what? So I might rain retribution down on a dead man?"

He fought against the weight of his own lie hanging heavy in his gut. The only words that came to mind were not his own, but those from a divinity training he thought he'd long left behind. "Avenge not yourselves, but rather give place unto wrath: for it is written, Vengeance is mine; I will repay, saith the Lord."

"And did the Lord take vengeance upon Christopher Pennington? Did your uncle die in pain, in shame? Will his name go down in history as a betrayer of his own people, as my father's has? Or did he die a good Christian death, his family all beside him? Did he meet his end with fortitude, certain of God's forgiveness for his crimes?"

The bitterness of her laugh, so pained, so despairing, broke something deep inside Kit. No one should ever have cause to feel so lost, so without hope.

He reached out, taking those small hands—so cold, despite the pool of sunlight in which she sat—between his own. He'd had to do it, had to hurt her, if he was to keep his uncle safe.

"I'm sorry," he said, knowing even as he uttered the apology how inadequate it must sound.

Her head jerked up at his words, her green eyes glazed with unshed tears. "Sorry? For what do you have to be sorry, Kit Pennington? For being born a legitimate, privileged Englishman, instead of a poor Irish bastard? For burying your uncle with the honor due a soldier, not the ignominy of a traitor? For having a family that loves you?"

He cupped her face in one hand, catching the drop hovering on the edge of her dark lashes with his thumb. "For your losses, my heart. For all your terrible losses. And for my being so utterly incapable of setting them right for you."

She shuddered beneath his palm, tears coursing down her face. Tears that he'd put there, he and his damned lead-pencil lie.

Kit pulled her tight against him, rocking her like a babe as she sobbed. How in the hell was he ever to make this right?

CHAPTER FIFTEEN

Warm. So very warm, the arms about her back, the cheek nestled against her temple. The chest rising and falling beneath her palm. How long had she sat with him here, down on the drawing room carpet, quiet, anchored, so blessedly empty?

Fianna burrowed her face further into the soft folds of a neckcloth, unwilling to break the spell. No, she'd simply keep her eyes firmly shut, floating, drifting, breathing in the salt of her tears, the starch of his linen, the sharp, soothing mint of the soap with which he'd washed. Time enough later to wonder what she would do, what her life could be, without the lodestone of vengeance urging her ever forward.

Her arm, caught between his body and hers, twitched with numbness. She willed it still. Kit would wake soon enough.

But he must have felt her stir. His arms tightened about her for a moment, but then, all too quickly, fell slack.

She stifled the urge to pull them back. But as he raised his head from where it rested beside hers, an involuntary sound of protest must have croaked from her throat, for his hand immediately rose to cradle her face against his chest. They sat there together without speaking, watching a beam of sun meander across the green-figured carpet.

"Will you tell me about him?" he asked, breaking the long silence. "About McCracken? He must have been an inspiring person, to win such devotion from you."

"Aidan McCracken. My father." How strange, to acknowledge their relationship out loud. To talk of him with someone who had never known him. Someone who did not immediately turn away in disgust at the sound of his name.

"He was a kind man," she said at last, her words coming stiff and slow. "He liked people, thought the best of them. Even after all the horrors he'd witnessed. Foolish, some said. But still, he was kind." *Like you.*

Kit circled an encouraging hand over her back.

Fianna took a deep breath, pinching her eyes shut. It was easier to speak without his clear blue eyes staring at her undeserving soul.

"So many assumed I'd been born evil—a bastard, the devil's spawn," she murmured. "But *Dadaí* would never tax me with my sins. *Máire*, he'd cry, pulling me up into his arms whenever he came to visit. *What good deeds has my sweet* cailín *done today?*"

"Is that your true name?" Kit asked. "Máire?"

She trembled to hear the Gaelic syllables on his English lips. "Máire was the name my mother gave me. Though no Catholic priest nor Presbyterian elder would allow me to be baptized with it."

She felt him stiffen beneath her. In anger? Or in sympathy? But his voice was even as he asked, "Your parents never married?"

She shook her head. "Aidan McCracken might have believed with all his heart that the Anglicans, Dissenters, and Catholics should unite in order to throw off the yoke of English rule. Yet somehow the son of a prominent Presbyterian manufacturer could never quite bring himself to wed an illiterate Irish Catholic."

"Then your real name—it's not McCracken?"

What might her life have been like, if her parents had married? If she'd been born a McCracken, rather

than an O'Hamill? If Grandfather McCracken had openly claimed her mother as daughter-in-law, had given her
the protection of the McCracken name, would Mairead
have stayed in Ireland? Or would the memories of her
dead lover still have been too painful, the sight of his
child too much to bear? Even then, would her mother
have left her behind?

"True name, real name?" she scoffed. "What matters
the name, if no one cares enough to claim the person
who owns it?"

"Would your father have claimed you, if he'd not
died?"

Fianna rubbed a fold of Kit's neckcloth between her
fingers. "I like to think he would. Would a kind man
reject his own flesh and blood?"

"Kind," he echoed, doubt in his tone. "I can't help
but find it difficult to picture a man of kindness leading
peasants into armed conflict." Kit's thumb stroked down
and up her temple, soothing away the sting of his
words.

"But he was more than just kind," she protested. "He
threw himself wholeheartedly into everything—political
debates, discussion about the family's linen
manufactory, arguments over how to alleviate poverty
and injustice. He had high spirits, and charm, and more
courage than anyone she ever knew, his sister always
told me."

"Not a peasant, then. How did such a man come to
agitate on behalf of the poor?"

"He'd been sent to Scotland, to recruit workers for
the family's cotton mill," she said, her words coming
with more ease as the old stories flooded her mind.
"And when he returned to Belfast, he started the first
Sunday school for the impoverished. Not just Presbyterians, but anyone who wanted to learn how to read and
to write, so they might gain knowledge for themselves,
no matter what religious sect they embraced. He believed with all his heart that if Christians living in Ire-

land would only join together, they could throw off the tyranny of English rule." She smiled, even now so proud of his boldness, his vision. "That's why he helped to found the Society of United Irishmen. Because he believed in a genuine brotherhood of man, irrespective of religion."

"But what of the violent protests of the Catholics? The burning of cottages, the destroying of crops, the brawling and killing? Did he condone it? Did he participate in it?"

"Ah yes, the English do so like to believe it was only the Catholics who turned to violence." When had her voice grown so bitter? She took a deep, calming breath. "But the Protestants did their fair share of maiming and killing, too, though the government-run newspapers never reported it. And of course, whenever culprits were caught and tried, Protestants were always found innocent, while Catholics ended up in gaol or sentenced to death. The magistrates were all from landed families, weren't they? Protestant families, who would convict a Catholic on the flimsiest of evidence. No, my father did not participate in mob violence, but he did extend substantial sums to meet the legal expenses of the unjustly accused."

Kit sat in silence for a long while, considering. "But he did participate in the rebellion," he said. "Did more than participate, according to my uncle. In the north, he was its leader."

"Yes, but not out of liking for the role," she said. "The man originally appointed general of Down was arrested before the uprising began, and then the general for Antrim resigned. My father didn't ask for the post; the men proclaimed him their leader."

"And then he led them to their downfall. And to his own."

She sighed. "He believed in Ireland, in its people. So much so that he was willing to die for them." *To die and leave his family behind.*

Kit shifted then, his hand moving from temple to chin as he tipped her face up to his. "As was my uncle," he said, his words quiet but firm. "Willing to die, for England and its people. Should a man of honor, one only performing his duty when he oversaw the execution of a rebel leader, be put down like a dog run mad? What kind of justice is that?"

Fianna shook her head. How could the eyes of a man who had reached the age of twenty-four still shine with such trust? Such steadfast belief in the honor of a man she knew to be anything but honorable?

Something dark and wild inside whipped her, urging her to strike against such blindingly innocent trust. To make him keen with the same sense of abandonment and loss that had driven her all these dark years. All she need do was tell him how his uncle had lied about her father after his execution.

But what use would it be to disillusion him? With Major Pennington dead, there'd be no chance now of forcing him to retract his lies against her father, no chance of redeeming her father's good name. No chance of returning in triumph to claim her rightful place amongst the McCrackens, of winning a true welcome from her grandfather, or from any of his kin.

Fianna lowered her head, pulling free from Kit's embrace. Had she truly become so spiteful that she'd undermine an honest man's loyalty to his family? Simply because she had lost the chance to earn the loyalty of her own?

It was more than spite, though, wasn't it? But even if he knew his uncle had not been quite as honorable as he once believed, would that make her any more so in his eyes?

No. She had sunk low, to be sure. But even she could not bring herself to hurt an innocent so.

She rose, crossing to the window to lay her forehead against a pane. But the sun had moved away; the glass held no warmth.

What to do now? Crawl back to Ireland in defeat? Or throw herself on the mercy of Sean O'Hamill?

No matter which she chose, she could no longer remain here. Not after revealing herself so painfully to Kit.

She took a moment to make certain her mask of impassivity was firmly in place before turning back to him. "I thank you for your hospitality, sir. But I fear you must have long been wishing my absence. If you give me a few moments, I'll pack up my belongings and be out of your way."

She took a few steps toward the passageway, but before she could reach the door, Kit moved to stop her.

"Oh no, Máire," he whispered, catching her by the shoulders. "No more pretending, not between us."

"Fianna," she bit out, shrugging free of his hold. "Máire no longer exists."

But he caught her up again, shook his head in denial. "Fianna. Máire. It's not the name that matters. Only what's between us. Don't pretend you don't feel it."

Her body urged her to step closer, to shelter once again within the confines of his arms. *A Mháthair Dé!* She willed herself not to move.

"Something between us? Whatever could you mean?"

He answered not with words but with touch, his fingers burning a path across her collarbone, then up the column of her neck. Was it anger that made the blue of his eyes spark like the hottest fire? Or something far more dangerous?

"We never did discuss terms," she continued, forcing her voice to splinter like ice beneath a boot. "But since you've not had the satisfaction of taking your pleasure of me, you needn't worry about compensation. Or perhaps you wish me to repay you for my room and board?"

He made not the slightest flinch at the coarse reminder of what they truly were to each other. Instead, he took a step closer, capturing her face between his palms.

"Oh, you like it when that's all the world sees, don't you? The icy fae queen, with no feelings to call her own. So high above us all, so unmoved by anything as mundane as a human emotion." His thumbs traced across her cheeks, catching against the trails of salt her tears had left behind. "But my waistcoat, still damp from your crying, knows it for a lie. No, that proud, disdainful mask won't fool me any longer, Fianna Máire McCracken Cameron. If you leave, at least be honest enough to acknowledge that it won't be because I wish you gone."

"More fool you," she said, praying her voice did not tremble. "But why should I be witless enough to remain?"

"For me. For this." And he lowered his face to hers.

The softness of her, the warm, yielding curves of her body—a dream, damn near a revelation, she'd been, the Fianna Cameron who had cried out her sorrows, then fallen asleep in his arms. And when she'd trusted him with the truth of her father, her small form nestled close against his chest, Kit had felt immense, boundless, as if he could drag down castles with his bare hands, save all the innocents of the world from every iniquitous blow. Anything, if only it were done on her behalf.

She intended to use you. To betray you. To murder your uncle, family fealty rebuked.

But she acted out of justice, and a loyalty to her family as keen as your own, conscience countered.

He'd tried to reconcile the two, asking her to consider what justice might look like from his uncle's point of view. But the challenge had sent that warm, feeling Fianna fleeing, even while her body remained in the room. Something wild and desperate clamored inside him then, an urge to grab her and shake her, that wintry fairy seductress who'd banished the woman he truly wanted. He wanted her back, no, *needed* her back, that woman who felt. Not because his uncle suspected her of treason. Not even because he'd promised the Colonel to use her to track down the Irish assassins. But because the loss of that Fianna had felt too much like other soul-withering losses he'd not been able to prevent—Benedict, to the Continent and his art; his father, to wasting disease and death; Theo, to grief and the blinding oblivion of drink.

He'd held his recklessness in check until, in that cold, impassive voice, she'd announced her plans to leave. Instead of watching her go, as a wise man, a rational man, would have done, he found himself kissing her, demanding, daring, *begging* that feeling human to chip her way free of the *sídhe's* icy hold.

But for the longest time, her lips remained cool and still beneath his own. He might almost have been fooled, but for the race of the blood in her throat, her pulse pounding so quick beneath his stroking thumbs. So very skilled at self-protection, she was, this woman with as many masks as she had names.

"You think to hide from me?" he whispered, pulling back to stare into her unrevealing green eyes. "To pretend you're nothing but a fair face? A fae without a soul?"

Dark, narrow brows arched in disbelief. "Is that not what all men want? A beautiful, empty shell? Pretty but vacant, ready to be filled with their own low desires?"

Kit scoffed. "What man would want the simulacrum, after once having glimpsed the substance of you?"

"My *substance*? Be glad you've not had more than a glimpse of my *substance*, Kit Pennington. It's not nearly so attractive as the veil that conceals it."

"But I have seen it, Fianna."

She tried to jerk free of his arms, but he held tight,

willing her to listen.

"I've seen the passionate, caring woman you work so hard to deny. I've seen your beauty and your anger, your independence and your loyalty. How much you care for your family. How you fight against what you feel. For me. For us."

His hands rose to frame her face, his fingers lightly brushing back the wisps of hair by her temples. "I see *you*," he whispered. "I want *you*."

"Then take me, and be damned," she whispered, yanking down on his neckcloth, pressing her lips to his.

Kit sank deep into the welcome of her mouth, reveling in a heat closer to the hearths of heaven than any fires of hell. Hot, and lush, and sweeter than anything he'd ever imagined, a pyrotechnics of taste and touch. With a gasp, his hands slid down the sharp blades of her shoulders, as if he might somehow pull the flaming whole of her entirely inside him, set himself alight on her flame.

The feel of her firm breasts against his chest sent his cock surging, pressing for attention into the softness of her belly. He pulled back, embarrassed, afraid she'd shy away at the evidence of his arousal. But instead, her arms rose to twine about his neck, drawing him even closer. Why did he keep forgetting she was no inexperienced girl, but a mature woman, one who'd warmed Ingestrie's bed, and perhaps many others'?

Experienced, perhaps, but she held her body with passive pliancy, offering herself, demanding nothing. *Take me*, she'd said; had she commanded past lovers to do the same? Had they simply taken, accepting what she offered, giving nothing in return? No wonder she'd been able to manipulate Ingestrie, if he did no more than greedily seize the reflection of his own desires, without any consideration for hers.

No, their exchange could not be one-sided, not if he wanted Fianna to stay beyond the time it took for his own passion to be sated. He needed not just to take, but

to give. To startle her beyond her protective self-posses-
sion, push her outside that clever mind. Bind her to him
with pleasure and with need. Make her care, as he was
growing to care for her, so it would become anathema
to do him, or any member of his family, harm.

And so he forced himself to slow, to turn the seductive weapons she'd used last night on him against her.
Tiny nibbles against a lip. Fingertips that skimmed over
the lightest hairs on exposed skin, then glanced away.
Breaths that teased against the tendons of the neck, the
sensitive lobe of an ear, fleet and thrilling as a whispered confidence.

Her body stilled, grew taut. With pleasure? Or in
fear?

"I'm right here," Kit murmured, tracing his tongue
over the curve of her ear. "Be here, too. Be with me."

She gasped, a shudder tremoring down her spine. Kit
pulled her closer for a moment, then drew back, just
enough so she might see the truth of what he wanted
from her, wanted for her, in his face, in his eyes.

"Fianna," he whispered, entreaty entangling with
command. "Touch me. Want me, as I want you."

Kit held his breath for what seemed hours, watching
her eyes widen, the black of the pupils almost eclipsing
the green. He swallowed as her hand finally, gently,
cupped his jaw.

"I am. I do."

A heady rush of triumph washed through him as he
scooped up the warmth of her into his arms, a rush that
only grew stronger at her cry of welcome surprise.
Without haste, he made his way down the passageway,
shouldering open the bedchamber door, kicking it
closed behind him. Kneeling on the bed, he set her atop
the coverlet, holding still as her slim hands gingerly
pushed aside his coat, then worked at the stiff buttons
on his waistcoat.

"May I?" he asked, fingers itching at the ties of her
gown. At her nod, he pulled the knots free, quickly

unlacing until the fabric fell open and down over her slim shoulders. She wore no stays, only a thin chemise held closed by a pale green ribbon.

As she worked, he toyed with that ribbon, undoing its bow, sliding its tip down the column of her neck, tracing it over the seductive arch of her brow. She shivered, but remained intent on her own task, tugging at his recalcitrant neckcloth with tantalizing, persistent fingers.

When at last it drew free, she murmured in satisfaction, then slowly pulled at the ties of his shirt. As it, too, fell open, she mimicked his actions, drawing one tie with painstaking care across his left collarbone, then the right, until he, too, began to shiver. He wanted to close his eyes, to concentrate solely on the sensation of touch, but he forced them to stay open, unwilling to give up the sight of her, so serious, so intent. But when her tongue began to follow the tie, tracing a warm, slick path up his throat, up the line of his jaw, his lids lowered of their own accord, his neck arching in response.

As she moved the tie to tickle against the lobe of his ear, he growled and pushed aside her hand. Clutching the tails of his shirt with both hands, he yanked the linen over his head, baring himself to her gaze.

His hands clenched as she took him in, drawing her gaze over the planes of his chest, the muscles in his abdomen and arms. Those green eyes darted lower, just for an instant, to the bulge behind the fall of his trousers. His cock tightened in greedy response, straining for freedom against the constraint.

Her eyes fixed on his, Fianna shrugged against her shift. His own eyes followed the garment's path as it slid slowly, so slowly, down her arms, over the small mounds of her breasts, falling to pool in a puddle of white around her slim hips.

"Touch me," she said, even as her own hand, light as a dragonfly, skimmed over his chest.

He reached out then, each hand cupping the weight

of a breast, marveling at their curves, at the responsive-
ness of each rosy tip as he circled it with the pad of a
thumb. When his fingers caught a nipple between them,
she moaned, the sound vibrating deep in her throat. His
grin of satisfaction disappeared, though, when her
hands jerked away to cover her mouth. Did she think to
push the too-revealing sound back from whence it had
come?

"Fianna," he said, one hand tilting her chin up so he
might meet her eyes. "I want to know what pleases you.
What makes you groan with wanting. What will make
you come apart in my arms. Tell me." Placing her hand
over his free one, he then moved both back to the swell
of her bosom. "Show me."

CHAPTER SIXTEEN

Fianna watched a shaft of sun drift over the drowsing form of the man beside her. She had been made for the shadows, for the murky dark of overcast days and moonless nights, but Kit had been formed for the glories of the light. It limned his curls, the whorls of hair on his chest, even his eyelashes, adorning each with hints of gold, as if he were a page she'd stolen from the Book of Kells.

She reached out a finger, skimming it over the very tips of his lashes, as if she might sweep free a tiny speck of that light for herself. But it came away empty. Of course. It was simply a trick of the sun, after all. She couldn't steal it, or him, not his warmth, not his heart. Only bask in them for a while, until the shadows claimed her once more.

With a sigh, she lay her head down on his shoulder, her hand tracing circles on his chest.

An arm stole around her shoulders, pulling her body close against his. The pad of a thumb stroked against her temple, then toyed with the damp curls beside her ear. She closed her eyes as his head turned, his lips and nose burrowing deep in her hair.

"Did I please you?" he whispered.

Oh, the vanity of the man! As if he hadn't even been there in the bed beside her, a witness to her hedonistic cries, to her body shuddering so completely beyond her

control. Even now, she could barely believe she'd allowed herself the luxury of indulging her desire. With
men she'd only seduced out of vengeance, disgust, at
both them and herself, had made it easy to keep her
own passions firmly in check. And with Ingestrie, disgust had been sharpened by discomfort and pain—she
never would have persuaded him to bring her to England if she had complained about his dreadful lack of
skill.

When Ingestrie would lift his clumsy weight off her
and roll to his side of the bed, she'd always felt a sense
of reprieve, the bone-deep relief of a sinner finally freed
from the stocks. But when Kit had pushed up on his
elbows, whispering worries about crushing her, she'd
pulled him back, one hand on his head, the other on his
tight, round buttocks, not nearly ready to give up the
comforts of his body. He'd laughed then, his breath
warm against her neck, and rolled them both until her
weight rested atop him.

"Heartkin? Did I please you?" he asked again.

Had he pleased her, indeed.

"Well enough," she replied in as dampening a tone
as she could muster. Best to turn the conversation in a
less dangerous direction. "But what is this word,
heartkin? I've not heard it before."

He laughed, the rumble in his chest echoing against
her cheek. "A love word, an endearment of my mother's.
She only used it when speaking to my father, never to
my brothers or sister or me. I think I rather envied him,
having that word all to himself."

Nodding proved difficult with her head pressed in
the crook of his arm. "Ah. *Mo chroide*."

"Ma chree?"

"Yes. What my mother called my father. *Of my
heart*."

He fell silent for a moment, his hand resting against
the curve of her shoulder. "She loved him that much?
Even though he wouldn't marry her?"

Fianna sighed. "I suppose she must have. But what does a child know of her parents' hearts?"

"Does she never speak of him, then?"

"I do not know," she said, the words thick in her throat. "I've not seen her since I was a child."

He inhaled sharply. "Was she hanged, as well as your father?"

"No. But once the English soldiers had finished dealing with the rebellion's leaders, she feared they'd turn their attention to those who had aided and abetted them. And so they fled."

"They?"

"Yes. My mother, and her father, and her brother." How strange, to speak of them and not receive a quelling frown in return.

"But not you?"

"No. My aunt Mary, my father's sister, agreed to give them coin, enough for passage to America. But I remained in Ireland, with my father's people."

She'd spoken in a flat, even voice, one that kept her emotions closely in check. But still his arms tightened around her. "They left you behind?"

"What kind of life could I expect, being raised by unlettered Irish peasants in a foreign, heathen land? Far better to accept the protection of the McCrackens, safe in familiar Belfast. They gave me warm clothes, good food, and an education that would allow me to make my way in the world as a gentlewoman. Just as my father would have wanted. Even my mother agreed it was for the best, Aunt McCracken said."

"Did she?" An unfamiliar undercurrent of anger edged Kit's voice. He rolled her to her back and propped himself on his elbow by her side. "And did you believe her?"

Fianna stared at his frowning face. "My aunt was a God-fearing woman. What cause would she have to lie?"

Kit waved a hand. "To shield herself from her own

unkindness, perhaps? For it was unkind—no, more than unkind, it was a damned cruelty—to force a woman to give up a child in order to save the lives of a father and a brother."

On the most difficult days of her childhood, those days when the townspeople whispered *bastard* behind her back and Grandfather McCracken's gaze skimmed right over her as if she did not even exist, Fianna often consoled herself by imagining a tearful Mairead begging and pleading with Aunt Mary to be allowed to take her child with her. She'd always felt sinful, afterward; her aunt and grandfather had saved her mother, and her mother's family, at great risk to themselves. To imagine their rescue as a crass exchange, or even worse, a bribe or a threat—no, it had simply been unthinkable to a child dependent upon their care.

But even if her mother had been compelled to leave without her, did that mean she had not grieved for her loss? Was there not room in a woman's heart for love and sorrow, as well as for fear?

Would Fianna herself not feel both when it came time for her to leave Kit?

Kit caught her cheek in a palm, turning her eyes to his. "Your mother loved you, Fianna. I have not the least doubt of it. And neither should you."

He made it sound so simple. So obvious. Was this what it would be like, to truly belong to a family? To be comforted, reassured, sheltered from hurt, even when one did not in the least deserve it? Or was it only because it had been Kit who had spoken the words, offered the comfort? Would she always feel so safe, if she knew she would wake up to find him beside her every morning?

She jerked her head free of his hand and rolled to her side, shunting away the ridiculous thought. If the son of a Presbyterian merchant could not fathom bringing a Catholic peasant girl into his family, how much more preposterous to imagine the son of an English viscount welcoming an illegitimate Irish whore into his?

And why should she even want to tie herself to a family who claimed as one of its own the very man who had murdered her father? Would she betray Aidan McCracken, then, just as surely as had the men upon whom she'd wreaked retribution?

A warm hand stroked down her back. "Fianna—"

"It matters little whether she loved me or no," she interrupted, jerking away from the bed and reaching for her shift, which had fallen to the floor. "It's the McCrackens with whom she left me, and it's to the McCrackens I must return. Though whether they'll accept me empty-handed, I've no idea."

She'd whispered the last words to herself, but he still must have heard. "Accept you? After forcing your mother to abandon you, did they then have the gall to make you feel unwelcome?"

"Unwelcome? They gave me shelter, and sent me to the meetinghouse and to school. Far more than many a peasant child ever receives. What more of a welcome could I expect?"

"What more, indeed," he answered, sitting up on the side of the bed to pull on his trousers. "And so you thought to buy your way into their hearts by killing your father's executioner?"

She stilled, pinned by his words. He made it sound so crude, as if an act of justice were some low, mercantile exchange. As if she'd disappointed him in some deeply important way. How dare he?

"I thought to support my family by redressing an injustice," she bit out, yanking her gown over her head. "To wipe away the care from my aunt's eyes, and make the smile return to my grandfather's face. The Penningtons are not the only ones who hold family loyalty dear, you know."

"But violence isn't the only way to right a wrong, Fianna," he said, pulling her closer to tighten her laces. "And rarely the best way, for it only leads to more of the same."

"Oh, and what would you do if your father's name
had been smeared in the mud, and he were no longer
alive to demand satisfaction from those spreading the
lies?" she tossed over her shoulder.

"I'd refuse to listen to such low gossip. Shun anyone
who did," he answered, tying off the laces and tucking
them under her skirt.

She crossed to the dresser, where one of her stockings lay. "Ah, there speaks a man who has never felt the
lash of disrespect. Simply ignoring gossip doesn't keep it
from spreading. Or keep those who listen to it from
shunning those caught in its net."

"All right, then," he said, rising to pace the room, his
feet and torso bare. "What of this? I'd gossip, too, but
I'd tell the truth. Tell it to everyone. Holler it from the
rooftops. Make a sermon of it. No, I'd print it up on
broadsides and hang them all about the town. Especially
across from the houses of the ones spreading the lies."

He looked so alive, so eager, with that wide, determined smile, those arms gesturing as if he might pull in
the entire world and make it believe whatever he would.
A soldier of words, armed with broadsides and hammer,
not pistol or sword.

Why could she not summon the scorn that such
naïveté deserved? She shook her head as she reached for
her other stocking, the one he'd abandoned on the
counterpane, then sat on the chair beside the bed. Before she had the chance to pull it on, though, Kit knelt
in front of her, a pamphlet waving from his fist.

"Do you have any of your father's letters? You could
publish them, just like Henry Hunt did after he was sent
to prison for his role at Peterloo. Or you could write his
life story. You said that fellow who wrote *Memoirs of the
Different Rebellions in Ireland* told only one side. Why
should you not tell the other?"

"A biography, of my father?" Her brow furrowed.
"Who would be interested in reading such a thing,

never mind printing it? No one in Ireland would dare."

"The press in England is restricted, too," Kit said, sitting back on his heels. "But not so tightly controlled as it is in your country. Why, I know any number of printers here who would be more than eager to pay for such an account. Do you remember Sam Wooler? His uncle publishes a radical journal, and I'm sure he'd be eager to include articles detailing the life of a man who played such a key role in Irish reform efforts. You could even have them printed as a book."

He sat forward, his hands gripping her knees. "Imagine handing such a volume to that grandfather you're so eager to please. Far more likely to bring a smile to his face, I'd warrant, than my uncle's head on a platter."

A frown began to form on her lips. But before they could shape a denial, he pressed a finger against them. "Don't say no, not yet. Not without considering the idea first. Come, we'll find Sam and meet with his uncle, and then you can decide."

He slipped on her stockings, tied her garters, and slid her shoes onto her feet, all before the tingle of his touch faded from her lips. Had she ever met a man of such unbridled optimism? It would almost be worth it, indulging his fantastic scheme, if it would bring such a smile to his face. What harm could it do to grant him a day, or two at most? It would give her time enough to think, to come up with a plan for what she might do with the rest of her life, now that retribution had slipped beyond her grasp.

And so when he stood, holding out his hand to her as if he were a gentleman requesting a dance at a ball, she placed her own within it, and allowed him to pull her in his wake.

"Thank you, Mr. MacGowan, for sharing your memories of my father. I'd no idea he'd traveled to Scotland to recruit workers displaced by the Highland Clearances."

Even now, after he'd spent more than a fortnight as her lover, the sight of Fianna Cameron's rarely bestowed smile still set Kit's insides all a-tumble. At present, her smile wasn't even aimed at him, but at the garrulous older man whom they'd been questioning. Only after a moment of standing transfixed could Kit shake himself free of its enthralling charm. Poor MacGowan, however, remained impolitely fixed in his chair long after Fianna had risen.

Kit exchanged an amused glance with Sam Wooler as they waited for MacGowan to regain his wits. Once Kit had told Sam of Fianna's connection to the Irish rebel McCracken, Sam and his printer uncle had done everything they could to help advance the project of writing the man's life history, including inquiring amongst all their radical acquaintances for any who might have known him. Over the past fortnight, Sam had brought several such men to meet with them in Kit's rooms, including MacGowan, who had once worked in the McCrackens' Belfast mill. As he had promised his uncle, he'd kept an ear attuned for word of political plots, but neither MacGowan nor any of the other fellows with whom they'd spoken had even mentioned the United Irishmen or their rebellious cause.

The old Scot had not been intimidated by his Mayfair surroundings, nor by the questions of a woman with the beauty and imperiousness of a monarch, as had most of the other men Sam had found. No, for nearly two hours MacGowan had told stories of Fianna's father without pause. But the sudden warmth of her smile, so unexpected in the midst of such a cool, collected face, seemed to have finally tied the poor man's tongue.

"How cruel, that tenants of such long standing could be summarily displaced, just to give their lands over to the grazing of sheep," Kit finally interposed.

MacGowan shook his head, as if waking from a spell, then scrambled upright. "Aye, sir, terrible cruel. Never thought I'd see the day when a laird would care more for a dumb animal than for a hardworking crofter. Nothing like your father, miss, those mean, miserly men who cleared us from their lands," he added, swinging back to Fianna like a compass point drawn to the north. "He never promised Belfast'd be anything like the Highlands, not like those false sayers who swore we'd grow fat on the land they forced us onto. Barren as an old crone's womb, wasn't it, though? Better to emigrate than to starve, McCracken said, and gave us his word that work at the mill in Ireland would pay well enough. And so it did."

The more he learned about Aidan McCracken, the more Kit's admiration for Fianna's father grew. That a man such as the one described by MacGowan—an intelligent, capable man who interacted with the poor with a rare ease, who did something, rather than just lamented over the plight of the displaced—should in the end succumb to the temptation of violence filled Kit with frustration and regret.

How much more painful must be Fianna's feelings? Confronted by that habitually impassive expression with which she held the world at bay, many might believe she felt nothing at all. No trembling mouth, no furrowed brow, ever betrayed her. But each time she heard some new piece of her father's past, he saw her grow ever more imperious, her jaw tighter, her chin raised just that bit higher. As if by sheer will alone she could deny the slashing hurt of his loss.

And yes, there, his hand had risen without his even thinking to move it, coming to rest in the small of her back, offering the comfort she'd never admit to wanting, nor deign to request. She didn't pull away from his touch, though, but instead curved into it, her body warm, even a bit yielding. A small sign of the trust they were beginning to build?

He allowed his hand to trace one reassuring circle, then another, against that curve before letting it drop to his side. He held the other out to their visitor. "Thank you for sharing your stories with us, Mr. MacGowan. You have no idea how helpful you've been. Please, let me summon my man to retrieve your hat."

Kit returned from seeing MacGowan on his way to find Sam and Fianna elbow deep in foolscap. "Do you think you can deliver the first installment by Tuesday week?" Sam asked, pushing his spectacles back up his nose with an ink-stained finger. "My uncle's saving several columns in the April edition for it."

"Perhaps, if all these notes I've taken can be arranged into some semblance of order," Fianna answered, staring down at the papers on the table in front of her with a fierce frown. As if she couldn't quite believe that they, like all good minions, hadn't already anticipated her needs and sorted themselves out accordingly.

Lord, he must be far gone, to find such imperiousness so dear.

"Good, good. Now here's the sample you gave me last week, back to you with some suggestions for amendments," Sam said, adding yet another sheet to her stack. "You present your ideas well, but don't be afraid of evoking your readers' sensibilities. You want them to feel the passion McCracken held for Ireland, his anger at the injustice with which his fellow men were treated. Then, when you begin to write about the rebellion, they'll have some sympathy for why he felt compelled to violence. See, as you do here."

Fianna glanced at the lines in question, her brows narrowing. "Are logical, rational arguments not enough to persuade, Mr. Wooler?" she asked, her eyes pointedly turned away from Kit.

Kit bit back a grin. He knew the exact line to which Sam must have pointed, for it had taken him nearly an hour to persuade the logical, rational Fianna to include even that one small appeal to readerly pathos in the sample that she'd penned. Not one to give much credit to emotion, at least not in the cold light of day, was Fianna Cameron. How she'd scoffed when he'd wagered her a kiss that Sam would praise the passage he'd insisted she add. And how very delicious it would be to claim that kiss from a woman far more comfortable reasoning her way through life than trusting her feelings. She might prefer to hide them—or to hide from them—but with each kiss they shared, he could feel them bubbling ever closer to the surface.

"The author's expertise, and the logic with which he presents his facts, can both help to persuade. But it's the appeal to sentiments that seals the deal," Sam said as he rose to his feet. "Ask Kit if you're having difficulties; he's a dab hand at it. My uncle even considered offering him a regular column in the paper at one time—The Radical Aristocrat, or some such nonsense, I think he planned to call it."

"He did?" Kit exclaimed. "Why did I never hear of it?"

"Because I knew a fellow as ambitious as you would never be content with such a mean task, Kit. Besides, we need you in Parliament. You never would have caved to Tory pressure on the army estimates resolution the way Norton did on Wednesday. Does your brother have no control over the man?"

Kit stared out the window, fighting back a scowl. Even if he'd been too busy with Fianna to read the accounts of parliamentary doings for the last week, why should he be surprised by this news of Norton's latest disloyalty? Or of Theo's inability to curb it?

But that was beside the point. He wouldn't stand for anyone criticizing a member of his family, not even someone as well intentioned as Sam Wooler.

"Come, Pennington, you know I meant no disrespect," Sam protested as Kit grasped his elbow and pointed him toward the door.

"I believe you have another appointment, Mr. Wooler?" Kit said, giving his friend a light but decisive push toward the passageway.

Sam stumbled, but turned with a chuckle. "Who would ever believe such a good-natured fellow capable of so much haughty disdain?" he quipped. "It must be your influence, Miss Cameron. Teach me, too, one of these days, how to make a man quake in his boots with just one look?"

With a quick bow to Fianna and a wink to Kit, the impudent fellow darted out of the room, cravenly pulling the door shut behind him.

Kit darted to the door to pursue his friend, but a sound he'd never heard before brought him to a halt.

Laughter? From Fianna?

As the silvery peals came closer, he almost feared to move, as if catching sight of a mirthful Fianna might be tantamount to spying on Melusine at her enchanted bath, a sight so forbidden that it would send the fairy a-fleeing, never again to be seen by mortal eyes. But when he felt her breath on the back of his neck, he couldn't seem to stop himself from turning and pulling her tight to his chest. Superstitious of him, perhaps, to keep his eyes pinched shut. But who but himself would ever know?

At long last, her laughter finally stilled, although she remained tucked against his waistcoat. "Most would say you're lucky to have such good friends, Kit," he heard her whisper. "I know it's not luck, though, but the worthiness of your own character that has won them to you."

His arms tightened at the wistfulness in her voice.

"Do you truly think him interested in my father's story?" she asked. "Or has he just agreed to print it as a kindness to you?"

Kit bent his head and rubbed a cheek against her temple. "It's you who are doing him a kindness, Fianna. And not just one for Sam, but for your own countrymen, too. It will go a long way toward discrediting the ridiculous idea that Irish Catholics' fanatical hatred for the English, and for their Protestant countrymen, was the sole cause of the rebellion if you can show that it wasn't only Catholics, but Protestants such as your father, who objected to the repressive policies of Anglo-Irish magistrates. And that would be a good first step toward easing the remaining restrictions on Catholics' civil and political rights."

"What an optimist you are, Christian Pennington! Only you would leap from writing Papa's biography to Catholic emancipation as if the two were no farther apart than the banks of a lazy country stream."

Another laugh bubbled up beside his ear, sending his blood fizzing beneath his skin. Kit pulled back and opened his eyes.

His breath caught in his throat at the wondrous sight of a Fianna in full smile. He watched as his finger rose, tracing the unfamiliar lines laughter had wrought on her brow. Laughter that he, Kit Pennington, had inspired.

Win a seat in Parliament; gain Catholics and other unfairly disenfranchised men the right to vote; make Fianna Cameron laugh at least once a day. All eminently worthy goals to which a man might aspire.

He tapped a finger lightly against her lip. "And only you would berate a poor fellow instead of giving him the kiss you so clearly owe him."

She would have bestowed only a quick peck if Kit had not caught her back when she moved to pull away and kissed her until her pulse pounded as fiercely as his own.

"Ah, no more of your distractions, Kit," she said, ducking under his arm as he bent to take the kiss deeper. "We should be able to finish the first section in good time, but I'm concerned about the latter ones. We've not been able to speak with anyone who knew *Dadaí* during the actual rebellion. Or at least anyone brave enough to admit it. How am I to give an accurate account of that time in his life if I have no facts about it?"

Kit frowned as Fianna moved back to the table and began again to rearrange the piles of foolscap. He knew at least one man who could tell Fianna something about those last days of her father's. But the trust he and Fianna had begun to build between them would crumble faster than a week-old biscuit if she found out he'd lied about Uncle Christopher being dead.

Might he visit the Colonel alone, though, on the pretext of needing more information about the United Irishmen and their purported assassination plot, and ease the old man into discussing McCracken's last days? It wouldn't be a pretext, not truly, since all the inquiries he'd made on his uncle's behalf to date had come to naught.

How, though, would he explain to Fianna how he'd come by such new intelligence?

"Oh!" A cascade of foolscap fluttered to the floor as Fianna's hands clapped over her mouth. Her green eyes looked up at him in mute appeal, as if it were she, not he, who was guilty of some betrayal. "I'm so very sorry, Kit!" she whispered between her fingers.

"Well you should be, throwing my rooms into such an untidy state." He kicked at a paper that had fallen close to his boot.

"No, not the papers. The letters!"

"What letters?" But by the time he had finished speaking, she had already dashed from the room.

When she returned, she walked with a far more decorous gait, though the hand that held out a packet of letters to him was not entirely steady. "That day your brother sketched me, while I unpacked the boxes he had brought—I found them then. But I didn't read them, not with Benedict there watching, and later, after we returned from the political meeting at the coffee-house and we—"

No blush, but there, that rise of the chin, the quickness of her words—had that evening affected her as deeply as it had him?

"Well, I must have forgotten them, is all," she said, pinching her lips tight.

Kit smiled. "And what does a packet of the late Lord Saybrook's letters have to do with your father?"

"They're addressed to your father, yes. But they were written by your uncle Christopher," she said, her eyes meeting his without wavering. "While he was in Spain, and Ireland before that. I'm sorry for keeping them from you." With a shove, she pushed the packet into his unresisting hands.

The yellowing paper crinkled between his fingers. He traced a thumb over one red seal, the Saybrook family crest over Uncle Christopher's monogram pressed into the wax. The same design in the signet Uncle Christopher had given to him.

"Of course, I wouldn't want to impinge upon your privacy, or that of anyone in your family," Fianna said, her voice low and tentative. "But perhaps, if you could read through them, and discover what he wrote of those days, whether he ever mentioned my father—"

Kit stared at the folded sheets, lost for words. Reading the correspondence of the dead was one thing. But prying into that of the still living?

He looked up at her, the negation forming on his lips. Fianna had no idea that Christopher Pennington was still alive, but still, she expected him to refuse. The very stillness of her body, her shoulders already set as if anticipating an expected, familiar blow, all spelled "rejection" as clearly as if she'd spoken the word aloud. No one who saw her tight, drawn expression could ever imagine it could glow with such splendid delight as it had only a few moments before.

Fianna needed to prove her loyalty to her father, and to her father's family. But she couldn't do it, not unless he first proved his own loyalty to her.

"It might take me some time to read through all of

these," Kit said, taking a seat at the dining table and setting the letters down on its polished surface. "A pot of tea would not come amiss."

No laugh this time. But before she left the room, she gave his shoulder a quick, hard squeeze, a touch he felt all the way down to his toes.

How could the mere touch of her fingers make him feel as tall as the oldest oak on the Saybrook estate?

CHAPTER SEVENTEEN

Kit was deeply engrossed in the letters when Fianna returned from the kitchen. Small lines rayed out from the corners of his eyes as he squinted to make out the cramped handwriting that crossed and recrossed the sheets. Good thing she had a tray in her hands, else she might have given in to the ridiculously sentimental impulse to smooth them away with the tip of her finger.

As she poured out, she stole glimpses of his mobile features, gauging the differing emotions that his uncle's letters evoked. She'd hardly envisioned Major Pennington an agreeable correspondent, but the frequency of Kit's smiles suggested that if his uncle's handwriting was not entirely legible, at least he'd taken pains to make what could be deciphered as entertaining as possible.

She prepared Kit's tea just as he liked it—no sugar, just a touch of milk—then set the cup down beside his elbow. He nodded, but seemed far too engrossed by his reading to pay it much heed. One letter in particular seemed to catch his attention; he read and reread it several times before setting it aside from the others.

Not until the day's light began to wane did he lay down the final letter. He shook his head, as if waking from a deep dream, then looked up and started, as if he'd not expected to discover her still sitting at the table beside him.

"Did you find anything of interest?" she asked, careful to keep her tone even.

"To me and to my family, of course. But I'm not certain if anything here will be of much use to you," he said, his brow furrowing. "Most of them date from the time my uncle was posted in the Peninsula, not in Ireland."

Fianna frowned. Another profitless endeavor, then.

His hand reached out, stilling her fingers as they tapped against her teacup. Taking the saucer from her hand, he replaced it with the stack of letters. "But you might recognize names of people or places that would mean nothing to me."

She looked up at the sound of Kit's laughter. How ridiculous a picture she must look, her mouth gaping open, the letters dropping from her suddenly numb fingers. But she'd simply never imagined he'd ever trust her enough to lay his uncle's private correspondence open to her.

She donned her most haughty expression as she raked the letters back into a neat pile. But it no longer seemed to daunt him, that expression, if it ever really had. He reached out a finger and tapped it against the nose she'd stuck so far up in the air, and she simply couldn't help it: she found herself laughing along with him, the sound strange but surprisingly warm in her own ears.

"He mentions no names, but the incident he describes in this note, here on the top—it sounds quite remarkably like something your father would have done."

How would Kit think her father likely to have acted? For good? Or for ill?

Instead of taking up the letter in question, Fianna leafed quickly at each note in the pile, rearranging them so they fell in chronological order. Better to be methodical, and read from start to finish, rather than allow emotion to overrun her better sense.

August 1797
Dear Brother
Belfast holds little beside the beauty of its situation to recommend it. A practical little town, with few architectural graces to draw the eye. Only the belfry of the Market House, the slender spire of the Poorhouse, and the cupola of a Papist church break the low line of the sky. Oh, and the masts of the ships in port, which you can see, all the way from the opposite end of the High Street. The older streets are ill lighted and badly kept, with pigs wandering at will. Come market days, the main thoroughfares grow crowded with booths and stalls, making it difficult for my men to conduct their patrols.

September 1797
You will laugh when I tell you that some of the city's inhabitants propose to begin a subscription, aimed at funding the revival and perpetuation of the Ancient Music and Poetry of Ireland. I wonder they need any funds at all, given the dearth of culture this land of barbarians can claim. Needless to say, I did not contribute.

October 1797
I thank you for the reminder that in no part of Ireland are the Catholics so sparse as in Antrim and Down. But it is a common saying that the Country will never know peace 'til Belfast is in ashes. With its prevalence of thatched roofs, the town could be burned to the ground in as little as an hour. As it is, we must rush out to stamp out a fire nearly every fortnight; just last night, one flamed up in a barn beside the barracks. The men of Belfast seem diligent about answering the alarms, but the town's poor water supplies could easily be overtaxed by a few well-placed tinders. The Irish agitators, of course, are too dull to hatch such a plan, but if the French should send aid. . .

January 1798
Many of the Dissenters here seem almost as rabid for

"relief" as do the Papists. One of the Presbyterian societies even suggests that persons of every religious persuasion should unite to agitate for political reforms. Presbyterians, tolerant of other religions? When icicles embellish hell, mayhap. . .

February 1798
More rumors of a French invasion, each more fearful than the next. Some say there is not one Papist in a hundred who had not confederated with the Frenchies under the most solemn sanction to extirpate the whole race of heretics (Protestants) from the island, and well I believe it. The unabashed admiration of the Irish for the rebellious French, and the colonists in the Americas, too—how can such admiration not be deemed traitorous?

For hundred of years, Englishmen have spared no efforts to civilize these Gaelic Calibans, but their incorrigible predisposition to insurrection has made every attempt come to naught. Savages, the lot of them.

Fianna fought back a bitter laugh. The Major, of course, did not include himself in that lot. He wrote nothing about the barbaric actions British troops had taken: nothing about the men whipped on mere suspicion of insurgent sentiment, or taken up for transportation without even a trial; nothing about the houses of innocent peasants burned to the ground when they protested against intrusive searches for hidden caches of arms; nothing about the barbarous murders English soldiers were granted free reign to commit, all in the name of peace.

Hardly surprising, that a man who would slander an enemy's reputation would gloss over the barbarities committed by his own side. But how could that same man fill his letters instead with such detailed inquiries about and advice to his three young nephews?

August 1797

I am not at all dismayed that my namesake did not take me much into liking at our first introduction. Christian is full young, and a babe does not retain much affection for every visitor by whom he is flattered and caressed. When he is older, we will be the best of friends, I am certain of it.

September 1797
Does Benedict still tend toward taciturnity? He is not a dull child, be assured, only a thoughtful one. Do not forget to offer praise and affection when he tells you his thoughts, and to assist him when he seems lost for words.

November 1797
Remind Theo that no boy learns his numbers without proper attention and diligence. A boy who is firm and collected, and not depressed by adversity, will soon be a man of great and noble deeds, worthy of the Pennington name.

Fianna ran a finger over the crease in this last note, pressing it back into a tight square. Not the polite family generalities she'd expected from a man taken up with military concerns, these frequent lines about Kit and his brothers. No, Major Pennington's questions and counsels suggested not only a deep affection for, but also an intimate knowledge of, each of his nephews' characters and interests.

Fianna raised her eyes, but Kit stood with his back to her, staring out the window. Did he think to soften her toward his uncle by showing how deeply the man was entwined in the heart of his own family?

But how could she begin to reconcile the kindness of this doting uncle with the crude prejudices against her own people that the letters so clearly revealed?

When Fianna reached the letter he had originally set aside, the one he suspected might refer to her father, Kit began to pace the room. Damn his uncle for teaching him to march with such military precision, his boots slapping sharp stings against the uncarpeted passageway floorboards.

March 1798
Unrest throughout the country. The establishment has declared martial law. No overt violence here yet, tho' we have witnessed our own share of disturbances. Two recruits beaten by a Mob, purportedly in retaliation for their striking down several townspeople in the street. But in truth angered by the army pressing their land in service of grazing our cattle. If the peace is to be kept, the soldiers must be fed, but can these peasants be made to see the sense of it? Of course they cannot.

A servant of Lt. Barber's was also struck down; when Barber laid his hand on his sword to defend him, one of the townsmen—a Presbyterian, of course—stepped forward and desired him not to draw it. Barber, tho', denounced him as a Rascal, naming him ringleader of the Mob. In return, the puffed-up fellow—the mere son of a mill owner —had the nerve to claim himself Barber's equal, and to demand satisfaction. Barber would not fight—he did not know him, and would not contest his honor with a man to whom he had not been introduced.

Politesse? Or cowardice? At least, more bloodshed averted. But for how long?

Fianna ran a finger over the prophetic words. Not long, indeed. The rebellion broke out at the end of May; Antrim attacked on 7 June; her father was captured, then tried and hanged only a short month later. But Major Pennington had written nothing about that time, at least not to his brother; the next letter in the pile, sent from Portugal, not Ireland, was dated August 1808.

Warm hands cupped her shoulders, thumbs tracing against the tight sinews of her neck. "Do you think it might have been your father? The man who attempted to stop the fighting, but who would not tolerate a slur against himself?"

"It does sound like him, doesn't it?" She turned her head, resting her cheek against the satin of his waistcoat. "My aunt might remember."

"Might you send a letter of your own, and ask her?"

Write to her aunt? Fianna forced down a stab of distress.

Before she could begin to shape her answer, a knock sounded from the front of Kit's rooms. Deep voices echoed from the passageway. Fianna shrugged free and moved to the window, unwilling to be seen in such intimate circumstances.

"Your brother, sir," Kit's man announced.

For Kit's sake, she hoped the high-and-mighty Theo Pennington had finally deigned to pay a call on his brother. But the odor of turpentine and charcoal wafting into the room suggested otherwise.

"Benedict." Kit smiled and reached out a hand. "Have you come to beg Miss Cameron to sit for you again?"

Benedict gave a brief nod in Fianna's direction before striding toward his brother. "In this poor light? What do you take me for, a dabbler? No, I've brought this letter from Oxford, which, since it arrived at Pennington House express, seems to be of some urgency."

"I thought you had given over your studies, Kit," Fianna said, crossing to his side.

"Actually, I completed them. But after Father's death, the dons offered me a fellowship, to tide me over until I was old enough to be ordained." Kit slid a finger under the letter's wax seal.

"Then why are you here, in London?" she asked, frowning. How had she come to know so little about the man whom she'd taken as a lover?

"Requested a leave of absence for Hilary term," he said, looking up from the note. "Ever since my father's death, the man he handpicked to represent Pennington interests in Parliament has been voting with the Tories instead of the Whigs, something of which Theo seems to be unaware. I hoped to persuade him of the necessity of requesting Norton to step down. And to support me as a candidate in his stead," Kit finished with a wry smile.

"You thought to stand for Parliament?" Fianna and Benedict both exclaimed. She could hardly tell which of them sounded the more surprised.

Kit grimaced. "Easier to picture me speechifying in front of a congregation than in the House of Commons, is it?"

"No, of course not, Kit," Fianna answered, placing a hand on his arm. "Who could doubt your skill after hearing the way you spoke at the Patriot Coffeehouse?"

"The Patriot? The place where all the radicals gather? Don't tell me you've taken up the cause of reform, Kit," Benedict said.

Under her hand, Kit's muscles tensed. "Father believed in reform."

"Yes, but moderate reform. Not wholesale enfranchisement of the uneducated rabble, for which Henry Hunt and his radical cronies are agitating. Has Theo truly agreed to support you, knowing you've become entangled with that crowd?"

Fianna's breath caught in her throat. Kit supported universal suffrage in England? Did that mean he also supported the rights of the Irish to the vote? Had she truly shot one of the few Englishmen who might be willing to speak in Parliament on behalf of her countrymen?

"But is not the Pennington credo loyalty to family above all?" Fianna asked, stepping between Kit and his taller brother. "Lord Saybrook would deny his brother the opportunity to serve, simply because their political views differ?"

"It's difficult to tell what Theo will do about anything these days, he's so busy trying to bury his grief in gambling and drink," Benedict said.

Behind her, Kit started, and Benedict's eyes shifted to

his brother. "Oh, I know you'd rather pretend otherwise, but I have no compunction about speaking the truth about our brother. I'm surprised you managed to catch him sober enough even to discuss your plans, never mind assent to them."

Kit's eyes flicked quickly over to her, then shot a quelling glance at his brother. "I haven't, not yet. When he failed to keep several appointments I made when I first came up to town, I simply chalked it up to his poor sense of the hour. You know he's always been loath to carry a timepiece."

Benedict snorted. "And how many weeks have you been in town together now?"

"I've had a few other distractions, Ben. Helping Miss Cameron in her search, and then in the research for her book—"

"Not to mention the week of bed rest you had to take after being shot." Benedict raised a sardonic eyebrow in Fianna's direction. How many of her secrets had Kit shared with his brother? Did he know she was the one who had aimed the pistol at Kit?

But Kit's eyes had turned back to his note before she could catch his reaction to his brother's words. "Yes, you're right. I should have pressed harder for another meeting. I just took it for granted that all would be settled, well before Trinity term began. It would have taken Theo some time to orchestrate Norton's departure, and to lay the groundwork for a by-election, and I could have easily finished out the term before I needed to campaign in earnest."

Kit's fingers snapped against the foolscap. "But now the dean wonders if, given my current engagements in town, I intend to finish out the fellowship they were kind enough to bestow on me. Having been informed of said engagements, it would seem, by a visiting Viscount Dulcie. Lord, how politely the dean words the most biting imprecations against one's integrity."

"Dulcie?" Benedict snatched the letter and skimmed

it through narrowing eyes. "Damnation! I told that
craven tale-carrier he'd regret it if he continued to
spread gossip about you."

Benedict set the letter down on the table, then
reached out a hand and grasped Kit's shoulder. "You'll
most likely find Theo at his ladybird's house, Kit, over
on Seymour Street. Two doors down from Ingestrie's.
Probably just rising from last night's carousal; if you
hurry, you might just catch him before he downs his
first bottle."

Kit grimaced as his brother strode to the door.

"I'd go with you, but there's a certain talebearing
lordling who needs to be taught a lesson first." Benedict
closed the door softly behind him.

"And he claims he cares so little for family loyalty,"
Fianna said, shaking her head. "Well, if your eldest
brother proves as little devoted to it as Benedict, you
should have no difficulty convincing him to support
your candidacy."

"Perhaps. Regardless, it won't do to put off the meeting any longer."

"No." Fianna frowned. "But you truly haven't seen
each other, all these weeks you've both been in town?
Did he not call on you after I—after you were injured?"

"I did not inform him," Kit said, reaching out to
grasp her fingers. "I didn't wish the rumors that I'd been
shot by a vengeful mistress to reach his ears."

"Or because you did not wish to have reason to think
ill of a Pennington?" she asked, her thumb stroking
over his palm to soften the bluntness of her words. How
strange, to be able to see so clearly to the heart of his
reluctance. "Blind loyalty to one's family will only go so
far."

"Mr. Norton's loyalty has certainly not been blind,
has it?" he said. Fianna refrained from pointing out his
obvious change of subject.

"But Theo's never been much for politics, and he
dislikes change of any sort," Kit continued, as if it were

she, not himself, that he had to convince. "Hearing about Mr. Norton's voting record may not be enough to persuade him that a man in whom my father once put such confidence needs to be discharged."

"Then give him a more compelling reason," Fianna said. "Tell him that the man drinks, or besmirches Saybrook's name in public. No, better yet, tell him that he's been accepting bribes from the Tories to vote against Pennington interests. A man such as your brother, one with little inkling about the true workings of government, will likely find such disloyalty difficult to stomach."

Kit's eyes brightened, his hands clenching around hers. "Do you have some proof that Norton's been accepting bribes?"

"Proof? What other reason could there be for such an abrupt shift in allegiance?"

Wheaten curls bounced against his temple as he shook his head. "I don't know, Fee. Norton always agreed with Father's positions in the past, but perhaps he's had a change of heart?"

"A change of heart? More likely, with your father gone, he's become susceptible to the influence of other men. Men who will seize their chances whenever they find them. Offering an MP incentives to change sides is part and parcel of everyday governing, Kit. Surely someone who envisions taking up political work himself cannot be so naïve as to doubt it."

Kit frowned, staring at the floor. "But an incentive is not quite the same as a bribe, is it? And to blacken another man's reputation, without any real proof—"

Fianna's jaw clenched. His uncle's scruples had not been so particular, had they?

She ducked to catch Kit's lowered gaze, then rose, straightening her shoulders. "If the goal is just, should one quibble over the means by which it is achieved?"

Kit took a step back, her fingers sliding from his grasp. "I'm no Machiavelli, Fianna, no matter how much I believe that this country is in desperate need of reform. I won't lie to my brother, about Mr. Norton or anything else. Not even to win a seat in Parliament."

What disappointment shone from those genial blue eyes! Fianna's hands grasped for a moment at the empty air, finally finding purchase in the folds of her skirt.

She'd let him close, far closer than she'd ever allowed anyone before. Too close, for he was beginning to glimpse just how vast the gulf between his own forthright, frank principles and her own more dubious morals really was. Had she truly believed he'd find her worthy after he finally saw the true Fianna Cameron, all her deceitful masks stripped away?

Freeing fistfuls of muslin, Fianna smoothed her palms against the wrinkles in her dress. Let him be disappointed in her. But she wouldn't allow his disappointment to prevent him from pursuing his dream.

Reaching for the lapels of Kit's coat, she coaxed him closer, as if proximity might melt away the doubt lurking in his eyes. "Then don't lie. Simply demand that your brother choose you over Norton. A man as loyal to his family as you—do you not deserve the same loyalty in return?"

Kit smiled, his hand reaching out to cup her cheek. "Such vehemence, all on my behalf? I don't know what I've done to deserve it, Fee. But I count myself full lucky to have the sympathy of a woman as fiercely loyal as you."

He bent and pressed his lips to hers, soft but insistent, as if seeking some physical confirmation that his words spoke the truth. She answered him with a fierceness she hadn't known she could summon.

"Go," she whispered, when the kiss finally broke.

She watched him out the window as he strode toward Oxford Street, proud and full of purpose, until he turned a corner and disappeared from view. She'd have to take more care, keep her masks more fully in place, if he was to be firmly on his way toward achieving his goals before true disillusion in the woman he'd taken as lover had a chance to overtake him.

And by then, she'd be ready to hear him speak the inevitable word.

Good-bye.

Fianna threw her quill down on the table, her groan startlingly loud in the silence of the empty drawing room. "Appeal to your readers' sensibilities" had sounded simple enough, but whenever she tried to revise her chapter in accordance with Mr. Wooler's advice, the results proved frustratingly maladroit. This line clumsy, that one maudlin, this last one utterly false—she'd struck through each one with increasing frustration, the ink blotting in ugly smears on the paper.

She raked her hands through the hair at her temples. Her father had used words to inspire the people around him; why couldn't she?

Perhaps that was the answer—use Father's own words, rather than her own. Where had she hidden them, those letters her father had written to his sister in 1796 and '97 when he'd been imprisoned in Dublin's Kilmainham Gaol? Candlestick in hand, she made her way back to her bedchamber, her eyes scanning the room. Yes, there, under the mattress, where she'd placed them for safekeeping the night she'd first arrived.

Somehow, she'd not been able to bring herself to share them with Kit, even now, when they were well into the project of writing her father's history. Still clinging to the one thing of Aidan McCracken's that was all her own?

Setting down the guttering taper on the bedside table, she flipped through the packet of letters.

15 November 1796
It is expensive to live here, plundered by Turnkeys, etc.
and still more so when confined with others who cannot
support themselves nor yet be left to themselves. I hate
money, it makes me melancholy to think about it.

He'd be proud of her, how she'd dealt with those
gaolers who'd extorted and stolen from him.

She turned to the next letter, written in an unfamiliar
hand. She'd forgotten the packet contained not only
letters from her father, but also ones he'd received while
at Kilmainham. This one, from his cousin Charles:

26 April 1797
I have nothing to tell you of except the barbarities com-
mitted on the innocent country people by the yeomen and
Orangemen. The practice among them is to hang a man up
by the heels with a rope full of twist, by which means the
sufferer whirls round like a bird roasting at the fire, during
which he is lashed with belts, etc., to make him tell where
he has concealed arms. Last week, at a place near Dungan-
non, a young man being used in this manner called to his
father for assistance, who being inflamed at the sight
struck one of the part a desperate blow with his turf spade;
but, alas! his life paid the forfeit of his rashness; his en-
trails were torn out and exposed on a thornbush.

Yes, that would be a story to engage a reader's sentiments. Well used to hearing of the barbarities committed by the Catholics in Ireland, the English were, but
not so familiar with the ones inflicted by their own
kind.

Had Kit's uncle ordered his men to participate in
such acts? Taken part himself? Or merely stood by and
allowed Irish Protestants to deal with those who
protested the English oppression his uniform so clearly
symbolized?

Fianna frowned. Fanning the flames of outrage toward a dead man would do little to help her tonight, would it? Fianna set the letter to the side, opening one written by Aunt Mary:

2 June 1797
It is a great pity the people do not always keep in mind that they should never do evil that good may come of it. What is morally wrong can never be politically right. Have you not observed that since the assassinations began the cause of the people (which had before been rapidly gaining ground) has gradually declined? When we once deviate from the path of rectitude it is difficult to return.

Fianna shuddered, her aunt's words an eerie echo of her barely averted argument with Kit. Or, if she were to be truly fanciful, a prophecy of warning sent by a kindly pooka, if a fairy horse could write as well as speak.

Well, she'd always known she'd have to keep the details of her quest to rehabilitate her father's good name a secret from Aunt Mary if she wished to gain her aunt's acceptance. Had her father agreed with his sister about what constituted justice? Or had he, like his daughter, believed that a vitally important end might justify a dubious means?

"Writing of Aidan's, is it, then?"

Fianna shot to her feet, clutching the letter close to her chest. How in hell had Sean O'Hamill entered Kit's rooms without her hearing him?

"Did I startle you, *cailín*? Or did someone walk over your grave, as the English are wont to say?"

"Sean!" Fianna could not quite meet her uncle's eyes, her body strangely awkward and unsure. Should she offer him a smile? Her hand? An embrace? Would he welcome any such presumptions of intimacy? Or draw away in disgust?

Settling on a cautious nod, she folded her hands in her skirts. "But how did you get in?"

"Oh, I have my ways," he said, taking a step into her chamber. "As you well know, we O'Hamill are a resourceful people."

"Of course we are. But I didn't expect to see you again so soon." Not after she'd written to him telling him of her mistake in believing Major Pennington still alive.

"Of that I've little doubt," he said, glancing about with curiosity. He bent down to pick up a cravat—Kit's —that had fallen on the floor. With a grimace, he set it down on the dresser. "As your last note made no mention of your current abode."

"Of course it did not," she said, her chin tilting high. "After the way you snarled and snapped at Mr. Pennington the last time you met? What, did you expect an invitation to dine? Like a cur in the streets, you were, and I a bone he'd snatched from your jaws."

"Ashamed of your uncle's manners, are you, Máire? How little family feeling you have."

"Family feeling?" Fianna said, shaking her head. "I was simply afraid you'd toss about more insults, or worse yet, start a brawl, and ruin my chances to find out what I needed to know."

"But why should you care if I brawl with young Pennington, now that you've no need of his help?" he replied, stepping closer to her. "I'd think a proper caílin would be glad to see a strong Irishman's fist in the face of the blackguard who stole away her honor."

"Not every situation calls for a violent response, Seanuncail."

Her uncle's eyes narrowed. "What, do you seek to unman us, just as the English do? Demand we suppress our pride, our patriotism? Stand idly by and watch while our women are violated as shamefully as is our country? Does not the despoiling of our womenfolk call for a strong fist?"

"You think me despoiled, do you?"

"Have you not been forced to trade your virtue in

order to achieve justice? And now, when justice has slipped beyond your grasp, is not that damned Pennington still keeping you here, forcing you to cater to his voluptuous pleasures?"

"No one has forced me to do anything, Sean." Her fist beat against her chest once, then again. "I chose to make an arrangement with Mr. Pennington, and with Viscount Ingestrie before him, in order to achieve my ends. *I* chose, *Seanuncail*. *I*. A bitter bargain, to be sure, but one that I made of my own free will. And my choice says nothing about you."

"It may say nothing of the uncle of Fianna Cameron. But it's O'Hamill blood that runs through your veins, Máire. And a smear on my honor if I allow a daughter of the blood to succumb to the blandishments of a deceiving Englishman."

He pulled at the valise that poked out from beneath her bed, lifted it to the mattress, and opened it wide. "Come, what reason have you to stay?"

Fianna reached out a hand to pull the valise closed. "What reason? Come, and I'll show you."

He followed her to the drawing room, where her papers lay in piles upon the table. She picked up the first few sheets of the manuscript and thrust them into his rough hands.

"We are working on it together, Mr. Pennington and I," she said as Sean's eyes quickly scanned the ink-smeared pages. "A history of my father, his life and his beliefs. A book that will tell the truth of Aidan Mc-Cracken and will restore his good name. Perhaps not here in England, but in Dublin, and in Belfast. Mayhap through the length of Ireland. A book that will make my grandfather proud."

Her uncle looked up from the pages, his mouth a grim twist. "But your grandfather has left Ireland behind, Máire, for the wilds of America. And he never learned to read, as well you know."

"You deliberately misunderstand me, Sean. You

know I speak not of Grandfather O'Hamill, but of my father's father. My McCracken grandfather."

Sean grimaced. "You think to make dour old Mc-Cracken take pride in you?"

"You think I cannot? Because I'm a bastard? A whore?" The nails of her fingers burrowed deep into her palms.

He lowered the manuscript sheets down on the table, shaking his head. "The fault lies not in you, *cailín*. It lies in himself. Ah, did I not tell Mairead, when that pinched sister of Aidan's came with her fancy carriage and fine promises, no McCracken would ever care for you as an O'Hamill would? What matter how many fine frocks or fancy books they could give, if they never welcomed you into their hearts?"

"But I can prove my worth, Sean. I can!" She grabbed up a sheet of the manuscript, shaking it close to his face. "If not by bringing my father's killer to justice, then by telling his true story and restoring his good name."

Sean's expression was grave as he grasped her trembling hands between his. "Máire. What family worthy of the name demands a child prove her merit before granting her its love?"

His words sent a cascade of icy memories tumbling through her brain. *Cold, unsmiling slip of a girl,* the women of Belfast had whispered when she first came to live with her father's family. *Fae-born,* the more superstitious murmured, hands restlessly tracing the sign of the cross as they jerked their menfolk away from the sight of her strange, uncanny beauty.

Unnatural. Changeling.

Bastard.

No one in her father's family had stood for such ignorant talk, staunch Presbyterians that they were. She'd been so very grateful—frightened, reserved child that she'd been—for the stern, haughty McCracken glances that instantly quelled slander and gossip in

Belfast's streets and kirk.

But had her aunt, her grandfather, any of her Mc-Cracken aunts and uncles, had they ever troubled to wonder what might lie beneath the impassive face of the girl they'd plucked from her mother's side when she was but six years of age? Had they ever told her those whispers were untrue? Ever told her she was worthy of their regard? Of their love?

Fianna shook her head, once, twice, trying to cast off the doubts Sean's words had raised. But hadn't Kit said almost the same, suggesting that Aunt Mary had lied to protect herself from her own unkindness, insisting that Mairead agreed it was for the best to leave her child behind?

Had she been wrong all these years, then? Wrong to work so hard, to plan and scheme, to prostitute herself, even, all in the hopes of winning her father's family's regard? Should a true family accept all its members, love them all, no matter how unworthy?

Might it not be her, but the McCrackens, who were unworthy?

But if she did not, could not, belong to the McCrackens, then what chance did she have of finding a family at all? Fianna pulled out of her uncle's grasp, turning away from the pity in his eyes.

"Why should you care what the McCrackens think of you, Máire? Does not O'Hamill blood run red through your veins?" A heavy hand came to rest against her shoulder. "Come. More important work lies in store for you, *cailín*, than wreaking vengeance on a dead man. Devil Pennington may be gone, but London still teems with the enemies of Ireland."

"And you think to turn enemies into friends?" she asked, turning to face him.

"Friends?" For the first time, a hint of passion shone from his dark green eyes. "Nay, there'd be no redeeming such as they. Say instead, wipe the filthy stench of their tyranny from this island, and from our own."

"Murder, Sean?"

"Nay, not murder. Justice! And you will be its herald, Hibernia and her harp calling to the sons of Ireland to pull their tyrants down." Sean grasped her arm, urging her back toward the bed. "Come, I'll tell you of our plans while you pack your bag."

Fianna took a stumbling step toward Sean, then pulled back against his grip. "But what of Kit—of Mr. Pennington?"

"What of Mr. Pennington, indeed? Or, say rather, what of Mr. O'Hamill?"

Fianna could not see the man who stood behind her. But even when it was hardened by suspicion, there was no mistaking the sound of Kit's voice.

How was she to explain why she was alone in his rooms with the man he'd once accused of being her lover?

CHAPTER EIGHTEEN

"A wise man would remove his hand from Miss Cameron's person. Are you a wise man, Mr. O'Hamill?"

Kit had never heard such ice in his own words before. But the sight of Sean O'Hamill's thick, rough hand gripping proprietarily about Fianna's arm— damnation, he wanted to break each and every finger. Especially after the older man jerked Fianna roughly behind him. As if it were Kit, and not himself, who posed her the greatest threat. Kit stepped farther into the room, waiting for the man's reply.

"Wiser than you, I'd say, Mr. Pennington," O'Hamill said at last, his chest thrust forward at a belligerent angle. "At least I make damned sure I've the right to touch a woman before placing hands on her. A pity you cannot say the same."

Kit's eyes narrowed. What right did O'Hamill have to touch Fianna? She'd never spoken of him, not once in the days since she'd welcomed Kit to her bed, and he'd not pressed her about it, knowing little but ill to come from the waking of a sleeping dog. Yet here the burly Irishman stood, laying hands on Fianna and casting aspersions on Kit's character with all the authority of a judge.

What was the man to her? Not a husband, nor a lover, as he'd once suspected, not when she'd given herself to him so freely, with such joy. Kit looked more closely at the man's green eyes, the familiar set of that stern mouth—

"Miss Cameron—she is your sister, O'Hamill?"

"No. Miss *O'Hamill* is the child of my sister. My niece."

"Your niece?" Kit felt his blood rising. "And here I thought it an uncle's sacred duty to keep a sister's child safe from harm. Particularly when she has no father to offer his protection and guidance. But perhaps it was your idea that she trade her honor for a chance at vengeance. Were you the one who set her in Viscount Ingestrie's way?"

O'Hamill growled, low and menacing. Kit's shoulders tensed, readying for the man to spring. But Fianna wrenched free of her uncle's grasp, setting herself between them. "Sean had nothing to do with my meeting Ingestrie, Kit. Nor with my decision to use him to get to England. I'd no idea Sean was even in England, not until we met him with Mr. Wooler."

"But after?" Kit replied, his eyes not on her but on O'Hamill. "You knew your niece was being kept by Ingestrie, but made no move to help her? Excuse me if I find your paternal instincts distinctly lacking."

"She made no mention of any such relationship," the Irishman bit out, shaking off his niece's restraining hand. "Now that you've informed me of it, though, you can be sure he'll pay the price for sullying the honor of the O'Hamill. No man has the right to touch her, not without my permission."

Fianna gasped, her eyes snapping green fire as she gazed back and forth between them. "The only man with the *right* to touch me is the one *I* allow to do so. At this moment, I'm not inclined to grant either of you the privilege. Sean, go now. And do not come again unless I summon you."

"Máire, you cannot—"

"No." Only one word, but uttered with the absolute authority of a woman who had long forged her own path through life. "No more. After I have concluded my work here, I will consider the merits of yours. Now leave us."

O'Hamill stared at her for a long moment, then at Kit, before turning on his heel and striding to the door. But before leaving, he wheeled around, his finger jabbing toward the manuscript pages lying on the table.

"Mad, it is, *cailín*, to think a few bits of writing will win you a place in the heart of any McCracken. Although not as distempered as fancying young Pennington here will carry you off to church and wed you out of hand, as I'm fearing you've fooled yourself into dreaming."

"Mad, perhaps," she answered, her eyes never wavering from her uncle's. "But my choice, Sean. *My* choice, not yours."

O'Hamill's lip curled, a scar at its edge puckering white.

Kit's jaw tightened, but Fianna laid a restraining hand on his arm before he could make a move in O'Hamill's direction. He looked down at it, then up into her eyes, seeing not the command she had issued to her uncle, but the vulnerability of a plea. Kit reined in his burgeoning temper, just barely. To compensate, he snaked a possessive arm about her waist, a silent challenge, but a challenge all the same.

A vein pulsed at O'Hamill's temple as he picked up a battered cap from where it lay on a side table. "So be it, niece. But when this fine *Christian* here tires of you, and tire of you he will, come to me, Máire O'Hamill. For I'll never turn a child of Aidan and Mairead's away from my door."

His eyes narrowed as he jammed the cap onto his head. "Even one who allows the honeyed promises of a Englisher to make her forget what she owes her family and her country. She'll remember soon enough, she will, once his promises prove as false as the devil's."

He slammed the door with such force, the echoes

reverberated right through the floorboards.

When had Fianna picked up his hand in hers, carefully uncurled his fisted fingers from around the gorse branch, the one he'd plucked from an early-flowering bush, anticipating the pleasure it would give her? And when had he forced one of its pointed spines so deep into his palm?

"Do you commonly go about stealing limbs from unsuspecting hedgerows?" she asked, dabbing at the welling blood with a lace-edged handkerchief. The handkerchief he'd given her, to replace the one she'd ruined wiping the scrape of the young Irish sweep. Would she leave him before he could gift her another?

"Do you believe him? Am I as false as the devil?"

"Hush, now," she crooned, wrapping the handkerchief tight about his hand. "You've made me no promises, Kit."

"No? Not in word, perhaps. But certainly in deed. Whenever a man lies with an unwed maid, the act itself is a promise. At least if the man cares anything for his honor."

"But I care so little for my own. At least if my uncle is to be believed." Her tight, pained smile made Kit's own lips thin. How deeply her uncle's words had cut.

"And I was no maid when you took me to your bed, as you well knew." Fianna kept her eyes lowered as she tied the linen about his hand in a tight knot. She grazed the tips of her fingers over her handiwork once, then again, before pulling them away. "Come, shall I find a vase and some water for this dangerous excuse for a bouquet?"

Kit caught her hands between his before she could move away. "Do you want to leave, then? I won't stand in your way, if that is what you truly want."

Fianna bent her head, her eyes avoiding his. "Why must you always push so, Kit? How can I know what I want, what I feel, before I've had a chance to think everything through?"

"Feelings aren't always subject to reason, Fee."

"But they must be," she said, jerking her hands free of his so she might pace across the carpet. "They have to be. How else may one protect oneself from wanting something one can never have?"

"What can you never have? A family?"

"Yes," she cried. "A family, one that looks out for its own, cares for its own. Loving and loyal, a family that cares about the happiness of its members. That helps them achieve their goals. A family like yours."

The corner of Kit's mouth turned up. "I think you overestimate the bonds of Pennington family affection, Fee. At least the filial ones."

"What?" she cried, her forehead furrowing with disbelief. "Do not tell me Saybrook refuse to support you over that disloyal Mr. Norton?"

For the first time, Kit saw a flush blaze across Fianna's face. Not one of shame, or of pleasure, but of anger. Cold, unfeeling Fianna Cameron, angry on his behalf? The disbelief that had been congealing inside him since leaving Theo's townhouse slowly began to thaw.

"Yes. Or, at least, no, Theo is aware of Norton's growing tendency to side with the opposition, and that steps need to be taken to stop it." He raised one corner of his mouth, hoping the smile conveyed self-deprecation rather than self-pity. "But he is not convinced that I am the man to take Norton's place."

"Why? Because your politics are too radical? Ah, did I not advise you not to reveal the depths of your beliefs?"

Kit shook his head. "Even if I had taken your advice, Fee, it would have been in vain. Theo already has another candidate in mind. One whose temper will not be a hindrance to him, as mine always has been to me, as my brother was kind enough to point out."

"What? Does he not realize that passion is what persuades others to join one's cause?"

Kit smiled. "Kind of you to term it passion, not temper. But Theo, I fear, is more afraid of alienating old friends than interested in winning new allies. Strong feelings, whatever name you give them, are far more likely to lead to the first, at least to Theo's way of thinking."

Fianna jerked to a halt beside the table, slamming her palms down on the stack of papers. "Then your brother is a fool. Was it not my father's passion that led men to embrace his cause? His passion that led men to dream about a new way to live, to fight for the chance to make a better life? And is it not your own passion that makes you such a powerful communicator? I'd be entirely unable to capture it, my father's passion, if not for the example you've set me every day since we began this project."

Kit stepped to her side, raising a hand to cradle her face. "Passion drawn to passion?" he asked, his thumb tracing over the curve of her cheek.

"I've no passion, Kit," she said, her words stilling his hand. "Cold and unfeeling, that's the heart of Fianna Cameron. Cold enough to cozen a man with a kiss, to take another into my bed in exchange for a ticket on the steam packet from Ireland. Cold enough to turn my back on my kin. What sign of passion is that?"

"Isn't wanting to be loved the deepest form of passion?" Kit returned, his lips pressing against her temple, against her throat, before he pulled back to stare into her eyes. "To shape your entire life around the chance of winning love, from your grandfather, from all your father's kin?"

"But what if Sean is right? What if the McCrackens never take me to heart, no matter how hard I work to reclaim my father's good name?"

"What if he is? Might your desire for family be fulfilled by your O'Hamill relatives, then? Have you not rediscovered an uncle you once thought long lost? An uncle who may, perhaps, even help you find the mother who was forced to abandon you?"

"Sean has no idea where my mother is. And while he may take me in, will he ever truly care for me? Love me? Even if he can somehow temper his pride enough to overlook the shame I've brought to the O'Hamill name, can I truly abandon my father?"

Kit tipped her head up so he could look deep into her eyes. "But your father has already given you what you so desperately want from him, Fee. His love. He gave his life in the hopes of winning a better one for you. What greater act of love could there be?"

Fianna shook her head, her eyes closed tight. Against tears? When she spoke, he had to bend close to hear her whispered words. "Have I truly been such a fool, then? Chasing after the love of a dead man? What kind of passion is that, to want something I can never have?"

The hurt in her broken laughter tore at something deep and low inside him. How strange, to find that love could rise even more quickly than temper.

He couldn't stop to wonder at it, though, not until the words roiling inside him had a chance to break free. He caught her face between his palms, tipping her head up so she could not miss the sincerity in his eyes.

"Then stop chasing a dead man. Stop longing for the family you lost, and dream instead of the one you've found. A family filled with so much love that even your passionate heart cannot help but be filled to overflowing."

She pulled away from him, her eyes narrowing. "A family?" she asked. "What family?"

He reached for her hands, pulling them flat against his chest so she might feel how deeply she had dug her way into his heart. "With me, Fianna. Become my wife, and make a family with me."

"Kit," she whispered, raising a hand to his oh-so-dear face, her thumb brushing against the evening bristles of his jaw. He'd tried to hide it with that wry upturn of a smile, but his brother's disloyalty had hurt him, hurt him deeply. And somehow, his hurt had affected her, made her jump to his defense as if it were instinctual. Praising passion not only to pay tribute to her father, but to offer Kit some small comfort for his pain.

And yet Kit, so ready to put the feelings of others before his own, had taken her clumsy consolations and transformed them into a balm not for his own wounds, but for hers.

Would she never reach the bounds of this tender man's kindness?

That he could imagine being married to a woman as flawed as she! How deeply it warmed her, even knowing that his offer of marriage had been made only in the passion of the moment. Perhaps, even, to avoid his own guilt at playing a part, however so small, in what Sean had so callously termed her "ruin."

Of course, as soon as the harsh light of morn brought him back to his senses, he'd realize what a mistake it had been to make such an impetuous, impossible offer.

But she'd not give him cause to regret his kindness. No matter how hard her heart had yearned when Sean had mocked her with the mere idea, she'd not accept what he offered. No, Kit would not have that pain, to know himself a man who would be forced to go back on his word.

But neither did she have the heart to burst the bubble of his so very kind intentions. Not tonight, not when he stood there, so proud and determined, so uncaring of how vulnerable his unthinking words had made him.

No, she might not be able to accept his offer. But she could show him how very moved she was by its tendering.

Her one hand joined its mate, then, framing his face

between her palms. "You do me great honor, sir," she whispered. "Will you allow me to honor you in turn?"

To answer the question that rose in his eyes, she pulled his head down to hers, and pressed her lips against his.

The kiss began with reverence, the merest skim of lip against lip. Nudging, bussing, a gramercy in each light touch. But the growl of pleasure that soon began to vibrate through Kit's throat called forth answering shudders in her own body, veneration transforming into need within the span of a single breath. Her hands moved to his shoulders and gripped tight, as if she might contain her own desire even as she heightened his. Nudging his lips apart, she set her tongue to exploring, searching out the secret places that made his blood pound harder, his breath hitch.

For hours, eternities, there was nothing in the world but this warmth, this closeness, this kiss. Only the scrape of the rough linen on his bandaged hand, caressing against her cheek, brought her back to herself, to her purpose: to give to him, as he'd so often given to her. She stepped back then, just one pace, far enough for his eyes to focus on the finger she slowly raised to her mouth. She licked its tip, then watched his eyes darken, his eyelids lower, as she used it to trace a winding path over his skin, from the nape of his neck to the sensitive valley behind his ear.

How different it was to weave a sensual spell over a man when admiration for his strength, rather than contempt for his weakness, lay at the heart of her. No disgust roiling heavy in her stomach, no shame at the bitterness of her own acts, no, not with a true man such as Kit. Only a bone-deep warmth, radiating throughout her entire body like the rays of the sun in highest summer.

His arms rose to pull her close again, but she grasped his hands in hers, easing them back down to his sides. "No, Kit. You give, and give, and give, all with no expectation of a return. But tonight, for once, you will be the recipient."

She pressed a finger against his lips before the words of protest could emerge. "Shhh. Would you truly be so unjust as to deny me the chance of bestowing pleasure?"

His arms grew slack beneath her hands as understanding dawned in his eyes. With a nod, she unwound the cloth from about his neck and draped it about her own. His eyes followed her hands as they pushed aside his coat, undid the buttons of his waistcoat, dragged the tails of his shirt from his trousers. She pulled at the ties of his shirt, then tugged both ends, drawing him low, low enough to allow her to pull the linen over his head, a slow, sensuous drag that raised the color in his cheeks.

Color flooded her own as she gazed upon his naked torso, its thews and sinews so different from her own. Surprised, she was, every time, to discover this taut, tempered muscularity hidden behind such a genial, angelic face. A man of contradictions, he was, of softness and strength, of kindness and courage, all linked together to make a fascinating, compelling whole. Yes, she would give this man what he wanted, even if he had proved too solicitous up until now to ask for it.

Blue eyes winked up at hers, then back down to her hands, as she pulled the length of his cravat taut between her fists. "Most men like to be in command during bed sport," she said, teasing one end of the linen over one of his wrists, then the other. "To force their will upon a woman, to prove their manly strength. But is it not a sign of courage when a man allows a woman to take the reins?"

She kept her eyes lowered as she raised his hands to the level of his waist, then looped the cravat about his wrists, once, then again. She bit her lips, struggling to contain the heady mixture of fear and desire that the pound of his pulse under her thumbs set flying. She'd thought to give him pleasure through such an act, but the ardency of her own response shocked her.

Would he be disgusted by her forwardness? Or would it please him, accepting pleasure at her hands? Taking a deep breath, she dared a glance, then found herself transfixed by the fierceness of the desire firing his eyes.

Drawing her small body up to its most regal height, she turned her back to him and stepped toward the passageway, one end of the neckcloth tight in her hand. The cloth drew taut, stopping her for a moment in her tracks. Before her heart could sink, though, the neck-cloth fell slack as he followed her lead, the cool winter-green of his soap and the hot whisper of his breath pricking at the hairs on the back of her neck. She smiled, pulling it tight once again.

The only light in his bedchamber came from the moon, which painted the carpet and the edge of the bed with traces of silver. She led him to the bed, pushed lightly against his chest. He fell back without demur, his lithe body sinking heavily into the mattress beneath him.

Fianna scooted across the bed, tugging on the neck-cloth, drawing his arms above his head. His fingers grasped at her skirts, but once she tied the end of the cravat to the side rail, she was able to pull free with ease. She smiled at the groan of frustration he could not quite smother. Before this night was over, she'd make him do far more than groan.

She skirted round the bed, eager to gaze on her handiwork. Kit lay half-clothed, his chest rising and falling so temptingly, her fingertips actually tingled in anticipation. His usual smile was nowhere to be seen; instead, his mouth set in a stern line, as if it took all his will to keep his body from fighting against its restraints. No fear marred his face, only the starkness of desire aching to be fulfilled.

She set out to map every inch of his fascinating body,

using just the tip of a finger to tickle against the light hair covering his skin. To tease and torment, not out of contempt or fear, but so he would know how much he was valued, how worthy he was of each second she spent at the task.

Down the back of his arm, up its tender inside, a light whorl amidst the curls, darker than the ones on his head, that lined the hollow beneath. Retracing the same path with tiny kisses, then again with a swirling tongue, forcing herself not to rush, not to give in to the pants and moans that her touch drew from between his lips.

"Tell me what you want, Kit," she whispered, one hand soothing circles across his chest, the other teasing at the band of his trousers. "Tell me, and I'll give it to you."

"You." His voice cracked, even on just that one short syllable. "You, Fianna."

"But I'm right here, sir," she answered, leaning down to lick against the taut nub of a nipple. "Ready and willing to meet any demand."

He groaned, shaking his head from side to side like an untamed horse fighting against the bit. But she would not give him satisfaction, not until he found the courage to speak his own desires. To acknowledge that he, too, wanted, that he, too, had needs.

"You," he finally bit out, his voice more of a croak than fully enunciated speech. "No clothes."

"Ah, me naked, is it? But it hardly seems fair, when you yourself remain half-dressed. Shall we do something to remedy that?"

His hands, jerking hard about the twisted cravat, made the bed creak as Fianna slithered down to the floor. She pulled off his boots, then his stockings, then laved the same attention on his muscled calves that she had given to his arms. He lasted far shorter, this time, before groaning his resistance, jerking his knee away from her mouth. She laughed as he reached about her waist with his strong legs and tugged her back up to the bed. Next time, she'd have to remember to tie his ankles as well as his wrists.

She would not think about that, that there might not be too many more next times. Instead, she took pity on him, slipping free the buttons of his trousers and lowering the fall. He planted his feet on the bed, raising his body so she might pull his remaining garments free. She did it slowly, tauntingly, her hands stopping to shape the muscled curves of his arse, to skim the tips of her fingers over the head of his wide cock.

"Naked. Now," he growled. She shivered at his tone, half sweet prayer, half guttural curse.

"As you wish, sir." Returning to the bed to kneel astride his muscular thighs, she reached behind to free the buttons of her gown. Her breasts, raised high by her task, seemed to transfix him, his blue eyes open wide, refusing to blink. As she shook the fabric down over her shoulders, the involuntary jerk of his hips nearly toppled her to the counterpane beside him. She caught herself with a hand on his shoulder, then pulled back before his greedy mouth could capture the prize of her newly bared nipple.

"Words, Kit," she reminded, her hand curving around her own breast. "Is this what you want?"

"Lord, yes. I'll go mad if you don't let me taste you."

"What else do you want?" she asked, dipping close, but still just beyond his reach. "Tell me, before your mouth becomes otherwise occupied."

"Oh, Fee, please." His groan sent a shaft of tingling pleasure straight between her legs. But she waited, until at last he acknowledged his own desires. "Your hand. On me. On my cock."

Shuddering, she lay beside him on the bed, pulling his leg over her hip to bring his beautiful cock within reach. Her fingers circled round the edge of its head, once, again; then she slid one finger down its length, marveling at its tensile strength. Ingestrie's demands that she touch him like this had always filled her with revulsion, but she only wanted to draw Kit closer, grasp him tighter, reward him for allowing her to explore this most vulnerable part of his body. Her hand grasped his base, giving an experimental squeeze.

He swore, then buried his head in her chest, as if he could no longer stand to be the only recipient of pleasure. His lips and teeth seemed already to know the most tender spots, the spots that made her moan deep in her throat. His clever tongue swirled about her nipple, and she allowed herself to become lost in the mind-numbing pleasure of it, just for a few moments. She came back to herself only when she felt her own hips begin to move against the hard, furred thigh that had somehow snuck its way in between her legs.

Panting, she pushed his hips to lie flat on the bed. How could she punish him for making her forget herself so? How could she make his pleasure even greater?

Kneeling between his legs, she took his cock in one hand, his tender cods in the other. Her fingers dipped and circled, teasing, tormenting, then drew to a halt as the most lascivious thought darted into her head.

"Are hands enough, Kit? Or do you want my mouth? Here, on you?" She skimmed her lips against his very tip.

He cried out, a sound that nearly undid her. But then he pulled away. "Fee, no, please."

She lowered her eyes. Had her boldness disgusted him?

He took a deep breath, then spoke, his words far steadier than the body that trembled below her. "Fee. Look at me. It's you I need. Just you. Take me inside you, now, before I burst out of my very skin with want."

Kneeing her way up the bed until her hips opened wide above his, she took him in hand and guided him to the slickness of her entrance. With her own moan, she lowered her body, filling herself with his heat and width.

He bucked and thrust against her, his fingers yanking against the neckcloth that bound his wrists. Her hips moved to meet his, pressing ever faster as she found she could angle her body on every downthrust so that the top of her nether lips shocked against the base of his cock. She'd never heard such sounds come from her own throat.

His jaw clenched, though he kept his eyes wide open. Close to spending, he was. The sight set her own body tight and trembling. She snaked a finger down her belly, eager to push herself to her own release, but his was there before her. Together, they circled her most sensitive flesh, driving, driving, until she stilled and shuddered, throwing herself over the edge. With a guttural cry, he threw his head back and his hips forward, following her into the abyss.

She came back to herself to find Kit's arms about her, one hand stroking down the curve of her spine, the torn neckcloth trailing from his wrist.

"God, how I love you, Fianna," he whispered, quiet and reverent, as if they stood in a churchyard rather than lay together in a bed.

As if love were the only thing that mattered. . .

CHAPTER NINETEEN

Kit guided Fianna into the clamoring Bishopsgate building, a protective hand at the small of her back. He smiled as her nose wrinkled at the less-than-pleasant smell. Had she never been inside a printer's shop? He'd visited Sam and his uncle here so often he'd become accustomed to both the thump of the press and the stink of the soot, linseed oil, urine, and heavens knew what else they used to make the inks and clean the metal type. Perhaps he should have warned poor Fianna.

"Kit! Well-timed. We've just now finished the binding."

Sam, who had been minding the counter, darted back into the depths of the shop. A moment later, he returned, a single volume balanced like a tray on one open palm. With an exaggerated courtly flourish, he presented it to Fianna. "Your book, my lady."

Her words had been bound not in leather, suitable for a gentleman's library, but in the newer, cheaper stiff boards covered in paper. Yet Fianna's fingers hovered over the title printed on its front cover with as much reverence as if Sam had handed her the rarest of illuminated manuscripts.

How expeditiously the Woolers had transformed her words into print. Over Fianna's bent head, Kit smiled his thanks to his friend.

Sam folded his arms over his chest and nodded. Sam's suspicions of Fianna had certainly faded, hadn't they?

Heavy footsteps sounded against the uneven wood floor—when had the thump of the press stopped? A man several years older and several inches taller than Sam bustled up to the front counter, wiping his hands on an already ink-stained apron. "Mr. Pennington. Do not tell me this elegant young lady is your collaborator?"

Kit's smile grew wider. "Miss Cameron, may I introduce Mr. T. J. Wooler, printer, publisher, and leading advocate for the rights of the English people. And, of course, Sam's uncle. Mr. Wooler, my writing partner, Miss Fianna Cameron."

Fianna made her curtsy, one more elegant than any he'd seen her offer any nobleman. "Sir, it is an honor to make the acquaintance of the publisher of *The Black Dwarf*. Rarely have I read so intelligent an advocacy of the rights of the people as in the pages of your newspaper."

"And rarely have I read so thought provoking a discussion of the Irish Rebellion as in the pages of this book, ma'am," Wooler answered, tapping a finger atop the volume in question. "Few in England have any idea that any Protestants joined Catholics in protesting the oppression of the Anglo-Irish landlords. A misperception that will change, I hope, if the critics aren't too craven to review your work."

"Not many men are willing to stand up for their principles the way you are, sir," Kit said. "Not if they know they'll be imprisoned for it."

"Bah." Wooler shook his head. "Who would not appreciate a holiday in Warwick Gaol?"

"The accommodations must have been very fine for you to have devoted eighteen months of your life to them, sir," Kit answered.

Fianna's eyes widened. "I honor you, sir." She curtsied again, this time in appreciation.

Wooler looked remarkably like his nephew as he waved aside their praise, the color rising in his round cheeks. "Someone will always be found bold enough to brave an arbitrary law, and publish truth, in contempt of penalties. Although I've rarely encountered any who can combine rationality and passion with as much success as you and Mr. Pennington have done here, Miss Cameron. Have you ever considered writing more regularly, say, for a weekly newspaper? I'd be well pleased to have you take up a pen for the *Dwarf*."

Kit's breath caught at the sight of eager interest flaring in Fianna's eyes. Lord, just imagine if she allowed the deep well of passion she'd kept so hidden to break free, even just in print. Railing against the injustices of the world not just to him, but to the entire English public, calling for wrongs to be righted, for the people to join together to claim their rights? By God, she'd set the world afire.

"Now, Uncle, I told you that Kit has his eye on a seat in Parliament," Sam said. "What time has he for scribbling?"

"Bah." Mr. Wooler waved a dismissive hand. "Any scoundrel who can bid the highest price can walk into the British House of Commons. But it takes a man of both courage and talent to challenge the people to become political actors themselves. Or," he added with a nod toward Fianna, "a woman."

"How kind you are to suggest it," Fianna replied, her fingers grazing lightly over the volume on the counter before her. "Perhaps after I've had a chance to read through the fruits of this current labor, and have set to rest my own doubts about my skills, we might speak again on the matter?"

"Of course, ma'am. You and Mr. Pennington will always be welcome in Sun Street."

After exchanging a few more pleasantries, Sam and Mr. Wooler returned to their work. The heavy, repetitive thump of the press once again began to shake the floorboards as Kit and Fianna made their way back to the street.

Kit handed Fianna into the cab they'd left waiting, then climbed up to take a seat beside her. With that hint of a smile on her face, how could he resist throwing an arm about her?

"Can you believe it, Fee?" he said, squeezing her tight to his side. "Did you ever dream you'd be holding a book in your hands, knowing that without you, it would never have come to be?"

"Without you, don't you mean? If you had not known Mr. Wooler and his uncle, or been unwilling to add polish to my dry-as-dust prose—"

Kit raised a finger to her lips, stilling her grateful outburst. "Without us, then, Miss Cameron. You and I, together."

Ducking under the brim of her bonnet, he replaced his finger with his own lips, a heady mix of pride, gratitude, and sheer joy electrifying his touch. The sum of earthly bliss, it was, to feel her respond with an ardor to match his own.

"Kit, we must stop," she whispered, even as she kissed a hot trail down the slope of his jaw. "Anyone can see us."

"Pull down the shades."

"The cab doesn't have any."

The sight of the blush high on Fianna's cheekbones, the knowledge that he'd been the one to put it there, almost made pulling away worth the effort. Kit dropped his head against the squabs and took a deep breath, willing his own blood to calm.

"Was the elder Mr. Wooler in earnest, Kit? About your writing for his paper?"

"About *our* writing for his paper, Fianna. He'd not want my overly enthusiastic prosings, not without the curb of logic you provide."

"You sell yourself short, Kit. Your words, they speak

to both the mind and the heart." Her eyes narrowed as he shook his head in denial. "They speak to mine. And if you can move my cold heart, how much more easily will you appeal to the readers of the *Dwarf*?"

"What of my political aspirations? Do you believe Theo is right, that it would be madness to pursue them?"

"Madness, no. But perhaps not the best use of your talents? Must not a politician keep many of his passions in check to be skilled in the art of diplomacy, in order to be successful in negotiating for his cause?"

Kit grunted. "I suppose I deserve that, after nearly undressing you in the midst of a public hackney."

"It was not meant as a criticism, Kit, but a compliment," she said, laying a hand against his arm. "Your enthusiasm, your passion, they draw people to you. And they'll draw people to your words, too."

Even though he stared down at the floor, Kit could feel Fianna moving closer on the seat, taking his hand in hers. "The men in power, men like your father and your brother, once had little need to consider the views of ordinary people like me, even when they made decisions that directly affected our lives. But today, some of those ordinary people are starting to believe that they can and should have a voice in the way their country is run. Public opinion matters, Kit, in a way it never has before. And your belief in them, Kit, your passionate belief that such people have the right to be heard, shines out in your writing. If you can persuade me that I've the right to participate, to make my voice heard, do you not think you can persuade others of the same? If you can fire such people with your own passionate belief in them, will that not be an accomplishment well worth the achieving?"

He'd never heard Fianna speak at such length, or with such overpowering emotion. And when he raised his head to hers, Lord, what utter confidence shone from those deep green eyes. How different from the doubt that dominated Theo's, or the tentativeness that shaded Benedict's, whenever Kit expressed his political views. Even Uncle Christopher had never looked at him with the absolute faith that animated Fianna's earnest countenance.

What more could a man want from a wife than for her to believe he could win her the world?

"I don't think I can do it without you, Fee," he said, turning his hand to grab tight to hers.

Now it was Fianna's turn to avoid his gaze. "I'm afraid you will have to, Kit. For finishing this book was only the first step in what I hope to accomplish. Now I must return to Ireland, book in hand, and hope it can begin the work of clearing my father's name. And of earning me a place in my father's family."

"A book with so much to accomplish needs to put its best foot forward," he said, struggling to keep his voice light. "Rebound in leather, I think, rather than this cheap board and paper. With gold tooling on the spine *and* the covers. Green leather, do you think, in honor of Ireland?"

She gasped as he plucked the book from her lap. How long did it take for a book to be bound? No matter; he'd make sure the bindery held it long enough for his express to reach Ireland and, if he were lucky, for a response to be sent in return. Yes, he'd formally request her hand from her grandfather, loath as he was to pay such a sign of respect to a man who kept his granddaughter at such a distance. He'd do far more, if it would bring her even a few moments happiness.

Such as admitting his lie about Uncle Christopher's supposed death. And bringing about a reconciliation between the two.

But first, the easy part. The letter to McCracken.

"Kit, truly, such extravagance is hardly necessary," she protested, reaching for the book.

"No, I'll not have your words shame you by going out in public nearly naked," he said, tucking the book behind his back. "Clothes do make the gentleman, or the lady, and people will judge a book by its cover. Now, what do you say to half-leather with marble boards? Or should we go for the extravagant full?"

Yes, he'd do far more, just to see another hint of that smile teasing at the corners of her lips.

Dear Aunt Mary:

~~I know how the rumors about my father's your brother's betrayal have grieved my grandfather your father~~

~~Do you remember the sermon Grandfather McCracken preached about the verse from Romans? For he is the minister of God, a revenger to execute wrath upon him who doeth evil~~

~~Please accept the enclosed volume as a token of my respect and affecti~~

The heavy hand with which Fianna crossed out yet another awkward opening to this impossible letter split the point of her quill, sending a huge blot of ink streaming across the paper. Had all her best words gone into the slim volume resting on the table beside her? Or could she not write because somewhere deep inside she still believed that no words, not even the ones bound between these stiff paper covers, would ever reconcile her grandfather to accepting her in his lost son's stead?

"Ah, your soul to the devil," she muttered, tossing the useless implement on the table and rubbing a thumb across her temple. She'd bring on the headache if she kept at this fruitless task much longer.

A sharp rap on the front door drew a wry smile to her lips. Surely her invocation hadn't brought Old Scratch himself to her door. No, Kit must have forgotten his key.

Her smile of welcome faded at the sight of a stranger on the landing. Well dressed, even dandified, he was, with his many-caped greatcoat, gold-topped walking stick, and creamy silk waistcoat intricately embroidered with tiny flowers and vines. The wrinkles in his shirt and the wilting of his cravat, though, suggested that he'd first donned them not this morning, but sometime the night before. A hint of something she could not quite identify—anger? unease?—teased about the corners of his mouth. Fianna's hand tightened around the knob, pulling the edge of the door tight against her side.

Sweeping the beaver hat from atop his head, the stranger made her an elegant, if perfunctory, bow. "Miss Cameron?"

She nodded. "You have me at a disadvantage, sir."

He did not seem to take umbrage at her lack of an answering curtsy, only tucked his arm behind his hip and thrust his chin in the air, as if to give her the clearest view of his person. "Ah, you do not mark the resemblance? How odd. People do say that out of all my siblings, it is Christian who most takes after me. But then, I am a good deal more mature than he. As, I understand, are you, ma'am."

Fianna blinked. He did look a bit like Kit, this elegant lord, far more than either resembled their middle brother. The same shade of hair hung over the same high brow; the same long, tapering fingers tapped lightly against the same sinewy thigh. But if he shared any of his brother's affability or kindheartedness, his air of fashionable ennui hid it from view. And if she read his sallow skin and bloodshot eyes correctly, dissipation, not passion, held him under its sway. No, she would not have guessed at their relationship, not even if Kit were standing right here beside him to acknowledge it.

"My Lord Saybrook." Fianna made a curtsy as slight as his bow.

With a careless wave of his hat, he gestured toward the room behind her. "May I?"

"I'm afraid your brother is not here."

"Of course he is not. I waited, you see, until I was sure he would not be." The corners of his lips rose, just the slightest bit. That hint of insolence was not at all reassuring.

Tightening her own lips, Fianna pulled the door wide. Her nose wrinkled at the fume of tobacco and spirits he brought with him into the room.

"Ah, Benedict's work, I see," he said as he followed her into the drawing room. "He always did admire green."

Fianna took a stance by the window, her hands folded neatly at her waist. Far better to let a potential enemy make the first move.

Saybrook held out his cane, hat, and gloves, as if expecting a servant to take them; when she remained still, he shrugged, then tossed the lot onto a side table himself. He then spent some minutes gazing about the room, examining its contents with the eye of a connoisseur.

Only then did he spare her his attention, considering her with the same dispassion he had paid to the furnishings and decorations. Then, after looking his fill, he lowered himself into the most comfortable chair in the room. He leaned back and stretched out his legs before him as if he were readying himself for a lazy afternoon's nap.

Such an obvious mark of incivility told her more quickly than any words that Theo Pennington knew at least some of who and what she was. And that he wanted her to be well aware of the regard, or rather lack thereof, in which he held her. No, this would be anything but a friendly visit.

"I received a quite interesting letter this morning, Miss Cameron," he began, in a tone as negligent as his posture. "Perhaps even upsetting, if one may admit to having feelings in this day and age. Might you guess what said letter contained?"

Fianna took a seat on the settee opposite, clasping her hands beneath her chin as if deep in thought. "I cannot begin to imagine. A billet-doux from your *chère amie*? A dunning note from your tailor?"

Theo Pennington's eyes narrowed. He might think to intimidate her, but she was not entirely without resources of her own.

"A peer of the realm would hardly find any such news the least bit disturbing," he answered. "No, the letter I received was of a more personal nature. From my youngest brother."

"Oh? But I understand Christian has written to you many times over the past two months, all without causing you the least alarm. Or perhaps I misunderstood; were you too prostrated by his news of Mr. Norton's disloyalty to pen even a line in return?"

"I took steps to address the issue of Mr. Norton, I assure you, ma'am. There was no need to inform Kit of every detail."

"How unfortunate that your brother has not the skill of reading minds. For then he might have known just what you were about, without your having to take the trouble to write him of every detail." Fianna gave him a polite smile, then lowered her eyes to the hands she had folded in her lap.

"He may not be able to read my mind, but I assure you, ma'am, I am well able to read yours." He leaned forward, his eyes intent upon hers. "And it holds nothing but trouble, trouble for me and mine."

"What, did Kit send you a copy of our little book? I admit, some might find it a bit outspoken, but I assure you, sir, nothing we've written can be legally prosecuted under the Gagging Acts."

"A book? I know nothing about a book. I am speaking of Kit's plans for the future."

"A future you've all but ensured he won't have," Fianna accused, her tone far sharper than she had intended. "Refusing to support his bid for Parliament shows a surprising lack of family feeling on your part, sir. Although perhaps one should not expect an Englishman to demonstrate loyalty, even to his own kin."

"I have enough family feeling to put a stop to the more ridiculous of his schemes. Bad enough to discover he's been spewing his fantastical ideas about the equality of man throughout the taverns and coffeehouses of London. Did he honestly think I'd allow him to do so in the midst of the House of Commons?"

"Afraid he'll draw the ire of one of your drinking companions, are you? Or cause one of your gaming connections to call in your debts?"

"Indeed not, ma'am," he replied, leaning back in his chair and resting his tented hands atop the slight paunch of his belly. "Afraid he'll be shunned by society for taking up with undesirable acquaintances."

"You consider me one of said undesirable acquaintances, my lord?"

Saybrook flashed a brief, chilling smile. "An Irishwoman? How could you be anything but? Oh, you've a compelling countenance, no doubt, although your person is rather slight to truly delight a man's senses. Tell me, what tricks of bed sport have you plied to bewitch him? For I cannot imagine any other reason he'd be fool enough to believe another man's doxy worth the time of an archbishop."

"Archbishop?" Fianna laughed to hide her confusion. Did Kit think to undertake her religious conversion?

"Yes, I thought you would find it amusing. What an innocent he is, our Christian, thinking he can rescue all the waifs and strays of the world. Even as a boy, he was always insisting on saving unwanted kittens from drowning, and rescuing smaller boys from the bullies. This time, though, I fear he has spent too much time with Aunt Allyne, listening to her tales of prostitutes miraculously returned to the path of righteousness. Or perhaps it was you who put the idea in his mind."

"The idea? What idea?"

Saybrook drew a letter from inside his waistcoat, tossing it contemptuously on the floor by her feet. "I would not have believed it, even of gullible Kit, if I had not read it myself. And in his own hand, so there can be no mistake. Imagine the scandal if someone besides myself had be the one to open his oh-so-touching declaration that he was to wed a whore."

Wed a whore? Fianna knelt down and took up the letter with a shaking hand. Surely Kit had forgotten his misguided offer of marriage. He'd never repeated it, not after that one mad night when he'd discovered her with Sean. And she'd certainly not brought it up again, no matter how often his whispered words of love tempted her to imagine a future with him. To believe the son of an English lord would marry an Irishwoman, let alone one who had been bent on executing his own uncle— why, she would have been a fool to spend even a moment dreaming of it.

Yet as she scanned the lines Kit had written to his brother, informing him of his intention to take one Fianna Cameron, spinster, to wife, the tight, anxious loneliness inside her, her everyday companion since childhood, began to dissipate, replaced by a lightness and warmth of which she could hardly remember the like. To declare such intentions to an eldest brother, the head of his family. To declare that nothing would sway him from his course. Such words from Kit, a man who held loyalty to family so very dear!

Fianna clutched the letter to her heart, as if its slight heft could keep her giddy, weightless self from floating clear up to the ceiling. What an idealist he was.

And how much she loved him for it.

"Oh, I would not be so quick to smile," Saybrook drawled, drawing Fianna back from the reverie into which she'd fallen. A keen, knowing expression had taken the place of his previous careless air. "You may have Christian under your thumb, but you'll not find me so easy to gull."

Reaching into the pocket of his frock coat, he pulled out not a pistol, as she had half expected, but a handful of sovereigns. "Do not misunderstand," he said, tossing them lightly from palm to palm. "I am willing to grant you something for your pains. A princely sum for an Irishwoman, would you not say? Particularly one of dubious morals."

With a quick jerk, he tumbled the coins into her lap. They clattered there for a moment until she settled them with a quelling hand.

With lazy but heavy grace, he rose and moved in front of her, his height and bulk clearly meant to intimidate. "Take them, and be gone before he returns."

Arrogant, stupid man. As if he were the only one with a flair for the dramatic.

Rising slowly from her chair, she forced him to take a step back or be pummeled by the weighty coins that rained down from her lap. They hit the carpet as softly as summer rain. "And if I refuse?"

He waited, watching a solitary coin that had landed on hardwood floor as it spun on its edge before, with a sickly wobble, it finally toppled to its side. When he raised his eyes, they burned bright with suppressed anger. "Then I'll not scruple to report you to the local magistrate as a drab of the lowest order. And insist on your prosecution as such."

"Kit will never allow it," she said, forcing ice into her voice.

"Oh, believe me, madam, he'll offer no protest. At least not after our uncle has given him a proper set-down. He may not have much respect for my authority, but he has the utmost respect for the Colonel. How he could ever take up with you after what Uncle Christopher suffered at the hands of your countrymen, I can't begin to imagine." He kicked at a coin that had landed near his polished boot, sending it spinning across the room.

"Your uncle," Fianna whispered, arms falling to her sides. "But I thought he was dead."

"Dead? Christopher Pennington?" Saybrook gave a sharp bark of a laugh. "Word of Kit's doings aren't likely to improve the old campaigner's disposition, but I don't imagine they'll send him to an early grave. How important you imagine yourself, Miss Cameron."

She hugged her arms tight to her chest. Important enough to win Kit's heart. But not to gain his loyalty, his trust. He'd reserved both for his own uncle, his own kin. Not for her.

She could not even blame him for it, could she? For now that she knew her father's enemy still lived, was not that cursed old familiar, vengeance, rising up inside her, its icy talons clawing away any softer feelings she had been unwary enough to welcome?

What right did she have to demand he hold justice for her family higher than loyalty to his own?

None. None at all.

She steeled her spine against the shudder that threatened to bring her to her knees.

Fingers pried open her clenched hand, pressing the smooth, cool metal of a sovereign within the nest of her palm. "Take it, and be gone," Saybrook whispered. "There's nothing for you here."

How foolish for an Irishwoman to allow her hopes to fly high as an air balloon. Had not the first balloon to wreck fallen to earth in Ireland? And had it not burned an entire street in Tullamore to the ground?

No, there could be nothing here for her. No matter how much Kit might think he loved her, he'd always put his own family first.

Fianna's fingers closed tight about the coin.

CHAPTER TWENTY

The twisted maze of streets with their dingy, straggling houses and crowds of idlers loitering about the gin shops surely would have sent any genteel Englishwoman into a fit of the vapors. But to Fianna, the soft vowels and harder consonants lilting off the tongues of its denizens felt uncannily familiar. The parish of St. Giles, which had once served as refuge for a colony of lepers, now housed another race of outcasts: her desperate Irish countrymen, who had flocked to the city in hopes of escaping the grinding poverty of their homeland, only to find themselves ensnared within the filth and squalor of London's most infamous slum.

Difficult, it was, to find Sean's rooms, the way the streets and courts darted in all directions, tangled as a ball of yarn after a kitten's pounce. Someone less determined surely would have given it up as a bad job hours earlier. But at long last, one listless fellow, leaning with stolid indifference against a post, nodded a lazy head toward the lane for which she searched.

The woman who answered her knock made no answer to her inquiry for Sean O'Hamill, only turned and plodded down the dank passageway. Fianna shut the door behind her and followed in the crone's footsteps, taking care not to allow her skirts to skim against the dirty walls. The building might once have held only one family, but the noise and smell suggested that now, each of its rooms housed an entire brood.

The old woman jerked her head toward the last door before trudging back to the front of the house.

Setting her portmanteau by her feet, Fianna raised a fist and knocked.

Her uncle gave no sign of welcome at the sight of her. But neither did he gloat, nor pinch his lips tight in reproach. He simply opened the door wide, gesturing her inside.

His room was far cleaner than the passageway that led to it, its wooden floor free of dirt, its single bed neatly made. Hardly enough room in which to swing a cat, here, but she'd made do with smaller. If, that is, Sean would have her.

He took her portmanteau and placed it by the bed. "Wish to talk of it?" he asked as he pulled out one of the two rickety chairs by the scarred wooden table.

"What is there to say?" Fianna sat down with a sigh. The need to find the Major had once pricked her as sharp as a spur. But now, after Kit, only lethargy greeted the prospect of resuming the search.

Her uncle took the chair opposite, resting his folded hands atop the table. "Oh, many a *cailín* likes to weep and wail over a lost love for at least a few days before turning her attention to more important matters. My shoulder's a strong one, if you've a need of it."

"I'd as lief swim back to Ireland in nothing but my shift."

Sean bit back a laugh. "Ah, what a bold, free-spoken child it is. That's the Máire I remember."

Hardly a child any longer. And wise enough to keep her thoughts to herself, even in the days when she'd worn skirts far shorter than these. But if it pleased him to think her courageous, she'd not say nay.

"Bold enough to ask for your help, in spite of the harsh words with which we last parted," she said.

He frowned. "Not coin for the passage home? I'll ne'er believe young Pennington's cowed a brave

O'Hamill."

"No, not coin. Only a place to stay. A pallet on the floor will do, if you've a blanket to spare."

"For the child of my sister? A blanket, mayhap even a pillow, for as long as she needs them." His lips caught somewhere between a smile and a grimace. "Lord knows I'd not wish any kinswoman of mine ill. But far better to suffer a broken heart than to turn a blind eye to one's duty."

"Duty?"

"To one's country and one's family. You've come to help our cause, just as you promised." He wrapped her hands in his two rough palms and squeezed. "And just when we'd thought all lost."

The eagerness animating his face sent her stomach tumbling. She'd come to ask his help in hunting Major Pennington, not to become entangled in whatever schemes he had afoot. How could she have forgotten the bargain she'd made?

Best to gather all the facts, though, before refusing him outright. "Just what is it that you wish me to do, Sean?"

"You sacrificed so much, Máire—your name, your family, your very virtue—all for the chance of killing a man already dead." He leaned forward, his eyes kindling with passion. "But what if that sacrifice was not all in vain? What if it freed you to strike a blow that truly mattered for your country?"

"A blow against what?"

His eyes narrowed. "Say rather against whom."

"Killing, Sean?" Fianna drew her hands from his. "I've little skill with firearms, not even my father's."

"You have Aidan McCracken's pistol with you? Where?" Sean knelt by the bed and jerked open her bag, rooting around in its contents without regard for her cry of protest. His face lit with the zeal of a martyr as he shook the firearm free from its wrappings and raised it to the light. "How fitting, for Aidan's pistol to fell his most fervent enemy!"

"What enemy? Sean, who are you targeting?"

"Why, no other than the Butcher of Ireland himself. Castlereagh." The name spit from his mouth with as much vehemence as if it were spread with rancid butter.

"Viscount Castlereagh? The British Foreign Secretary?"

"Foreign Secretary now. But he had the gall to call himself Chief Secretary of Ireland in 1798. Was it not Castlereagh who gave the orders then to quarter troops upon the people, to steal their horses and carriages? To demand forage and provisions from the starving populace? And then, did he not put down the rebellion with the brutality of a savage? And was he not responsible for this damned Act of Union, with its false promises of greater rights for Irishmen? Any true Irish patriot should be glad of the chance to send the bastard to his grave."

"You wish me to shoot Castlereagh," she said, her voice as dispassionate as she could make it.

"No. As much as you might relish such a task, Máire, I'll be reserving that right for myself."

But the thought of Sean committing murder, rather than herself, gave her no relief. "Then what is it you want of me?"

Sean returned to the table and grasped her upper arms. "Our most comely men have been trying to turn the head of a housemaid, any housemaid, in his employ. To use her to gain access to Castlereagh's house. But there's no Irishwoman amongst them, and the English ones all look on us with scorn."

Her brows furrowed. "And you wish me to try for a post?"

"That's one idea. Or you might befriend a footman or a groom in the bastard's employ."

"Befriend? Or seduce?" Fianna jerked free of her uncle's grasp. "Just what is it that you're asking of me, Sean?"

"Come now, surely it won't come to that. Not if you use the talents with which the good Lord has blessed you. Your comely face. Your beguiling ways." His expression hardened. "And if any man offers you insult, he'll be repaid tenfold. The O'Hamill honor will be avenged. On all accounts"

A sudden, sick fear darted into her mind. "Did you avenge the O'Hamill honor when my father violated your sister, Sean? Did you betray Aidan McCracken to the English?"

Sean's ruddy face paled. "Christ Jesus, Máire! How could you think such a thing? I loved Aidan, loved him like a brother."

"But he debauched your sister, did he not? Got a bastard on her, never married her. Why was that not a smirch on the manhood of the O'Hamill?"

"Damn it, Máire, it was Aidan! He was fighting for us, not crushing us under his boot. His love for Mairead did us honor."

"But mine for Kit does you none?"

"It's not love that you feel, *cailín*," Sean answered, the line of his mouth grim. "Or it won't be, not once you know the falsehoods that rogue's been whispering in your dainty little ear."

Fianna dropped back in the chair. "Major Pennington?"

Sean leaned against the table, his fit of temper already put behind him. "Discovered it yourself, did you? And left him over it? Ah, there's a wise child."

Fianna caught back a curse. "How long have you known?"

"That yon Pennington lied to you? A few days now. Doubted old devil Pennington cocked up his toes without my hearing of it, despite the tale young Christian spun you. Spent some time tipping a glass in the taverns about town, I did, the ones where old soldiers like to gather and talk of old times. Places no *cailín* would find a welcome. Took some time, but at last I turned up a fellow who'd served under the Major—no, Colonel, he is now—in the Peninsula."

"And you did not think to tell me?"

"Am I not telling you now?"

Now, days later. When it best served his purposes. Fianna leaned forward, hands gripping the edge of the table. "You know where he is, don't you?"

"As well as young Pennington does, to be sure." The sourness of her uncle's smile would have curdled milk, if there'd been any on the table.

"Then tell me, and let me be done with it," she bit out from between clenched teeth. Sean's reminder of Kit's falsehood had stung. As he damn well knew it would.

"Ah, and are you forgetting our agreement so soon, *cailín*? My help for yours, was it not?"

"The Major's direction, in exchange for beguiling Castlereagh's servant? A harsh bargain, even for an enemy, *Seanuncail*, let alone a member of one's family."

Sean's eyes narrowed. "Any person unwilling to devote himself—or herself—to the cause of Irish freedom is no kin of mine, Máire."

"The crow's curse on you, Sean. You're as blindly devoted to your murderous purpose as Kit is to his family."

"Quick, you are, to realize it. Quick enough, no doubt, to track the Major down without my help, now that you know he still lives. What would it take? A day or two? A fortnight, mayhap, if you were truly unlucky?"

Fianna jerked from her chair and crossed to the window, staring out at the milling mob. So many people in St. Giles. But not a one, not even an uncle, that she could call her own.

She felt him come up behind her, his hand falling heavily on her shoulder. "But why wait? Does not this pistol sing to you of vengeance, if only you've courage enough to grasp it?"

Fianna stared at Aidan McCracken's pistol clutched in her hand. When had she taken it off the table?

She turned, caught by eyes so very like her own. She'd wanted so desperately to belong to a family. The McCrackens. The Penningtons. Even, perhaps, the O'Hamills.

But belonging always came at a cost, did it not?

"I've courage enough, *Seanuncail*," she whispered, tilting her chin high.

He gave her shoulder a squeeze. "Of course you do, Máire. Of course you do. Are you not an O'Hamill?"

He strode back to the table and snatched up a pencil. But he paused before placing it to paper, his green eyes boring into hers. "And if I give you Pennington, you'll give me Castlereagh? Or do all in your power to help me bring him down?"

Fianna swallowed back the bile rising in her throat and nodded.

As Sean began to scratch out Major Pennington's direction, the voice of Fianna's grandfather echoed in her ear. Not Grandfather McCracken, but her other, barely remembered O'Hamill one.

Never forget, Máire, the three greatest rushes—the rush of water, the rush of fire, the rush of falsehood.

Who would feel the greatest rush from falsehood today? Kit? Sean?

Or herself?

You are kind, sir, to offer her your hand, and the protection of your name. But we cannot in all good conscience recommend such a course. Tho' it pains me to write it, Maria was ever a strange, quiet, unfeeling child, tainted as she was by her Irish Catholic upbringing. My father also fears her moral sense is not all that it should be. The last letters we had from her hint that she thinks to take God's will into

her own hands, wreaking vengeance against those she believes have wronged her. And what is to say that some-day she will not regard you as in the same light, and turn against you? Nay, do not trust your future happiness to the keeping of such a woman.

Now, you will say she is passing lovely, but do but remember your Proverbs: Favour is deceitful, and beauty is vain; but a woman that feareth the LORD, she shall be praised.

"Ho, sir! Have a care!"

The cry from above jerked Kit to a halt, just in time to prevent his imminent collision with a ladder. His eyes hitched to the workman perched at its top, bucket and cloth in hand. Devil take it, he'd almost brought a pail of dirty water crashing down on his head. And on the damned letter he'd received just this morning from Fianna's aunt, the contents of which had absorbed so much of his attention that he'd not paid the least heed to his surroundings. How had he walked all the way back to his rooms without taking notice?

Kit waved a hand in apology, and the workman responded in kind. "Gen'lemen," the man muttered, shaking his head as he returned to the washing of his windows.

"Has the beauteous Miss Cameron taken to writing you love notes, Kit?"

Benedict stood leaning against his front door, his stern face struggling to hold back a grin. His brother had witnessed the entire ridiculous episode, had he? Well, at least word of his absentmindedness would go no further than his own family.

"Back to try your hand at drawing Miss Cameron again, are you, brother?" Kit asked, shoving the note deep in the pocket of his greatcoat. He'd no wish to share its cruel contents with anyone, family or no.

Benedict shook his head as he followed Kit inside. "Can't seem to make any of my portraits come right since I've been back in London. Viscount Dulcie's been bruiting it about that an artist who's lost his touch must go all the way back to the beginning, and take up still life again. As if I were a child with his first drawing master! Bah."

"Then why are you here?" Kit asked as they climbed the stairs.

"A summons from the esteemed head of our family."

Kit halted in front of his door. "From Theo? What reason did he give?"

"None. But since he wished to meet here, not at Pennington House, I've hopes that it's you rather than me who's being called onto the carpet." The corner of his brother's mouth turned up in the hint of a smile. "What have you been up to, brother of mine?

Oh, only informing the head of his family of his intentions to wed a woman entirely unsuitable for a gentleman of his rank and station, as no doubt Theo would rage. But damn, he was tired of stuffing his desires into the confines of the mold his family set before him. Why should Theo care if a third son of a viscount married outside the *ton*? No matter whom Kit married, within a generation or two his descendants would only be a distant branch of the noble line.

But care Theo did. Enough, it would seem, to interrupt his round of dissipations and call in person to make his objections known. And to gain the higher ground by making himself right at home in Kit's absence. For there his brother sat, in the middle of the drawing room, arms crossed, eyes narrowing as he watched his younger brothers enter.

But of Fianna, there was no sign. Had she gone out before Theo's arrival? Or had she hidden herself in a back room?

"Theo," Kit acknowledged, tossing his hat on the table. "Apologies for not being home to receive you. Benedict tells me you wish to speak with us?"

"I did, yes."

Kit gritted his teeth as Theo gestured to them to take a seat, as if he were lord and master here rather than Kit. Benedict sat, but Kit remained on his feet.

His elder brother leaned back in his chair. "But it seems there is no longer a need. I've taken care of the problem, and with far less difficulty than I had anticipated."

"What problem?" he asked.

"The problem of your unfortunate infatuation with Miss Fianna Cameron. Did he inform you, too, Benedict, that he intended to wed the wench?"

"Marriage, Kit? Truly? I'd not the least idea." The look in Benedict's eyes, equal parts surprise and concern, had Kit clenching his fists.

"As head of the family, Saybrook had the right to be informed first," Kit said. "Despite his less-than-admirable performance since taking on that role."

Theo's lips tightened. "And you've kept this family's concerns so close to heart, have you, Kit?"

"More so than you," Kit snapped. "What head of family would allow his own member of Parliament to vote against his interests for months on end? Would drink away the nights and sleep away the days instead of paying attention to the duty he owes his name? Would hear that his brother's been shot, and not take the least trouble to pay him a call?"

"And you would do so much better, would you, Kit? By taking up with radical rabble, as if you're ashamed of our noble lineage? By allowing the woman who shot you to become your mistress?"

Benedict gasped in surprise. No, he'd not shared that bit of the story with his middle brother, had he? How the hell had Theo discovered it?

Theo leaned forward, his round cheeks ruddy. "By having so little pride in the Pennington name that you'd share it with a hardened whore?"

Fury drove Kit across the room. "Don't you ever use such foul words in my hearing again, Saybrook," he hissed, hands gripping the arms of Theo's chair. "And especially not in hers. Fianna may not yet be a member of our family by law, but she soon will be, whether you say yea or nay."

Theo pushed up from the chair, forcing Kit to take a step back to avoid a collision. "I wouldn't be so sure of that if I were you, brother. Have you not noticed her absence from this intimate family coze?"

"She's just gone out for a walk," Kit said, willing the words to be true.

"Yes, but it's likely to be a walk of some duration. Quite eager to leave, your wild Irish girl, after the two of us had a chat of our own."

"You're wrong," Kit said. "She'd never leave, not without talking to me first."

"You would know best, of course," Theo said with a careless shrug. "Although why one would require a heavy valise for a brief afternoon constitutional, I'm sure I cannot say."

The smugness in his brother's voice made Kit's ears burn. He raced down the passageway and shoved open the door to Fianna's room. But no portmanteau rested at the end of the bed; no hairbrush lay on the bedside table. He yanked each dresser drawer open, one after the other, each rattling as empty as the one before.

Kit strode back to the drawing room, fists furled, ready for once to allow his temper free rein. Benedict, his eyes widening, set himself in Kit's path before Kit could get anywhere near Theo.

The feel of his middle brother's palm on his shoulder did little to assuage the flow of blood pounding in Kit's temples. "What did you say to her, Theo? Did you threaten her?"

Theo crossed his arms. "I simply made it clear she'd never receive my consent to your ill-advised matrimonial plans. And gave her a bit of gold to tide her over until the next gullible gentleman crossed her path."

"What, without even talking to Kit first?" Benedict

asked. "A mite interfering, no?"

Theo drew himself up to his full height. "I am the head of this family, as even our youngest brother acknowledges. As such, I will do as I see fit to protect its members. Even if I have to pay for the privilege."

Kit shook his head. Haughty Fianna, deigning to accept blood money from a Pennington? Impossible.

"She refused you, didn't she, Theo? Refused your filthy lucre."

Theo's jaw clenched, but his tone remained even. "Oh, she may have put up a token protest, at least at first. But she changed her tune quickly enough. The Irish will always take the easy way out, won't they?"

Benedict frowned. "Really, Theo? You sound like Uncle Christopher, spouting such prejudicial drivel."

Uncle Christopher? The blood drained from Kit's face as he pushed past Benedict. "Theo, did you say anything about the Colonel when you spoke with Fianna?"

"Uncle Christopher? I suppose I might have. Why should you care about that?"

Kit grabbed the lapels of Theo's frock coat, jerking his brother close. "Damn it, Theo! You don't understand. I told her Uncle Christopher was dead."

"Dead? Lord knows we've all wished the cantankerous old fellow to the blazes every now and then. But why should your lightskirt care about the Colonel's health?

Kit's hands dropped, his stomach plummeting. "Because when she pointed that pistol at me in the Crown and Anchor, it wasn't Christian Pennington she intended to threaten. It was *Christopher* Pennington. The English army major who ordered the execution of her father during the Irish Rebellion."

For long minutes, the slow *tick, tick* of the mantel clock was the only sound in the room. His brothers' silence, heavy with disbelief, clung to Kit like a pall.

At long last, Theo cleared his throat. "And you offered her shelter? A woman intent on harming our uncle? Why would you do such a thing?"

Kit pulled his hair in his hands. "I didn't know she was the one who shot me. Not when we first met."

"But you knew when you invited her here," Benedict said, his expression even more stony than usual. "That's why you asked me not to mention our uncle in her presence, not because you feared his antipathy to the Irish might give her pain."

"It was only a suspicion. You wouldn't expect me to condemn an innocent woman without any proof, would you?"

"But you found proof, no? And still you allowed her to stay?"

"Yes," Kit cried, his voice thick in his throat. "But by then, it was too late."

"Because by then, she'd seduced you, made you forget what you owe your family," Theo snapped.

"No. Because by then, she *was* my family." Kit slumped in a chair, his head heavy in his hands. "I love her, Theo. I was afraid she'd leave if she found out I'd lied."

Theo took a step back and ran a hand over the mantel. "And so she has. Left, I mean. Poor sod." The clumsy sympathy in his brother's voice grated like chalk on a slate. "Shall we take him to the tavern across the way, Ben, help him drown his sorrows?"

"Before you make yourself or either of us incoherent with drink, we need to find out what's become of Miss Cameron."

"What? When I've just gotten rid of the wretch? Whatever for?"

"Because if she thinks Kit has betrayed her," Benedict answered, "what's to keep her from returning to her original plan?"

"Original plan?"

Kit raised his head, his eyes bleak. "To make Christopher Pennington pay. With his life."

CHAPTER TWENTY-ONE

"So you've come for me at last, have you, daughter of Aidan McCracken?"

Major—no, Colonel now—Christopher Pennington looked nothing like the monstrosity that had haunted Fianna's nightmares for decades. No dark, looming figure of evil, mocking her feeble attempts at vengeance; not even the tall, haughty officer Aunt Mary had described, striding about Belfast as if the whole of Ireland should bow down to him in homage. No, the man sitting upright in the narrow tester bed was small and wizened, his hair (at least the little that remained of it) faded almost to white. He wore not a uniform but a nightshirt, its wrinkles mirroring the creases lining his forehead and bracketing his grim, set mouth. Even from across the chamber, the fetid odor of the sickroom hung heavy in the air.

But the frail man did not tremble, not even when she raised her father's pistol and aimed it at his heart.

Christopher Pennington might be old and crippled. Might even be dying. But no one could ever accuse the man of being weak.

Fianna stepped into the room, nudging an elbow to shut the door behind her. More than unwise, it would be, to take her eyes off the vile lie-monger, no matter how unthreatening he appeared.

"Been long expecting me, have you, sir?" she whispered, stepping onto the room's thin carpet. "For my part, I've been awaiting this moment for years. Eternities."

Pennington's eyes shifted, tracking her as she moved across the room. "Ever since you saw me give the signal for the hangman to kick away the stool from under your traitor father's feet?"

Fianna ignored the bite of pain his words were clearly meant to provoke, maintaining a slow, even pace toward his bed. She would not be distracted. Not now, when she finally had her prey in her sights.

"No, Major. I assure you, I had eyes for only my father that day."

Pennington's eyes were the same blue as Kit's, that pale blue that washed the sky on an unclouded spring day. But they held none of the warmth that his nephew's did. Only a determination as stark as her own.

He folded gnarled hands across his lap. "Typical of the Irish, to allow a child to witness its own father's execution. Barbarians, the lot of them."

"My mother forbade me to go," she answered, stopping beside the chair someone had set next to the Major's bed. He'd not be inviting the likes of her to sit, now, would he? "But my uncle would not dishonor Aidan McCracken's sacrifice by refusing to bear witness. Nor allow Aidan's only child to, either."

"Ah yes, your uncle. O'Hamill, isn't it? Hatching even grander plots than even your misguided father ever dreamed. As if he could singlehandedly wrest Ireland from British rule." The Major's mouth twisted in an ugly sneer. "He's a damned fool if he thinks assassinating anyone in the government will forward his cause."

"Even Lord Castlereagh?"

"Even bloody Castlereagh. Why, if I'd thought it would free my country from that wretched bog in which it's mired, I'd have put a bullet through him myself, years ago."

She gestured with her father's pistol. "Unfortunately

for you, it appears I'm the only one with a weapon here today."

Pennington's hand rose, sending her jerking away in alarm. But instead of reaching for her father's gun, his fingers curved, beckoning her closer. "One pistol is more than enough for what needs to be done today, don't you agree? Come now, *cailín*, come and finish what you've begun."

Yes, it was time to finish this, once and for all. Lifting one hand from the pistol, Fianna felt for the reticule hanging by her side. Laying it on the end of his bed, she reached a hand inside and pulled out the sheet of foolscap she'd been carrying with her ever since her arrival in London. With a flick of her wrist, she tossed it on the bed. "But you're the one who will finish it, Major, by signing this confession."

"Confession?" Pennington snorted, his bushy eyebrows rising. "What, do you believe me a Papist? I don't recall converting, wench, despite the efforts of several of your Irish priests to persuade me of my soul's dire peril."

"I care nothing for your soul," she bit out. "All I want is your signature."

"Acknowledging what? That I oversaw the execution of your father? It's a matter of public record."

"No! Your admission that you spread malicious and baseless lies after his execution. That you falsely cast him as a traitor to his own people. Sign it!"

With a finger, she nudged the paper closer. But instead of reaching for it, the Major leaned back against the pillows. His brows drew down over those pale blue eyes as he folded recalcitrant arms across his chest.

"No."

"No?" Her free hand returned to the pistol, jerking it higher. "Do you deny that you did it?"

His eyes narrowed. "Of course not. I'd have done anything to stop that foolish revolt from escalating any further. A damned idealist, Aidan McCracken, with his love for Ireland and its craven, stupid peasants. If they'd been able to turn your misguided fool of a father into a martyr for the cause, they'd have kept on, maiming my men, suiciding themselves. Well, I pulled the air from their sails right enough, didn't I, showing them how he'd betrayed them in the end. And he did, you know, even if it wasn't in the way I made them think. He betrayed them by making them believe they had a chance in hell of achieving that 'United Ireland' he so loved to dream of. What chance did that feeble cabal of rustics have of defeating His Majesty's armed forces, even if they'd gone a bit to seed? So yes, I lied about your father. I asked him, practically begged him, to give up his fellow conspirators in exchange for his own life. But all he ever did was smile, and refuse."

Fianna's lips pursed, holding back the retorts she longed to utter. Focus on the task at hand, and the emotions would take care of themselves. "Do you wish to write your own account, then, instead of signing mine? I'll bring you a fresh sheet of paper—"

"No. I'll not deny I did it. At least not to you."

She swallowed hard, the dawning realization bitter in her throat. "But you will to everyone else."

The man nodded. "I'd hardly wish my family to find out the dishonorable depths to which your hellish country drove me, would I? All my nephews take the gentleman's code of honor quite to heart, you see. Especially Kit."

Yes, especially Kit.

Fianna's eyes narrowed. "I'll tell him, Major. I'll tell Kit all you've done."

"And you think he'll believe you, over a member of his own family?"

"Yes. He loves me. I'm a part of his family now."

The old man snorted. "Kit, love a lowborn Irish harlot?"

How strange, to find the blood rushing from her cheeks at the Major's insult. As if she'd never been mocked before, and with words ten times more vile than his. Fianna shook her head, as if she could will away the betraying emotion.

"Oh yes, wench, I know how you whored your way to England, using that fey face of yours to beguile Talbot's idiot heir." The Major leaned forward, his hands fisted in the sheets. "Do you think I'd let a slut like you ensnare a beloved nephew? Love, bah. Kit may feel lust, but lust soon fades when the rottenness at a woman's core comes to light."

"And what rot lies in your bones, Major? What kind of man is it who allows the soldiers under his command to pillage the homes and businesses of civilians without restraint? Who watches while they commit every kind of atrocity on the bodies of unwilling women? Who utters no protest when innocents are tortured, even murdered, in a fruitless search for yet another imaginary cache of hidden weapons? England takes pride in her soldiers, sir, but how long would Kit's pride in you last, if he had the least inkling of all the evil you've countenanced?"

"Do you think I take any pride in my service in Ireland?" Slashes of red burned across the man's sunken cheeks. "I was trained as a soldier, not a constable. I should have been fighting against France, not stuck with the dregs of the British army, subduing a barbaric populace. God, how I begged to be transferred to another regiment, any regiment, as long as it was serving far from that blasted, bloody land."

"Enough!" Fianna hissed. "You may have lost your pride, but I lost my father, my mother, my entire family." She jerked the pistol toward the paper on the bed. "And unless you sign, I'll make sure you lose yours."

Pennington sat back in the bed, his back resting against the headboard. "Please. Just try to blacken my name to Kit, and see how long his tender regard for you lasts."

The muscles in Fianna's arms quivered from the weight of the pistol. She tensed, forcing her arms to hold straight. "If you don't sign, I'll kill you."

The Major spread his arms, palms up in invitation. "Go right ahead, my dear. I'm more than ready to meet my maker."

A Mháthair Dé! How could she return to Ireland, to her father's family, without the means to redeem his name? She risked drawing a step closer, so she might press the pistol's muzzle against Pennington's chest. "I'll do it, damn you. I will!"

A strange smile fluttered about his lips. "I'd expect no less of an Irisher. Bloody violent beasts, the lot of you."

A violent beast, was she? And what of him? Yes, he deserved to die, the lying, hypocritical bigot. Fianna waited for memory and rage to fill her with purpose, as it had when she'd brought down the other men who'd dared to betray her father. But her thumbs did not move to raise the flint. For all she could see was Kit, kneeling over the limp, lifeless body of his uncle, his kind eyes now as hardened as the Major's, cursing his uncle's killer, cursing her, to damnation.

Fianna stared down at the gun between her hands, then back up at the Major's face. How long had she been standing there, lost in the nightmare vision? Long enough for him to snatch the pistol from her hands, if he'd truly wanted to. . .

She began to shake her head, waiting for her jumbled thoughts to come into some semblance of order. "You want me to do it, don't you? You want me to kill you. Why? Are you mad?"

The Major's lips thinned, but he said not a word.

She took a step back, then another, allowing the weight of the pistol to pull her arms down. "No. Not mad. You want me to prove it, don't you? Prove that your contempt of my people is warranted. Show Kit how vile I am, how I could never be worthy of a place in the high-and-mighty Pennington family. In any family of honor."

Christopher Pennington's eyes narrowed. "Misplaced your bravery already, my jade? Are you sure you're really Aidan McCracken's get?"

"Yes, I'm Aidan McCracken's daughter. And Mairead O'Hamill's. Both had courage, far more than I thought I could ever muster."

The Major's lips thinned into a cold smile. "Not far wrong, were you?"

Fianna stared, unseeing, at the pistol in her hand. "Was I? I always thought I had to prove that I belonged, that I deserved a place in the McCracken family, by bringing you to justice. And now, too, that I'd sacrifice anything to be worthy of the O'Hamills. Worthy of Sean's regard."

"Then prove it, girl," Pennington hissed. "Pull that trigger!"

She looked up, realization tingling in her chest. "But if I kill you now, what would that prove? Only that I'm just as bad as you think me, a violent Irish beast. You'd die with a smile on that cold face, knowing in your heart that you were so much better than me, than any Irisher. Knowing that Kit would hate me forever for betraying him."

Fianna shook her head. "No. I won't let you do it, Major. I won't play the violent beast your hateful prejudice would have me." She lowered her arms, pointing the pistol toward the mattress. "I'm not the unworthy one, Christopher Pennington. You are."

The Major's lips pulled back, baring his teeth. Without warning, he lunged forward, snatching the pistol from her unprepared grasp.

His breath coming in short, sharp pants, he raised her father's firearm, aiming it at her head. "Damn you, wench. Damn you for a disloyal coward." His hands trembled as he raised the flint to full cock.

The blood pounded in Fianna's ears. She could not

allow the Major to pull that trigger. Kit would be even more devastated by his uncle's betrayal than he would have been by hers.

Taking a deep breath, she stepped closer, laying her two hands atop his. She stared at those deep blue eyes, so familiar and yet so distant. "Will you truly shoot the woman your nephew loves, sir? Kit has forgiven you for much, but I wonder if even his loyalty would survive such a blow."

A hint of the vulnerability that so often shone from Kit's eyes glinted in his uncle's. Would it be enough?

Fianna took a step back, then another. Drawing her skirts wide, she knelt into a respectful curtsy. "Bid you good day, sir."

Turning her back on the man for whom she'd spent a lifetime searching, she straightened her shoulders and stepped toward the door.

Kit's heels drummed against the dirty floor of the hack. A trip from Marylebone to Bloomsbury should take no more than a quarter-hour. But this carriage was moving slower than a slug. Damnation, he should have just commandeered Theo's horse and ridden ahead.

Theo's cane tapped lightly against Kit's boot. Kit bit back his scowl. Theo had every right to take him to task, if not for fidgeting like a boy, then for placing the uncle they all loved directly in harm's way. But neither Benedict nor Theo had said a word of censure, not back in his rooms, and not here in the carriage.

Kit closed his eyes, pressing his head back against the squabs. How had he allowed his passion for a woman to blind him to what he owed his family? To what he owed his uncle, his godfather, a man who had always taken the greatest pains to look out for Kit and his concerns?

But would Fianna really do his uncle harm? Even now, every feeling rebelled against the notion.

He'd taken the cold, haughty *leannán sídhe* as the mask, the warm, loving woman in his arms as the truth of her. But perhaps it had been just the opposite. Could love have made him so utterly blind as to mistake the concealment for what it concealed?

A hand, rather than a cane this time, forced his leg to still. Lord, when had he started the tapping again?

Kit jerked his knee out from under Benedict's hand, unable to meet his brother's eyes.

"She'll not know where to find him, even if she's still intent on seeking him out," Benedict offered.

"Yes, we'll reach him long before she will," Theo added. But still he pounded the head of his cane against the roof of the hack and chided the driver for his sloth.

Still loyal, the both of them, even to a brother who had betrayed their trust.

How long would that loyalty last, though, if Uncle Christopher came to harm because of him?

Kit threw open the door of the hack as the vehicle drew up beside Aunt Allyne's house. Leaving Theo to deal with the driver, he jumped to the pavement and rushed up the stairs. The knob of the front door offered no resistance to his touch. Unlocked, damn it all to hell.

"Sir!" One of the footmen Kit had hired hurried down the passageway, dismay evident on his face. "My apologies, sir, I did not hear the knocker."

Kit waved off the man's apology. "Bates, has a young woman—"

"A beautiful young woman," Benedict interrupted.

"A strikingly lovely young woman," Kit said, with a glare at his brother, "come to call on the Colonel?"

"No sir. No callers today, not even the physician."

Benedict's shoulders slumped against the wall in relief. But Kit could take no comfort from the words. How easy for a woman, alone, moving with stealthy grace, to enter without the footman noticing at all?

Taking the treads two at a time, Kit raced up the staircase. Four broad strides took him to Uncle Christopher's bedchamber. His nightmare—Fianna, with cruel smile and smoking pistol, his uncle, tangled in sheets and blood—had it come to life?

Kit pushed open the door.

No blood.

No Fianna.

But, damn it all to hell, no Uncle Christopher, either.

Kit took a step into the room, his breath rasping. The Colonel was not in the bed, although its mussed sheets said he'd occupied it not long before. Curtains drawn; not in the chair by the window. No steam or clatter rising from the bathing chamber. A *leannán sídhe* might transport the emotions of a man she beguiled, but his body? How the hell had Fianna spirited a fully grown man out from under their eyes?

A shuddering moan raised the hair on the back of Kit's neck. It had come from the far side of the bed.

Two strides brought him around the bed frame. Uncle Christopher lay sprawled, facedown, on the floor beside it.

Falling to his knees, Kit reached out a hand and turned his uncle onto his back. He could find no gunshot, no knife wound, not even the least sign of blood. All he saw was the twisted, wasted lower limbs of a soldier who had sacrificed his ability to walk while defending his country.

And a pistol—Aidan McCracken's pistol—clutched tight in his uncle's hand.

Uncle Christopher's eyes fluttered open.

"Did she do this to you, sir?" Kit asked, helping the older man into a seated position. "Did she threaten you, push you from the bed?"

Kit tried to ease the pistol from his uncle's grasp, but the Colonel held on to it with the tenacity of a drowning man clutching at a lifeline. Could he be afraid, even of Kit?

"Colonel? Did she hurt you?"

His uncle's eyes focused on Kit's face for a moment, then glazed over once again. With a groan, he tipped his head back against the bed, his Adam's apple a prominent, vulnerable bump against the sunken skin of his neck.

"No, damn her heart." Kit had to lean closer to catch his uncle's whispered words. "Enticed her here, didn't I? And gave her every opportunity. Practically painted a target, right here on my chest. But still, she would not do it."

"Enticed her?" Kit raised his eyes to his brothers, who now stood by the door. Did his expression look as bewildered as theirs? "Whatever can you mean, sir?"

"Aye, enticed her. Made certain her devil of an uncle knew precisely where to find me. She'd not be able to resist such an invitation, not a child of mad Aidan Mc-Cracken's."

The man's fall from the bed must have injured his brain. What else could account for such strange talk?

"Why would you wish to see Miss Cameron, Colonel?" Benedict asked, kneeling by his uncle's side. Yes, his brother's soothing tone might help calm their uncle enough so that they could safely move him to the bed.

But Uncle Christopher shook off the hand that Benedict laid on his shoulder. "Why? Because it's time I laid down this blasted guilt that's been hanging about my neck these five-and-twenty years."

"Guilt?" Kit asked. "Come, sir, what has guilt to do with an honorable soldier?"

Uncle Christopher's eyes snapped open as he grabbed at Kit with a shaking hand. "No, you wouldn't understand, would you, Christian, how a man's honor and his loyalty to his country could ever come into conflict. Because I made damn sure you never would. I made your father swear he'd never allow you to join, no matter how hard you begged."

Kit sat back on his heels. "But it was Father—"

"No," Theo interrupted. "It wasn't. Before he died, Father told me of his promise to Uncle Christopher, and made me promise, too, never to purchase you a set of colours. And to not breath a word of it to you."

Kit stared at Theo, then his uncle, struggling to find the right words. "Why, Uncle? Why didn't you wish me to join? When the army was your life?"

Uncle Christopher shook his head "Such the idealist you were, Kit! Always championing the weak and downtrodden, always convinced that goodness and right always win out in the end. How could I bear to see such spirit ground into the dirt by the ugly realities of a military life?"

"Ugly realities? You've never spoken of such, sir."

"Of course not! What man would want to talk about taking food from the mouths of the impoverished to keep his own soldiers from starving? About watching his men and their flintlocks mowing down poor bastards armed with nothing more than pitchforks and pikes? About the dishonorable things he's forced to do to women and children? Cruel things, foul things, things to which you, a gentleman, would never stoop." Uncle Christopher's eyes bored into Kit's. "Only to wake up one day to find yourself doing them all the same, your beloved honor lying dead in the dust beside you."

Kit's brain reeled. He'd long left behind any youthful illusions he'd once cherished about the infallibility of the British military. Men charged with defending their country did not always act with wisdom, or even honor, as he'd witnessed firsthand on the bloody grounds of St. Peter's Field. But to hear his uncle suggest that such behavior was not a horrible aberration, but the norm? Even for an officer of the Colonel's caliber? Impossible!

"What has any of this to do with Miss Cameron?" Benedict asked.

"She was supposed to end it! And she brought the

pistol, yes," Uncle Christopher cried, shaking the weapon in an unsteady hand. "But would she give me the satisfaction of taking away my sorry life? Of relieving me of this burden of guilt I've been carrying for more than twenty years? No, far too cunning a bitch, that get of McCracken's. She'd not end my misery, no, not she. She wants me to feel how bitter it is, to see a nephew who once worshipped me as a hero now stare at me with disillusionment and contempt."

Kit's fists clenched at the Colonel's ugly slur against Fianna, but the words that followed pulled him up short. "Why would you believe I'd ever hold you in contempt, Uncle?"

"Because she'll tell you the truth of it," Uncle Christopher cried. "The truth of what I did to her father, to her family. If she'd murdered me as she was supposed to, you'd have taken her for a liar. But now—"

Kit's insides turned to ice as his intuition made the connection. "Was it you who spread the rumors that McCracken had turned apostate? That he'd betrayed his own men, all for the chance of a pardon?"

Kit grabbed his uncle by the lapels. "Did you, sir? Did you besmirch a gentleman's honor? Did you lie?"

Uncle Christopher stared at Kit for a long moment, then gave one short, sharp nod. "I'd have done far worse if I'd thought it would end that bloody, pointless uprising even one day sooner."

Kit's hands fell to his sides. *My God.* How had he never seen it? The dutiful, loyal soldier, never speaking of his time in Ireland—it was all a mask Uncle Christopher had donned, wasn't it? A mask hiding the sins he'd committed, a mask intended to protect poor, kindly Kit from the harsh truths of the world.

A mask to protect himself from his own shame.

A mask, yes, a mask just like the ones Fianna wore. Why, though, had it been so much easier to look beyond hers than to see the one behind which his uncle hid?

Theo dropped to his knees by Kit's side, laying a gentle hand on Uncle Christopher's sleeve. "Sir, please, let us remove you to the bed," he said. The Colonel's grim words still hung in the air, unacknowledged.

Yes, that would be just like a Pennington, wouldn't it? To ignore their uncle's bitter revelations, pretend he'd never mentioned anything about the dishonorable things he'd done. If you were loyal to your family, then you overlooked the frailties of its members, pretended they had no weaknesses, did you not? And above all, you hid all signs of flaws from anyone outside the tight family circle.

Hadn't Kit spent his entire life doing the same? Accepting his father's decisions about Kit's future without protest. Pretending Theo's fall into debauchery after their father's death was only a bit of harmless carousing, rather than the debilitating grief that he'd never been allowed to voice. Following his family's lead by steering the conversation away from Uncle Christopher's time in Ireland whenever outsiders happened to bring up the topic in casual conversation. To save him discomfort, they'd all reassured themselves. But had it not been just as much out of fear of what he might reveal, and an unwillingness to share his pain?

The intention behind such blindness might be a kind one, but too often only injustice resulted. Injustice against Fianna and her family, who had suffered so much because of his uncle's silence. Injustice against Kit, never allowing him to know the complex man behind his uncle's shiny, heroic façade. But most of all, injustice against Christopher Pennington, a man who had suffered in silence for years under the burden of his guilt, with no way to expiate the pain of his sins. For how could you ever be forgiven for an injustice no one, not even yourself, would acknowledge you'd even committed?

No. Kit would no longer allow himself to be blinded by a loyalty that refused to see.

"Uncle," he said, moving to kneel beside his brother. But the Colonel shook free of both Theo and Kit. With painstaking effort, he dragged himself to his feet. One arm leaned on the bed behind him, supporting his shaky weight. His eyes clouded as he slowly raised the other. The one still holding Aidan McCracken's pistol.

With a quick shift of his wrist, Colonel Pennington pressed its barrel to the center of his chest.

Kit's heart nearly burst out of his chest. "Bloody, bloody hell," he heard Benedict whisper. But Kit only had eyes for the pistol, wavering in his uncle's trembling hand.

"Uncle, no." Kit rose to his feet, but stilled as his uncle brought the pistol to full cock.

"I can't stand it, Christian," Uncle Christopher said, an unfamiliar tremor in his voice. "The dishonor I'll bring to this family, once all these secrets come out. I won't stand for it. Now step back, and allow me to finish this."

Kit shook his head. "I'm sorry, sir. So very, very sorry."

"Sorry?" Uncle Christopher's eyes watered. "For what do you have to apologize, Christian?"

"For forcing you to be someone you're not. Forcing you to hide your pain, to keep it inside and allow it to fester. For refusing to see the truth of you, the noble and the cowardly, the sacred and the profane. For being so blindly loyal, I couldn't imagine injustices you might do, or help you to lift their painful weight from your soul."

"Then see justice served. Allow me to die, as I deserve!"

Kit shook his head as he reached out, laying both his hands over his uncle's. "Being blindly loyal may be unjust, but what is justice if it is not tempered by mercy? *What doth the Lord require of thee, but to do justly, and to love mercy?* No, if taking your life would have truly served justice, sir, Fianna would have pulled this trigger herself."

Drawing a deep breath, Kit slowly pushed the pistol's hammer back to half cock. Then, with painstaking care, he drew the weapon from the Colonel's unresisting grasp.

With a groan, Uncle Christopher's upright military stance crumpled. Before his body could reach the floor, Benedict and Theo each caught him underneath an arm. Setting down the pistol, Kit took his uncle's feet; together the three brothers laid their uncle gently back on his bed.

Uncle Christopher's eyes fluttered, but did not open.

"Summon his man, and call for the physician," Kit said as he tucked the coverlet over his uncle's chest. Theo nodded and left the room.

Pulling up a chair beside the bed, Kit sat and reached for his uncle's hand. Benedict took up a stance close behind him.

"You think Fianna acted from mercy? And not from love, Kit?" Benedict murmured, his tone low. "Love of you?"

"I don't know. I love her. Love her so much that it hurts. But she—" Kit couldn't bring himself to finish the thought.

"You love her." Benedict took a deep breath. "And since the Penningtons seem to have discovered a new penchant for truth telling, I'll say what I've been thinking ever since I heard you utter those words, back in your rooms. You love her, but you don't trust her."

Kit turned to stare at his brother. "Trust her?"

"No. Not entirely. You would have told her that Uncle Christopher was still alive if you did."

"Is that what you think? Not that I lied at first, but that I kept lying because I didn't trust her?"

"Yes," Benedict answered, his arms tight against his chest. "You'd never have kept such a secret from me, or from Theo. Not from a member of your own family."

"No. I wouldn't." Kit swallowed down the painful

lump in his throat and looked up at his brother. "I love her, but I've lost her, haven't I, Ben? Not because she betrayed me. But because I betrayed her."

At Benedict's nod, Kit dropped his head into his hands, fingers pressing hard against his skull.

Minutes passed in silence until at last Theo returned with Mr. Acheson. Kit moved to stand beside his brothers as the physician began his examination.

"Do you know where Miss Cameron might have gone, Kit?" Benedict asked.

Theo's eyes narrowed. "As long as she doesn't return here, why should any of us care for Miss Cameron's whereabouts?"

"Because Kit does," Benedict answered. "He loves her. And he needs to tell her the truth."

"I know where she's gone," Kit whispered, his stomach roiling at the realization. "God in heaven, she's gone to an uncle as mad-brained as our own. To O'Hamill."

CHAPTER TWENTY-TWO

The smell of roasting pork, rich ale, and men's bodies after a hard day's work washed over Fianna as she took a few cautious steps into the interior of the Green Dragon Tavern. The patrons of this establishment were a different sort than those who frequented the Patriot Coffeehouse. Workingmen both, but the laze of contentment, rather than the fire of injustice, held sway here. A haunt of men employed by England's wealthiest families, mayhap, men far more likely to take pride in their employers' rank than to chafe against their own lack of status. No, Sean would be giving no incendiary political speeches at the Green Dragon.

Why, then, had the note she'd found in his rooms after her return from Major Pennington's asked her to meet him here?

Heads turned and eyes widened as she threaded through the crowd, once again the only woman in a very public room. But no one offered challenge or insult. Good manners? Or fear of the man glowering from a table at the corner of the room?

"It's done, then?" Sean asked, pushing out a chair for her with his foot. "You've taken care of the Major?"

She answered with only a curt nod.

He waited for her to elaborate, but she remained silent. How could she explain her choice to her uncle, when she could barely understand it herself?

Sean stared for a moment, then gave his own brief nod. Raising his tankard toward the serving maid, he gestured for her to bring another. "A toast, then, *cailín*. To one less butcher in the world."

Christopher Pennington might still be alive, but he was a broken man, unlikely to do any further harm to the innocent. Fianna raised her tankard to Sean's, then drew a deep, bitter sip.

Sean stretched an arm wide over the back of the chair beside him. "An interesting place, the Green Dragon," he said, looking not at her but at the men jostling about the tavern's bar.

Fianna set down her own tankard, pushing it away from her. She'd never been partial to ale. "This is not just a simple celebration, then, Uncle?"

A grim smile slashed across Sean's face. "See that fellow behind you? The lean one by the counter, putting on airs as if he were the very cock of the walk?"

Fianna turned slowly in her chair, bending down as if to retrieve something that had fallen to the floor. She glanced at the men by the bar out of the corner of her eye. Not the rotund one in blue, nor the one with a laugh as high-pitched as a woman's. Ah, that one—tall, thin, and surrounded by a claque of fawning plauditors. Still wearing his livery, his dark hair cut in a manner far more similar to that of Ingestrie's dissipated friends than any servant she'd ever seen. A high opinion of himself, this one had, and no mistake.

"Castlereagh's head footman," Sean said as she returned her attention to their table. Her uncle spoke in a low voice, but intensity underlaid each word. "My friends and I have all tried to ingratiate ourselves with the arrogant bastard, but we're far too lowly for the likes of him. You'll soon bring him to a better sense of his own worth, though, will you not, *cailín*?"

Fianna frowned. "And how will I be doing that, *Seanuncail*?"

"Why, by playing to his *amour-propre*, of course.

Flash those green eyes, fawn over him as if he's the Second Coming, and you'll soon have him jumping to do your bidding."

"After I've gained a post in Lord Castlereagh's household?"

Sean shook his head. "Castlereagh's grown suspicious. Won't allow any new servants about his London house or his person, only those from his own estate. Besides, this way will be quicker."

"What way, Sean?"

Reaching across the table, Sean took her hands in his. "Just use the talents with which the good Lord has blessed you, Máire. Surely a *cailín* handsome enough to seduce not one but two English lordlings will have no trouble leading a mere footman astray."

Fianna stiffened. "You wish me to seduce him?"

"I wish you to have him so crazed with lust that he'd do anything you ask for the chance of slaking it."

Pulling her hands from Sean's, Fianna turned and stared at the man in question. Difficult, it was, to summon the glamour of allure for a man other than Kit. This one was so caught up in his own performance as ringleader of the sycophants who surrounded him that he didn't notice her looking at him at first. But when a few of his cronies began laughing and clapping him on the back, gesturing in her direction, the footman deigned to turn his eyes to her. His stare contained more insolence than admiration, as if he took it as the natural course of events that all eyes in the room should come to rest on him. He raised his tankard to her, then, with a wink and an overfamiliar smile, drank deep.

She could not quite contain the shudder that racked her body at the sight. Could she truly allow such a man to lay hands on her person?

"He's an arrogant sort," she observed, careful to keep revulsion out of her voice. "What if he won't accept such a bargain? If he insists on slaking his lust before he offers anything in return?"

Sean smiled. "It will be your task to see that it doesn't come to that, now, won't it?"

She could not smile in return. "But if it does?" she insisted.

Her uncle's eyes dropped to the table, then shifted to the other side of the room. Unwilling to meet hers? She held her breath, waiting for his reassurance that he'd never ask such a thing of her. No true kinsman would ever ask such a thing of a member of his family, would he?

But the words never came.

"You wish me to prostitute myself?" she asked flatly.

Sean shrugged. "Have you not done so already? And for a far lesser cause?"

"No! It wasn't like that. Not with Kit."

"But Ingestrie already had the use of you, Máire, even before young Pennington," Sean said, impatience edging his voice. "A bit late to turn overdainty, is it not?"

"Overdainty? What, because I sacrificed myself to Ingestrie for passage to London, and offered my love to Kit, now any fellow is entitled to my person? Whether I say yea or nay?"

He frowned, his green eyes finally rising to hers. "What matters who else you lie with? No decent man will have a *striapach* to wife."

Whore. The foulness of the word Sean had uttered with such casual, unexpected cruelty sent the bile rising in her throat. Why had she assumed his offer of shelter would come hand in hand with acceptance, perhaps even love? The memory of the brave boy who'd comforted her when their neighbors whispered or shouted *bastard* must have blinded her to the reality of the grown man before her. He might defend an innocent child, yes. But offer respect to a woman he deemed irretrievably fallen?

Why had she expected him to feel any differently than did the rest of the world?

Because Kit did, something deep inside her whispered.

She pushed back in her chair, squaring her shoulders as she faced her uncle. "No, Sean. I won't do it. I'm finished pretending to be who I'm not."

He folded his arms across his chest, anger tightening his lips. "Pretending? Once a whore, always a whore, *cailín*. No matter how gentlemanlike the rogues who debauched you."

She slapped her hands down against the table. "Kit is no rogue. And I am not a whore."

The scowl slashing across Sean's face made even her cold blood begin to race. "What, you would do such shameful things, and yet refuse to atone?"

"Atone? For what must I atone?"

"For the dishonor you've brought to the O'Hamill name!" His shout, and the fist he slammed down against the table in its wake, stilled all conversation in the room. But the harshness of his glare persuaded any eyes bold enough to catch his that it would be far safer to turn back to their own concerns than to inquire about his.

The ale twisted in Fianna's gut. So this was what her uncle truly thought of her?

"Come, Máire," Sean said, his voice lowered. He sat back down in his chair, gesturing for her to do the same. "You've brought justice to the Major. Why shirk now from enacting justice on a far larger scale?"

"Sean, how can you ask me, a member of your own family, to whore for you? To be so loyal to your cause that I must sacrifice every finer feeling in order to achieve it? Can you not see how hurtful it is, knowing a member of my own family holds me so cheap?"

"But why? You're a fallen woman, Máire. You can never be pure again." His rough hands flexed against the tankard he held between them. "And when will you ever have such a chance to make amends? Do this, and prove you're worthy of Ireland. And of the name of O'Hamill."

Fianna rose to her feet. "But my name is not Máire O'Hamill. Not anymore."

Sean sneered. "And you think the McCrackens will welcome dear Maria to their table, now that she's done away with the Major?"

"No. I'm no longer Maria McCracken, either. I'm Fianna Cameron. And Fianna doesn't need to kill Major Pennington, or whore for you, to prove her worth to you or to anybody."

"No. The only one she has to prove herself to is Fianna Cameron."

Sean's mouth hung open, but the words had not come from him.

"And anyone with eyes can see you've more than done so, over and over again," Kit Pennington added with a decisive nod.

Kit drank in the sight of Fianna, thirsty as a desert nomad whose last sip of water was only a distant memory. He could spy no obvious injury from her confrontation with Uncle Christopher. But she hid her hurts well, especially the ones to her heart. Only when he had her safe back in his rooms, back in his arms, would his worry be assuaged.

If she would come. . .

"Kit, how did you—"

The scrape of O'Hamill's chair interrupted her. "So— you'll use me to gain justice for yourself, Máire, but betray me to the English? Now who holds family loyalty so dear?"

"No," Fianna cried. "I didn't betray you, Sean. I don't know how Kit found us."

"Sam Wooler told me how to find O'Hamill's rooms," Kit said, placing himself between Fianna and her uncle.

"You left his note on the table."

A cruel, derisive expression drew down O'Hamill's brows. "But you betrayed *him*, did you not?" he hissed at Fianna. "How long do you think he'll go prosing on about how worthy you are after he finds out what you've done to his uncle, eh, *cailín*?"

She jerked her head toward Kit, the life in her eyes dimming. What, did she think he'd condemn her for confronting the man who had slandered her father?

"I know precisely what she's done to my uncle, O'Hamill. She's taught him a painful lesson, one that I'm certain he won't soon forget. One about both justice and mercy."

"Mercy?" O'Hamill's eyes burned with incredulity. "What, did you not kill him, then?

Fianna drew her shoulders back, tilting her arrogant nose in the air. The combination of strength and vulnerability in that oh-so-familiar stance sent shivers down Kit's spine.

"I did not," she said. "I told you true, I'll not be using violence any longer to achieve my ends." She took a step closer, laying a hand upon her uncle's arm. "And, I hope, neither will you."

"I'll have little opportunity to do so, once you hand me over to young Pennington here," O'Hamill said, bitterness edging his voice.

"I'll not be handing you over to anyone, Sean. But please, give over this mad scheme against Lord Castlereagh. Killing just leads to more killing, more bloodshed. Work with us, work to persuade the people to agitate for peaceful change. It's the only way to achieve justice for our people, our country."

But O'Hamill paid no heed to his niece, all his attention now focused upon Kit. "How many officers of the law have you brought with you, sir?"

Kit spread his hands. "None, sir. My only intention in coming here was to find Fianna."

"And found her you have," he snarled, jerking Fianna in front of him as a shield. The point of a knife pricked at the pale column of her neck. "Now, what will you do to keep her?"

Kit's body tensed. Her own uncle, threatening her? And they called Fianna a bastard—

"Now, O'Hamill, there's no need for violence," he said, spreading his open palms in appeasement.

"Certainly not," Fianna concurred. A sharp elbow to O'Hamill's gut and a hard stamp on the instep of his foot sent the knife clattering to the floor.

As O'Hamill clutched at his stomach, Fianna bent over to retrieve the fallen weapon. She ran a finger along its edge, shaking her head. "Hardly sharp enough to cut a man's throat, Sean. You ought to keep your weapons in better order." With a quick jerk, she stabbed the knife into the table between them.

The room around them had grown unnaturally quiet. Kit waved a hand toward the silent crowd. "Nothing here to gawk at, good sirs, just a small family squabble. All is in good order, I assure you."

It took a few moments, but the tavern's patrons gradually turned back to their own concerns.

"What, still here, O'Hamill?" Kit asked, placing a protective arm around Fianna. Not that she needed much in the way of protecting. Still, she might take some comfort from it, knowing she had an ally close to hand.

O'Hamill shook his head in bewilderment. "And you'll stand by and allow this, Pennington? Allow me to stroll free, without summoning the watch or the king's soldiers?"

"Miss Cameron has shown great mercy to my uncle today. What sort of gentleman would I be if I did not show the same to hers?"

"Please, Sean. Go," Fianna added. "But know we will be sending a letter to Lord Castlereagh, informing him of your plans and warning him to take precautions. It might be wise if you returned to Ireland at your earliest opportunity."

He nodded, backing away from the table.

"I've Theo's carriage outside," Kit murmured, giving her shoulder a squeeze. "Will you take a turn about the park, and grant him some time to pack before you return for your things?"

Instead of answering, she turned back to her uncle. "After I've had a word with Mr. Pennington, I'll come by to pick up my valise. Perhaps it would be best if you and your belongings were gone by then?"

Sean gave a brusque nod. "Rent's paid up through quarter day, if you need a place," he said before turning on his heel and striding to the tavern's door. Not entirely without family feeling, then. As long as it did not come into conflict with his cause.

At the threshold, her uncle turned back, staring at her as if he wished to fix her image in his mind. As if he knew it would be many a long year, if ever, before he'd catch sight of his sister's child again.

"Good-bye, *Seanuncail*," she whispered, hardly loud enough to hear herself. But perhaps Sean guessed in spite of it. A grim smile slashing across his face, he nodded once more, then pulled the door closed behind him.

CHAPTER TWENTY-THREE

After the din and bluster of the tavern, carriage wheels turning over cobbles sounded as silent as the scamper of a mouse. Theo must have had the coach newly sprung; in his father's day, the ride had never been this smooth. The interior hadn't changed, though, its seats the same azure as the Saybrook coat of arms, the velvet nap almost entirely worn away from the front-facing seat where he'd placed Fianna. He'd wanted to sit down beside her, draw her into his arms to persuade himself that she'd not been injured in the encounter with his uncle, or with her own, but he'd taken the seat opposite, wary of his welcome. For once in his life, no easy words came to his lips. What did one say to the woman one loved but had betrayed?

Kit placed his hat and gloves on the seat beside him and cleared his throat. But Fianna kept her eyes fixed on the squalid streets of St. Giles.

Perhaps action would serve better than words?

Kit reached across the coach and laid Aidan Mc-Cracken's flintlock on the seat beside her. "Perhaps not quite true to say 'With Christopher Pennington's compliments,'" he said with a wry smile. "But certainly with mine."

Fianna cradled the pistol between her hands, running a single finger over the Gaelic engraving, just as she had the first night they'd met. But this time, the movement conveyed no hint of seductive enticement. Only the deepest of sorrows.

At long last, she tore her gaze from the pistol and raised her eyes to his. "Are you not afraid I'll turn it on your uncle again, Mr. Pennington? Or this time upon you?"

The cold formality of her words set his heart a-pounding. "Oh, Fianna," he said, raking a hand through his hair. "What can I say to make you understand how sincerely I regret what I've done?"

Fianna's lips tightened. "Regret? For what have you to be sorry, Kit Pennington?"

"For not trusting you. For lying to you, making you think my uncle was dead."

"You thought I was a threat to him. Of course you would do anything in your power to keep your own uncle safe."

"At first, yes. But later, after I—" Kit rubbed a palm up and down his thigh. "After we became lovers. I should have told you. I should have trusted that you'd not harm a member of my family."

"Should you have? Truly? When I was not even certain of it myself? I tell you, Kit, when I entered Major Pennington's rooms today, I hardly knew what I intended. Force him to confess his guilt? Or murder him, just as he killed my father?"

"But you didn't kill him, did you?"

"I wanted to," she whispered, her head bowed. "You don't know how much I wanted to pull this trigger."

"I know how much you care for your father, how bitter it must have been to come face-to-face with his executioner." Kit drew the pistol from her slack fingers, then cradled her hands between his. "But when the time came, did you choose vengeance?"

She grimaced. "A coward, was I, to give it over?"

"No. No coward would choose mercy over vengeance. But you did. As anyone who cares for you should have known you would." His hands squeezed hers tight. "Can you forgive me, then, for allowing my loyalty to my uncle to blind me to who you truly are? I swear, I never meant to betray you, Fianna."

"Betray me? Kit, such a thought never crossed my mind."

Kit moved to sit beside her. "Why did you leave, then? Theo said that he put the fear of God into you, and of course you gave in to his bribe. I knew you'd never be so craven, but if you felt I'd betrayed you—yes, that would be reason enough to leave."

"It was not your betrayal, but my own, that preyed upon me."

Kit frowned. "How did you betray me?"

"Oh, perhaps not betray. But I put your loyalties into unbearable conflict. How could you care for both me and your uncle, knowing how much I hated him, hated what he'd done? You care so deeply for what is right, what is just, Kit. If I told you how he'd lied, and you believed me, how would you ever have reconciled justice with the loyalty you owed him?"

She sighed, pulling her hands free of his. "It wasn't fair, asking you to choose between your love for your uncle and your love for me. So I chose for you."

Kit gave a bitter chuckle. "You chose for me? This, from the woman who objected so strenuously to me, or her uncle, or any man, making decisions for her? Do I not deserve the same respect as you demand for yourself?"

"Of course you do, Kit," she whispered. "But you had already chosen, hadn't you? After allowing your family to direct your path for so long, you'd finally chosen something you wanted, just for yourself: a political career. And I won't stand in the way of that, not something that matters so much to you. Oh, Saybrook may object now," she added, placing a hand over his mouth to stop his protest. "But you'll make a fine member of Parliament, Kit. Your brother will see it, once you've rid yourself of the millstone of an Irish courtesan from around your neck."

Kit jerked her hand down. "I think your feelings for me are blinding you to the truth, Fianna. It smarted, what Theo said of me—that I'm too outspoken, too hotheaded, to be successful as a politician. But now that I've had the chance to consider it, I cannot in all confidence say he's wrong. I *am* short-tempered and I believe strongly in my own opinions. And I like to be in control. Brokering agreements between contending parties, making concessions when I know that I'm in the right—I don't think it would sit well with me, not for very long."

"Then you'll enter the church, as your father wanted. And once again, we come to the end of our time together. For I doubt many of your priests bring their courtesans along when they take up their duties in a new parish."

"No, not the church," Kit replied, shaking his head. "Many men seek to help their fellow men by working for God, yes. But I don't want to just help individuals; I want to change the society in which they live. If not through the law, then through the power of the written word. Did you not feel it, Fianna, the fire, the joy of language, when we wrote your father's life together? Have you ever felt so powerful, so *alive*, as when we took up our pens and brought his principles, his world, to life? Aidan McCraken may have died that day in 1798, but through us, through the book we created together, his ideals will live on."

Fianna frowned. "But that's all finished, Kit."

"That book, yes. But there are still so many ideas to write about, so many people to tell them to! A hundred years ago, nay, even fifty, people like my father and his fellow aristocrats could make decisions about our government without any regard for how the people felt about them. But now, more and more ordinary people are realizing they can play a role in government, too. If I can write—essays, pamphlets, articles for newspapers such as Wooler's—and persuade the common man that his opinion matters, that he has a role to play in the disposition of our nation, why, then I'd have done something truly worthwhile. Something that truly matters."

Kit placed a palm upon Fianna's cheek, tilting her face to his. "But I need you, my *leannán sídhe*, to make it happen."

"Your *leannán sídhe*?" she said, jerking away from his touch. "What, you want me to play your muse? I'm to sit about and look pretty, am I, and inspire you to ever-greater compositional glory?"

"No, Fianna, that's not what I meant!" Kit rubbed the back of his neck. "It wasn't I alone, inspired by you, who wrote that life of your father. It was you and I, working as partners, as a team. Your cool logic, your analytical mind; my feelings, my ability to evoke a reader's emotions—together, we created something more than either one of us could have done alone. And we can do it again, Fianna. I know we can. Put us together, and our words will remake the world."

"What a dreamer you are, Kit! You imagine us as writing partners?"

"Writing partners, yes. But not just that." He reached out again for her, cupping his palms over her slim shoulders to draw her close. "Damn me for a greedy fool, Fianna, but I want all of you. I want you for my colleague and my helpmeet, my lover and my friend. But most of all, I want you for my wife."

"Wife? But why, Kit? Why should you want to tie yourself to a mongrel of a woman like me?"

"Because I love you, Fianna. I love the woman you've made of yourself, with so little help from any of your family. Your courage and your keen mind, your calm objectivity and oh-so-regal manner. The way your green eyes snap when you're vexed, the way you sigh when I kiss you here, right behind your ear. How devoted you are to the truth, no matter how painful it may be, how many people's feelings get hurt when you tell it. And because I think you may love me, too, Fianna, even if you can't bring yourself to believe it."

Fianna drew a harsh breath. "Have you forgotten the price the *leannán sídhe* demand in return for their gifts of inspiration, Kit? A man's life force."

"You won't harm me."

"Oh, not literally. But still, I'd drain you, kill your spirit, just the same. Do you not realize what censure you'd bring down upon yourself, an English gentleman with a viscount for a brother taking an Irish whore to wife? Oh, you'd scorn it, at least at first. But it grows heavy after a while, the constant oppressive contempt people sow with such a free hand. Believe me, I know. I've lived with it these five-and-twenty years."

"Are you not brave enough to love me, then?" Kit asked. "You've never said the words."

"Damn you, Kit. How could you ask it, after what we've shared? But no matter how you imagine yourself in love with me now, you must know that I'm not worth a future of nothing but shame and scorn."

"Not worth it?" Kit fought back the urge to shake some sense into the stubborn woman. "Did you not boldly declare to your uncle that you didn't need to prove your worth to anybody? Did your actions not say the same to mine?"

Fianna said nothing in reply, only bowed her head. Kit swallowed, hard. "Ah, were you wrong, then? Fianna Cameron will never be worthy, not of the McCrackens, or the O'Hamills, or any man who dares to love her prickly self, no matter how loudly she declares the opposite. No, not unless she, Fianna Cameron, can come to believe in her own worth."

Fianna's lips rounded in an O of surprise. Yes, one's own shames bit deep, as Kit had discovered this afternoon. But she'd taught him the importance of facing the truth, and he'd be damned if he allowed her to shy away from what she'd been hiding from for so long.

Kit slid his hands from her shoulders to her cheeks, willing her not just to listen, but to truly *hear*.

"Talking with my uncle today, I saw that I've been blinded for too long by my loyalty to my family. But you're being blinded by *dis*loyalty, Fianna, disloyalty not to your family, but to yourself. You only see your mistakes, your flaws, and judge yourself unworthy. But I see all of you, a woman made of both flaws *and* strengths, ambiguities *and* truths. And I'm as certain as I am that the sun rises each day that you're worthy of everything. Especially of being loved. Can't you trust yourself and believe it, too, Fianna?"

He watched as the delicate muscles in her throat worked, swallowing not bitter sorrow, but the far-less-familiar draught of hope. "I stood up to your uncle," she whispered at last. "I stood up to Sean, too, did I not?"

"Yes, love, you did."

"Why then should it be so hard to stand up for myself?" Tears glittered in the corners of her eyes.

"Because you've had the misfortune of not having any of your family set you the example. But that's a misfortune I vow you'll suffer no longer, heartkin. Will it help, knowing I'm standing by you?"

"A little. And perhaps, if you kissed me—"

Kit needed no further invitation, pressing his lips against hers with all the urgency of loss just barely averted. The passion with which she answered him, her hands reaching around his torso to tug him closer, suppressed sobs turning into sighs, sent heat radiating throughout his body.

How long they kissed before they were interrupted by the cough of the coachman and his polite inquiry —"Once more around the park, sir?"—Kit had no idea. More than a few minutes, if the swelling of Fianna's lips and the disarray of her bodice were any indication. With a smile, he tugged her clothing to rights, then gave the driver his direction.

"Does this mean you've accepted the inevitability of

joining your fate to mine?" he asked, tucking her close against his side. Yes, right there, against the heart that beat with so much more vitality, simply because she was near. It would be a long time before he'd let her from his sight again.

"All your family will object," she said. But her voice lacked the assurance he'd grown accustomed to hearing. Tread lightly, but press on, and he might just persuade her.

"Not all my family, surely. Aunt Allyne is always after my brothers and me to marry and ensure the continuance of the Pennington line."

"Your aunt! But surely she'll be scandalized! Do you not recall that she and I have already met, at the Guardian Society?"

"Oh, but these days, Aunt Allyne's so busy trying to find a suitable husband for my sister that she scarcely remembers her own name, never mind the face of every penitent prostitute to whom she's offered her aid."

"Lord Saybrook, then. I did take his bribe, after all."

"A bribe we'll be certain to pay back in full, from the copious remunerations we're sure to reap from the glory of our writing. Oh, he may threaten to cut me off without a sou, but he well knows that the income from the small property gifted to me by my paternal grandmother is more than enough to keep us afloat. And if he wishes for us to remain on speaking terms, he'll soon learn not to say a word against you."

"And Benedict?"

Kit smiled. "Yes, Benedict will likely be angered. Having such a striking model as sister-in-law is sure to rankle. Perhaps if we invite him to dine on a regular basis, and allow him to sketch us to his heart's content? I'll leave it to you to make sure he washes the charcoal from his hands before coming to table."

"And your uncle Christopher?" Fianna said with a sigh as she rested a cheek against his chest. "He for one will never accept me. How will you stand to be estranged from a man you hold so dear?"

"If there is any estrangement, it won't be caused by me, love. I'll continue to visit him, as long as you do not object. And if he refuses to welcome you, too, why, that will be his loss, won't it, now? But I think he might surprise you. The two of you have more in common than you might think."

No, it would not be easy, forging a family from such stubborn, antagonistic members, both of whom felt far safer keeping their darker feelings to themselves. But he knew how important family was to Fianna, and would do everything in his power to make her feel welcome in his.

But first, he'd have to convince her to become a part of it.

"Is Fianna Cameron the only other name you've used, besides the ones given to you by your O'Hamill and McCracken families?" he asked as the hack pulled up in front of his rooms.

"Cameron's only one of the many surnames I've adopted over the years," she answered, accepting his hand out of the carriage. "But I've always come back to Fianna. My mother loved to tell stories of the brave warrior Fionn mac Cumhaill and his *fianna*, the landless warriors from different tribes all across Ireland who joined together to protect the country from invaders. Mother said that in days long past, both men *and* women were welcome in the *fianna*."

"A fitting name, then, for a warrior such as yourself," Kit said, unlocking the door to his rooms.

"I'm glad you think so."

Oh, so tempting, that knowing smile lurking about the corners of her mouth. Kit bent to capture it, knowing he'd have to be satisfied with the chase alone. For as many times as he caught it, it would always come back, more wise, more tantalizing than before. The blood coursed hot through his body at the thought of the hours, the days, he'd devote to its pursuit.

"Then it's only Cameron I'll be asking you to change," he said when he finally lifted his head from hers.

He'd never seen her eyes so befuddled, half confusion, half darkening desire. "Change? What do you want me to change?" she asked, her hands drifting down from where they'd been entangled in his hair.

"Your name, heartkin. Will you change it? Leave Cameron behind, and take Pennington in its stead? Will you join my family, Fianna? Even if at first we're its only members?"

She shook her head, her eyes wide. "You truly mean it, don't you, Kit? You mean to marry another man's courtesan."

"You're no man's anything, Fianna. Unless you choose to be. Will you choose to be mine? As I've chosen to be yours?"

Fianna bowed her head, taking one deep breath, then another. Was she steeling herself to stand firm against his disappointment? Or searching for the courage to banish her own? He waited, his heart pounding in his ears.

But when she finally raised her eyes to his, the love shining from their green depths stole the breath from Kit's throat. "You've shown me that love is not something you must earn, but the most precious of gifts, given without conditions. And I accept your gift, Kit Pennington. Will you accept my own in return?"

Could a man's heart leap clear out of his chest for joy? "Yes," Kit answered, reaching about her waist and lifting her high in the air above him. Spinning her a dizzy circle to his assenting chant—"yes, Yes, YES!"— Kit wondered that his own feet, too, did not rise to float above the floor.

They fell, laughing, into a tangle of silk and skirts on the tufted green settee. "But Miss Cameron, I'm afraid I do have one infinitesimally small condition before I say 'I do.'"

He half feared he'd set her back up, but she knew him too well now to mistake teasing for gravity. "Your condition, sir?"

Kit pulled Aidan McCracken's pistol from his pocket and placed it in her lap. "That you never wave this blasted firearm in my direction again."

"Oh, Kit," she said, half laughter, half dismay. "I never did apologize for shooting you, did I?"

"Come, we've had enough of apologizing for one day, have we not? Can you not think of better things to do with this fine moonlit evening?"

Fianna cocked her head and gave a sly smile. "Shall we begin an essay on behalf of Catholic relief, then? Or perhaps a pamphlet on the evils of the Seditious Meetings Prevention Acts?"

Kit growled, grabbing her up in his arms. "Tomorrow is soon enough to begin with all that. But tonight, I have other plans for that feather pen you so admire. Are the *leannán sídhe* ticklish, I wonder?"

Yes, his heart sang. To make her laugh like that, her head thrown back, her mouth a rounded O, her eyes shining with uncomplicated pleasure—yes, if he could do that, at least once a day, why, then, how much harder could it be to change the world?

THANK YOU!

Thanks for reading *A Rebel without a Rogue*. I hope you enjoyed it!

If you have the time, would you consider writing a review of *Rebel*? Reader reviews on Amazon, Goodreads, and other social networking sites are especially valuable for e-books. I'm grateful for all reviews, and if you take the time to write one of *Rebel*, you have my thanks.

If you'd like to know when my next book becomes available, you can sign up for my guaranteed-infrequent newsletter at blissbennet.com, follow me on Twitter where I'm @blissbennet, or like my Facebook page at www.facebook.com/blissbennetauthor.

AUTHOR'S NOTE

It's amazing how a few short sentences from a primary or secondary research source can prove to be the catalyst for an entire novel. I first came across the lines reprinted above while reading a biography of Irish social reformer and abolitionist Mary Ann McCracken. Though well-known in late 18th and early 19th century Belfast for her progressive social beliefs and her activism on behalf of the indigent and the enslaved, today Mary Ann McCracken is primarily remembered as the younger sister of Henry Joy McCracken, one of the leaders of the northern rebels during the Irish Rebellion of 1798. Arrested by the British after the rebels' failed attempt to seize Antrim in June, "poor Harry" was offered clemency if he testified against other United Irishmen leaders. He refused, and was tried and executed in Belfast on July 17, 1798.

Shortly after her brother's execution, Mary Ann Mc-Cracken was informed that the impetuous Harry had left behind an illegitimate child, and that "his inability to make provision for her had been his only sorrow in his last moments" (McNeil 194). Taking the burden of the four-year-old child's provision into her own hands, the unmarried Mary Ann helped the girl's Irish mother and family to emigrate to America, then moved the child, whom she called Maria, into her father's house in Belfast.

What would it have been like, I began to wonder, to have been that child? To have been born the bastard daughter of an Irish peasant, to have lived with a rural Irish Catholic family for the first years of one's life, and then suddenly to find oneself uprooted and thrust into a genteel city family, one with Scottish roots and Presbyterian beliefs? And, on top of it all, to know that one's father had been executed as a traitor? As I thought about this "what-if," the idea for Fianna and her quest to redeem her father's reputation, and to win a secure place in her father's family, was born.

By all accounts, the actual Maria McCracken grew up beloved by her aunt Mary Ann, with whom she lived in Belfast (except for time at a boarding school in Ballycraigy) until her aunt's death. Even Maria's own marriage did not separate them; "it was a foregone conclusion that Maria would bring her aunt to the new home," her biographer writes (McNeill 300).

A happy child and adult, though, does not a romantic heroine make. I hope Maria's descendants will excuse the major liberties I've taken in imagining a far different course for the fictionalized characters I've loosely based on her life.

The letters that appear in chapter 17, those purportedly written by Fianna's father, are taken almost verbatim from actual ones written by Henry Joy McCracken to his sister while he was imprisoned in Kilmainham Gaol in 1796–97 for his United Irishmen activities.

You can read more such letters, and find out more about the real Mary Ann McCracken (a far more fascinating woman than I've depicted in my fiction), in Mary McNeill's *The Life and Times of Mary Ann McCracken: A Belfast Panorama*. Dublin: Allen Figgis, 1960.

SOMETHING ABOUT BLISS

Despite being born and bred in New England, Bliss Bennet has always been fascinated by the history of that country across the pond, particularly the politically volatile period known as the English Regency. So much so that she spent years writing a dissertation about the history of children's literature in the period. Now she makes good use of all the research she did for that five-hundred-plus-page project in her historical romance writing.

Bliss's mild-mannered alter ego, Jackie Horne, muses about genre and gender on the _Romance Novels for Feminists_ blog.

Though she's visited Britain several times, Bliss continues to make her home in New England, along with her husband, daughter, and two monstrously fluffy black cats.

FIND BLISS

On the web at www.blissbennet.com
On Facebook at www.facebook.com/Blissbennetauthor
On Twitter @blissbennet

A sneak preview of Bliss Bennet's next book,
A Man without a Mistress

February 1822

"You'll feel differently, my dear, once you are married. . ."

Sibilla Pennington sighed, her gloved finger tracing smaller and smaller circles on the tufted velvet of the carriage seat.

One hundred and forty-seven. Great-Aunt Allyne had uttered the phrase "You'll feel differently once you are married" one hundred and forty-seven times during their all-too-lengthy journey from Lincolnshire to London. As if once Sibilla exchanged maidenhood for the married state, this devilish penchant for risk taking she'd developed since Papa's death would miraculously be replaced by the demurest of haloes and wings.

Only someone who had spent as little time with her over the past year as her aunt would believe the daughter of the fifth Viscount Saybrook likely to be tamed by matrimony. No, she had as little intention of changing her unconventional opinions as she had of participating in this year's Marriage Mart, despite what she had implied to her brother. For did not her promise to her father come first? She'd risk far worse than another quarrel with Theo to keep her word to Papa.

Still, she'd have to exercise at least a modicum of restraint if this devil's bargain were not to come crashing down about her head.

"Is it not a wife's duty, ma'am, to keep herself well informed?" she asked in as innocuous tone as she could muster. "So she might appear to advantage in the polite world, and be a credit to her husband?"

"Well informed, yes, but to read the newspapers? The political columns? No proper young lady would even consider such a thing," her aunt said with a delicate shudder.

Sibilla shoved her reticule, which held a tightly furled copy of the *Times*, farther behind her back.

"If only your father had listened to my advice and allowed you to remain in London with me three years ago, rather than curtailing your come-out in that quite shocking fashion," Aunt Allyne continued. "But he never would listen to the guidance of a poor female, not when I advised him about the dangers of filling your head with talk of radicals and reform, nor when I cautioned him about waiting too long to find you a suitable husband. If you had but stayed in town, surely you'd be a happy wife with a child or two by now, and this unwonted interest in politics would be long forgotten."

Aunt Allyne could imagine her happy, with Papa barely a year in his grave?

She clenched her hands in her lap, wishing the kid of her gloves did not protect her palms from the sharp bite of her fingernails. Physical pain could often distract from pain of the emotional sort.

"Aunt, your offer to keep me in London was all that was good and kind. But my father's health truly did benefit from my company. And missing the rest of my Season did not strike me as so great a loss. As you yourself noted, so few of the young men that year seemed inclined to marry," she hurriedly added at the sight of Aunt Allyne's frown.

"Ah yes, you are quite right," her aunt replied, apparently appeased. "Only three marriages of any consequence in the year '19, and only five the year after, all involving only the most handsome gels. And with your looks. . . of course, beauty is as beauty does, dear child. But perhaps it was better to wait. I find you in far better countenance now than when you were only seventeen."

Sibilla turned to stare out the window, determined to avoid the pity in Aunt Allyne's eyes. She'd long understood that she would never embody the slim, fair, fashionable ideal held by the *ton*, but her aunt's forthright sum-mary of her charms still stung. Shorter than the average, with eyes of the plainest brown and straw-colored hair that did not so much curl as wildly corkscrew in all directions, her face would hardly turn even the most short-sighted of male heads.

But the only male head she needed to turn during this Season was the one belonging to her eldest brother, Theo Pennington, the new Viscount Saybrook. And turn it not in her own direction, but toward his duty. Theo had little liking for politicking, but surely her offer to act as his political guide would convince him to follow in Papa's footsteps and speak in Parliament for reform. Hadn't her father, after all, chosen to share with her, rather than any of her older brothers, all he had known about the House of Lords? And wouldn't Theo, who had never shown the slightest interest in political goings-on, need her to smooth his way into Whig circles by acting as gracious hostess, rather than marry her off as expeditiously as possible?

Her heart began to pound at the thought of seeing her brother again. Even though Theo had long been the brother to whom she felt the closest, since their father's passing—no, since that last bitter parting shortly before it —they had each acted as politely as strangers the few times they had crossed paths. But she must make him understand why every peer who believed in a temperate reform of the government was vitally necessary if England did not wish to see the grievances of the poor erupt in riot or revolt. Surely then he wouldn't allow his antipathy to politics, or their personal disagreements, to stand in the way of his duty.

Still, perhaps it would be wise to recruit an ally or two.

"Do you know if Theo is acquainted with Lord James Dunster, son of the Marquess of Tisbury?" Yes, and what other aristocratic names appeared most often in the Parliamentary Intelligence column of the *Times*? "Or Mr. Harold Hardwicke, cousin to the Earl of Trent?"

"Oh, I *am* pleased to see you finally taking an interest in potential suitors!" Aunt Allyne's wrinkled face creased with a smile. "But do not worry yourself; Theodosius and I will choose to whom you should be introduced. Now, my Bible is in my valise, but I do have Miss Hatfield's *Letters on the Importance of the Female Sex* to hand. Shall we take up from where we left off?"

Ah, the enervating strictures of Miss Hatfield. Something between a groan and a sigh escaped Sibilla's lips.

"Now, now, no need to take on so, my child." Aunt Allyne gave Sibilla's knee a kindly pat. "The Season will soon start in good earnest, and you will have your chance to meet the most eligible *partis.*"

Heaven help her if her plan failed, and she must accede to her aunt's idea of an eligible marriage partner! She could picture him now, declaiming her aunt's favorite commonplaces as if they held the wisdom of the ages: *An idle brain is the devil's shop, Miss Pennington. You catch more flies with honey than with vinegar, Miss Pennington. A little learning is a dangerous thing, Miss Pennington, especially for an unmarried lady with an unseemly interest in politics. And when you are married, surely you'll think the same. . .*

The coachman's "Hollah!" brought the disagreeable litany to a blessed halt. Berkeley Square, at last. Before a groom could drop from the seat above or a footman scurry from the house beside, Sibilla opened the door of the carriage. One nimble jump and she was on the pavement; three quick steps brought her to the portico-covered door.

"My dear girl, have a care! Lady Jersey resides at number 38, and you would not wish to risk making a poor first impression on one of Almack's most esteemed patronesses!" Aunt Allyne called from the door of the carriage.

Paying no heed to her aunt's chidings, she pushed past the footman and stepped through the just-opened front door.

At last! Pennington House, the London residence of the Viscounts Saybrook for the past sixty years. The memory of the last time she had been here, that tantalizingly brief month during the spring of her seventeenth year when she and Papa had talked politics and hatched plans, debating into the wee hours over potential suitors, made her smile. How differently the words "When you are married" sounded when uttered by Papa!

But then Lord Saybrook had grown sick and died, and all their plans for forging a marital alliance that would also forward the cause of political reform fell by the wayside. *Yes, I'll see that Theo takes up the cause in your stead,* she'd whispered by her father's deathbed. *And I won't forget it, either. Not like Jane Carson, and Cissy Hubbard, and the others who abandoned politics as soon as they married.* Husband and household, bedding, breeding, and babies, all left wives far too little time for any pursuit beyond the domestic. No, far better to remain right here, at Pennington House, working by her brother's side, than to risk taking on a husband.

"Theo! We're here!" She raced up the main staircase in a manner certain to earn her the label "unladylike" in most *ton* households. Shedding her pelisse and muff, she rushed down the corridor, opening doors right and left. "Theo?"

Dust shrouds had been removed from the furniture, and the windows, recently cleaned, gleamed with light. But each room felt empty, unlived-in; the smell of polish, not people, greeted her at every door. Had she truly expected Pennington House would still hold her father's scent, tobacco and sunshine and starch, even after it had vanished from the house where he had died?

"Miss? Please, allow me." A tall man in Saybrook livery bowed, then opened the only door on the corridor that still remained closed.

Her brow wrinkled, then cleared. "Hill, isn't it?" At the footman's answering nod, she added, "Please, Hill, where might I find my brother?"

The footman smiled. "Remember me, do you, then, miss? Ah, your father's daughter, to be sure. You may find

Master Benedict in what we are to call his *studio*, in the attic next to the maidservants' room. Master Kit has taken lodgings in Duke Street, I believe."

"But I'm looking for my eldest brother. Don't tell me that sluggard is still abed?"

She hesitated at the threshold of the room Hill revealed. The music room, with its overstuffed armchairs and gleaming pianoforte, purchased by Papa just before he brought her to town that last time. How he loved it when she played just for him. Her fingers begin to trace out the notes of his favorite ballad against her thigh.

She jerked them to a halt, her hands clenching.

"My apologies, miss. I haven't seen Lord Saybrook these many months."

"Months? What, is he not residing at Pennington House?"

Hill started, his eyes growing wide. "No, miss."

Chagrin must have made her exclamation sharper than she had intended. But to come all this way, and discover Theo not even here. . .

Sibilla pressed a palm, hard, against her sternum. Had she been the one to drive him away, with her cruel words and stinging accusations over their father's sickbed?

"Thank you, Hill. That will be all," Sibilla said, dismissing the servant before he could catch sight of the tears threatening the corners of her eyes.

Descending the staircase at a pace far more sedate than she'd taken while climbing it, Sibilla made her way back to the entrance hall.

"Oh, my dear girl, what luck. Not a soul on the square witnessed your untoward flight." Aunt Allyne juggled a bandbox, a book, and her reticule by the front door. "The dear Lord looks after his orphans and strays, so he does. Now come, meet Bridget, the abigail I've—"

"Aunt," she interrupted, "Hill tells me Theo is not living here. Why did no one inform me?" *Papa gone, and now Theo, too?*

"Ah, brothers," her aunt answered as she allowed Hill

to most properly divest her of her outer garments. "Such provoking creatures! They do say that sisters are ever so much more obliging. Even if your father had been my brother rather than my nephew-in-law, I doubt he would have listened to my advice and agreed to allow you to remain in London rather than traipsing down the country-side to nurse him. After your mother died, Saybrook always did like to keep you close to pay him court. But your nursing didn't help much in the end, though, did it, my child? 'Ashes to ashes, dust to dust,' just like my own dear Mr. Allyne, may they both rest in peace."

Sibilla bit her lip, hard, determined not to allow her grief to show. It would only lead to another of her aunt's sermons on accepting death with perfect resignation to the will of the Almighty.

"But just think, my dear," Aunt Allyne said, linking her arm through her niece's. "Once you are married, you'll no longer be troubled by such trying creatures as brothers."

One hundred and forty-eight. *One hundred and forty-eight!*

Sibilla bit back a most unladylike curse. Surely she'd be able to persuade Theo to take up his parliamentary duties long before the count could reach a thousand. . .

Across Mayfair, in the London residence of the Earl of Milne, Sir Peregrine Sayre, too, was counting. The number of acres one needed to enclose to feed the average herd of sheep. The number of men brought into the Guildhall Justice Room each week for thieving, and the number of those who were convicted and transported. And, most recently, the number of men who had voted against the disenfranchisement of Grampound, the first move toward reforming representation in Parliament. And, of course, the number of favors Lord Milne would need to provide to reward them for said support. Praise heaven he'd finally been able to convince Milne to champion the bill, despite the earl's conservative leanings. One fewer time he'd have to compromise his own principles just to keep in his patron's good graces.

Per sighed, laying down his quill to rub the tension from between his brows. Such glorified accounting hardly did justice to his skills as a politician, garnered over six years of working with the earl. But Milne had seemed unduly anxious of late. Best to humor him, especially when he was so close to persuading the earl to support his candidacy for a seat in the House during the next election. If Per had to count all the fleas on all the rats in all the alleys of London to set Milne's mind at ease, then by God, count fleas he would.

Before Per could take up his quill again, a long arm clad in the richest superfine reached over his shoulder to snatch it up off the desk.

"Still totting away, my good fellow? If one didn't know any better, one might believe my father ran a counting-house. How will I ever live down the shame?"

Viscount Dulcie, Lord Milne's scapegrace of a son, perched on the edge of the desk, twirling the stolen pen between nimble fingers. With others, Per's natural reserve held him aloof, but somehow he could never stand on ceremony with the irreverent lord.

"Do my ears deceive me? Or did I truly hear the word *shame* emerge from your lips? Surely Lord Dulcie has no acquaintance with the sentiment?" He made a lunge for the fluttering quill, but Dulcie danced away, just out of reach.

"How could I not feel shame when all the world blames me for your absence from society? If you do not take steps to address the gossip, my good name will soon lie in tatters."

With a swift feint, Dulcie darted in, attempting to tap the quill against Per's nose. But this time Per was quicker, catching the smaller man's arm and turning it behind his back.

"What has your good name to do with my refusal to waste my time on parties and routs?" Per had cultivated a reputation for indifference with the ladies of the *ton* for a purpose and had little interest in abandoning it without good reason.

"Beast! Give over or you'll rip the seam. Here, have your dratted pen, for all the good it shall do you."

He gave a grunt of satisfaction as Dulcie let the feather drop from his fingers.

"A bully as well as a recluse!" Dulcie accused, rubbing at his arm in an aggrieved manner, as if Per had actually done him an injury. "No wonder they can't stop chattering about you. Ladies will hanker after the enigmatic, violent fellows, fools that they are. And then they have the gall to blame me when you ignore them."

"Of what, precisely, stand you accused, besides the abuse of perfectly good pens?" He lifted the feather to reveal the top of its shaft tipping over at a drunken angle.

"Why, of encouraging your most unnatural *tendre* for me, of course, dear boy," Dulcie replied, his lips quirking in amusement. "For what other reason would the ladies of the *ton* believe you would squirrel yourself away in our house, eschewing all their charms?"

Per uttered a silent curse. Dulcie typically took care to keep his liaisons with those of the opposite sex far from the public eye, wary of allowing any whiff of scandal to touch his family. But had Milne's increasing insistence that his son marry and produce an heir led his son to rebel and deliberately court scandal? And was Per to be sacrificed on the altar of Dulcie's dramatics?

If such rumors—no matter how patently false—were to reach Lord Milne, Per's dream of sitting in the House of Commons would die a speedy death. And how then would he work toward parliamentary reform, toward giving the people of England a real voice in the running of their own government? How would he ever make restitution for the suffering he had caused?

"Surely, Dulcie, you didn't—you haven't—"

"Of course not. You think I'd share the story of your crushing rejection?" Dulcie gave a dramatic shudder. "Why, no man's *amour-propre* could withstand such a blow! If only I'd known then how often you frequented whorehouses that first year you came up to town, I'd never have mistaken your true proclivities. You must tell me, why ever did you stop?" The viscount settled in Per's chair, chin propped on his hands, eyes wide with curiosity.

How the hell had Dulcie caught wind of that old scandal?

For a moment, Per had the urge to give in to temptation and confess his own past mistakes. But if he spilled his budget to a gossip such as Dulcie, the entire *ton* would soon know that he'd haunted London's brothels and gaming hells during that ghastly year after he had come up from Cambridge for reasons completely unrelated to his own amusement. A rumor of lewd behavior with Dulcie would be nothing to the revelation of those sordid secrets.

If, in fact, such a rumor even existed. . .

He took a step toward Dulcie, frowning as suspicion grew.

"Now, you've no need to punish me for bearing bad tidings," Dulcie said, jumping up from the chair and holding out his hands in supplication. "Indeed, I bring you the means to dispel such scandalous tittle-tattle. All you must do is drag yourself away from this tedious pile of papers and accept the dinner invitation my parents will so kindly extend. Chat amiably with a chit or two, turn a page of music for another, and you'll quiet the gabble-mongers forthwith."

"One dinner invitation? No balls? No routs? No tedious musicales?"

"Only dinner, Per. Lady Butterbank will be in attendance, so if you snub me, we're certain to dispel this scurrilous scandalbroth brewing among the gossips. Lord knows that woman loves to tattle."

"Yes, almost as much as you do." He retreated to his chair, crossing his arms in disgust.

Dulcie chuckled. "Lady Butterbank does give me a good run for my money. But I see no reason not to throw her a juicy bone now and again. You'll attend, if only to give her a reason to rise the next morning?"

He found himself unable to maintain a grudge in the face of Dulcie's good humor. "If I must," he conceded.

"And, if you would," Dulcie added in a suspiciously offhand manner, "you might consider a Miss Pennington as one of the recipients of your somewhat dubious charms. Another nobleman's daughter up from the country, ready to make her bow to the king, my mother tells me. Ill dressed and whey-faced, I'll wager. And from bucolic Lincolnshire, no less!"

"Dulcie," he growled, eyes narrowing as he rose from his seat to tower threateningly over the far shorter viscount. "If I discover you've created this ridiculous rumor only to extricate yourself from yet another of your father's matchmaking schemes. . ."

The viscount raised one eyebrow as he backed through the door. "Why the earl thinks I'd have anything to say to a schoolgirl who has spent far more time communing with cows and cabbages than engaging in intelligent conversation, I cannot begin to imagine. But you, Sir Peregrine, should be more than suitable."

Per lunged, but caught only the sound of laughter as the viscount beat a quick retreat.

In truth, this Pennington girl must be a gorgon if Dulcie required *his* help to free himself from her clutches. Perhaps he would attend the Milnes' party, if only to watch the sport as the earl tried once again to entice his son into the matrimonial lists. And might he even teach Dulcie not to tease him with false gossip?

The corner of his mouth quirked as he tapped his quill against the table. Just what words should he whisper in the ear of the whey-faced Miss Pennington to suggest

Viscount Dulcie harbored a *tendre* not for Per, but for her?

A Man without a Mistress
Available from all major retailers
December 2015